C000007711

Heart of the Few

By

Jon Duncan

Pine Tree Press

This book is a work of fiction. Names, characters places, organizations, and incidents are either a product of the author's imagination or are used fictitiously. Any resemblance to actual events, organizations, or persons, living or dead, is entirely coincidental.

Published by Pine Tree Press, 3330 Darby #412, Simi Valley, CA 93063

ISBN 978-0-9993486-0-4 Print version

ISBN 978-0-9993486-1-1 eBook version

Second Edition

For my wonderful wife.

Your love will always be my most precious gift.

Being loved deeply by someone gives you strength,

Loving someone deeply gives you courage.

- Lao Tzu

Fifty-Four Hours Earlier

Lightning split the void, a white-hot slash torn in an obsidian sky. Thunder exploded in her ears as the aircraft lurched with such violence the woman expected any second the black bomber would be torn to pieces. Her body crushed into the seat as the plane shot upward, shuddered and abruptly fell hundreds of feet toward the earth as she floated weightless, restrained only by the straps. The bomber slammed into an updraft hard enough to throw her head forward, her teeth cracked together with an audible sound. Another bolt detonated behind them. In the flash, she saw the contorted face of the pilot as he struggled against the storm, his hands welded to the controls.

Somewhere over the Channel, miles from the Dutch coast, the aircraft collided with a gale that was brutally attempting to tear it apart. The pilot glanced over at the woman just as the plane gave a savage shudder. He gritted his teeth and screamed above the din, "Damn you. You're gonna get us all killed and for what? Stupid girl."

She looked across the two feet separating them.

"I don't give a damn if you get killed—it's me I worry about," the pilot snarled.

Once again, the aircraft abruptly fell hundreds of feet and careened off an updraft, every rivet strained to hold it together.

The pilot fought against the turbulence, tried to level the plane. "What's so damn important that I have to risk my life for you?"

"My mission," she yelled above the raging storm, a mission she knew could win the war. "And that's all you need to know."

He laughed, "We're done here, I'm not dying for you. Your mission can go another night, we're getting out of this storm." The muscles in his jaw stood out, his eyes narrowed to slits as he slammed the throttles forward and turned the aircraft.

The woman unzipped the top of her flight jacket. Her hand slipped inside and wrapped around the grip of a Luger stored beneath her arm. In a quick, precise movement she freed it and shoved the barrel against the pilot's temple. "Get back on course," she shouted above the deafening roar in the cockpit.

His head turned slightly, his eyes wild, pinned to the corners. "You bitch," his lips formed. "You wouldn't dare."

"You'll do what you're ordered to do, or I'll shoot you right here," she yelled. The pilot turned toward her, the black muzzle a few millimeters from his eye. "I'll probably die anyway, so if I kill you now, does it really matter."

Rage covered his face as he turned away from her stare and pulled the throttle back. The pilot looked down, scanned the instruments and mumbled to himself as the compass slowly spun back, wobbled and then centered on the correct course. She rested the ice-cold weapon on her lap, her finger close to the trigger.

Ten long minutes ticked by second after second as she sat next to him without a word between them. She knew the risk she was taking and in the frigid night, a bead of sweat formed beneath her leather flight helmet and ran down the side of her face.

"Finally," he roared as he reached down to adjust a dial.

On the instrument panel, she watched a round gage spring to life, two needles jumping up and down, his attention riveted on it.

"There's the homing beacon. Now I can be rid of you." His words spat out in a hiss. "Get ready to jump—and quite frankly, I hope you do get killed."

The woman slipped the pistol back into the holster and zipped the flight suit. She unbuckled as the plane lurched and threw her toward the pilot, her forearm deliberately catching his chin. Their eyes met and she saw nothing but hatred looking back at her. She staggered toward the bomb bay as another clap of thunder slammed against the aircraft, a fury of sound bounced around the empty bomber as sweat ran down her spine.

"Positions!" the pilot yelled.

Tied into a small desk in front and below the pilot, she watched the navigator unbuckle and grab at anything to steady himself. Another bolt of lightning exposed him hammering arms and elbows against the heaving plane as he stumbled back toward the center of the aircraft and the bomb bay.

"Twenty seconds." the pilot screamed, the sound of his voice barely heard.

A section the size of a grave and just as black opened in the plane's belly. Hurricane winds tore through the breach as the woman took station, her legs in the mouth of the abyss whipped by stinging wind. She snapped a steel ring onto a thick metal loop tied to the aircraft's ribs and yanked, assured herself the static line was secure and the parachute would deploy some ten feet below the bomber's belly. She looked down into the abyss, her body shook, almost out of control, her terror focused in the black void.

Unable to hear anything except the roar of wind as it ripped through the bomb bay, the navigator pressed in so close she could smell his breath. He screamed in her ear, "Standby." She felt his boot thump onto the back of the parachute, her heart jumped against her chest, her breath now coming in rapid gasps.

An amber light above the open bomb bay came to life and the navigator's boot gave a slight shove. She gritted her teeth, her eyes now tightly shut, her chest heaving. It took all the courage she could muster to release her grip on the metal supports and open her eyes. She crossed arms, one hand on each shoulder and peeked through slits at the amber light. It flashed green and the boot shoved. Eight hundred feet above the ground she tumbled out into the frenzy of the storm, glanced against the bomber's wet belly and fell away. A half-second later, a black silk canopy burst open with a bone-jarring jolt and she screamed.

Enveloped in emptiness, swinging like a metronome, she began to count, trying to estimate the time left until the ground rushing toward her would one way or another end the horror.

Nine, ten, the sting of wind driven rain on her face. Fourteen, fifteen. Brace for impact. A sheen, water on grass, she slammed against the ground, her breath ripped away. Gale force winds snatched her parachute and, on her back, gulping for air, she skid across the soaked ground. Her hand rammed repeatedly against the release until the hasp finally snapped open and the parachute tore away. She lay in a puddle covered in mud as air, welcome air, finally came in panted breaths. The woman rolled onto her belly, unzipped her flight jacket, and retrieved the gun from beneath her arm. Her thumb freed the safety and she slowly scanned as much of the muddy field as she could see in the enraged storm. Lightning flashed. She saw some fifty meters away a stand of trees that seemed to hover above the earth, the canopies violently flailing back and forth. Several long, slow breaths satisfied her lungs as her heart eased back into her chest as she focused on the thrashing trees.

Off to her right something appeared, a pinprick at the side of her vision. She stared at an area beneath the writhing canopies and waited. She counted five seconds and a pinpoint of light flashed once, twice, paused and blinked once more. Coming onto one knee, the black weapon trained on the light, she reached into a pocket by her thigh and removed a small military torch. Peering into the rain, she flicked it on once, a pause and then two more times in quick flashes.

After what seemed like an eternity with every fiber of her body on razor edge, two figures began to emerge from the rain. They approached cautiously, their flashlights scanning a narrow beam over the slick wet soil, their own weapons pointed at her.

Their lights now some thirty feet away, she offered in a loud but carefully controlled voice, "Have you seen my dog?" She hunched over making herself the smallest of targets, her weapon trained on the approaching men, poised to fire.

The taller of the two shouted, "Remarkable, I'm looking for a dog as well." The sound garbled by the wind, but unmistakable. Their weapons slid beneath sodden trail jackets as they closed in on her.

She stood as they came to a halt a few feet away. The fat one removed his hunting cap, "Ruddy awful night for sightseeing." She pointed her flashlight on his round, chinless face and he smiled, his teeth yellowed and gapped.

"Electra, welcome to England," he said.

Chapter One

Pilot Officer Jamie Wallace sat alone in a musty Victorian railway car that belonged in another era. His legs were crossed at the knee, a misfolded copy of *The Times* and the grim news it shared lay on his lap. Out the window glass, the verdant hills of western England slowly rose and fell as if to mimic a placid ocean that stretched toward the horizon. Fertile fields dotted with saffron and blue blossoms that bore Holstein dairy cattle, standing motionless in the shade of thick oaks, while farmers toiled and turned the rich soil beneath a warm, lazy sun.

To Jamie, the view seemed like a blurred photograph, smeared and out of focus, its content meaningless. His mind was captive elsewhere, locked in a future from which he could not escape. An obligated future, one that would soon engulf him in the cataclysm of war and the senseless slaughter and destruction. He knew too well how close death and loss resided. It harried his heart and left him feeling alone and apprehensive. He wasn't at all sure he had the courage, or the perseverance to see it through. Would he also lose his life, be one of those robbed of a future and forever remain twenty-three, never blessed with the love of a woman or the gifts a full life could offer?

A squeal from the compartment's door startled him, brought him back into the shabby compartment. He turned away from the window to see a long-legged, ginger haired woman of about twenty with round, green eyes the color of spring. She stood in the now open doorway, her head cocked to one side, a tumbler of whiskey in hand. Her unpainted lips eased upward at the corners of her mouth in a Mona Lisa smile.

"Are you Jamie Wallace?" she said. "If so, your pal Miles sent me to fetch you. He said to look for a RAF Officer, a sandy blond with easy curls and you fit the bill."

She stepped into the compartment and held out the tumbler. Jamie noticed a flash of light flicker from a diamond on her ring finger and was disappointed, "I'm Jamie Wallace. You say Miles *sent* you?" He tossed the newspaper on the seat and stood.

"That he did." The royal blue of her naval uniform was an agreeable contrast next to her buttermilk skin and tailored quite well. There was a relaxed air of confidence about her, something he admired in women and she spoke with a light Scottish accent that softly rolled off her tongue.

"Why didn't he come himself?" Jamie cinched his tie and took the tumbler from her hand. "Then again, if I'm going to be absconded, I would much prefer it be done by a beautiful woman, even if she is already taken." Her smile broadened. "May I ask your name?" He downed the whiskey.

"Madge Camden," she extended her hand and he took it. "Miles is wedged into a booth between some other pilots, so he asked that I find you. We've quite a smashing party going on in the lounge car but, if you care to be alone, I'll let him know that as well."

Jamie forced the last of his dark thoughts into hiding. "No, I've been alone for the last hour. It's time I rejoin the living."

Her head nodded ever so slightly, her smile vanished. "I'm unable to spend time alone these days, it's simply too frightening," she said. "My fiancée is a gunnery officer aboard *HMS Ratherham*, a destroyer on convoy duty in the North Atlantic. When I'm alone, it's all I think about and the fear rattles me."

The look in her eyes betrayed a flicker of confidence lost. "I understand. When was the last time you were together?"

"A month ago." The smile came back to her face, "But today I'm headed for Cardiff where *Ratherham* is to dock early this evening. We're due for two weeks together. After which, he's to be assigned to shore duty for the duration." This time her eyes betrayed her joy.

"How wonderful for you both." Maybe they would be of the lucky, the one's able to make a life together. Jamie set the empty tumbler on the newspaper's front page directly over a column title: Two Destroyers, Sixteen Merchants, Lost in Convoy Battle. As a rule, the government never made public the names of ships lost and he hoped *HMS Ratherham* was still afloat and not one of the two destroyers at the black bottom of the North Atlantic. *One can hope* he thought as he quickly blocked her view of the paper and said, "Well then, shall we join the party?"

They made their way out of the Victorian carriage, through the passageway and into the alcove outside the last car of the train. The Government paid for lounge that served alcohol gratis to anyone in uniform. It was conceived to be a welcome home for the thousands of souls rescued from the beaches of Dunkirk and it proved to be a reward most took ample advantage of. Even with all the rail noise in the alcove, when he opened the door, the sound of tipsy voices and laughter rose above the din.

The lounge car was longer than a normal carriage and curved at the far end to accommodate the bar. Sets of green leather half-circle booths lined the left side of the coach and small polished round tables with two fixed chairs ran along the other side which together with the booths formed a center aisle. While the car was crowded with personnel, there were still seats open at the booth closest to the oak bar around which a few people stood. What surprised Jamie was that a substantial number of the uniforms were filled by women, either Woman's Auxiliary Air Force (WAAF) or like Madge, (WRNS) Woman's Royal Naval Service. What didn't surprise him was that they attracted most of the attention.

Jamie and Madge managed to get three steps into the lounge before Miles' voice rang out. "There you are. Over here lad," as he motioned with his hand for them to join him and four other pilots in the second booth.

They squeezed around an army sergeant talking with two WAAFs seated at a table and as they approached, Miles raised his pint. "Thank you for fetching him Madge."

She smiled and put her hand around the back of Jamie's arm. He leaned over as she came close to his ear, "You go speak with your friends, I'm going to the bar," she said. "Shall I bring you a whiskey?"

"Why not? It's on the house, so to speak." She smiled and as she walked away, he watched her wend a path through the gaggle standing in the aisle and disappear.

"Gentlemen, this is one of the best blokes in all of England, Jamie Wallace," Miles said to the pilots seated around the table as he approached.

An officer closest to the aisle on the far side of the booth stood and extended his hand. "Hello Jamie, Miles has gone on quite a bit about you. I'm Eric Locke, 41 Squadron's Commander."

He was several inches shorter than Jamie and a few years older, but quite fit. His looks were that of a film star, but his legs were too short to be one. Jamie shook his hand, his grip firm and confident. He could sense Eric was the kind of man you wanted by your side in a brawl. His coal black hair was parted on the side with a razor-sharp line which added to the no-nonsense countenance about him. Jamie's first and most lasting impression was that Eric Locke was a leader, a man he could follow. "Have a seat," Eric said and motioned toward the empty space across from him.

Eric started with an introduction of the other three pilots. The man next to him was an aristocratic and refined Sikh. He introduced himself as Raj Singh and appeared larger than most pilots, tall enough that Jamie wondered how cramped he must be in a cockpit. He spoke with the type of accent usually reserved for graduates of Oxford and yet, beneath the gloss there was an intensity about him that led one to believe he was a fierce warrior. Next to Raj, was Billy Fiske, a simple looking man who was about the same size as Eric. He smiled a broad smile and immediately let Jamie know he was a yank from Brooklyn and only an Acting Pilot Officer. There was something about Billy that made him feel as if you had known him all your life. Next to Billy was Miles, his red hair scattered about his head as usual and a pint in his hand. The last pilot introduced himself as Harry Baum, a shy Jewish kid from the midlands, his accent betrayed him as most likely from Manchester.

"Well met to all of you," Jamie said as he slid in next to Harry.

Eric lay his forearms on the table. "I understand you and Miles have been friends for a long time."

Jamie looked at Miles and thought of their exploits together. "Miles and his family moved to Newent when we were both about twelve. We've been friends ever since." Jamie said.

Eric nodded. "And you and Miles joined the Aviation Cadet Program together three years ago. What made you do that? Miles said he did it because you did."

"I don't know about that, but for myself, I've always loved aeroplanes. Besides, the two pounds a month was a good incentive for a lad with no money. Why do you ask?"

"Wondering what got you interested in aviation and the RAF. I understand you volunteered for active duty when your brother went to France with the expeditionary forces and that he was listed as missing at Dunkirk." Eric leaned back in the seat, "Also, you and Miles received your wings two days ago, finished at the top of your training class and are waiting for a squadron."

"I think Miles has covered it all," Jamie laughed. "We're to report to the Air Ministry for our squadron assignments day after tomorrow."

"Suppose I can save you the trouble?" Eric took a sip of his pint and looked at him over the glass rim, "I'm in need of two more pilots to fill 41 Squadron. So, I thought we'd chat a bit and see if you're interested. What about you, Miles?"

"Absolutely, I'd much rather be with a squadron I know than walking in cold."

"And you Jamie?"

Jamie ran a finger over his lips thinking of how oddly fate worked. He looked over Eric's shoulder and saw Madge approaching with his whiskey. "What would we be flying?"

"Spitfires," Eric said, "and they're the latest and best in the entire RAF. That's why we're here. We're on our way to Cardiff to pick up the last four of our new Spits."

Madge set the whiskey in front of Jamie. He slid over and patted the seat cushion next to him. "Please, join us," he said to her as the others made attempts to stand. "Do you all know Madge? She's on her way to Cardiff as well, to meet her fiancée. He's on a destroyer arriving in from convoy duty."

Billy Fiske held up his pint. "We met her when Miles came over to the booth. Welcome back," he said through a grin and his Brooklyn accent.

After a few seconds, Eric looked Jamie in the eye and said, "So, what do you say, ready to join the finest squadron in the RAF?"

Jamie smiled. "It feels right, Eric. I think 41 will be a good home."

"Welcome to the squadron, to both of you," Raj said as he swilled his glass of what appeared to be water in the condensation left on the table. "Miles mentioned you had a brother at Dunkirk, an Army Sergeant, Michael I believe." He paused a moment and looked up from the glass. "We were there, you know. Lost four of our own covering the evacuation. I understand he's missing?"

Jamie looked at his mahogany face, "We received a letter a few days after most of the soldiers returned. It informed us Michael was listed as Missing in Action. We all took that to mean he was killed or captured, we didn't know which. A week ago, they let us know he'd been found and was in hospital somewhere near London. They moved him to Gloucester yesterday and today, he was to be released and go home. We know he was injured but not much more."

"They had a bad time of it, Jamie, a very bad time. There were thousands of them, all crowded shoulder to shoulder with nowhere to hide and the bastards would bomb and strafe them right there on the beach." Raj took a sip of the water. "We did everything we could to keep them off the lads, but it was impossible. A few of the Germans always managed to get through. So many died right there on the beach. I'm happy your brother wasn't one of them. No matter what his injury, he made it out alive."

"And for that I'm grateful," Jamie said.

"That's the first time I've heard anyone speak about what Dunkirk was like for the boys," Madge said as she sat forward towards the table. "The government's kept things like that out of bounds for any discussion. They don't want us to know the truth. A few days ago, they banned the ringing of church bells for the duration. The bells are now to be used to signal an invasion is in progress and I'm sure the Germans are right now preparing for just that. It's high time they told us what's really happening."

The truth of her statement brought silence to the table. It was a long moment before Eric spoke. "You're right, Madge. The truth does need to be told. The people need to know how tenuous our position really is, we're barely hanging on. But as to an invasion, the Germans will have to defeat the RAF first and that's something I assure you they will never be able to do."

She took a breath. "I'm sorry. It seems I've been rather boorish, I didn't mean to destroy the mood. It's that all of it seems so frightening."

The door to the lounge snapped opened, the clacking sound of the rails leaked in ahead of a white-haired Conductor, his dark blue uniform a little faded, but the brass buttons polished to a gleam. He walked toward the rear of the car announcing in a voice above conversations, "Next stop, Newent."

As he passed their table, Miles downed his almost empty pint and set it down, "Sorry to break this up, but that's our stop. Ready, Jamie?"

"One second you two," Eric let out a little laugh. "I'll expect you both to report the day after tomorrow before noon at the Uxbridge main gate. I'll take care of the Air Ministry. At the gate they'll direct you to me and 41 Squadron. Welcome aboard."

The Mona Lisa smile came from Madge as she looked over her shoulder and stood to let him out of the booth. He smiled back at her, knowing they most likely would never see each other again.

The train lurched as brakes were applied, the squeal of steel on steel well above the other sounds in the lounge. Miles rose behind him and said, "A pleasure Madge and Eric, we'll see you day after tomorrow. Come on Jamie, they'll only stop for a minute or two." He turned and headed off to retrieve his gear.

"Right behind you," Jamie said. He looked at Madge and wrapped his arms around her. In a whisper he said in her ear, "When *Ratherham* docks, I know everything will work as you dreamt it would. Take care of yourself."

She leaned back and stared at him, her eyes a little wet. "You as well, Jamie Wallace. Don't let anything happen to you." She rose onto her toes and kissed his cheek. "Please be safe."

That was something he knew he couldn't promise.

Chapter Two

It was the kind of morning when most people took delight in the promise of a new day. But for Lord Randall Ashford, every eighteenth of June brought a surge of memory, a cacophony of images as intense as the night they were created. A rain-soaked night, the shimmer of amber light on a wet London street and the love of his life cradled in his arms as she struggled for her last breaths.

It had been fifteen years to the day, his wife Mary, the only woman he ever loved, was struck by a drunken hack driver as she waited for him by the curb. Her loss and the guilt of his failure to protect her always resided right below the surface. He ran a hand through his graying hair and relived the terror of arriving home with Mary's blood caked on his uniform and the fear filled eyes of his then six-year-old daughter as she stood before him and said, "Where's Mummy?"

The memory followed him as he stepped from his study onto a Mediterranean porch that spanned the entire length of his ancestral home. He stood silent between ornate urns filled with blood-red geraniums and gazed out over a breeze stippled lake surrounded by five-hundred acres of rolling grounds and forests. It was his home, the place of his birth, and at Kensington Manor, there was a solace he could find nowhere else. As the memories began to diminish, he felt an arm reach around the small of his back. He turned to see the face of his daughter, Livy. It was as if he was looking into her mother's eyes, she was so much like her.

"I know what you're feeling. I miss her too." she said.

He put his arms around her as if she too might vanish. "It's a hard day for us both." He managed a smile as she looked up at him. "You are so much your mother's daughter, including her hard-headed obstinance," they both laughed as she took a step back and in his heart he knew he was rapidly losing her. She was taking her own life into her hands and would soon be leaving the Manor to walk into a world he had tried to shelter her from, a world he was convinced she knew nothing about. "I assume you're still going through with obtaining your WAAF assignment?"

"I thought we quit this discussion last night." She flopped two towels over the stone railing and adjusted the strap of her white swimsuit tighter around her neck. Her eyes narrowed a bit and she crossed her arms over her chest, one bare foot tapped a consistent four beat rhythm. "There is no further need to speak of it, I'll not be left out of this war. I will do my part and you are to do nothing to prevent that. Agreed?"

Randall held his hands up in resignation, "You're a grown woman, Livy, and you make your own choices. But, think about this first. You have no idea what's coming, what the Germans are like. It was a damn fool idea for you to join the WAAFs. You're the last Ashford, the last of our line," he swept his hand around as if displaying the estate to a newcomer. "Someday all of this will be yours and you being injured or worse because of a foolish decision is something I can't live with."

"Nothing's going to happen to me. I can assure you of that." She picked up one of the towels, "Whatever assignment they give me, I'm sure it won't be anywhere close to danger. We'll drop this conversation because I've made my decision. I'm going to take an assignment and a swim as well." She turned from him and headed down the porch stairs toward the lake.

"You haven't much time, don't forget Churchill's speech to the House of Commons," he called out to her.

She looked over her shoulder without missing a step, "I wouldn't miss it."

So adamant, determined to do "her part," and so headstrong he knew he couldn't stop her. What infuriated him was that she refused to listen to reason. The whole thing was a silly idea, one he had to quash immediately and that's exactly what he did. Only, she didn't know it.

He turned away from her and noticed Harold Ryder, the Manor's butler, as he stood a few inches inside the French doors to his study, "Lord Ashford, Stewart Menzies and Sir Gordon Howell have arrived."

Randall nodded, "Thank you, Harold. Show them in." With a little apprehension, he entered the manor. Churchill would not have sent these men to Kensington Manor unless what they brought was of grave importance. Whatever burden they came with, he suspected it would be disagreeable.

Randall stood by the side of his desk as the two approached. Metropolitan Police Commissioner Gordon Howell came towards him, his face framed with compassion, something a little unusual for the normally stoic policeman. He looked at Randall from under thick sandy-blond eyebrows and rested one of his ham-hock hands on his shoulder, "I know how difficult this day must be for you." Sir Gordon Howell was with him outside the restaurant doors when the taxi jumped the curb and took Mary's life into the past.

"Good to see you, Gordon," he shook his old friend's mutton hand and attempted a smile, "I'm plodding my way through." The other man stepped from behind Gordon's bulk. Stewart Menzies, Chief of the Secret Intelligence Service, MI6. He was a man Randall knew only by reputation. "Finally, we meet Stewart."

There was odd countenance about the man. He was thin with deep set, almost black eyes that spoke of an immense treasure of secrets residing behind a rather bland and quiet, patrician face, the kind of face that would easily disappear in a crowd, become invisible. The kind of face that should belong to an intelligence man.

"Lord Ashford, a pleasure," Menzies said in a flat, toneless voice.

Randall motioned to the chairs in front of his desk. "Gentlemen, have a seat." The two men settled into burgundy leather wing-backs as he said, "Winston rang me early this morning to say he had arranged this meeting, but he was quite secretive about the subject. So, tell me what's going on?"

Randall moved in behind his desk and noticed the worry on Gordon's face as he slid forward in the chair, his hands clasped together, his shoulders hunched, the weight of his elbows pressed into the soft leather.

Gordon's forceful baritone voice started the meeting, "Winston has requested we inform you of a situation that has only become clear during the last week. What we are about to disclose may not leave this room." He paused a moment as the weight of his statement hung in the air. "We believe somewhere in and amongst the highest levels of our Government, a traitor exists. He is delivering to the enemy intelligence of the highest quality, some of our deepest and most guarded secrets."

Randall felt his gut tighten and he focused on Stewart Menzies. "Do they know we've broken Enigma?"

Menzies barely moved his head from side to side. "No, we believe they still think Enigma is unbreakable."

Randall leaned back in his chair, slightly relieved and looked back at the Police Commissioner. "Gordon, obviously, this traitor must be found and I'm sure you're well into that task, but why involve me? I'm not a security man."

Gordon Howell didn't move, "When the war started, we apprehended every agent the Germans had in Britain. They were offered one of two choices, either they work for us or be executed." Randall nodded, he'd heard that before. "Of all of the agents working for us, to a man, not a single one knows anything about a highly placed mole and I can assure you they are telling the truth." Gordon looked at Stewart Menzies seated next to him, as if it was his turn to speak.

"I'm afraid this entire matter is quite different than anything we've seen before." Menzies said. "We believe this mole is a sleeper agent, one that's been in Britain for quite some time. He is shrewd, ruthless, and most likely a member of the aristocracy. But unlike a common sympathizer, he is a Nazi."

"You asked why you are involved," Gordon said.

"I did, I still don't understand."

"They're out to destroy our air defense system, the one you created and because of that, we believe you and your daughter are in danger. You have a security detail with you everywhere you go, but your daughter is vulnerable. For the last week we have instituted a policy of shadowing individuals we believe the Nazis might harm. Your daughter is included in that policy."

"You believe they would use my daughter as what ... ransom?"

"We do." Gordon nodded.

"Well then, I agree with your precautions." Randall paused a moment and said, "However, that being said, there is a small issue. Today she is to receive her WAAF assignment. I've made my objections quite clear to the clerk handling the matter and I believe he's going to comply with my wishes, but one never knows, after all she did sign up."

"At this time, an assignment of any type for her would not be advisable. There's too much risk involved." Gordon paused a moment and then shrugged his shoulders, "Perhaps a friendly nudge from Special Branch might ensure his cooperation." He reached into a coat pocket. "What's the man's name?"

"Mueller, a Warren Mueller. He's at the WAAF section of the War Office."

Gordon wrote a note in his policeman's notebook and returned it to the pocket. "Before the morning is over, he'll receive a little push from Special Branch. That should settle it, no assignment."

For a few moments, silence overtook the study which was finally broken by the bland voice of Menzies. "The enigma intercepts we believe intended for this traitor detail a concerted attempt to discover any weakness that might allow the Germans to cripple the air defense system."

Randall sat forward, his elbows again on the desk, "I doubt this traitor, or anyone else for that matter, will have any concept I was involved. But, if they are successful and find the plan, they'll quickly discover how to blind the RAF. Without radar, Fighter Command will be defeated and their invasion will succeed." He looked at Gordon who still hadn't moved, "You must have suspicions as to who this traitor might be?"

Gordon Howell shook his head. "I have over one hundred officers from Special Branch assigned to the task, but so far, we have nothing. Which brings us to the second reason we're here. The defense plan must be secured."

"Oh, I agree. For now, it may be the most precious document in the realm," Randall added.

Gordon continued, "Some of the precautions already taken include incinerating the two reserve copies as well as any other portions released to individuals or departments. As of today, only your original and

Churchill's copy exist." Gordon paused, his eyes focused on Randall, "The document must be protected at all cost," his meaning clear.

"I understand," Randall said as a knock came to the door.

It opened and Harold Ryder took a single step into the room. "My pardon, Lord Ashford but you requested to be informed when the courier arrived. He is here, sir."

"Give us a moment Harold." When the door closed he said, "Gentlemen, I must see this courier."

As the two men stood, Gordon said, "We're finished Randall. It's a nasty business my friend, especially for you today."

Menzies rose and Randall shook hands with the two as they left. For several seconds, he sat and stared at what seemed to be blank papers on his desk. Silently, the walnut door opened and Harold announced, "Lord Ashford, the courier, Squadron Commander Beck."

Randall motioned for the courier to sit in one of the chairs facing his desk. He was curious when he looked up at the Squadron Commander as he crossed over a Persian rug and took a seat facing him. The man had a familiar look about him, but one Randall couldn't quite place.

"I know you, don't I?" he said.

The man set a leather briefcase on his lap. "Yes sir, I was at the manor about ten years ago with my father, Samuel Beck."

Randall cocked his head to one side and said, "Are you Banker Beck's boy?"

"Yes sir. My name is Aubrey Beck."

He looked older than he should have, his dark hair wearing thin at the crown and graying at the temples. Randall guessed he was midway into his thirties and he looked as if sleep had turned its back on him. He wasn't at all the somewhat handsome young man of his memory.

"It's been a long time, Aubrey." He extended his hand and the younger man took it, rising from the chair. "And how is your father? I haven't seen him since all this trouble started."

"Very well, sir." Aubrey said as he slipped back into the comfort of the chair.

A vague memory came back to Randall, something about Aubrey and a young woman in Guernsey. He assumed he must have got her pregnant, but he wasn't sure. Whatever it was, it caused his father to turn him out, disown him from the family's wealth. As he observed the man across from him, Randall noticed the lack of wings on his uniform. "How long have you been in the RAF, Aubrey?"

"A little over four months, sir. Doing my part for the war effort."

Randall nodded and understood. Aubrey had been granted an officer's commission based on his family's name, he hadn't earned it. There were far too many of this kind of officer. He'd seen his type get men slaughtered in the Great War from their incompetence and as a naval officer, he resented them—all of them.

"What have you brought me," he said, knowing full well what Lord Beaverbrook had sent.

Aubrey spun the briefcase and struggled to unlock it. His hands shook as he fumbled and attempted to insert the key. "I have the latest production figures," he said as he finally clicked the lock and opened the case. He slipped out a sealed folder stamped with a large red X and labeled "Most Secret." As he handed it to Randall, he took a breath and started over. "These are the aircraft production estimates and timetables you requested. I'm also instructed to say that Lord Beaverbrook and the Ministry have asked, that if possible, all aircraft plants be camouflaged so as not to be visible from the air. They believe the Germans will begin to expand their attacks well past the Channel in an effort to destroy our industrial capacity, a prelude to invasion."

"We've taken those steps and as to an invasion—no other military option is rational. Hitler must destroy us or lose the war. It's that simple." Randall thought of the secrets being delivered to Berlin and the fragile thread England hung by. "If he doesn't, he's finished."

He broke the seal and opened the folder. "Give me a second, Aubrey. I want to look over what's in here."

Randall dropped the stack of papers on his desk and began leafing through them. He stopped at a page that outlined the capacity of the aircraft factories and calculated it would take six weeks to replenish the fighters lost in the failed defense of France. Far too long a time when the Luftwaffe held a four to one superiority. If not for radar, the RAF would lose.

With the conversation paused, he looked up and noticed Aubrey gaze around the study, taking in the ornately framed oil paintings that posed various Ashfords whose lives had passed into history. He watched Aubrey scan by them and stop at the silver frames aligned along an intricately carved baroque table containing photographs of people and places that spoke of Randall's life.

He looked back at the papers and completed his mental calculations. Thoroughly discouraged, a few seconds later he slipped the stack into the government folder and looked at the RAF officer who was staring at a family photograph, one showing his daughter and her mother taken at their seaside cottage a month before her death. It showed Mary smiling, her shoulder-length hair flowing in a brisk wind. She lovingly held a much smaller Livy by her favorite spot above the cliffs that overlooked the Channel.

He remembered the happiness of that day and wondered if he could ever feel something like that again. "Is there anything more, Aubrey?"

"Lord Beaverbrook also requested that you accompany him to a cabinet meeting with the Prime Minister, after his speech to the House of Commons."

Randall thought about those very words coming from Beaverbrook not more than an hour ago. He stood and said, "You go and tell Beaverbrook I'm on my way."

Aubrey stood and took his hand. "I will, sir. Is there anything else?"

"Nothing I can think of. I'll be at the House chamber as soon as I can."

Aubrey smiled and said, "Thank you, sir," the entire time reminding himself how careful he must be around this man—someone this powerful could be very dangerous. As he turned to leave, he heard the sound of a woman humming, it seemed to float into the study like a Siren's call. It hung in the air as she appeared framed in the open doors, backlit by the sun.

Water ran off her smooth skin and pooled beneath her feet. Dressed in a one-piece white suit that almost transparently clung to the curves of her hips, she gracefully scooped up a towel folded over the railing. Centered between red flowers, she daubed at the moisture falling off her shoulder-length auburn hair and he couldn't take his eyes off her.

"That's my daughter, Olivia. You remember her, don't you? Livy, come say hello to Aubrey Beck."

Surprised, the young woman turned toward the open door. He saw her squint, her eyes accustomed to the sunlight. "I'll be there in a moment. I need to dry off a bit."

His mouth open, Beck watched her and an idea for his salvation began working in the recesses of his mind. She wrapped a towel around herself and crossed the threshold to her home. The face was stunning, as if sculpted by the magic of Renaissance hands, something delicate and expressive, yet strong and deeply moving. A far cry from the awkward little girl he remembered.

Her penetrating indigo eyes captivated him as she approached, her wet bare feet leaving prints as she came across the sun-heated floor. She extended her hand. "Aubrey, a pleasure to see you again, it's been years, hasn't it?"

Soft, but firm and cool, her skin touched his and a hunger began to burn inside him. He tried to speak, but his mind went blank and all he could manage was a smile and a dip of his head.

"I think she was eleven or so when you saw her last. Grew up a bit, wouldn't you say?" As Aubrey tried to compose himself Lord Ashford turned to his daughter and said, "Livy, you need to hurry or you'll miss Winston's speech. Are you coming to Whitehall with me?"

She shook her head. Aubrey watched little water droplets sparkle as they fell to the floor. "Alana's coming to fetch me, she's home now from America. We plan to take the train into Westminster and meet you there. I didn't realize we were running late, but we'll be there on time. I wouldn't miss this for the world." Her exquisite face smiled at him and the voice said, "A pleasure to see you again, Aubrey."

Feeling as if his feet were stuck to the floor, he watched as she passed by him, opened the walnut study door and closed it softly behind her.

Chapter Three

The House of Commons was filled to capacity. Livy and Alana managed seats in the gallery because Lord Randall Ashford ordered security to rope them off. They sat together on a green leather bench in the front row overlooking the House floor as Winston Churchill paused delivering his speech.

He stood with hands draped on either side of a rather plain boxwood podium. Slowly, he raised his eyes toward the balcony and Livy almost believed he was looking at her alone. He gripped his coat lapels and began again with that graveled voice and unmistakable cadence. "Hitler knows that he will have to break us in this island or lose the war. If we can stand up to him, all Europe may be free, and the life of the world may move forward into broad sunlit uplands. But if we fail, the whole world, including the United States, including all that we have known and cared for, will sink into the abyss of a new Dark Age.

"Let us therefore brace ourselves to our duties, and so bear ourselves that if the British Empire and its Commonwealth last for a thousand years, men will still say, *this* was their finest hour."

For a few heartbeats, the entire chamber was silent and then spontaneous cheers erupted. Above the floor in the gallery, Livy stood with the multitude and applauded as proud tears welled in her eyes. She reached into her WAAF jumper, retrieved a linen handkerchief and daubed them away. "Alana, there is no other place I'd rather be than here. We've just seen history, something that will be spoken of a thousand years from this day. Those Nazis are unbelievable. My blood is up and I am starving to have a crack at them."

Livy glanced at her childhood friend. Alana's silky-black hair was tied in a tight roll at the nape of her neck and contrasted with her sky-blue uniform. Her extraordinary face turned, her chestnut eyes set as if in stone. "What if the Nazis win?" she said. "What happens if the RAF is destroyed, we're invaded and we lose the war?"

The cheering suddenly sounded hollow, as if Livy had taken a step back from the world. That thought had never occurred to her. She looked away from Alana and back to the Commons floor below, the members cheering and gathering around Churchill, her father standing quietly behind him, dressed in his dark-blue uniform of a Royal Navy Captain. Seeing him so resolute, her confidence gathered. "Not a chance, my dear. Hitler has no idea of the quicksand he's walked into. The last despot who planned to invade England died an outcast on some godforsaken island in the South Atlantic."

Alana shook her head. "Don't be so sure. The Germans scare me, they seem invincible. They took France out of the war in less than six weeks. It would make me far happier to see some sort of peace offered than to risk our complete destruction."

Livy replaced the handkerchief. "Peace is out of the question. Hitler can't be trusted. He's proven that and like Churchill said, if we stand up to him, he'll lose the war. I think saving civilization from a Nazi world is worth fighting for. I'm proud to be a part of it."

Alana's smile was stiff. "I wonder if it's that simple."

Livy put her arm around her shoulder as she looked down and caught sight of her father walking alongside Lord Beaverbrook with Aubrey Beck trailing behind. Her father looked up at her and with a wave pointed toward the huge ornate doors to indicate they should meet him in the central lobby outside the House chamber.

It took several minutes for Livy and Alana to get through the jostling crowd jamming the narrow stairwell and navigate through one of the eight hallways leading to the octagon-shaped lobby. Her father, Beaverbrook, and Beck stood near the center speaking with a tall white-haired man who was dressed in an exquisite gray pinstripe suit that must have come from a Savile Row tailor. As the two squeezed through the crowd, she heard his voice—a melodic, almost hypnotic baritone and definitely American.

"Randall, I really don't know," the man was saying as they approached.

"Ah, here they are," her father said to the American. "This is my daughter Livy and this young woman is her friend, Alana Eaton. Alana is the daughter of Member Wilfred Eaton, from Gloucestershire and an old friend of mine. These two have been inseparable since their early school days." He turned to them both. "Girls, you both know Lord Beaverbrook and Alana, you might remember Aubrey Beck from years ago. This gentleman"—he swept his hand toward the tall white-haired man— "is someone I have known for too short a time, Paul White. He's responsible for the entire operation of CBS News here in London and a great friend to the people of England. We've been attempting to coerce Mr. White to help us convince President Roosevelt that America should enter the war."

Paul White shook his head and with a laugh said, "Anything to do with convincing the President of something like that is far above my meager talents."

"I don't believe a word of it," her father said, smiling at him. "By the way, Paul, Alana is American—or part, at least."

"Really," White smiled and extended his hand to Alana. "A pleasure to meet you, and which part of you is American?"

Alana slipped her hand into his and said, "My mother is from Chicago, but I was raised in England with my father, you see my parents separated when I was very young." She paused for a moment and then said, "Mr. White, will America come into the war, or are we to go it alone?"

He smiled and shook his head, "I really don't know. I've met with the President on several occasions though I'm certainly not in his confidence. But, the American people are a funny lot; their opinions can change very quickly. Right now, most remember the last war vividly and have no desire to again be a part of something like that. There's a well-funded group called The America First Committee and they have no intention of allowing America to get into what they call foreign entanglements." He winked at her, "However, we do have a special place in our hearts for the underdog. For now, though, my best guess would be absolutely not. America won't enter the war, at least not anytime soon." He held Alana's eyes for a second and turned to Livy.

She took his hand and thought this was a man of intellect and a great deal of confidence, "A pleasure to meet you, Mr. White."

Her father interjected, "I believe you're both taking your assignments today, aren't you?" He forced a tired smile at her.

"We're to be the War Office no later than two," Livy said as she noticed Alana shift her eyes toward Aubrey Beck.

"Well then, how about some lunch?" her father offered to the group. "Lord Beaverbrook and I have at least an hour until we meet with the Prime Minister. So, how about it? The fare offered here is superb."

Paul White checked a gold pocket watch and slipped it back into his vest, "I'm game. But first let me mention I'm having a cocktail party a week from this Saturday. I'd be honored if all of you could come. I'm holding it at the country home I've rented in Kent, and if you can make it, I'd enjoy your company."

Alana was the first to respond. "With all the bad news, I'd enjoy a party right now. I'll definitely agree, Mr. White."

He looked at her and smiled, "Wonderful, and the rest of you?"

They all looked at one another, nodding agreement.

Aubrey Beck spoke up. "I guess we'll all be joining." He looked at Livy, "How about you, Miss Ashford? I trust you'll agree."

She paused a second, her head tilted to one side. "I think that would be fun and I might even get you to apologize. The last time I saw you, you referred to me as a skinny little waif."

"And for that, I deserve to be drawn and quartered," Aubrey said, beaming a smile.

"Well, that seems to be settled." Livy's father clapped his hands together and said, "Now, how about a fine Burgundy with—"

A stern-looking security man interrupted. "Pardon me, sir." He nodded to Lord Beaverbrook, "The Prime Minister has requested that you and Lord Ashford follow me."

"What's happened?" Beaverbrook said, his words quick and ominous.

The security man studied the group for a moment and said, "The Germans have come inland far beyond the Channel. As we speak, they are attacking the Chain Home Radar installations at Ventnor and other key points all over southern England. The Prime Minister has called an emergency meeting of the Cabinet. I was ordered to find you and bring you both immediately."

Chapter Four

There was a time Jamie would stand on tip toes at the second story dining room window to watch rain splatter on the cobblestones of Broad Street. It would begin slowly at first, dark spots on the stone globes. With time, water would gather, start to trickle in the deep valleys and he would imagine little wending rivers that flowed between high mountains, filled with tiny, invisible sailboats bound for destinations known only to his mind. Sometimes their voyage would last minutes and sometimes seconds until the rivers were gorged and the water rushed over the mountains in torrents that wiped away the imaginary towns and microscopic people and Jamie would turn away from the window.

On this afternoon, the street was dry and the mountains merely stones as he and Miles stood before Wallace's Butcher Shop directly across Broad Street from a pub called the Red Lion. The shop's windows were decorated with roughly painted Union Jacks, *Welcome Home Michael* stenciled across the glass in simple red, white, and blue letters.

Jamie stopped in front of the window, "You coming in?"

"I'll say a quick hello." Miles patted his shoulder, sensitive to the turmoil his friend must be feeling. "Don't worry about Michael," he said. "The lad was the toughest kid in all of Newent and no matter what his injuries, he'll come out on top. He always did." His eyes narrowed a bit. "As for your father, I'll wager that his anger has blown over and he'll welcome you home."

"I'm not so sure. Nothing feels right about this, it's as if I've become a stranger." He looked through an unpainted section of the window and saw Julia Weiss, Michael's fiancée, setting the final additions to platters for an already gathering party across the street. "I've turned a corner, Miles, and began a path from which I can never return."

His friend's eyes scanned the window and then looked back at him. "I feel much the same. This isn't really home anymore and for the two of us, I believe our adventures have barely begun."

Jamie nodded, "Well, I guess we should make the most of it for now. We have little time until we report to Uxbridge."

He paused a moment as he took hold of the knob and then opened it. A little bell that hung over the front door tinkled as he entered the shop and Julia looked toward him. "Jamie you're home!" she exclaimed.

Her dark, almost black hair was pinned back exposing a face and soft, round brown eyes that could best be described with a biblical passage. There was something about her that could light up a room. From the first time he saw her with Michael, he knew they were meant for each other.

He dropped his kit bag beside the entrance. "Julia, it's great to see you." She pushed the sausage tray further onto the porcelain counter and ran up to him, placing a quick kiss on his cheek.

She stepped back and said, "Miles, I'm so happy you're here too. It will mean so much to Michael."

Miles placed his kit bag next to Jamie's, "Hi Julia." She gave Miles a hug and looked back at Jamie. He instantly understood the fear written on her face.

"You don't know anything about Michael's injuries either, do you?" he said.

She shook her head. "No one does. I'm so scared, Jamie."

As he was about to speak, his mother's voice came from the cutting room at the back of the shop. She entered the front room staring at her hands as she wiped them on an apron tied around her waist. "Oh my, look at the time! Robert will be in a snit if we don't get the food over there before he returns. He was a bit of the terror this morning."

She looked up from the apron and spotted them. Her face surprised, "Jamie, for the last two days we've been trying to get hold of you. Why didn't you ring us? Your father is absolutely furious."

Pushing into her mid-fifties and heavier of late, she was still an attractive, gentle woman with graying strawberry-blond hair. Soft hazel eyes were set on either side of a nose exactly like his, one that turned up ever so slightly. "Hello Miles, it's good to see you," she said.

"Thank you, Mrs. W." Miles grinned back.

Julia turned to Jamie and whispered in his ear, "Please, we have to talk." She looked in his eyes and then faced his mother, "Rachael, I'm going to get these over to the party. Miles, can you help me?" She picked up the tray of fresh sausage and with Jamie holding the door, Miles followed her with his own tray as she darted across the street.

Jamie looked toward his mother, "Mum, I didn't ring you because there are no phones. They shut 'em off."

"What? We called the aerodrome yesterday, Commander Brook something—your father spoke with him."

"Wing Commander Brookwall," Jamie said. "Of course, he has a phone, but with the security blackout after Dunkirk, for the last two weeks they haven't let us off the aerodrome, much less speak to anyone on the outside."

She threw up her hands in exasperation. "Why did you ever do this? Join the RAF. We already gave one son to the war; we don't have to give another."

"It was right for me mum, but what about Michael, what have they told you?"

"Nothing. Two days ago, an Army officer came and told us to come fetch him today. He's been discharged from the Army and that's all we know. Your father is so worried about him; he's right on the edge."

She quickly took in a breath to compose herself. "But we'll have plenty of time to talk about this later." She put a loving hand on his cheek. "Jamie, when your father sees you, pay no attention to what he says. He's still angry that you left, but he won't mean his words. It's the worry over Michael, that's all."

He wrapped his arms around her. As for his father, he would deal with that later. "It'll be all right, Michael always lands on his feet." He picked up a basket of hot scones wrapped in a red checkered cloth and the two headed toward The Red Lion.

Jamie placed the basket in a space between food trays on a table set beneath a window across from the bar. At almost every other table, the conversations centered on the same question: Will they or won't they invade? The threat of Germans waging war on English soil was far too real and with the Army almost destroyed at Dunkirk, people were frightened England would fall like France.

Most of the younger men wore uniforms and those that didn't had either just enlisted or were awaiting induction, all but one—Squeaky Jenkins. His thin little body the military determined couldn't meet the rigors of combat. Although he hadn't said a word about it, Jamie knew the rejection devastated him.

He put a hand on Squeaky's shoulder and said, "Hello lad, how are you?"

Squeaky leaned back in his chair and smiled up at him. "Hey there Jamie, good to see you. Did ya finish with pilot training?"

"Both Miles and I got our wings two days ago. What about you? What are you up to?"

I've been blacking out all the signs that name the town and streets. They think it will confuse the Germans when they invade, as if they can't buy a detailed Michelin map anywhere from Paris to Berlin. 'Tis a foolhardy idea, but as long as they pay me, I'll oblige 'em."

"You got 'em all done?" Jamie laughed.

"Nope, I left a few. I wasn't gonna miss this thing for Michael. If the Germans invade in the next two hours, they'll know they're in Newent and it'll be my fault." He grinned and took a swig of his pint.

"Hey Squeaky," Miles said over Jamie's shoulder. He looked towards a girl they both knew seated across the table. "And, hello to you Lizbeth. Seems like ages since I've seen you. You look smashing."

"Hello to both of you," she said twirling a blond ringlet around a finger.

"Lizbeth, how are you." Jamie said. She was quite a girl and had been a hot issue with Miles during their time at upper school. She was the type of girl that could stop you in a second with merely a look. Miles moved in and corralled a seat at the table across from her.

Squeaky looked up at Jamie as Lizbeth and Miles seemed to pick up from where they left off years ago. "Anyway, I didn't get a chance to tell you. I'm giving up me painting career. Old Smitty gave me Jack's job at the garage, you see he's in the Navy now. I'll be sellin' motorcars. How's that for a lucky break?"

"Good for you. In fact Squeaky, I'm in the market for a good motorcar. Can you find one for me?"

"Of course, you'll be my first customer." He raised his pint. "Oh, I forgot to tell you Julia is over there at the end of the bar. Asked that when I saw you to send you over, she said it was real important."

"Thanks, Squeaky. Please keep an eye out for me though, pilots with a motorcar have a leg up with the girls." Jamie motioned to the barkeep that the next pint was on him. "I got your next one Squeaky, cheers." He looked toward the corner and spotted Julia.

The century old, polished rosewood bar curved back toward a wall against which Julia sat sipping tea in one of the quietest places in the pub. Jamie approached and she motioned to the stool next to her.

Julia put her hand on his forearm and said, "I'm happy you're here. I've felt quite alone these last few days." She looked into her teacup and said, "The day your mother told me Michael was missing, my world fell apart. He was everything to me. We had plans, knew what our life would be like and in a flash, that all went up in smoke."

Small ripples ran across the surface of her tea. He reached out to steady her shaking hands. "I can see there's more happening. What is it, Julia? You seem like you're on the brink."

"I'm frightened," she said. "I'm in love with Michael, the Michael I knew. What happens if that's all changed? Suppose he has no legs or arms or he's badly burned? I don't know what I'd do. I've been in absolute turmoil for the last two days."

"I can imagine." Jamie nodded.

"When I found out he was alive, I was so thrilled—he was coming home to me. Then the fear set in. How is it possible to feel so much joy and so much fear at the same time?"

"I think all of us feel that way—the joy and the fear seem to be jumbled up together."

A slight rumble began to roll across the oak floor. The sound grew until it seemed to shake the entire pub. Everyone was stomping on the dark wood planks. It was called The Lord's Thunder, an old tradition that originated at a time when knights in armor greeted their king after victory in battle. Suddenly, cheers erupted throughout the pub and Jamie knew Michael had arrived.

Jamie escorted Julia through the crowd toward the front door. With his arm around her waist, he could feel her body shaking and knew this moment would decide everything for them. His father stood a few feet inside the door, but his brother was nowhere in sight. As they got closer, he caught a glimpse of a wheelchair and a leg wrapped in plaster then Michael's face came into view.

Jamie recoiled at the sight of him. He was in uniform, the left pant leg and the sleeves from both shirt and coat removed. He was pale and so very battered, the left side of his face was one massive bruise, his arm cradled in a sling and his leg covered in plaster from ankle to mid-thigh. His light blue eyes were in stark contrast to the remnants of dark circles below them, but they were bright and full of life. Michael turned his head, spotted Julia, and his wonderful cocky smile appeared on his face.

She bolted to him and ever so gently gave him a kiss that told Jamie all would be well. For the first time in his life, Jamie saw tears fall from Michael's eyes. They kissed again and Jamie thought with all the madness overtaking the world, there wasn't anything that could be more right. As Julia pulled back, Michael looked over from her kiss and smiled at him.

"My God, you look terrible!" Jamie said.

"I'm still a little topsy-turvy, but my war is over. From the looks at it though, yours has just begun. I can't believe it—my little brother a fighter pilot." His voice was tired but clear and contained the same quality of optimism he always carried.

Jamie laughed. "When you went missing and I thought you were a goner, being a pilot seemed like what I should do. I think I wanted revenge more than anything." He shook his head, "I can't believe it— you're alive and home."

A steeled tone from their father interrupted. "Michael, time to get the honors going. You can speak with him later. Your mothers got a table set—all the special things you like." Jamie's father forced the wheelchair toward the table reserved for him. It caused Julia, still holding on to Michael's hand, to stumble and pushed Jamie a step back. His father gave a cold stare in his direction and said, "You, I'll talk to later."

He pushed Michael's chair close to the reserved table and raised his arms to quiet the crowd as their mother came to stand next to her husband. "Please, be still a moment." The noise began to diminish and at the proper time he said, "I wanted to take a second to thank all of you for coming to welcome our Michael home."

The Lord's Thunder erupted and Robert once more raised his hands. "Thank you. I know he appreciates it as much as Rachael and I do."

Cheers and applause filled the pub. The patrons were caught up in the excitement, but the entire time Michael sat in his chair shaking his head, "This isn't right. I don't want this."

"Jamie," he said, "help me to stand."

From behind the chair, Jamie helped his brother to stand, surprised the bulk of his rugby body was so diminished.

Michael stood, his right leg strained to carry the weight. He held up his arm like a policeman stopping traffic. "Thank you for your welcome. It's more than anything I expected." The Lord's Thunder started again and he held his hand up, the Sergeant stripes prominent on his coat sleeve. "Before this evening is over, I hope to speak with each of you, but for now, I want to spend a few minutes with my brother."

After they had Michael settled in his wheelchair, he leaned his head back and said to his parents, "Would you make the rounds for a few minutes and thank everyone? I wish to speak with Jamie."

"If that's your wish," Robert said with a glare towards Jamie. "That's not exactly what I had planned. These people want to hear from you and about the medal King George personally gave you, I've told everyone about it."

"The medal isn't important, but if you want, we'll do that later. Right now, I want to speak to Jamie." Michael was the carbon copy of their father, he said it with an authority that left no room for further discussion.

Julia squeezed in next to Michael and took his hand as Jamie sat across from them. "The look on your face little brother is bloody priceless," Michael said with a quiet laugh.

Jamie smiled, "Well ya big ox, you scared the hell out of all of us. For weeks I thought you were either dead or a prisoner in some Nazi concentration camp. What happened?"

Julia gripped Michael's hand tighter.

"I'll tell what I can remember. But first draw me a pint." Jamie signaled to Beth Dugan, the pub owner and she nodded. He looked back into Michael's eyes and that was when he saw it, the hollow veil that shrouds images that would never be forgotten. The same veil he saw in the eyes of so many of the soldiers who survived Dunkirk or the instructor pilots who had seen combat in the skies over France. Michael simply nodded at Jamie as if he understood and began, "The retreat from France was bloody, very bloody. Every time we got a battle plan, before we could move the Germans were already ahead of us and we'd walk straight into an ambush. It was as if they knew where we were going before we did. It was uncanny and it happened too many times to be coincidence. Their last ambush was on the first of June, a mile or so east of Dunkirk, at a little place called Bray Dunes."

Beth Duggan, came and placed three pints on the table. Michael took a long swill and continued, "That ambush took out our entire platoon and killed our Lieutenant. I took charge of the six men still alive and we ran for the beach. In the process, we were able to scavenge a machine gun and set it up in a sand dune. When they came at us, it was with a vengeance because we'd killed so many of theirs. After about ten minutes of fighting, we ran out of ammunition and I ordered the four lads that were left to make a run for it. I didn't want the Krauts to get the machine gun, so I took the shoe laces from one of the dead boys and tied a grenade to the breach, pulled the pin and ran like hell. I ran and ran until I managed to get to a boardwalk that had a large concrete privy. As I dove for cover, a Stuka screamed down and dropped a bomb right on top of me. I remember the heat and flying through the air and that's all until I woke up in a London hospital five days later."

He pushed back from the table a bit, got his good leg under it and took a swig that half-finished his pint. Jamie pushed his pint in front of him. "I'm so grateful you're alive."

Michael looked down at his hand as Julia's gripped it so tight her knuckles blanched. He managed to twist his hand free and then picked hers up and kissed it. He looked at her and said, "So am I. My war is over thank God."

Michael finished off his pint in one long gulp and picked up the one Jamie pushed in front of him. "That tastes so good, it feels like years since I've had one."

Jamie waited as he took a draught and then asked, "What about your injuries? What have the doctors said?"

He shrugged. "Well, I won't be playing any rugby. The blast took off half my calf. The rest of this is from shrapnel. It's gonna take some time to mend, but in the end, I'll be fine."

Amid the shock Jamie felt a strong hand grab his shoulder.

"Come with me. We have a bit to discuss," his father said as he made a beeline to a section of the bar near the door.

Jamie slowly stood. "Back in a minute." He walked over to his father and said with a calm confidence that seemed to shock him, "All right, I'm here. What is it you want to talk about?"

"Don't take that tone with me, boy."

"What tone?" Jamie's hands clenched. "What's on your mind?" His father had always treated him as if he were second class, the cast-off son that could never match up to his older brother. He never said anything; he'd simply push it down as if it didn't faze him, but his anger and disappointment simmered below the surface.

His father started in, "Can't you see your brother? Can't you see he has needs? But why let that bother you. You don't think about anyone else, what they might need—no, not Jamie Wallace. You only think of yourself. When Michael was deployed to France, when we needed you most, what did you do you? You joined the bloody Air Force." His fist slammed on the bar. "You never even spoke to me, got my permission. You've never listened to anything I said, never lived up to the responsibilities I set for you. You're not a soldier, Michael is a soldier. You chose the damn Air Force over your family. How could you leave your mum and me to fend for ourselves? How could you do that, Jamie? Can't you see your brother's going to need a lot of help in the next few months? How can you leave us like this? Don't you want a part of the shop one day?"

"The shop belongs to Michael, it always has and it isn't what I want for myself."

"Oh, it's not good enough for Jamie Wallace I suppose because you're a pilot now, like that's supposed to mean something. Your brother was almost killed and you decide you're leaving us once again when you should be here?"

"It is something I must do. Can't you understand that?"

"No. To hell with those that fed you, with the business that paid for everything. No, that's not what Jamie wants and all that's important, what Jamie wants—and now you show up here."

"I came to see my brother. I came to see him before I have to go to my duty station." Once again, he pushed the resentment deep into the pit of his stomach. "I don't have a choice. I'm under orders and I will report to my duty station as ordered."

"Then, I suggest you go and right now!" His father turned and headed toward Michael and the crowd.

Jamie seethed, the rejection he'd endured as a child churning inside him. He watched his father lean over and speak to Michael, then he turned and left the Red Lion. He marched across the street, threw open the butcher shop door and snatched his kit bag and coat leaning against the wall. As he turned to leave, he came face-to-face with his mother.

"Where are you going?" she said.

"I'm doing exactly what my father told me to—I'm leaving. I'm going to my duty station."

"Please, don't take your father too seriously; he's been under a tremendous burden. You know he doesn't mean what he said. It's the times, Jamie. It's making us all a little mad." She placed her palm on his cheek. "Where will you be? I must know."

He looked at his mother, knowing how her heart was breaking and said, "I can't tell you, you know that. I love you, mum. Take care of Michael; Julia will help you."

Miles came up from behind her. "Jamie, what's happened?"

He gave his mother a kiss, slung the kit bag over his shoulder. "I'm leaving, going to London. I'll see you at the aerodrome on Wednesday morning."

"Wait a minute," Miles said, "we came here together and we'll leave together." He took a step into the shop and lifted his kit bag.

"What about Lizbeth?"

Miles looked over at The Red Lion and back, "Looks like she'll have to wait for me."

Jamie smiled, kissed his mother goodbye, and with Miles at his side, the two set off up the hill toward the rail station.

Rachael crossed the cobblestones of Broad Street and watched her youngest son set out toward the war. They had almost reached the corner where they would disappear when she heard the pub door open. Her husband stepped out and stood on the stone step beside her. Over all their years together she knew his mind from the expression on his face. He suddenly had realized there was a chance, a very good chance he would never see his son again.

Rachael looked up at him. "You're a fool, Robert Wallace. You're a damn fool."

Chapter Five

"Are you cozy with Aubrey Beck?" Alana said as they passed Horse Guard's Parade on their way to the War Office.

Livy looked at her as if she'd lost her mind. "Whatever gave you that idea?"

"He pants after you like a dog in heat." She stared at her, demanding an answer.

"That's absurd." Livy paused a second and then laughed. "Though I did have a little mess-up this morning."

Alana nodded as if she wondered what might come next. "And what is a little mess-up?"

"Remember that one piece I bought when we were in Marseille two years ago?"

Alana rolled her eyes, "The one that shows too much when it's wet?"

"That's the one," Livy laughed. "This morning I grabbed the first thing I could find and took a swim. Afterwards, I went up on the porch behind my father's study to dry off. Aubrey was inside."

Alana stopped and pulled on her arm. "You went parading around in front of him in that suit, wet? No wonder. He wants you in his bed."

She pulled her arm away. "Alana, please. The last time he saw me I was eleven. I'm sure he still thinks of me as a little girl."

"Sometimes you're so naïve." Alana said it in a way that made Livy irritated and she walked a little faster. "You stay away from him, he's a bad penny that one. If you weren't willing and he wants you, he'd take you with force, believe me. He's that type of man."

"Stop it! I may have made a fool of myself this morning, but that's as close as he'll ever get to bedding me. Now enough of this." They both walked in silence for half a block and then Livy asked, "By the way, how was America?"

"America?" Alana said and her tone changed. "It was miserable. America is filled with uneducated slovenly people. They remind me of mongrel dogs. There are far better places in the world that deserve their wealth and resources, and besides, the weather was terrible, it was cold and raining. I couldn't wait to come home."

"Good Lord, what's got you going?"

Livy looked away from her as a red double-decker bus slowed to a stop and disgorged some twenty or thirty uniformed workers. They followed the crowd and made their way toward a breach in a sandbag wall some twenty feet high that surrounded the first floor of the baroque limestone War Office. Turning left, they passed the armed guards at the front gate, went up the outer stairs and entered into two and one-half miles of corridors dedicated to protecting the British Empire.

It was surprisingly quiet and dark inside the massive lobby, as if the meager light the chandeliers offered was swallowed by the deep-stained wood covering the walls. The two approached a matronly woman sitting behind a table beneath a blue sign that read "Assignment Desk." Her WAAF uniform jacket strained against silver buttons as she thumbed through index cards in a box. Without looking up she said in a thin scratchy voice, "Identity cards and orders."

They handed them over.

The woman riffled through their papers and studied the identity cards clasped between her thick fingers. She lifted her head and narrowed her eyes as she looked over Livy and Alana. "Ashford and Eaton, well, well." Still holding their papers, she crossed thick jelly-like arms over an ample chest. "Haven't you girls got something better to do than get your hands soiled? What are the likes of you doing down here with the working classes?"

"Obviously, receiving our assignments," Alana said with an authority that took the old matron by surprise. "So, give us directions to the correct office and you'll have done your job."

The woman's face took on a red hue as she extended the papers and dropped them on the table. "Up the stairs, turn right, second door on the left." Her eyes never left Alana's.

Livy sensed a rage building in her friend and grabbed up the papers. She quickly said, "Many thanks."

She pulled Alana away from the table and said, "Good Lord. I thought you were going to throttle her. Perhaps you should try to see things in better perspective."

"That shrew! How dare she speak to me like that?"

Livy forced out a breath. "Come on, Alana, let it pass. That philistine is not worth it."

They reached the top of the polished wooden staircase, turned right and headed down a long dusky corridor. Half-way down a sign stuck out above a solid oak door that read *Assignments*.

Livy turned the brass knob and opened the door. Summer sunlight flooded into the office, in stark contrast to the oppressive hallway. Although blackout curtains framed each of the windows, they were pulled back, exposing a bright blue sky dotted with thick swollen clouds. The room looked and smelled as if in another incarnation it might have been a medical suite. Victorian furniture sat around a wide low table that was perched on a burgundy rug woven somewhere in deep in the Far East. Light-yellow walls, a richly stained wainscot, and lavender-flowered upholstery gave the waiting room a homelike feel, something completely inconsistent with its purpose.

They handed their orders to a clerk sitting behind a frosted glass partition and took seats in oversized armchairs by the windows. Across the low table, three girls about their same ages sat on a long couch against the wall chattering away in thick East End accents. Their identical Air Force uniforms gave away that they too were waiting for assignments.

A round-faced girl in the center sat quiet, pale white hands neatly folded on her lap. Her head was bowed as the two bookends chattered back and forth. The girl on the left moved in quick staccato rhythms. The bright-red polish on her fingers flashed as her hands spoke in a cadence matching her voice. With her hands moving like a maestro's baton, she said, "Blimey, how can this take so long? It drives me mad."

The other bookend she'd called Lucy was tall and thin and had rolled her bleached hair so it piled up on top of her head, making her seem even taller and thinner. She looked a little awkward, as if she and the world didn't quite fit together. But Livy sensed something about her, an intelligence far beyond that of her companions. The girl bent over to speak around the girl in the center and said, "Rita, enough! You've been complaining since we got here."

Alana reached over and tapped Livy's arm. "Doesn't that tall girl look exactly like Miss Kretschmer—our seventh-form science teacher? She could be her daughter."

Livy's eyes moved down to the magazine she'd picked up off the table and a smile burst on her face. She whispered, "I was thinking the same thing and I'll bet she's just as smart. Has that sort of look like she might live in the lab."

A door at the far end of the room opened and a short balding man in a brown suit and a spotted yellow tie came out. He took two steps and said in a loud voice, "Eaton, Alana, serial number 227163."

"Right oh," Alana said, raising her hand.

"Well … are you waiting for an invitation? Quickly now, don't waste my time."

"Hey!" Rita declared, her hands flashing. "We was here first. We been sitting here for twenty minutes," she said as she rose from the couch and pointed at Alana. "We was here before them."

"Good for you. And, you'll be taking your turn when I am ready for you. Now, *sit* down." The little man motioned Alana through the door and closed it behind them.

Infuriated, Rita looked at Livy. "And what makes you so special?" she said in a voice filled with contempt as if she knew what the answer would be. "Likes of you don't have to queue at all, now do you, dearie. You have servants to do that for you, don't ya."

"Rita!" The thin girl said, "Stop it! She's no more responsible for her lot in life than you are for yours—so get off it."

"Don't lecture me, Lucy! It ain't fair!" She pointed at Livy, "Why do these two toffs get preference?"

Livy frowned, she'd had enough of Rita. "I'll give you some advice Rita, next time do what we did, make an appointment first." It wasn't the truth but it would have the desired effect.

Rita's head snapped around and she glowered at her. "How the bloody hell would you know if we made an appointment or not?"

"Quite simple actually," Livy responded. "There's no one else here. If you have been here for twenty minutes, at least one of you would have already been interviewed. And, it seems that's not the case. So, you didn't bother to make one."

Rita was about to lash out at her when the quiet girl in the center stirred. "My name's Patricia," she said, "but I'm called Totty. Forgive our Rita here—she didn't mean it. You see, she just lost her brother somewhere near Abbeville. They don't know if he's alive or if not, where he's buried."

She looked a little differently at Rita. "I'm so sorry, forgive me, Rita." Livy leaned forward in the chair a little. "My name's Olivia, but I'm called Livy. Are all of you waiting for assignments?"

Lucy slid forward on the couch and said, "Well, they are, but I know mine. I'm a nurse. They have me stationed at St. Thomas Hospital, across the river from Westminster Palace."

The door at the opposite end of the room popped open. Alana and the little man in the brown suit appeared. "Thank you, Miss Eaton." He looked around the room and focused on Livy. He said in a loud voice, "Ashford, Olivia, serial number 221774."

Livy shrugged, rose from the armchair.

"Good luck, Livy. I hope you gets a good one," Rita said, now with a slight smile.

Livy returned her smile and said, "Thank you Rita and I wish the best for you and your family."

She paused in front of Alana, a little worried about the look on her face and said, "Well, what did you get? Is it that bad?"

"It's foolish. I should have something better, more important. I'm a driver assigned to my father." With a resentful look on her face, Alana said, "I'm to be his personal chauffeur."

Livy grimaced and followed the little man into the offices. As she entered a narrow corridor, he closed the door behind them. Passing by him, she noticed the man's brown suit was rumpled and his faded tie twisted in an odd way, as if he was trying to hide a stain from his morning's tea.

Without saying a word, he set off at a nervous pace down the corridor with Livy behind him. They went by what looked like empty exam rooms on either side and came to an office at the end, its glass-windowed door open.

He passed the threshold and said, "My name's Warren Mueller. I'll be assigning you to your duties. Have a seat." He closed the door behind them and pointed at two chairs perched in front of a heavy wooden desk that looked like a discard from another office more important to the war effort. File cabinets stood along either wall, hiding bookcases filled with stacks of paper. Mueller sat at his desk in front of the windows, the stunning summer day now looking as if it were painted on the glass.

He picked up a thin file with Ashford, Olivia, Serial Number 221774 written in bold letters. He opened it, and she cringed seeing that horrible photograph snapped at her induction pinned to the top. Excitement began to churn as she thought how she would soon have a chance to do something worthwhile, to make her contribution and finally begin a life of her own, one not bound by the expectations and demands of a Lord's daughter.

"Miss Ashford, please allow me to thank you for coming in. It's not often I see women of your family's stature in here." Mueller thumbed through the few papers in Livy's file, looked up and said, "At this time Miss Ashford, I have nothing for you. However, I do want you to check back with me by phone in a month or so."

She was stunned. "Nothing for me! How is that possible? We're at war! Everyone can do something. How can you possibly have nothing for me?" Her thoughts went immediately to her father.

"As I said, at this time we have nothing for you. All of my present assignments for someone with your qualifications are filled. Something might come up in the next month or so and that's why I asked you to call. At least that would save you a trip. I don't want to waste your time. Thank you and please give your father my regards."

All of a sudden it was very clear, all except how he did it. "My father!" Aware she had snapped the words. "He told you not to assign me anything, didn't he?"

"Why would you say that?" Mueller stammered.

"Because you don't even know him, do you? And now you want me to give him your regards? What is it you want him to know, that you did exactly what he told you to—refuse me an assignment?"

His eyes opened wide, as if he'd been found committing a crime. Before he could utter a word, a commotion came from outside the office and the door burst open.

"Dammit, Mueller! Where the hell is my girl?" A man burst in, as large and imposing as his voice. "You told me I'd have her three weeks ago," his Canadian accent fired the words at Mueller, "then last week and yesterday and still you have nothing. We're ready to go and because of you, my entire production is shut down. What the hell am I supposed to tell the ministry?" He gripped the back of the chair next to Livy as if he were about to rip it apart.

"Peter, believe me I'm trying. We simply don't have any girls with a college education or a degree in English. As soon as I can find one, I'll deliver her right to you. My hands are tied; I don't have anyone like that." Warren Mueller rolled his chair back from the desk as if the other man was going to jump over it.

"No more damned excuses!" He slammed his fist into the top of the chair. "The ministry has forced me to use a WAAF girl for security reasons, and you're going to provide one — right now!"

The man he called Peter was dressed casually, he wore a white cotton shirt and dark slacks. A blue ascot with small white dots filled the void in his open collar. He was tall with wavy blond hair, pale eyes, and a face and frame that belonged to a rugby player.

"I'll do the best I can. I'll go back through my files and see if I can find someone that matches your needs. I'm sorry, I can't do more." Mueller said, squirming in his chair.

"I'll not wait any longer." He looked over at Livy sitting in the chair and pointed. "What about her? What's your assignment?"

Libby smiled at her luck—a reprieve. Hiding her excitement, she said, "Assignment? I don't have one."

"You don't have one?" he said sarcastically. The sandy-haired man looked over at Mueller and back to Livy. "You know anything about making films?"

"No sir, I don't, but I do have a degree in English literature." Livy said with a grin.

"English literature, huh." His head snapped back to Mueller, whose face was ashen. "There you go—she's perfect. I'll take her."

Mueller jumped out of his chair. "No, that won't work. I have something else in mind for her."

Peter extended a huge hand toward her. As she shook it, he said, "My name is Peter Watt. I'm a BBC motion picture director and I need a script girl. If you're interested, I'll take you over to Pinewood Studios and we'll start right now. You want the job?"

Still shaking his hand, Livy stood, barely able to contain her excitement. "Yes, yes I do. That would be terrific."

"Oh no! That's not possible. She's . . . she's Lord Ashford's daughter." Mueller seemed to have trouble getting the words out.

"So, what? Who the hell is Lord Ashford? I have a job to do and I'm not waiting any longer. She's mine. Let's go, Livy. Mueller, have her paperwork follow."

"But you can't. He's strictly forbidden it." Warren Mueller sounded as if a promised promotion had just evaporated in front of him. He straightened and said with his best authoritative voice, "No. You can't have her. She is not to have an assignment and that is directly from Lord Ashford."

"Mueller, you can tell Lord Ashford from me to shove it up his ass." He latched on to her arm and out of the little man's office they went.

Alana stood wide-eyed in the office lobby as they banged through the door. Livy laughed at the look on her face as she and her new employer flew through the room, Peter still holding on to her arm. As they reached the office's outer door and as he pulled it open, she looked back over her shoulder at Alana.

"Don't worry; I'll fill you in later." She felt excited like an adventurer on a ship leaving the quay, her own life about to begin.

Chapter Six

Aubrey Beck careened along a country lane lined with tall, thick hedges and spots of overgrown trees that formed a shadowed canopy. For most of the journey southeast of London, Aubrey fixated on an image of Livy Ashford standing on a stone porch in an almost transparent bathing costume, beads of water rolling down her legs. The thought of simply taking her, like he had so many other women, thrilled him, but this conquest had to be different. It must be carefully planned and executed. He wanted her, but more than that, he needed her wealth and power and that made everything Livy Ashford even more exciting.

He smiled as he slid more fuel into the purring engine and his Aston Martin roadster responded. The silver-gray machine shot through the hills and fields of Kent, hugging the curves and undulations of the narrow road. Twice he was forced to slow and cling to the far left—once for a rusting tractor and now for a flatbed filled with sheep awaiting the slaughter. As he squeezed by, three Spitfires roared low overhead, positioning themselves for a landing at RAF West Malling a few miles to the east. He suspected they were low on fuel after grappling with Germans over the coast as they attacked the radar installations he'd so carefully mapped a week ago.

Aubrey slowed the Aston Martin and turned right onto an unpaved wooded trail. A few minutes later, he creeped over the crest of a hill and into a ravine with a brook running down its center. Adjacent to the gurgling water sat a weather-beaten hunter's shack, hidden from prying eyes by a cover of ancient oaks. Pools of sunlight dappled the soggy ground as he shut down the engine, reached under the passenger seat, and pulled out the stolen documents. He slid out of the leather seat, his shoes sinking into soft damp earth and set off toward the shack, summoning all the courage he could muster.

The door squealed as he pushed it open and took a few steps into the single room. Before him, in a shabby brown armchair, the nightmare figure he dreaded sat staring at him through narrow, empty black eyes.

"I trust you have the documents?" The words crawled from the man's lips.

"I brought everything you requested," he said with a forced smile.

The thin aristocrat they called the Doctor picked at a fingernail and got up from the chair. His face was refined but sharply angular and disturbing. He was dressed like an undertaker, in a black suit and white shirt, with a black string tie hung around his thin but powerful neck. The man's polished shoes came to a point and made a cold scraping sound as he walked across the wooden floor toward him and Aubrey was forced to look away.

Nervous and feeling the angst of withdrawal, he took a step back and changed the subject. "Where's the Irishman? I thought he would be here too and when will I meet this Electra?"

"The Irishman will be along shortly and as for Electra, all in good time, Mr. Beck." It was a statement of fact, one not to be questioned. "Now, what have you brought us? Your last parcel was quite helpful as you can see from today's actions against the radar stations."

"I brought the latest production estimates." Aubrey swallowed hard, thinking about the dangerous game he was playing. "But the materials you've asked for have become increasingly difficult to obtain and the value of the information much greater. The risks posed to me are increased and as such, my price must go up."

Silence filled the room as beads of sweat formed above Aubrey's lip. The Doctor slipped his right hand into his pocket and moved closer, each step seemed more menacing than the last, the man's eyes never leaving his. The front door screeched and Aubrey jumped.

"Ah, you're here." The girth of the Irishman entered the cabin. Cradled across his left forearm was a double-barreled shotgun, open at the breach, and in his right hand were a brace of gray doves held by the heads. "I assume you've brought the goods we requested."

Aubrey found his voice and said, "I have—the latest aircraft production figures straight from the ministry." He held up a sealed manila package and offered it to the round-faced man as if it were a token of peace.

The Irishman flung the doves into a sink and turned his back on Aubrey. He hung the shotgun on hooks secured to the wall and rested his pocketed vest and hunter's cap on a peg as he said, "Well done, Aubrey. Let me see what you have."

He turned away from the wall and passed between the two men. He snatched the manila package from Aubrey's hands and slid a stubby finger under the seal to break it. The Irishman squeezed into the lone armchair and began to sift through the pages. Without looking up, he said to the Doctor, "Be so good as to bring me a malt, will you?"

The Doctor picked up a bottle from a table a few feet away and poured the deep amber liquid into a clouded glass. As he gently placed it in the Irishman's hand, he said, "Mr. Beck and I were discussing how he believes his efforts are worth more. He said the risk he's taking is not commensurate with our offerings."

"Is that so?" Looking up for the first time, the Irishman stared at him. He tilted his head and paused.

Aubrey held his hands behind his back to stop them from shaking as the silence dragged on until finally, the Irishman nodded. "I understand. We certainly want to properly reward you for your efforts. I'm sure Electra will agree. What you've brought today is exactly what we asked for."

"Those documents were difficult to obtain and their retrieval demanded extraordinary risk." It was a lie. A smile formed on Aubrey's face.

"My friend," the Irishman's pushed a lock of red hair off his forehead, "would you get Mr. Beck his reward?"

The Doctor went to a cabinet above the dead birds and took down a square wooden box and an envelope. He went over to Aubrey, the sound of his shoes crawled up Aubrey's spine like an insect.

"Here you are, Mr. Beck—enjoy them both," he said and handed him the payment.

A quick check of the envelope revealed the promised two thousand pounds in small notes. Aubrey lifted the lid of the box and was relieved to find it filled with a fine white powder, which he sampled and a feeling of relief washed over him.

"Better?" The Irishman pushed back, deeper into the armchair, crossed a thick leg over a knee and cradled his fingers under his chin. He seemed to calculate his next move, eyes fixed on Aubrey. "Your next little project is the most important one we've ever entrusted you with. You've performed fairly well so far and you've been properly rewarded for your efforts." He paused a moment, tapping his chin. "But, this particular job is critical and will be worth ten thousand pounds and a quarter kilo of your drug. Is that agreeable?"

Aubrey's eyes widened. His mind settled on the thousand pounds and how it would go a long way to satisfy his debtors as well as his continued safety. It would give him enough time to properly seduce Livy Ashford into a marriage that would resolve his problems.

"What can I do to assist you?" To Aubrey, his words sounded almost panted.

"Wonderful," the Irishman said with delight. "Your next assignment will be to obtain the order of battle for the RAF in southern England."

"The location and strength of all RAF units in southern England?" This time, he had panted the words.

"Precisely."

Aubrey's mind raced. He had no concept of how he could possibly obtain something like that, only a handful of people would have access to it. They were asking for the essence of the entire RAF defense for Southern England. He rubbed a nervous hand across his mouth, pushing away the sweat above his lip. "That could take some time."

"Perhaps, but time is a luxury we don't have. We must have that information. You see, control of the air over the Channel and southern England is a requirement for our invasion. It's a simple necessity to ensure the destruction of England." The Irishman stood, placed a brotherly hand on Aubrey's shoulder and said, "For too many years, my people have lived in slavery under an English boot. You can help end that. A victory now will assure your future in our new world and we won't forget those who helped."

Aubrey could care less about a free Ireland; his interest was far simpler: taking the payments, drugs and plotting a method to get to Livy Ashford. He nodded and said, "I'll find a way."

The Irishman patted his shoulder. "I knew we could count on you. Tomorrow, you'll receive orders assigning you to RAF Uxbridge. From headquarters there you should be able to obtain the order of battle."

Aubrey nodded again and the Irishman continued. "Go back to London and await your orders. We'll be in touch, but I do expect to have this information quickly." He shook his hand. "Till next week then."

Aubrey walked to the door and pulled the rusted knob. The door screeched in protest as he opened it. He left the weather-beaten shack and made his way up the small ravine toward his Aston Martin, hearing the sound of the brook and feeling the squish of rotted leaves beneath his feet.

Tucked behind the one-room shack, hidden from view by a false wall, Electra tapped out the word eagle and flipped a switch to shut down the radio connected to a directional antenna one hundred meters away that peeked above a small forested hill. The transmitter was powerful enough to reach France where it would be received and then rebroadcast to Abwehr Headquarters in Berlin. The code word eagle added at the end of the message assured the message was genuine and Electra had not been compromised.

The screeching of the door told her he had left. It wasn't the right time to speak with Squadron Commander Beck—not yet. That discovery would be saved for later. Electra sat at the equipment-laden table and read the mission orders; assess the reliability or eliminate an informant called Jack Reed. Berlin's decision had been made.

She leaned back in the wooden swivel chair, closing somewhat tired eyes to sharpen her wits. She thought about the conversation that had just taken place in the other room and whispered to no one, "It's good to have you sweat, Beck. You're one that could be very careless." Electra picked up a half-filled glass, the aroma of the malt blend soothing her disturbed thoughts about Squadron Commander Beck.

In the distance, the rumble of an Aston Martin starting its return journey was her cue to open the hidden door. She stepped around the double bed and entered the small Spartan room.

With a quick nod and a sharp click of his polished heels, the former SS doctor said, "Ten thousand pounds and a quarter kilo? Awfully generous, isn't it?"

"I have no intention of giving him either. When we have obtained the order of battle, his usefulness will be at an end," Electra said, her voice flat and cold. "You, Herr Doctor, will have the pleasure of removing Mr. Beck from this world."

"Thank you, that is something I look forward to." Again, the pointed shoes clicked as an odd smile formed on the Doctor's wafer-thin lips.

"You both gave an excellent performance and I'm very pleased." She looked into the black eyes of the Doctor, "I want you to carefully monitor the Squadron Commander. There's something wrong with that man. He could easily result in danger to us and more importantly, the failure of our plans. Have you done as I instructed?"

The Doctor smiled, "Yes, over the last few weeks I've introduced more concentrated cocaine, methamphetamine and heroin into his drug cocktail. We've also included psilocin, a psychotic dependence drug, within in another week or so he'll be hopelessly addicted."

"Excellent."

The Irishman held a hand up, the palm out. "There is one caveat however."

"And what is that?" Electra said.

"The concentration of the drug is such poor Mr. Beck will definitely become addicted, but also quite mad in a short amount of time."

She smiled and said, "That's all right. His usefulness to us will be over by then. I'll leave Mr. Beck and his mission in your hands." Electra looked into the Doctor's black eyes and said, "After we have obtained the information, you will wait until I order you to terminate Mr. Beck. It will be done on my instructions only, is that clear?"

"Very." The razor smile never left the Doctor's lips.

She moved to the door and took hold of the knob. "I have received an assignment from Berlin that will require my attention. I expect on your next contact with Beck you will obtain the battle plan." The door screeched in protest as it opened.

A few moments later Electra started a motorcycle hidden in the woods behind the shack, slipped out of the ravine and onto the road toward London.

Chapter Seven

A thick fog rolled off the North Sea and up the Thames Estuary, throwing a blanket over the East End of London that dampened sounds, shrouded footsteps and conversations. Electra moved carefully in the blackout, counting the same steps taken in daylight a few hours before.

She adjusted the jacket armband, made sure her hair was tucked beneath the helmet. She pulled the chinstrap tight and smiled. No one ever paid attention to an air raid warden—the perfect hiding place was in plain sight.

Preparing the Jack Reed mission, a week before the parachute jump into England, Electra designed the weapon she would use. Exact drawings were made and hours were spent with the finest German engineers. The effort resulted in something precise and lethal. It mimicked a battery-powered torch. Every refinement was made and tested, down to the knurls around the steel barrel that would ensure a firm grip. The On-Off switch was designed to release a taut spring loaded with seven inches of stainless-steel spike and thrust it through a hole in the reflector plate to shatter any nearby bone or tissue, instantly bringing death. As she walked on the darkened streets of London, a wry smile crossed her face and a thrill coursed in her blood. In the next few minutes perhaps, the device she conceived would be used for the first time.

Off in the distance, Big Ben chimed as she turned south onto the narrow ancient street labeled Saint Michael's. Halfway down, a blackened doorway offered a perfect view of The Shepherd's Name, a pub frequented by dockworkers from this run-down and very rough section of London. It was near closing time and Electra stood hidden, awaiting a prey that out of habit would soon leave the pub.

In the gloom that covered the city, she saw a sliver of light shoot through the mist as two men left the pub, the second one holding the blackout curtain a little too long. They exchanged a few words. The smaller of the two tipped his hat and the larger one turned his back on him. He crossed Alie Road and headed straight toward the narrow sidewalks of Saint Michael's.

She stood in the cavern like doorway and waited for the right moment. When it came, she stepped out and blocked the big man's path. There was no question he was the target; the huge frame, the sheer bulk from a life's work on the docks, exactly replicated the well-studied photographs. His massive hands were stuffed into the pockets of a worn peacoat and a stevedore's hat was cocked on a head bent forward as if he were pushing into a titanic gale. This man was her quarry.

"Jack Reed?" It was more a statement than a question.

Taking his hands out of his pockets, the huge man said in a Cockney mumble filled with alcohol and threat, "And who wants to know?"

"A Scotland Yard Inspector," she returned with the ring of authority. "I have a few questions you must answer."

Jack Reed spit on the ground. "And if I don't, what are you going to do about it? I've already told you Coppers everything I know. And you think you could take me in?"

"If need be, but if I were you, I'd be a lot more alarmed by my armed colleagues waiting for you to make a mistake."

Big Jack Reed looked around in the darkness, gave a grunt and said, "Girly coppers pretending to be wardens and you're gonna take me in. I don't think so." He looked around again. "You're bluffing. I don't see no one."

"Not very bright, are you? That's the point—I don't want you to see them. So, you'll answer my questions and be done, or your reprieve is revoked and you'll spend the rest of your miserable life inside a cell at the Tower of London. Or maybe we'll hang you as a spy—I'm not sure which." Electra hammered a pointed finger into his chest. "The Yard has a long memory, Mr. Reed. We haven't forgotten your past crimes, nor have we forgotten your association with our Nazi friends. You cajoled a reprieve because you snitched on of their agents to save your own skin. But we're at war now and that makes everything different. Do you understand? I would imagine your friends at the Tower would love to have a few minutes with you alone—that is before they cut your throat." Her eyes were merely slits that stared at him.

Fear rippled across the big man's face and she smiled a flat smile. Big Jack Reed would do whatever she commanded.

"Ok, what more you wanna know?" he said, his voice absent the threatening tone.

"That's better. You cooperate, you'll stay out of the Tower and maybe even stay alive." A hiss like menace carried in her voice. "First, why did you help the Nazis and what information did you pass along?"

"I've been over this a thousand times. You know all that."

"I want to make sure you're telling the truth, perhaps."

The big man slipped his hands back into his coat pockets and said, "I did it for the money. I gave the bloke dates and times ships would arrive and depart, as well as their cargo and that's all. I didn't know he was a bloody German, not till much later. I thought he was tryin' to get a leg up on his competition. But either way, it don't matter, I wanted the money."

Electra put a thumb on the switch. "What was this man's name? And what other contacts are you aware of in his organization?"

"The bloke's name was Richard—that's all I know. As for other contacts, there were a few, but that'll cost you. I kept quiet about that before, but now that we're at war, well let's say I'm a patriot. For the right price, I might remember some things."

"For the right price you're a patriot? My God, man, your country is at war and you want to withhold information for money?"

"We all have our needs and wants, Inspector. I'm sure good King George wouldn't mind parting with a few quid to find out me secrets. So, have we a deal or not?" Reed squinted and she knew he was wondering how much money he could ask for.

"I could run you in right now and you would never see the light of day."

"Aye, and you'd never get what I know. There is more about these Nazis and their plans inside me head than I ever told. Why not think of it as somethin' for the war effort?" The large man winked and gave a wicked smile.

Her thumb hovered over the trigger; the decision was made. Jack Reed was a hazard to their carefully placed agents.

"Very well, you win. What's your price?"

"Ah, now, that's better on your part. You'll get what you want and I get my money. One hundred quid would be a tidy sum. That's what it'll cost you."

"So, you'll help out your country for a hundred pounds."

He paused a moment unsure of himself. "So, Scotland Yard . . . you agree to the price and you get the names and places I know. You don't and you get nothin." His smile revealed missing teeth.

"I agree, you'll get your money. Come to the Yard tomorrow morning at ten and ask for Inspector Donaldson. I'll have your money waiting and you'll get it after you give me a list of names and places and anything else you know. Is that clear?"

"I'll be there, Inspector. You get the money and I'll tell you everything I know."

Electra took a step to the side and motioned for him to move on, saying, "Tomorrow then and you better perform or you'll be a guest at the Tower for the rest of your life."

Jack Reed gave a snort and a short salute. He started down the street and as he passed by, the torch came within an inch of the back of his skull. The steel spike fired, severing the brain stem and slicing through the frontal cortex, exploding bone behind the forehead. Reed's body thudded onto the cobblestones like a stack of newspapers thrown from a lorry, the spike protruded from a gaping hole that gushed black blood.

Electra yanked out a handkerchief and pulled the spike from above his open, lifeless eyes. She wiped the steel clean as she watched Jack Reed's blood pool onto the cobblestones and run to the gutter.

She turned and walked away down the gentle hill of St. Michael's Street and vanished like a wraith in the floating fog.

Chapter Eight

Jamie burst from inside a cloud into a frigid sky three thousand feet above his target. Once again, Red Flight had been directed quickly and precisely to intercept the incoming German raiders. But this time was different, they were already some thirty miles inland and these aircraft weren't the lumbering dive bombers that were so easy to destroy, these were the fast and well-armed twin-engine Heinkels, the Nazis' best bomber.

Strapped into the cockpit, he felt sweat trickle down his chest as the radio crackled, the voices broken, filled with static. Squadron Leader Eric Locke came garbled over the earphones, but Jamie could make out "Tally Ho," their battle cry. Jamie pulled on the stick and rolled the fighter left onto its back, pointing the nose and the six heavy machine guns at the black bombers below. He rolled upright and pushed the rudder, aligning his gun sight some fifty yards ahead of an unwitting black Heinkel.

Locke was the first to open up from long range, sending tracer bullets flashing by the German crew sealed inside. It caused the bombers to scatter, with Jamie's target turning abruptly left, away from the others, exactly as he expected.

He stepped harder on the rudder, his thumb held over the red trigger and he waited as his prey inched toward the gun sight ever so slowly. A second passed and another, each feeling like hours, until the sight touched the tip of the aircraft's nose and Jamie pressed the trigger.

The Spitfire seemed to jerk back as it spewed out a deadly stream of ammunition that smashed into the Plexiglas protecting the crew and walked its way back over the nose and onto the wing. White-hot bullets slammed into the right engine and it exploded in a ball of fire.

Jamie flashed by the stricken bomber, his Spitfire careened through the debris. Black smoke and red-orange flames trailed behind the aircraft as it began its long two-mile fall to earth. He banked hard to the right and pulled back on the stick, the G-forces crushing him into the seat. Like moving a stone anchored to the earth, Jamie shoved the throttle forward and the Merlin engine responded as fuel rushed into the hot cylinders and the Spitfire screamed upward into an empty sky.

He strained to turn his head against the weight pressing on him, seeking his companions somewhere above. He searched for tiny flashes on the blue canvas, but there was only emptiness. He was alone.

Livy and the film crew stood outside the bunker at RAF Uxbridge staring at twisting, turning contrails far to the south, long white lines drawn against the cerulean blue as if by a frenzied spider spinning a web in a windstorm. Occasionally they would see a puff of orange, followed by a black corkscrew as it spun down toward the Kent countryside, the death of someone unknown, a friend or foe caught up in and now consumed by the depredation of war.

Cameraman Mickey McCarty stared at the battle as sunlight glistened off his white beard. "My God, what have we done?" he said.

From prior conversations, Livy knew he was reliving memories of the last war, a time when he stood on the battlefields of France with a hand-cranked motion picture camera. He shook his head and looked at her. "There're a lot of young lads that won't be coming home tonight. We're doing the same damn thing all over again."

She didn't say anything; no one did. The crew stood open mouthed, heads tilted toward the heavens, not making a sound as visions of war filled their eyes.

After a long moment, Peter Watt brought them back. "Come on, we've got a job to do and standing here won't get it done."

The silent crew gathered their equipment and followed him down into the deep bunker housing Group 11 Operations Uxbridge, the focal point for controlling the radar defense against the German onslaught in the skies above.

A large cotton-ball cloud offered Jamie a perfect hiding place and he took it, pulled the stick back climbing the Spitfire headlong into the soft void. A straggler didn't have a chance, if the German fighters found him, the remaining time in his life would be nil. He reached down, balled his fist and thumped the radio, attempting to clear it, but all he could make out was scratchy mangled voices that sounded a thousand miles away.

Outside the Spitfire it was minus ten degrees and yet, inside his flight suit, Jamie was drenched in sweat. A bead slipped beneath the rim of his leather flight helmet and ran down into the oxygen mask covering his face. He tried again and again to make the radio respond and finally gave up. He sucked in a deep breath and listened to a hiss of silence in his headphones.

He leveled off, slowed the charging Spitfire and started a turn to the right when the cloud hiding him vanished. He scanned the sky and found he was behind and below three bombers flying in a tight V formation heading north. He started after them.

His body shook as he banked and shoved the throttle to its stop. He grabbed the loop atop the stick with both hands and pulled back, pointing the nose at the black underbelly of the center Heinkel. The Spitfire clawed higher and higher as the lead bomber began to fill his gun sight.

Jamie slid his thumb over the trigger and pushed, the six machine guns erupted and tore into the German, shredding the thin aluminum skin. The black machine shuddered as it rose, hovered in space for a heartbeat and in a blinding flash, exploded, ripping the wings off the other two planes. All three mangled carcasses helplessly tumbled toward the earth. His explosive bullets had detonated the bombs stacked so carefully in the center aircraft's belly.

He pulled harder on the stick, dodging what was left of the vaporized raiders. Shards of metal and flesh peppered Jamie's aircraft, tearing at its skin and leaving oil and blood smeared across the canopy. He saw a large piece of the bomber's engine coming towards him, the propeller still attached. It seemed to float across the sky, slowly spinning until it slammed hard into the Spitfire.

Thrown violently onto its back in a flat spin, the fighter shook like a truck running over railroad ties. Smoke began to flood the cockpit as he struggled to grasp the latch holding the canopy, it thickened until he could no longer see.

His eyes burned, his throat tightened as his hands scrabbled through the cockpit until he found the release lever and pulled as hard as he could. With a loud bang, the canopy was ripped from the plane, sucking the acrid smoke out into bitter air that now roared beneath his flight jacket and froze sweat to his skin.

Jamie slammed the rudder opposite the flat spin until finally the aircraft stopped rotating, dipped and fell end over end toward the ground. He jammed the stick forward, praying the Spit would stand on its nose, and it did. Shaking violently, Jamie managed to nudge the aircraft upright, the nose rose and flopped all over the sky, but she was under his control again—barely. Wind tore through the open cockpit and pulled at his oxygen mask as he struggled to keep the Spitfire flying. He glanced down at the instruments and found the compass. Thick smoke belched from the plane as he set a course for Uxbridge and safety, wondering if he'd make it.

Chapter Nine

Aubrey Beck glanced at the frenetic contrails to the south and slowed his Aston Martin to a stop. A down-faced corporal in full battle dress approached from the one-man gate shack and said, "Identification."

"My God boy, I've been coming through this gate for several days and you still can't recognize me?" Aubrey snapped. He saw the other two guards grin from behind the black-and-white striped pole barring the road.

"Orders, sir. Identification." The young corporal wasn't intimidated. He reached out his palm and stared at Aubrey without the slightest smile.

Looking past the gate, Aubrey fished in his jacket and pulled out his identity card, which was immediately snapped up by the corporal. The man studied it for longer than necessary and slowly passed it back to him. He saluted and motioned for the other guards to lift the barrier.

"You may pass, Squadron Commander," the guard said, a smile rising.

Aubrey snatched the identification card, threw the Aston Martin into gear, and sped off toward Hillingdon House, a century-old manor home that served as Group 11 Headquarters. He thought about what he'd say to the wing commander. Reporting for duty two hours late could be a problem and being a little hungover wouldn't help either. But, what a night he'd had. She was only fifteen and so delightful. Girls from the seedier side of London grew up so fast. He smiled at the memory of Bethany—or at least that was the name she'd given him—naked on the bed. She'd known more than most of the women he took his pleasure with. Quite a satisfying experience, even if he'd had too much to drink and equally too much of his drug in the hours before he'd requisitioned her services. Aubrey forced her image from his mind and focused on the Wing Commander, as well as on the excuse he would make up and how he would steal the order of battle. He had to find a way, get the promised ten thousand pounds and more importantly, a quarter kilo of his drug.

He came to a stop at the manor house and started up the walk. As he reached the outside stairs, the front door burst open and out marched Wing Commander Lester Hardington-Smythe with an aide in tow. Aubrey stood startled at the bottom of the stair, his plan not fully developed.

"Wing Commander." He snapped to attention and gave a smart salute. "I . . ."

"Nice of you to join us. You're more than two hours late. Where the hell have you been?" Hardington-Smythe said, looking out beneath recalcitrant gray eyebrows. "My God, you look horrible. Have you been drinking?"

"Of course not, sir. I had a rather uncooperative tire on the way down. I apologize for the delay." Aubrey surprised himself at how much that sounded like truth.

Hardington-Smythe bounded down the stairs, looking his newest charge over. Without stopping he said, "Well, no matter. I haven't got time to discuss it. I'm due at Whitehall for a conference. In the meantime, Beck, I have a duty I need you to look after."

Aubrey trotted to catch up.

As they rushed toward the staff car, the wing commander spoke over his shoulder. "The ministry has seen fit to send a film crew here today, of all days! I assume they're making some propaganda film or such. I want you watching them like a hawk. The last thing I need is more bad publicity, understand? I have enough on my hands without those damn fools running around here taking pictures."

They reached the powder-blue sedan. Gray-white smoke belched from the tail pipe. Aubrey cheerfully offered, "I understand, sir. Leave it to me, I'll make sure they behave."

Hardington-Smythe scowled and looked Aubrey up and down as he slipped into the backseat. "Make sure you do. Now get yourself down to the bunker and stay all over them. If they come out and want something else, you stick with them and get rid of them fast as you can. Be polite, but get rid of them. I want them off my airfield." The wing commander slammed the door and the dusty sedan sped off toward London, throwing specks of clay onto the legs of Aubrey's uniform.

This would be Aubrey's first time in the bunker. A muddy path took him to a small concrete block house with stairs on the left side leading down to a blue wooden door. There were no signs, no guards—just traces of wet mud covering the concrete from feet going up and down, in and out of the bunker. The chipped wooden door creaked on rusty hinges as Aubrey opened it. He went down flight after flight of damp, dimly lit concrete stairs, ending at a landing some sixty feet below the surface. The space before him was barely large enough to house a sergeant seated at a desk peering out from behind round glasses and two imposing guards at his side, all intently watching him approach.

"I'm Squadron Commander Beck. I've been ordered to shepherd our visitors while they're on the base, keep them out of trouble." He said with an air of command. "I just spoke with the wing commander."

"Yes sir, we've been waiting for you. He came in about two hours ago and left this note." The sergeant handed a small envelope to Aubrey, who immediately tore into it.

He slipped out the handwritten message and read the same information he'd been told that emphasized getting the film crew off the aerodrome quickly. "Thank you, Sergeant. Where are our visitors?"

The man's eyebrows rose above the dark round rims, "Why, they're inside, sir. Awaiting you, I would presume."

Aubrey made a move toward a metal door at his left, but before he could reach it, one of the armed guards opened it to another world.

The dark musty stairwell gave way to a room filled with noise and activity. RAF officers sat at stations above a sunken floor. They peered over a railed partition at several uniformed women below working around a large map depicting southeastern England and a slice of northern France and Belgium. Detailed instructions were delivered to them through headsets as the women used long poles to position small labeled blocks of wood representing the incoming German raiders. From the constantly updated map, an overview of the battle could be discerned and the fighter squadrons quickly and effectively directed to intercept the bombers.

Aubrey glanced at the note, making sure he had the director's name right and took the narrow wooden stairs down to the concrete floor below. His charge of civilians stood in a corner of the lower room listening intently to a flight officer. "The map shows us the relative positions of the German aircraft." He turned and gestured to the bank of officers working phones behind the overhead railing, "At a glance, the controllers know which squadrons are available and how to direct them toward the incoming raid.

"However, today is a little different. So far, the Germans have stopped after reaching the coast. But as you can see, they're well inland and truthfully, we don't know where they're going. Possibly London, but I don't suspect that even the Germans wouldn't stoop so low as to attack civilians. We'll simply have to see where they're headed and react accordingly. The personnel here ..."

"Excuse me, I'm sorry to interrupt." Aubrey tried his best command voice. "The Wing Commander has asked that I assist you while you're here. I am Squadron Commander Beck and which of you would be"—for effect, he glanced again at the note— "Peter Watt?"

A tall, rather athletic man with unruly blond hair snapped, "I'm Peter Watt."

Aubrey extended his hand, noting a lavender silk ascot filling the opening of his shirt collar. "I'm to be your liaison while you're here. I want to welcome you to RAF Uxbridge."

The man ignored his hand. "Good. I believe were almost done here and then we're on to the airfield." Watt glanced over his shoulder, away from Aubrey and said, "Mickey, have you got everything?"

A man with a white beard and a motion picture camera over his shoulder said, "Need a couple of shots from up above and were done. The airfield next?"

"Yup, that'll be the best part," Watt said, making his way to the stairs.

His attitude infuriated Aubrey. "I'm sorry, but that's not going to be possible. The airfield is off limits."

The burly man stopped on the stairs and spun around. "Off limits! Horseshit. The airfield is the main reason we came down here."

"I'm sorry. But the airfield is too dangerous. Believe me, it's for your own safety." The man's Canadian accent and crude language were irritating Aubrey's already frayed nerves.

Watt rushed down the stairs and ran up to Aubrey, forcing him to take a step back. "I was told by the ministry we could film anything we wanted and I'll be damned if we're leaving here without filming the aircraft and pilots. If you have a problem with that, I'll make a quick phone call."

"Aubrey! What a surprise!"

He turned to see Livy Ashford coming around the map board. Her auburn hair and exquisite eyes riveted his attention. "Livy! Good lord, what are you doing here?"

"It's my assignment, my contribution to the war effort," she said with a smile.

"Well, it's wonderful to see you."

"Thanks. But, Aubrey, why can't we see the airfield? It's the most important part of the film. The people must see the courage of our pilots. They're saving us from an invasion. Think of what that will do for the public spirit."

He responded in a voice meant to carry. "I'm sorry, Livy, the airfield is off limits. It is not a place where one saunters about. Far too easy to get killed out there, what with spinning props and the like. It's out of the question."

Peter Watt looked at Livy with a smile on his face that irked Aubrey. "So, you two know each other—wonderful." The man gave Livy a quick wink and said, "You have a quick chat and we'll be upstairs to finish and move on." She nodded, and the big man spun on his heels, following the rest of the crew to the balcony above.

Aubrey's plans for her begged for an answer and he wasn't going to take no. He came close to her and whispered, "I assume you're going to Paul White's party and that you might need a lift. I would be happy to fetch you even Alana if you wish."

She whispered back, "I don't know. I haven't seen Alana since we got our assignments. But I think we were going to drive down there together."

He assumed a practiced look of disappointment and watched her eyes for some sign of compassion. Not seeing any, he looked toward Watt's back as he reached the top of the stairs and said, "Who the hell does he think he is? What an arrogant . . ."

"Aubrey, he's a very important man. He put his entire motion picture career on hold to work for the ministry. I'm told he has Churchill's ear and is probably doing his bidding. It might be prudent to let us film the airfield. Aubrey, do this for me. I'll be in your debt." Livy reached out and touched his arm.

At first, he thought she was bluffing. But even if she wasn't, he didn't give a damn about the fool calling Churchill. He'd been told what to do and if anything happened, he would blame it on the wing commander. Yet, her touch ignited a fire through him. "So, you want to see the airfield," he smiled. "I need an answer about the party. Say I pick you up at three? Otherwise, I imagine the airfield won't be available, at least not today."

She cocked her head and looked at him through quizzical eyes as if pulling up a memory. After a brief moment, she ran her tongue across her upper lip and smiled. "Fair enough—you win. I don't know about Alana, but I'll go with you."

"Good, it's settled," he said, thinking of how he'd just initiated his seduction of Livy Ashford. "All right, but you stay off the active airfield and you leave when I say. Agreed?"

"Agreed." She nodded. "Come on, Aubrey—let's go upstairs with the crew."

He followed her, watched how she moved and almost laughed when he saw her throw a quick smile and a wink toward Peter Watt. How foolish of her.

The Spitfire was shaking so violently, Jamie couldn't believe it was still in the air. Over the last few minutes he'd been debating with himself whether to stay with the aircraft or jump. Thick, bitter smoke bellowed out of the engine and leaked through the floorboard into the cockpit. It left a trail even a novice pilot could follow. He could taste the overheated oil and metal through the oxygen mask and a burning heat from below the floorboard bit at his legs.

Jamie searched the skies behind him for both enemies and friends, but he couldn't see a thing—not another aircraft in sight. He looked down and checked the instruments. The engine was running rough, the Spitfire losing oil pressure and altitude. It was going to be close, very close. In another few minutes, he would be too low jump and there'd no longer be any question about what to do, he would have to stay with the Spitfire.

At one point, he thought he saw far in the distance behind him a formation of dark specks, but they disappeared before he could make anything out. Tugging the shoulder straps tighter, he struggled to maintain control over the stricken aircraft and focused on the horizon. A large green open patch formed out of the haze—Uxbridge. He might make it.

"Where the hell are the airplanes? Even more important, where the hell are the pilots?" Livy knew the irritation Peter Watt felt toward Aubrey Beck was about to boil over as he turned and shouted, "Mickey, may as well set up here and get a few establishing shots—of what, I don't know." Peter pointed to an air raid ditch a few feet away from the crew. "And watch out for that damn ditch. I don't want to lose anyone in all this mess."

Following a step behind Aubrey, Livy heard Peter continue to rant as she slipped by folding chairs and a half-played chessboard to step into the shack. The floor was littered with mud, the walls unfinished and the outside clapboard in several places showed light drifting through.

In a corner by a single window, a corporal sat at a desk, his back to them. His powder-blue shirt had the sleeves rolled up and on his bare head was a mop of dark-brown hair that looked like a perched, unkempt animal. The corporal set down the receiver from one of the hand-crank telephones and ran pale hands through his hair. He pushed the chair back from his desk and saw Aubrey, he jumped up and saluted.

"Morning, sir," he said.

Aubrey casually returned his salute. "I'm escorting this film unit. They're going to take a few shots here and they'll be on their way. I don't want them bothering you, so go back to whatever you were doing."

Livy felt as if she was looking at a young boy. "Corporal, how old are you?"

A red flush appeared on his cheeks. "Seventeen ma'am, but I've got me parents' permission."

"I'm so sorry. I didn't mean to embarrass you. I was surprised—you look so young."

"Young? Ma'am, we all are—every one of us."

From outside the window, Peter Watt slammed his hands on the sill. He looked at the boy and said, "The airplanes—where the hell are the airplanes?"

The corporal was taken aback. He pointed to the sky and said, "They're up, sir. Probably won't be back for at least a half hour or so, you see."

"Great!" He glared at Aubrey. "It seems we have no choice but to wait." Peter Watt almost spat out the words. He turned from the window and stormed past the vacant beach chairs and headed toward his crew busily setting up the camera. Livy saw him through the window as he looked up toward the south and yelled, "There! Mickey, get that! I want that!"

Everyone in the film crew turned to stare and point at the sky as Mickey started to roll the motion picture film. She and Aubrey ran out of the shack and searched the southern sky. Off in the distance, an airplane trailing billowing black smoke and orange flame was headed straight for the airfield.

"Mickey, are you getting this? I can't believe that thing is still in the air." Peter Watt shouted. "Come on, boy, you can do it. Bring her in."

"This is wonderful stuff," Mickey said, looking through the camera. "Come on, lad. Keep her coming." The lens focused on the stricken aircraft, Mickey exclaimed, "There's a bloody prop sticking out behind the pilot."

A few moments later the crippled Spitfire barely cleared the trees lining the field, its landing gear down. A broken piece of propeller now clearly could be seen sticking out behind the cockpit. Smoke and flames scraped the belly and the pilot, with goggles covering his eyes, peered out around the windscreen trying to see ahead.

Livy put her hand to her mouth. "Oh, my God, he's not going to make it."

Air raid sirens started to wail.

"Everyone—quick, into the trench!" Aubrey yelled. The crew followed him—all except Mickey, who stayed above running the camera and Livy, who stood frozen as she watched the burning airplane while the sirens wailed on.

From behind her, Peter yelled, "Livy! Mickey! Get in the trench!"

Livy jumped into the trench and peered out as the plane hit hard and bounced back into the air. It hit again and abruptly turned to the right, heading straight toward the camera, fire belching below its shattered wings. The nose shook back and forth as the engine coughed, poured out smoke and died. The plane kept rolling fast, right for them. Mickey jumped into the trench for safety, abandoning the camera as the growl of approaching bombers filled the air.

A huge explosion went off close to the tree line, and another and another, the bombs dropping closer and closer to the film crew huddled in the ditch. Angry red explosions erupted all over the airfield. Livy ducked, covering her ears as a bomb exploded nearby in a deafening blast and she chanced another look. The pilot jumped from the aircraft and ran through the smoke, dodging craters and flames as bombs exploded around him. The sound was vibrating her body and with each explosion, a slap of heat and pressure flew through the trench, the bombs coming closer.

Livy crouched down and screamed as each bomb slammed to earth and shattered the ground, pounded the air around it. She prayed for her life and safety, fear and horror thick in her blood when something heavy crashed on her back and she was shoved facedown into the bottom of the wet trench as she heard bombs whistle by, exploding one after another. Mud and dirt crunched in her mouth and covered her eyes.

As quickly as the attack had come, it ended and the world around them went eerily silent. Livy, sat up in the mud as the weight slowly released, her face and clothing covered with the sticky wet earth. She smeared dirty hands across her face, trying to see through the thick mud sticking to her skin and eyes. Shaking with fear, she felt a gentle touch on her shoulder. Someone began wiping her face with a soft cloth and she could finally open her eyes.

It was the pilot—the goggles hanging around his neck. His face was blackened everywhere from smoke except where the goggles had protected him. As he wiped the mud off her face, she noted a sparkle of humor in his apple-green eyes.

"I'm so sorry, miss. I didn't know you were there when I jumped in." On the pilot's face sat an odd, quirky grin. Then he cracked a smile and laughed.

"You . . ." She spat out some of the grit. "I can't believe it. You're more dangerous than the Germans. Look at me!"

"I'm so sorry." His smile grew wider. "I'll pay for the cleaning—I didn't have time to look. But at least we made it. My name's Jamie. Jamie Wallace." He laughed again and she saw that grin.

Something about him reached deeply into her, his touch as he wiped mud from her face, his smile and voice, but most of all it was his eyes, soft and penetrating. It scared her, made her want to run. He helped her stand and said, "Are you, all right?"

As she started to say something, a long howl came from above the trench. Both of them turned toward the sound and looked out on Aubrey Beck. He held his head in his hands as if it was about to explode. Livy's eyes widened when she saw what remained of his Aston Martin. It lay upside down, smashed and burning.

"My car! Oh, my beautiful car!" Aubrey walked around it, stammering. The sight of him almost in tears, pacing back and forth with his hands on his head made Livy burst out laughing. *So much for a ride to the party*, she thought.

Jamie took her hand and helped her up and out of the trench. The aerodrome was on fire, with several of the hangars and buildings burning.

The people on the base were scurrying in every direction but not in panic. They seemed disoriented and confused, but set about their duty to look for survivors as ambulances approached, their emergency bells ringing above the clamor.

Lorries and equipment were flipped over and burning, littering the tarmac. Gaping holes peppered the ground throughout. In one of the craters a water main had burst, spewing white water high above the black smoky ruins.

She turned her head and grabbed Jamie's arm as shock coursed through her, where the shack had stood; only smoldering rubble remained. Livy screamed as Jamie tried to pull her back, away from the sight. But it was too late. There, in among mangled beach chairs and a chessboard, lay the torn and decapitated body of a seventeen-year-old corporal, his blood soaking the soil.

Chapter Ten

"I'm so happy to be out of that damn uniform," Alana said as she turned off the wipers. "I hope there will be dancing. The sun's come out and I want to dance."

"Dance?" Livy stifled a sigh. "All I want is to forget this last week." The images of a young corporal at a burning airfield still haunted her.

Alana glanced in her direction. "What is it? What's bothering you? Did something happen?"

"I'm not supposed to talk about it." All the while, her inner voice begged to release the fear radiating inside.

"Come on. It's me, Alana. You can tell me; it won't go any further." She slowed the black Wolseley sedan to take a sharp curve in the country road.

"Let's drop it. We're not to say anything about what we've filmed." Alana could be so persistent. She would never give up until she got what she wanted.

"Filmed? Is that your assignment—filming?"

"I work for the Ministry of Information. I haven't had the chance to tell you. We're making a record of the war, the sort of stuff you see on newsreels and such."

The narrow road straightened out, and Alana looked at her. "Exciting. How did you get that assignment while I'm stuck driving my father around in this beat-up black box."

"Timing, that's all, pure luck. At least that's what I thought when it happened. Now, I'm not so sure."

"My goodness, Livy, what could possibly have you in such a dark place?"

"Well, I guess it won't make a difference; it's certainly no secret our air bases are being attacked." Livy looked at her hands as she tried to block the images. "I was at one of them when it was bombed."

From the corner of her eye she saw Alana's head turn in her direction. "Good Lord, you could have been killed."

"Perhaps, but I don't think so. That's not what's bothering me. It's the others—the ones who didn't make it. The noise, the burning petrol and flesh—I can still smell it. And then, there was this young pilot who brought in this awfully damaged Spitfire right as the bombing started. I was in the air raid trench with the others and when he jumped in and landed right on top of me, shoved me face first into the mud."

"Really! You got his name I hope." Alana eyes were huge.

"I did, but that's not important." Livy was silent for a few seconds. "When it was all over and the Germans had gone, he tried to clean off my face with that scarf they wear. He was gentle and caring and so good-looking. I knew he was someone I would be interested in and that scared me far more than anything the Germans could do."

"Scared you? What are you talking about?"

"Suppose I did spend time with him, found I loved him and he was killed? I don't want to feel that kind of pain ever again." She turned her head, the weight of her own loneliness competing with the memory of her loss. "I hate this God-awful war."

Alana kept her eyes on the road and silence returned. After a few minutes, she came to a break in the trees lining the right side of the road. A sign was posted on a stick with an arrow pointing to the opening. She slipped the Wolseley through it onto a gravel driveway that led to the front of a large ocher stone-and-pantile homestead.

Several motor cars rested on an expanse of mowed lawn dotted with small gardens spilling over with red dahlias and orange daylilies, their intense color striking against the deep-green oaks and pale willows that surrounded the country home. As Alana stopped on the grass, next to several identical black government automobiles, she reached out her hand and gently touched Livy on the forearm.

"On the by, thank you for ridding us of Aubrey Beck. I don't know how you did it, but it worked," Alana smiled.

Livy nodded, "It wasn't anything I did, his car was destroyed in the bombing at the aerodrome."

"Whatever happened, it worked out nicely." Alana laughed, "Livy, today is a day to forget. Forget about rationing, forget about the Germans, that pilot and everything else. This is a day to live your life. Let's make the most of it. Come on, have a little wine and put a smile on. Enjoy the people we meet and most of all, have fun." She shook her head back and forth, "No worries, no war."

Livy pulled on the door handle. Stepping out, she said over the corner of her square-shouldered dress, "I'll give it a try. It would be heavenly to forget about everything even if only for a few hours."

Livy and Alana entered the home and stepped out onto the ground-level patio, the rays of an afternoon sun peering out between huge gray clouds. Like the front lawn of the small estate, bright flowers grew in circular beds as if borrowed from a landscape painting. A large light-green willow occupied the center of the rear lawn by a little brook, its feather-like branches drooping toward a wooden bench nestled beneath.

Chords from a piano inside the den rolled through the open windows and lay beneath the murmur of conversations by the sixty or so invited. On their way to the bar, Livy surveyed the crowd mostly consisting of men in uniform speaking about the war and women in various colors and styles speaking of anything else.

Alana seemed to mumble something to the bartender and motioned toward the crystal glasses set up on an adjacent table as Livy looked at the faces around her, hoping to not see one specific face. She recalled the gentle way he'd cleaned the mud off her face, the humorous look in his eyes. She remembered how she felt as she looked at his grin and heard his laugh as she sat in the ditch covered in mud.

Off to one side of the flagstones, she noticed her father in an animated conversation and she blanched as she recognized the man her father pointed his finger at—a red-faced Peter Watt. She closed her eyes and sighed, knowing neither man would give in to the other and that she must be the topic of their row.

"Hello, are you there?" Alana pulled at the cotton sleeve of her cream-colored dress.

Returned to the moment, Livy said, "Thanks, I'll take the same," having no idea what she ordered. Livy took the filled glass and said, "Excuse me a moment. I have something to take care of."

She took off in the direction of her father attempting to contain whatever damage he was causing and left Alana standing at the bar. As she came within ear shot of the two men, Watt said, "I don't really give a damn. She's mine, she's good, and she's on my crew. That's all there is to it." She could hear anger spill over in his voice.

Livy arrived and quickly interjected, "I think I'm the subject of this conversation, so wouldn't it be better if you two see fit to include me in it? What's this all about?"

"It appears your father doesn't approve of the work we're doing." Watt seemed furious that someone had the audacity to question the value of anything he did.

Her father looked at her, his eyes afire. "Livy, I don't want you dithering on something as foolish as filming things. Actually, I don't want you in the WAAFs at all, but you went against that too, didn't you?" He spoke with the authoritative voice of Lord Randall Ashford—a man not to be trifled with.

Her eyes narrowed and her teeth clenched. "Would you come with me, please? I need to speak with you for a moment."

She plopped the crystal stemmed glass on a small table, turned her back and walked into the house with her father following as she knew he would. He would never leave that kind of challenge half finished.

She entered White's study, turned and folded her arms. "What do you think you're doing?" Her father straightened. "Finally, something comes my way, something I want to do and you decide to destroy it because it doesn't fit your idea of what's acceptable for me. I am not a little girl anymore and I will decide what is right for me." As her father's eyes narrowed, she added, "Not you."

"One second, young lady. As long as you live under my roof, you'll do as I say."

Livy ground her teeth, digging her heels into the thick carpet. "Fine then, I'll move out. Alana has a flat in London. I'll move in with her."

"Absolutely not! That's completely out of the question." His cheeks glowing. "You'll not be running around London like some tart."

"Tart? I beg your pardon! This conversation is finished. How dare you." Livy brushed past him on her way out.

"Livy, stop." Her father pleaded.

She turned to see him standing in the study as if he were the only one left in the world. "How dare you call me, your own flesh and blood, a tart? You don't understand, do you? For some reason, you think this is something frivolous. Well, I assure you it's not. I am starting a life and it's my life, not yours, to command. Now, I have to go try and repair whatever damage you've done with Peter." Livy started toward the door.

"Livy, please," her father said. "I'll apologize to Mr. Watt." She turned to face him, his eyes were downcast. "Sometimes, I forget you're becoming a young woman, one I'm very proud of." He paused a moment, looked at her and continued. "I worry about you and your safety and unfortunately all I seem to do is get in the way.

"The night your mother was killed, a part of me died with her and the thought of losing you isn't something I could bear. You are so much like her and I worry for your safety in what will soon become a very terrible time. I'm sorry for treating Watt the way I did. I'll apologize and make it right."

He looked into her eyes and she saw something she had never seen before. This great man she loved dearly, a man of courage and strength, one she had depended on throughout her life looked like a lost and broken little boy. Somehow, she sensed this wasn't about the WAAFs or Peter Watt and films. It was about a father grieving for the loss of his daughter, the loss of a child to the world outside, and about a man seeing the bitter truth of his own loneliness.

Her heart broke as she saw the anguish on her father's face and then she did something few upper-class children would—she embraced her father and gave him a kiss on his cheek. "We should rejoin the party," she said softly.

On the patio outside, Jamie Wallace was very uncomfortable. The collar on his uniform was choking him. He kept pulling at it as if he couldn't breathe. The party, the powerful people, their wealth, and a home of this size made him feel out of place, like a trout groping the air at the bottom of a skiff.

"You look like you're about to pass out. What's the matter, guy?" Raj Singh laughed, his pearl-white teeth beaming out from his mahogany face.

Jamie stopped pulling at his collar. "It's this party. I'm feeling out of place. I'm a working class stiff. Christ, my family owns a butcher shop— what am I doing here?"

Miles Stafford smiled and put his arm around his friend, "I feel the same way. My dad was a coal miner in Wales, but hey, it's not like we had a choice. That new squadron commander ordered us to be here and since that's the case, if they offer me food, I'm gonna eat it and if they offer me drink, I'm gonna drink it."

Raj smiled. "Rather!"

Miles started laugh and it caught on with the others. "Got me a Stuka yesterday lads, Locke confirmed it. Four more and I'll catch up with you, Jamie."

The laughter continued as Jamie shook his head at Miles. It was amazing—only a few weeks with the squadron and they were already as close as brothers. It was the danger that intertwined them, as well as their utter dependence on one another for survival. It was a bond only those who faced combat together could ever know.

An overweight man looking to be in his fifties approached. He was dressed in an expensive charcoal-gray pinstripe suit that hung open around his middle. Beneath his round face and second chin, a small black bowtie hung a little cocked off the collar.

"Welcome boys, I'm Wilfred Eaton," he said, shaking hands with each and listening to their names as if he would remember them. "So, tell me boys, are we killing off the Germans?"

Miles was the first to speak. "I think we're doing fine, sir. Jerry knows when he comes over we'll be right there to knock him down."

"Wonderful. How many are you shooting down? Ten, twenty, more?" Eaton asked.

Jamie grew uncomfortable. He remembered the pilots that didn't return. "Mr. Eaton, we leave all the talking to others."

"Come on, lad, I'm a Member of Parliament. You can certainly tell me." His smile almost forced.

"As a member of Parliament, you should know better than we do," Singh said, clearly clashing with this conversation.

After a few moments, their silence was broken by the approach of another man dressed in a Royal Navy uniform. This one had a strong countenance, with a confident face and hair graying at the temples. He looked distinguished, a man of experience, of importance, Jamie thought.

"Gentlemen, my name's Randall Ashford. It's a pleasure to meet you. I'd like to thank you for protecting our country. It's greatly appreciated."

"But you're a naval officer, we should be thanking you," Jamie said.

"Oh this." He motioned to his uniform. "Young man, I'm only a has-been from the last war. They called me back to command a desk for a short time, that's all."

"Don't let him fool you, boys," Wilfred Eaton quipped. "He's an intelligence man and a member of the House of Lords."

Randall laughed, "Wilfred, you make it sound far more dramatic than it is. Honestly lads, I push a lot of paper around a much-cluttered desk and that's all." He looked at the Member of Parliament standing beside him. "By the way, Wilfred, where have you been? I haven't seen you since Churchill's speech. I take it you've been out of town?"

"I spent a few days in Coventry touring aircraft production factories—a wonderful look at what's going on there." He took a sip of his cocktail.

Randall nodded, "Maybe we can try again for that breakfast, I'd like your opinion of our production facilities and how we might speed up the process. We need more aircraft and quickly."

Jamie watched the bowtie bounce as another sip went down. But before the man could answer, their host, Paul White strode up with Squadron Commander Beck following close behind.

"Randall," the American said, "there's a phone call for you. I'm sorry but it's Whitehall, I believe. Sounded urgent—you can take it in my study."

The naval officer smiled as if this was something that happened all the time—a call from Whitehall. The man shrugged his shoulders; "Gentlemen, I'm afraid I'll soon be on my way back to London."

A call from Whitehall Jamie thought and again he felt very out of place until the man shook his hand. He looked into Jamie's eyes as if taking the measure of an equal and said, "Fine to meet you, young man. I hope to see you and your friends again soon." He turned to the others, "Gentlemen, I must take my leave. Thank you, Paul, for this lovely party. I'll see myself out."

Surprised, Jamie watched the man enter the home and thought, I actually liked him. Growing up all he heard was *'the toffs'*, as the upper-class was referred to with vehement distaste, the ones his father continually blamed for all the ills of the nation and yet, Jamie would fly with the man anytime. It was the highest compliment a fighter pilot could give.

Paul White looked at Jamie and the other pilots and said, "Lads, are you having a good time?"

Before any of them could answer, Aubrey Beck interrupted in a voice that Jamie felt was condescending. "Gentlemen, I don't think I mentioned this, Mr. White is the head of CBS News in London so mind what you say."

Wilfred Eaton bit into a cucumber sandwich and between chews said, "Hold on, Aubrey. Don't tell them that. I want these lads to tell me the truth about what's going on up there. I want to know if the RAF can stop the invasion. That's what everyone wants to know." He slowly turned his head and looked straight at Jamie, his dark unblinking eyes focused, "You think you're ready to stop the invasion?"

Jamie's anger rose. Something about this man grated on him and without thinking he said, "If they try it, I promise you there will be a lot of dead Nazis floating in the Channel."

Eaton finished swallowing his sandwich and said, "Well now, that's what I wanted to hear. Finally, I have something I can say to the House of Commons."

Now you've done it, Jamie thought. He looked over at Squadron Commander Beck expecting to find some sort of admonition but instead he was greeted with a blank stare. A moment later he realized he wasn't staring at him at all, Beck was looking somewhere over his shoulder. Jamie turned, took one glance and spun back around. She was there, walking straight toward their little group along with another girl.

He nudged Raj Singh with his elbow.

"The girl, she's here. She's right behind us," he whispered.

"Great, we finally get to meet this phantom maiden," Raj whispered as the two women entered the circle and stood next to Paul White.

"Gentlemen," Wilfred Eaton said, dabbing the corners of his mouth with a soiled napkin. He leaned over and gave the dark-haired girl a quick kiss on the cheek. "Let me introduce my daughter Alana and her friend, Livy."

She turned, her beautiful eyes meeting his. As his friends announced their names from a place that sounded far away, he noticed the look on her face. It was cold, as if he didn't exist. Damn, what else could go wrong? He offered a smile at the auburn-haired beauty to no result.

Miles poked him in the ribs, bringing him back to reality. "I'm Jamie. Jamie Wallace." He said, still looking at her.

She blinked twice with her eyes still focused on his and with an almost non-expression said, "We've met, haven't we, Mr. Wallace?"

Jamie's mouth hung open.

After a second, Miles blurted out, "Christ, are you the mud girl?" He started laughing. "Jamie said you were beautiful, but he hadn't done you justice."

He noticed a tiny flush on her face. She paused a second, her eyes burrowing into him and said, "Is that how you refer to me, the mud girl?" Jamie thought he could see teasing in her eyes but he wasn't sure.

His nerves were jangled and he pulled at the collar of his uniform. He tried to speak, but his tongue felt covered with cotton. "I … I just told them a little bit about you and how we met."

Paul White laughed and said, "I've been a news hound all my life and I can smell a good story from a mile away. What is this mud girl thing?"

She looked over at him and said, "It's nothing really. We were at an airfield the other day when it was attacked by the Germans. I was taking cover in an air raid trench and this young man decided to jump into it, right on top of me. I ended up face first deep in the mud."

"Jamie Wallace. So, you're the one!" Alana gave him a look that penetrated right through him. "Livy mentioned you on our way here. I'd say you made quite an impression."

The group laughed, Jamie blanched, and Paul White said, "Well, that's a new story for my records. Not quite Romeo and Juliet, but it'll do."

Livy paused a moment as everyone looked at her and said, "It was an accident, a simple mistake. It was the attack I remember—not getting soiled with mud."

From inside the country home, the radio blared. The latest popular tune jumped out the windows. He watched as some of the guests inside start to dance—if one could call it that. A choreographed silly strut to a song called "The Lambeth Walk." Alana looked at the group and beckoned them to follow her. "Hey, come on everyone, let's dance. It's fun."

Most of them acceded and followed Alana into the house where some of the guests were lined up prancing and singing the lyrics: *"You'll have it all, doing the Lambeth Walk, hey!"*

"That is one of the most ludicrous things I've ever seen. I absolutely detest that song," Livy said, shaking her head. Jamie watched the sun glisten off her auburn hair as it swung from side to side.

Without the mud on her face and clothes she was even more beautiful than he remembered. There was something about her, a grace, intangible but very real. The cream-colored dress she wore accented her eyes and her coloring perfectly. Her scent was captivating. He wanted to speak with her, get to know her; he wanted to be near her.

"Would you like to take a stroll in the garden? It's so peaceful and beautiful," he said, praying she would say yes.

She looked at him, her upper lip slightly curled to the side. She was going to say no, he was sure of it. "Why not? We'll get away from that horrible song."

Elated, Jamie took her arm and they left the flagstones for mowed grass, "Livy, please allow me to apologize and offer to pay for cleaning your uniform. I honestly had no idea you were in the trench. I was looking for the first place I could hide."

"I know that. As far as the uniform goes, it's already done." She paused. "But thank you for the offer."

She directed a slight smile toward him and he was thrilled. They approached the wood bench beneath the willow and he said, "I love these trees. There was a big one on a hill near my home. As a kid, I used to spend a lot of time in the summer lying beneath the branches wondering what my life would be like. I would pretend I was a knight in armor riding over the fields to some big adventure, you see. Saving the damsel in distress or something, like in Ivanhoe."

She gave a soft laugh, the sound like bells. "One of my favorites. But I always wanted Ivanhoe to marry the Jewess. I think that would have been a far better ending."

"Ah, Rebecca, the lovely Rebecca. That's the kind of story I wanted my life to be like." He smiled at her.

"And now you're a fighter pilot. Did you ever think you'd be doing something like that?"

"No, never. Not in my wildest dreams could I have come up with that. I fell out of that willow tree I told you about—broke my arm and cut my head wide open. Never did climb it again. You see, now I'm scared of heights."

"Scared of heights, a fighter pilot?" She smiled at him and this time it was warm and it filled him. They sat at the bench beneath the willow as a muffled rumble of thunder came from far away, the sound of coming rain.

"Livy, I would like to make this whole thing right. Would you have dinner with me? I know of this great little place next to the Thames. Best food in London."

She was silent for an eternity. "No, I don't think that would be a good idea."

"It's just dinner. An apology for being so clumsy, I promise." It was as if the wind had abandoned his ship, left him stranded in the breathless Sargasso Sea.

"It's not that."

"What is it? Is it me?" He closed his eyes and nodded. "Oh, you already have someone."

She smiled at him, "That's not it. There isn't anyone right now." She looked into his eyes. "It's that I don't want to know you. Or anyone else, for that matter—not until this war is over."

He paused searching for words, but none came.

It was as if she could sense the loss he was feeling. "Jamie, I won't get close to anyone right now. At the airfield, I truly saw the war for the first time. Not the war they want you to believe—the real thing. War is death and horror. It's the loss of all you love or care about in a flash of cordite and blood."

He leaned forward about to speak, but she stopped him.

Her eyes focused on her hands. "That corporal at the ready shack was killed less than five minutes after I spoke with him—he was seventeen with a full life before him and a few minutes later he was dead, his body torn to pieces. It broke my heart.

"You're a fighter pilot, Jamie, and one day you might not come back. I never want to know that kind of pain, the same pain that young boy's family is feeling right now. So, thank you for the dinner invitation, but the answer is no. I trust you'll understand."

He leaned toward her. "I do understand. But, I'm not going to die. The Germans will never get me. Somehow, I know that and not living a life while you have it . . ."

Before he could finish, Paul White's voice carried across the lawn. "Come on, you two, the Murrow broadcast is about to start."

"Jamie, let's go. I don't want to speak about this anymore." She was looking at the ground.

As they walked back towards the house, his disappointment was palpable. It was as if all the dreams he'd had beneath a great willow had just vanished. He would never know this woman. Their lives would go on but in different directions and he would probably never see her again. To his surprise, as they walked toward the house, she slipped her hand around his arm, as if she was aware of how he felt.

In the den of White's home, the guests were crowded around a radio set in the corner. They stood or sat, some sipping wine or spirits and others dark tea. Jamie and Livy stood behind a long sofa filled with men and women ready to hear the evening CBS broadcast to America. He felt alone as she dropped her hand from his arm and Paul White came to stand next to them.

A voice came on the radio, "Now we take you to London and our correspondent, Edward R. Murrow. London, this is New York. Take it away."

A wonderful baritone voice took over. "This is London. The dark-gray clouds that hung around most of the day have finally opened up and a rain is falling. The soldiers with me on this roof—I won't tell you where—are still on station at their antiaircraft guns. Behind us, searchlights scan the skies and Moaning Minnie—what Londoners call the air raid siren—wails a hard-stony sound, and we don't know if it's a test or the real thing. We must wait for that answer.

"The war news comes to this ancient island in waves, large and ferocious, threatening its existence. The massive army that conquered Europe in a few weeks has dug its claws into the blood-soaked French soil ready to pounce across some twenty miles of Channel. The airfields scattered across southern England are in tatters and the few machines left to the Royal Air Force do their best to hold back a mighty Luftwaffe as it prepares the way for an invasion, one that may arrive at any moment.

"America, if England falls, so will the world as we know it. We can no longer stand on the sidelines. Sleep well, America—your safe for now, but your time will be coming. This is Edward R Murrow reporting from London. And now back to New York."

One of the guests switched off the radio to silence in the room. Livy leaned forward to see around Jamie and said to Paul, "I hope Americans will take to heart what Mr. Morrow said. It's the truth. We really could use the help."

"I have a feeling help will be coming. Though, I hope it won't be too late," Jamie said. "Do you agree, Mr. White? America will join in, won't they?"

"I can't say. Murrow and I were discussing that very subject over a lunch in Chicago a little over a month ago, right before he came to England. He's a lot closer to Roosevelt than I am and he didn't know what the President was thinking. I believe Roosevelt will play this very close to the vest. The political landscape is fraught with trouble and with the America First folks and the Congress being so intensely against entry into the war, it's anybody's guess."

"You were in Chicago this summer? I thought you'd been in England for quite some time." Livy asked with a curiosity.

"Oh, I went home for two weeks—it was my mother's birthday. Although I enjoy the city, I was very happy to come back to England. Chicago was so hot and muggy; I couldn't stand it."

Jamie noticed Livy cock her head to the side; her face puzzled and wondered why.

Chapter Eleven

After two days of rain and with it a respite from flying, the morning sun was out and unfortunately, so were the Germans. Red Flight of 41 Squadron had already flown two sorties and the dirty white clock on the wall of the rebuilt shack read ten minutes after eleven. There would be almost another nine hours of daylight, a long and dangerous day.

Jamie walked outside the shack and took the last empty seat. Closing his eyes, he leaned back in a torn wicker club chair dangling his arms over the sides, his hands almost touching the trampled grass. He guessed this chair, like the others scattered about, must have been scavenged from some junk pile close by. The bottom of the seat was ripped to the point that at any second he might fall through. But he liked it better than the striped beach chairs the other pilots occupied, little folding things discarded from the garages of seaside vacation homes.

The sun washed warmth into his chilled body. He still shook, either from adrenaline or the frigid temperatures at altitude or fear. He didn't know which and he really didn't care. It was just part of the job, part of the reality of his life. The glamor and adventure of being an invincible fighter pilot had left him three days ago at Paul White's party.

He kept seeing images of her face, heard the soft lyrical quality of her voice—words that told him gently but firmly to go away. Worst of all, he could understand why. It wasn't long ago he thought his brother might be dead and he felt the same loss and pain she desired to avoid. He wanted to tell her life will go on and to live whatever days they have to the fullest, but he was never given the chance.

As the sun shone on his face, sleep slowly wrapped her arms around him and the world outside slid away into one beneath the feathery leaves of a willow tree with her face smiling beside him. Exhilarated, Jamie left the ground soaring through a cloudless sky. He was free, flying higher and higher, his heart light and yet filled. He looked at the patchwork of ground far below him, at the lush green earth fertile with the gifts of a future and abruptly he could no longer fly. He fell like a stone, faster and faster, spinning uncontrollably as he dropped toward a certain death. He screamed, raged at fate stealing all he ever dreamed of, leaving him hopeless and lost. He raged against the horror, the futility of his life and again he screamed.

"Jamie. Hey, Jamie, wake up." Miles was shaking him. "God, man, you were bellowing like a bloody banshee."

Shrugging off the sleep, awareness flooding into him, he noticed the other pilots scattered about the well-trodden lawn outside the shack. They were staring at him, not with laughter or smiles but blank faces because they too were each tormented by the same dream and the same sour taste of a lost future. Once again, he pushed down the fear churning inside him.

Miles smiled and said, "The meanies got you. Sneaky little bastards, aren't they?" He put his hand on Jamie's shoulder, "The squadron will be standing down in another ten minutes and we'll be free for an hour or two. It'd do you good to go back to the barracks and see if you can sleep and if not, at least rest." The look on Miles's face spoke of their trust, a bond between brothers and yet, a cold premonition from the dream told him that one of them was about to die.

He slid out of the torn wicker chair and stretching the kinks out, decided to keep his mouth shut about any foolish intuition of impending death. From the corner of his eye, he noticed a mud-covered RAF staff car chug to a stop by the shack.

Squadron Commander Beck opened the driver's door. He stepped out and motioned for him to come over.

Jamie walked to him and snapped off a sharp salute, which was casually returned. He said, "Morning, sir, what can I do for you?"

"Hello, Jamie, as far as anyone knows, I'm not even here. I came to speak to you about Livy, as a friend. I've known her family a long time and thought I might help answer any questions you might have about her."

It took Jamie off guard. He remembered how the man had been constantly peering at them from inside the house as they sat on the bench under the willow. On the return journey from White's party when Raj and Miles badgered him from the rear seat wanting to know everything about her, he remembered how Beck's knuckles had turned white as he gripped the steering wheel when Jamie refused to say anything.

"Help me? I don't understand."

"Jamie, it's obvious you're interested in her. I could tell by the way you looked at her." He said it like someone he had known for a lifetime. "My job is to take care of you pilots. I want to help you if I can, not as an officer, but as a friend."

"I don't know what you can do. I really don't know her. I just thought she was beautiful and might be something special, that's all."

Beck looked at him like an older and wiser brother. "Well, let's start with her name. Do you know who she is?"

"I know her name is Livy."

"Do you know her surname?" Beck put his hands in his pockets. Jamie shook his head, "No, never heard it."

"It's Ashford, Livy Ashford. Does that mean anything to you?"

Where the hell is he going with this? "Not really."

"Remember that Royal Navy captain from the party?"

"Sure, Randall something."

"That's right, Lord Randall Ashford, her father. Do you really think you'd have a chance with someone like that, someone with her position in life?"

Jamie paused a moment, the reality stung him. "He's her father?" No wonder he thought and he's a Lord to boot. "I only wish she'd told me the truth."

Everything became crystal clear. It wasn't that she didn't want to know him out of some fear he would die, it was that he wasn't good enough for her. He wasn't of her social status; he was nothing but a penniless butcher's son. He was of the lower classes, a nobody to her, his disappointment now complete.

"I didn't think you knew, you see. I don't say this to pain you, but it would never work. Her father wouldn't allow it even if she wanted you, which she wouldn't. I didn't fancy you chasing after something that would end in disaster, something that could never happen," Beck said with compassion in his voice. "You're one of my finest pilots, Jamie; believe me, I only want what's best for you."

"Well, thanks for that and as for Miss Livy Ashford," he said bitterly, "I have no interest in her and I know it's the same with her—she has no interest in me. There's really nothing left. Hell, there wasn't anything to begin with."

"Well, that's good to know. You're better off that way." Jamie read genuine relief on Beck's face.

But there was something more Jamie needed to know that might make his loss easier—easier to forget her and move on. "There is one thing. Any truth to the rumors we'll be moving to RAF Hornchurch? That would be great. It's a hell of lot better than this place and nowhere near it or the Ashfords."

Beck smiled. "I haven't heard that rumor yet and even if I did, I couldn't say anything about it—you know that."

Jamie took a tentative breath and said, "Well, anyway, thanks. I appreciate your concern and taking the time to—"

The clanging of a scramble bell came from outside the shack, and the new corporal screamed out the window, "Red Flight, scramble!"

Jamie took off toward his Spitfire as fast as he could run, the bright yellow Mae West bobbled around his neck. He caught up to the other pilots as some were already climbing into their machines, the propellers spinning, making the aircraft sway back and forth, the heated engines anticipating a fight.

Aubrey Beck watched Jamie—aided by one of the mechanics—slip on his parachute and buckle into the Spitfire. He closed the canopy and pushed the throttles, bringing a deep rumble from the whirling Merlin engine, the wind making Aubrey lean forward, his uniform fluttering against his body. He smiled as Jamie left the ground and promptly returned to the staff car, assured his plans for Livy Ashford were still intact.

"That was easy—what a fool," Aubrey said to himself as he drove away from the shack toward Headquarters RAF Uxbridge and the second part of his plan.

He was intrigued by Jamie's question about moving 41 Squadron to Hornchurch. It solidified an idea roaming around the recesses of his mind. An idea that might be solution to his dilemma, get him ten thousand pounds and of course, his drug. He smiled as he drove toward Hillingdon House, thrilled with how clever he was.

Yesterday, after an early evening tryst with young Bethany, a short dirty-looking man had approached him. His face was almost skeletal, white stubble peppered his chin and the odor of cheap gin permeated his tattered clothing. He plunked a small typed note into Aubrey's hand, tipped his hat and said, "Thank you, Gov." as he quickly disappeared down a dark East End street. The note simply said "46 Shoe Lane 7 p.m. tomorrow."

The thought of the Doctor, his hawk-like face and the black soulless eyes, struck a chord of terror in Aubrey. He was a killer, one that fully relished inflicting pain, something he knew the creature could be very good at and one talent Aubrey never wanted to experience. But now, he may have found a way out from his failure to get the Order of Battle.

A few minutes later, he jerked the blue staff car to a stop outside Hillingdon House and ran in. Once again, he was late. Aubrey slipped past the guards and staffers, making his way directly to the wing commander's office. He paused for a second to straighten his uniform and swat away some of the dust left from Jamie's propeller. Properly setting his officer's cap beneath his left arm, he opened the door.

"Squadron Commander Beck reporting as ordered," he said to a blank-faced aide.

Without acknowledgment, the aide simply pushed a small lever on the squawk box and said, "Squadron Commander Beck is here, sir."

"About damn time! Send him in." The scratchy voice belched from the little speaker.

Aubrey opened the oak door and entered.

"My God, Beck, your uniform is a travesty, where the hell have you been?"

Aubrey snapped to attention and gave a sharp salute. "Sorry, sir. I was on the field with the pilots as they scrambled. I assume they're after another incoming raid, a busy day, sir."

The Wing Commander sat at his desk, his thumb and first finger squeezed his lower lip. "Correct. It's a deep penetration raid headed toward London or the Thames estuary—we're not sure which. Have a seat, we have something to go over."

He sat in one of the two upholstered armchairs across from the desk.

The wing commander paused a moment, observing him. "You're not a flyer, are you, Beck?"

"No sir, never learned to fly, actually, never wanted to."

"Hmm, a squadron commander that's never flown. Unusual, but not unprecedented. I remember in the last war my squadron commander didn't know a damn thing about airplanes. But that was a different era, wasn't it?" He waited for a response but Aubrey only nodded in agreement. "You haven't been here very long, and I haven't had time to discuss much with you, but you've done a fairly good job with the pilots and helping me when I needed it. I wanted to thank you for that. Beck, you're being transferred."

Aubrey's eyes widened. He was amazed at their efficiency; he hadn't expected the transfer to come this fast. He'd left the note for the Irishman at the communication drop only a few days ago, a note saying Uxbridge was a failure and there was nothing here to obtain—at least nothing that would get them what they wanted. He quickly feigned disappointment, "Transferred, to where?"

"Here are the orders." He passed over a single sheet of typed paper. "You're being assigned to work on special projects for a Member of Parliament. All I know is you're to report to Whitehall immediately. So, get your things and get going."

Aubrey looked up, he wanted one more thing. "Sir, may I ask you something before I leave?"

"Certainly, but be quick."

"While I was working with the pilots, one of them asked if 41 Squadron was being moved to Hornchurch." He looked over at a large map on the wall of Group 11's sector and noticed all the pins stuck to it were in different places from just a few days ago. "Is that what those colored pins on the map are—our squadrons and their current positions?"

"Only for today, Aubrey."

"So, you're moving the aircraft around, changing their locations?"

"Almost every day. We move them from home airfields to satellite fields, change the mix of squadrons and move them from base to base. That way, we keep the Jerry guessing. He can't hit us because he doesn't know where we are or how many we are. When they attack an airfield, unless we're caught sleeping, we won't be there and the damage will quickly be repaired. Then we come back with the aircraft and we're ready to go. Those little pins help me keep track of what we're doing. Works quite well—a flexible order of battle, I call it."

"So, 41 Squadron is moving to Hornchurch. The pilot was right?"

"Well, sort of, unless I move them again. Their gear was packed this morning; it's already on its way. They'll be going to Hornchurch to cover the Thames estuary. Oddly enough, close to where the Jerrys are attacking right now."

"Is that by design?" Aubrey said, actually impressed.

The wing commander simply smiled. "Is there anything else?" Aubrey shook his head. The wing commander looked at his watch. "You should be going. You're relieved Beck, be at your new post by morning."

He saluted and shook the Wing Commander's hand. Taking one last look at the map, he left the office, the general positions of the aircraft committed to memory.

Chapter Twelve

High, in an almost cloudless sky, Jamie took his hand off the stick, held it out and watched it shake as if it belonged to someone else. Once again, the Merlin engine sputtered and coughed as if it also felt the strain. This was his third flight in the new Spitfire and during each of the other two he'd experienced the same trouble—the engine had nearly quit.

London lay well behind them as the Thames estuary and the eastern coast of England slipped beneath, leaving a wide expanse of a choppy North Sea filling Jamie's view. Red Flight took the high cover, behind and a thousand feet higher than the other three flights of 41 Squadron. Three groups of four aircraft each set in a diamond formation, a total of twelve Spitfires against far too many Germans set on their destruction. For today, Jamie would be flying wingman for Miles, with Raj covering Locke, the flight leader.

The squadron headed slightly north of due east. A course completely different from all their other sorties—those had headed south toward France and the Channel. It confirmed Jamie's suspicion they would be moving.

He flicked on the talk switch and said, "We're a fare distance out, Red Leader. Where are we landing when this is over?"

"We'll head to Hornchurch, you'll find your gear there." Eric Locke responded. "Now stay off the blinkin' radio. Unless you see something, cap it."

Jamie knew the adrenaline was flowing like water in every one of the other pilots. They all knew that combat and maybe death was only a few minutes away. All of them were on edge, waiting for their call sign, Mitor, and the intercept instructions. Jamie took slow deep breaths from the oxygen mask, hoping it would calm the turmoil he felt inside. The girl he thought he might have something special with tossed him away like rubbish. And yet, when he closed his eyes, he saw nothing but her. Since the party, every time he flew, the shaking got worse and terrifying thoughts crept into his head. Maybe he won't be coming back, maybe she was right and the war would claim him.

"Mitor, this is Control, angels one seven, intercept 195, 100+, ten miles, over."

Locke confirmed the instructions as ice clawed up Jamie's spine. His flight would now wait to follow Locke's turn to the intercept course. They would hold back, giving space for the German fighters to follow the other flights as they attacked, a trap designed to kill. Locke held back a few more moments as Jamie sucked on the cold oxygen. Finally, over the radio Locke said, "Red Flight, tally ho."

Jamie pulled the stick to the right and the Spitfire arched over, steering into the heart of the tiny black specks, the raiders headed toward London. High cover meant that Red Flight's target would be the Nazi fighters, the ones chasing the other three flights of 41 Squadron as they dove into the fray. They would be approaching out of a high sun blazing behind them. On the first pass, the Germans would never see them coming.

Far below, Jamie could see the other flights of his squadron tear into the bombers, dropping two in flames, damaging another three, an angry swarm of small gray-green fighters chasing after them. But now the German would become the hunted.

He nosed the Spitfire over, screaming down out of the sun.

He slammed the throttle forward, coaxing every bit of speed from the engine, the aircraft tearing through the crowded sky. Black bombers filled his gun sight, but he ignored them, his eyes focused on a dark shape ahead as it slipped behind one of 41's pilots, seeking his death.

Jamie moved his thumb away from the trigger and held his fire as Miles pulled in behind the German. His only job is to protect him as he went after the fighters.

Miles was slightly ahead and to the left, smoke pouring from his guns, the hot barrels spitting explosive lead that raked the fighter and tore it to pieces. With Jamie behind, they screamed past the condemned pilot, orange flames curling around his body as he lived his last few seconds. The two careened into the fray, into what seemed like hundreds of fighters twisting and turning in a chaotic and very small sky. Their contrails corkscrewed over the cold blue and left traces of singed air like slashes from the claws of an enraged beast.

He followed close behind Miles, pulling hard, up and to the left, G-forces pressing him down into the seat, the harness now loose like an untied shoe. He squeezed every muscle in his body, trying to push the blackness away as blood drained from his head. Through what looked like a tunnel, Jamie saw the distance between himself and Miles increasing. He wasn't keeping up. Miles was losing him.

"Red Three," Jamie called for him. He could barely get the words out from the weight pressing against him. "I can't keep up. Ease off, ease off." He shoved the unmoving throttle forward, but it was already against the stops. He pulled back on the stick with all his strength, trying to keep up, speed bleeding away. Then in an instant, two miles above the earth, Jamie's engine coughed, sputtered, and quit.

The Spitfire fell out of the sky.

He watched in horror as Miles climbed away and a gray-green fighter slipped in behind him. It followed for a second and with a fury opened up on his friend.

"On your six, Miles, on your six!" He screamed over the radio. Red-orange fireballs flew toward Miles, smashing into his aircraft. "Break right, break right!" Jamie yelled as he looked down into the cockpit and tried to restart the engine, pulling and resetting switches franticly. He looked up and saw Miles rolling over, his aircraft on fire, spinning and twisting toward the earth, orange-tinged smoke streaming behind it.

Jamie's voice burst into the radio, "Miles, get out! My God, man—jump!" He pushed the nose of his silent Spitfire over, hoping to see a parachute as flames thickened over the aircraft and his friend disappeared from sight.

Sweat poured from his face and ran into his eyes as he pulled levers and pumped petrol into the fuel-starved engine. As he flipped switches back and forth, something flashed by above his vision. He snapped his head up and around as an orange fireball hurtled over the canopy followed by another and another. "Christ!" he shouted, rolling over and heading straight toward the earth. The Spitfire wrenched as flaming rounds slammed into the engine and burrowed huge holes in the metal, the pistons shattered and flew out across the frigid sky. Swarms of fireballs, glowing like lava, walked their way back toward the cockpit. Jamie sucked hard on the oxygen and screamed as a stream of fireballs buried into the center fuel tank and the Spitfire exploded.

Chapter Thirteen

A blue-black antiaircraft gun pivoted in a circle, its crew cranking the hand-powered wheels furiously. Unused polished steel barrels pointed upward, pretending to throw exploding shells at a phantom enemy floating high in a midday sky.

"Cut." Peter Watt's booming voice carried throughout the cast and crew rising above the murmur coming from the streets of London. "And that, ladies and gentlemen, is a wrap."

Cheers and applause broke out among the film crew; the long haul was over not only for the day, but for the film. The shooting was complete and most of them would get a hiatus during final editing. Livy had two full weeks to do anything she wanted.

"Remember, crew party tonight at Thirsty Bear on Stamford Street and I damn well expect every one of you to be there," Watt said with his hands on his hips. "Thank you all for a great job. However, two weeks from tonight we start again." He said to groans from the crew. "Come on, I'm not that bad to work for."

Mickey McCarty took the film magazine off the camera and pulling on his white beard for effect said, "Well, I'm not saying you're an ogre—maybe just one in training." More applause and laughter came from the close-knit crew and a huge smile settled on Peter Watt's sturdy face.

Off to one side, Livy leaned against a parapet surrounding the large flat roof over St. Thomas Hospital as the crew began to disassemble the lights and camera. She wondered how something that could take hours to set up could be taken down and packed away in minutes. Physically, she was bone tired and was relieved to be done with the early crew calls. This final day of shooting had started at four in the morning on a sound stage near St. John's Wood and now it was a quarter to one. She felt like a marathon runner who had just crossed the finish line.

Livy turned around and looked across the Thames River at the Houses of Parliament and Big Ben. A cold tremor ran down her spine as an impending gloom settled over her. This morning, the Germans had bombed London. It brought the threat even closer to home. England was about to be invaded and all she could do was wait for it to come, her feelings of dread and fear increased and intensified from one day to the next. She worried about her father and what would happen to him after they came and something else inside her kept returning—a young man she tried to avoid thinking about and couldn't.

Livy opened the canvas gas mask satchel that she used as a handbag after tossing the contents. Poking around in the interior, she found a pack of Players cigarettes and popped one into her mouth. She began to rummage once more, this time after matches.

A lit Zippo appeared before her. "Angel, what's going on?" Mickey McCarty said as he put his arm around her shoulder. "You look down in the dumps."

He lit her cigarette, "Thanks, Mickey." She blew out a blue column of smoke and rested her head on his shoulder. "I'm all right; it tires me sometimes, that's all."

"The work or the war?"

She smiled at him, "Both, I think."

"Well, we have two weeks to be away from this mess, but as for the war, we're all feeling like that."

"I'm scared, Mickey. Scared of what will happen when the Germans invade, they'll torture and murder my father. I know that because of his position as an intelligence officer. He's the only family I have left and I can't fathom the idea of losing him."

She pointed to the east at dark smoke rising from fires on the docks bombed less than three hours ago. "Look over there. Now they're bombing London in daylight." She looked up into his gray creased eyes. "Mickey, I've also made a horrible mistake. One I am sure I'll live to regret."

"You're too young to have anything to regret."

"I met this pilot—"

Mickey laughed. "Yeah, at the airfield, right? The one that crashed you into the mud."

"How did you know that?" She'd never mentioned him to anyone on the crew.

"My dear, I've been a cameraman for most of my life. There's very little I miss. I saw how you looked at him and how he looked at you, even though you were covered head to foot in mud." He laughed again and smiled a knowing kind of smile.

"I love you, Mickey."

"I'll even wager that you told him to bugger off, didn't you?"

Livy's eyes widened. It gave away the surprise she felt. "Well, not in so many words, but essentially yes."

"I had a young lass tell me the same thing as I got on a train to France in 1915. She didn't want to know me either. Said I might get killed and she couldn't stand the thought of going through something like that. Right, ain't I?"

"You are. That's exactly what I did."

"Livy, let me say something I hope you'll listen to. There is no promise you'll be alive tomorrow either. Look at the smoke over there—people just died there. They woke up, sipped their morning tea and had no idea they were about to die, now did they? They hopped a bus, went off to work like any other day and that was their last day on this earth."

He stepped back and placed his hands on her shoulders. "God didn't give you notice of when you'll die. All he did was give you the tools to live each moment to the fullest and what you do with that is all that matters. You go back and tell this lad you're going to live your life the best you can every minute and that life might include him. It's one thing to let go of something you don't know about, but it's an entirely different thing to toss an opportunity because you're afraid of what might happen.

"If you give in to fear, that's all you'll ever know. You'll never know what might have been, what you missed. Lass, it could be the best thing of your life. So, don't miss it, war or not. That girl by the train that didn't want me in 1915—she's been my wife of twenty-five years and the life we have together means everything to me. What would we have tossed away if the fear had won?"

Livy wrapped her arms around the cameraman. She stood on her toes and kissed his cheek; the beard tickled her nose. "Thank you, Mickey. You're wonderful, I know what I need to do. I'm sure he'll understand and maybe we can start over."

She nestled against him for a moment and pulled back. "I know this sounds foolish, I shouldn't even say something like this, but he's in trouble. I've been thinking about him all morning. I know something is wrong. I need to find him, tell him I'm sorry and hopefully after that," she shrugged her shoulders, "well, we'll see."

The darkness receded. Jamie was aware of a growling wind blowing against him and a wet sensation along the left side of his neck that ran down to his chest. He was falling, spinning, seeing glimpses of sky and ground and had no idea where he was.

Like a ghastly figure emerging from shadow, realization crept slowly into his mind. He was strapped into the armored seat, as he twisted and turned in a long fall toward the earth. Numb from the cold and disoriented, he struggled to pull his flailing arms into his body and tried time and time again to reach the buckle holding him fast until his fingers finally wrapped around the latch and he pulled with all the strength he could muster.

A sharp clack of metal and he was released; the straps tore away and he was thrown from the tumbling seat. Now free and careening through a frigid empty sky, he managed to slip his hand into the parachute ring and pull. It deployed against the wind and with a loud snap, it opened and yanked him backwards, arresting his fall.

The roar subsided to a whisper as he swung back and forth in the harness, his world rocking from side to side as darkness returned to overwhelm him.

Livy left the film crew and antiaircraft actors on the roof and went down the stairs into the hospital. At the nurses' station she asked, "Excuse me, where's a phone? Is there one nearby I can use?"

A doctor, his glasses sitting far down on a crooked nose looked up from the chart sprawled out on the counter. He pointed and said, "Down the hall—you'll see it." He went back to writing in his chart.

She walked down the hall and some fifty feet away saw a phone hanging on the wall. As she approached, a large woman dressed in a faded blue and white flowered dress that covered her like a tent scooted out from a patient's ward and grabbed the receiver.

Livy leaned against the wall, her arms folded across her chest and noticed a rude stare from the woman. A few seconds later, she gave up and pulled on the exit door next to the phone. She took the narrow staircase to the floor below, her footsteps echoing against the lime-green walls. At the landing, she opened the hallway door below, but there was no phone perched next to it. She let go and heard the hiss of an automatic closer. She ran down another level and opened the door. Hung on the wall unattended was the phone she needed.

Livy flipped open the satchel and digging deep, fetched the note with Aubrey Beck's number, soiled by powder spilled from an errant compact dropped into the canvas cavern. A quick call to him might work.

She stuffed a half-pence into the round slot, and waited for the operator to finish before she spoke, "Uxbridge 9172." Counting the rings, she reached eleven before hearing "Squadron Commander Beck here."

"Aubrey, its Livy."

"Livy, what a nice surprise, it's good to hear from you." His voice was almost too composed, too pleased and it grated on her. "You barely caught me; I was just leaving. I've been transferred to London."

"I need your help. Where's Jamie?"

"Jamie Wallace? What do you want with him?"

"Where is he? Can you find him, please?" She gripped the receiver tighter.

"Livy, one moment, tell me what's going on."

"Aubrey, I need to speak to Jamie. Where is he?"

"The last I saw, he was flying away from the field. He's somewhere with his squadron, my dear. But, tell me what's going on. He's not of your kind. What do you want with Jamie Wallace?"

The last comment incensed her. "I don't think that's any of your business." *What do you mean my kind?* "I think something's happened to him and I'm asking for your help. If you can't help me, I'll find him another way."

"Christ, Livy, what do you mean 'something' has happened?" His tone turned cooperative.

"I have this feeling he's in trouble. Aubrey, can you put me in touch with him or not?" The words left her mouth like a jackhammer.

"Is he important to you? What are you saying?"

"Aubrey, blast it, can you help me find him." She said through her clenched teeth.

There was a pause on the phone. "I'll do what I can. Where can I reach you?"

That stopped her cold. She had no idea where she could be reached and her mind whirled to find an answer. Parliament was a short walk across Westminster Bridge, but she certainly didn't want her father to know about Jamie, not yet. She could go to Wilfred Eaton's office, Mary Bolton, his secretary would be there and she would understand.

"I'll be at Wilfred Eaton's office in ten minutes. I'll wait for your call there." She paused a second and said, "Thank you, Aubrey," and rang off.

The line disconnected and Aubrey slammed the handset down. He thought he'd ended any problem with Jamie. There was absolutely no way he was going to help her. If anything, he wanted Jamie out of the way. If Livy has an interest in him, that could ruin everything.

Aubrey started to think. Suppose he were to find something tragic happened. He didn't have to tell her until he was ready. Maybe he could use the information to get to her even quicker. He laughed. Maybe he'd get lucky and learn that Jamie had been shot down and killed. That would be wonderful. It would make everything so much easier. But if not, he could use whatever he discovered to his advantage. Nodding, he thought; *Not bad.*

Chapter Fourteen

Ice-cold water reached out to drag Jamie down, deeper into darkness. Something gripped his body, trying to tear it apart as a faint consciousness oozed into his mind. He squinted and a sharp pain stabbed his eyes. Little by little he realized he was looking at a sun pasted high in a clear sky. A murmur of voices floated above his head, like the babble of babies, creating pinpricks of confusion as he struggled to decipher the noise. He heard his own voice rolling thick from his mouth, "The straps, the straps," and wondered what that meant.

Hands grabbed at him and suddenly, the tugging seemed to stop. The searing light disappeared, a comfortable shade covered his eyes.

"Where am I? Is this heaven?" Jamie stumbled through the words but got them out.

"It's all right lad, you ain't dead and it ain't heaven either. We managed to get your parachute off, boy. It was dragging you out into the bloody river." The man's voice sounded hollow, but he understood the words.

The fuzziness and buzzing in Jamie's head began to fade and his vision cleared. Every fiber in his body felt ripped apart. His mind struggled to understand what happened, but nothing came through the freezing cold that seemed to envelope his body. The left side of his head was pounding and of all things, he heard applause and voices as the hands pulled and pushed him into a seated position. His head rolled from side to side as he tried to look at his surroundings. He sat covered in mud at the base of a high earthen wall, a wide brown river behind him.

"Lucky the tide is running slack or you'd have been a goner, that's for sure." The voice came from someone standing above him, blocking out the sun. "Let's get you to your feet. Think you can stand?" The voice carried authority and Jamie instinctively followed the instructions, feebly standing on elastic legs that wanted to buckle.

"Your Spit didn't make it, son. It crashed into the Thames behind you." This came from a different voice. "Can you walk?"

Jamie looked to where the voice was coming from and saw a police uniform.

"I believe so," was all he could get out. Jamie tried to step forward, but he couldn't move. The mud was too thick, his legs too weak and his feet were stuck in the clay. He tried to move again and fell to his knees. Several hands rushed to him, picked him up and carried him over to the bank. Jamie figured those were the ones who'd just saved his life—the ones also covered in the same thick mud.

The group reached the top of the berm to cheers from a crowd of people standing along it. The men set Jamie down on his wobbly legs and the crowd gathered around him. He slid the leather flying helmet off his head. A few women standing nearby gasped and turned pale.

The policeman looked at him and said, "Criminy lad, you're covered in blood; let's get you to a hospital."

"That can wait. I'm all right." His voice sounded slightly above a whisper. "I've got to get back to my squadron. They don't know where I am."

"Lad, we'll phone the commander and let him know. But first, we'll be going to the hospital. Come along, son."

Muddy water beneath Westminster Bridge moved ominously upriver as Livy crossed. Not a soul appeared. Only a few black taxis and a single red bus took a chance to dart over the river, worried another attack might come at any moment.

She finished the bridge, scurried down a small set of stairs, reached the Parliament buildings and entered a door by the clock tower that would lead to the second floor and Wilfred Eaton's office. When she arrived at the landing, she paused to catch her breath and check her watch. It had been seventeen minutes since she'd rung off with Aubrey. She hoped he hadn't already called.

She hurried through the corridors and approached the door to Wilfred Eaton's outer office. Alana popped out of a stairwell directly across the hall holding a stack of military folders.

"Livy, what are you doing here?" she said.

"I need your help."

Alana held the folders cross handed across her chest and said, "All right, give me a second to deliver these and we'll talk. Come in."

Livy followed her into the neat, organized outer office and couldn't help but notice that Wilfred's longtime secretary was missing from her place at the desk. Livy pointed at the empty chair and said, "Where's Mary?"

"Gone, she's with her family. My father needed someone temporary to replace her. That's why I'm here."

Out of nowhere the phone started ringing, the jangle of bells startled Livy. Alana picked up the receiver and said hello, listened for a moment. "Of course, Admiral. I'll be sure to let him know."

She rang off and eyed Livy. "The requests never seem to stop. Now, what is it you wanted to tell me?"

"This will sound somewhat loony," Livy pleaded. "But, I think Jamie has been injured. I want to find him."

"I thought you were done with him," she huffed. "I'm surprised at you. What happened? How did you hear he was injured?"

"I didn't. I just feel it."

Alana looked at her as if she had lost her mind.

"Have you retrieved the folders?" Wilfred's loud voice carried through the half-open door. Alana motioned with her head as she went into her father's office and Livy followed.

Sunlight and fresh air with just a hint of scorched wood floated in from the open windows overlooking the brown river. Member of Parliament Wilfred Eaton, dressed in a dark blue three-piece suit and striped bowtie, stood by one window reading from a red-trimmed folder as Alana dropped a stack of identical ones on his desk. Livy knew from the color they contained sensitive material.

"Father, dinner with Admiral Creighton has been delayed until nine this evening. I just took his call and by the way, look who's here."

Wilfred finished reading and turned from the window, looking over spectacle rims. "Well, well, Livy Ashford." He paused. "It certainly was good to see you and your father at Paul White's party. How lucky we are to have a servant like him at a time like this." He turned further to include Alana. "Are you two planning a lunch or plotting something else?" He beamed a smile at the two women.

"Nothing like that, sir. I need to ask a favor," Livy said.

"A favor?" Wilfred riveted his attention on her. "My dear, ask, and you shall have it."

Livy had enough time to cool down from her trek across the bridge and tried to logically evaluate her feelings. Now she wondered if she was being a fool. There was no evidence or facts, only a sense in her heart that Jamie was in trouble. If it turned out he wasn't and she had caused all this commotion, she would face that later.

"Has Aubrey called?"

Wilfred gave her an odd look and said, "Aubrey? Aubrey Beck?"

"Yes, sir. Has he called?"

"No, why would he call here? Livy, what's going on?"

"Member Eaton, I have a suspicion a friend has been injured. He's a fighter pilot named Jamie Wallace, stationed with Aubrey at Uxbridge. I asked him to find out if anything happened and he's going to phone me here. Your office was the closest place I could think of to take the call."

Wilfred Eaton slowly nodded and let out a breath. "Now let me get this straight. You have a friend called Jamie Wallace. Wasn't he at White's party?" Livy nodded. "I think I remember him, a nice boy. So, you have this feeling he's in trouble. So, you called Aubrey to find out and he's supposed to call here to tell you what? That your feeling might be accurate? Is that about, right?"

"Sir, I know how mad that must sound—"

Wilfred held up his hand stopping her. "We'll get Aubrey on the line and sort this out. Alana, call Uxbridge and get me Squadron Commander Beck. We'll get to the bottom of this, my dear. I promise. Let's hope your feeling is merely that and nothing more. I'd hate for anything regretful to happen to that boy. We have enough of that happening to our young men right now."

Aubrey checked his watch and smiled, enough time to visit Bethany before his meeting with the Irishman and that hideous Doctor. Thinking of the fifteen-year-old and the wonderful things she knew about pleasure, calmed his anxiety. He was unsure what might happen when he told them he had nothing to give them except maybe a better way to destroy the RAF and make their invasion possible.

He took a quick pick-me-up from the drug-filled snifter he carried in a pocket while he drummed his fingers on the desk. He'd been holding for at least five minutes with Operations, waiting for an answer. If one had the authority, it was far easier to go thru Operations than Casualty Section for information on losses. Almost all losses would be gathered by Ops listening to the radio as one pilot reported another had "bought it." Of course, officially, loss assessments would be done by Casualty Section, but for a quick count, Ops was far better.

Finally, the WAAF girl picked up the phone. "Squadron Commander, I have your information."

"All right, let me have it." Aubrey said in a cold professional voice.

"41 Squadron reports two losses: Flight Sergeant Miles Stafford and Pilot Officer Jamie Wallace."

Aubrey's heart jumped a beat. "Both killed in action?"

"That's the information we have. Both aircraft destroyed, no sighting of chutes." The WAAF clerk responded as if she had said the same thing many times.

"Very well, thank you. I'll hold this information confidential until Casualty Section informs the families." Aubrey thought, issue resolved, sometimes things work out for the best and he smiled.

The flight surgeon at Hornchurch put the otoscope on a porcelain tray next to the exam table and washed his hands in a small sink. Jamie lay on his back looking up at a plaster ceiling that tended to spin every time he blinked. His flying clothes lay in a mud-and blood-soaked heap on the floor after every stitch had been cut from his body by a team of nurses, not one of whom was much older than he.

He felt as if he had been thrown from a five-story building. Every inch of his body ached, his head pounded like kettle drums from a symphony, and the eighteen stitches sewn in a zigzag above his left ear felt as if he'd been stung by a rabid bee. Cold hospital air blew on the portion of scalp where they had removed his hair, making him think they had clipped the entire side of his head. All in all, though, things had worked out for him, by all rights he should be dead.

"Well, son, your flying days are over for a while," the doctor said as he dried his hands. Jamie looked at him, surprised. "Your left eardrum is ruptured, but I think you'll be fine, given a little time."

"What does that mean, Doctor? I'm off flight status?"

"Exactly."

"For how long?"

"Might be just a few days, but more likely a week or two. Your eardrum must seal before you can fly at altitude and there's something else I want to check. I'm sending you to St. Thomas in London for a neurological exam. Though there are no fractures and I don't think anything has happened, the trauma to your head might have resulted in a concussion, so I'm not taking any chances. We don't have the equipment here, so you'll be on your way in a few minutes." The Doctor tossed the damp towel next to the sink.

"I'll know a lot more as to how long you'll be down after I've evaluated their findings. I think you're fine, but you're grounded. You know son, you're very lucky to be alive. Looks like you've been given a second chance at life."

A thought of Livy flashed across Jamie's mind, but he was far too tired and beaten to try to process what it meant. "I have to go to London, now? What am I going to wear? You cut up my clothes."

The white-haired doctor laughed and patted his shoulder. The creases on his face turned up with his smile. "We'll find you something. A driver will be in to get you and you'll be on your way. Don't worry about reporting in. Your status has already been forwarded to your squadron. Good luck, lad." With that announcement, the flight surgeon left the exam room.

Grounded—that was about the worst word a pilot could hear and yet Jaime was thrilled. The thought of having a week away from combat was a relief. It would also give him a chance to go to Newent and pick up his car. The day before he jumped into the trench on top of Livy, he posted a check to Squeaky for £30 to find him a motorcar and he did. RAF pilots with a car were first class with the girls and at the time, he thought meeting one might take away some of the loneliness. Now it seemed like a foolish idea, but he wouldn't go back on his word to Squeaky.

Alana went to the outer office. Livy heard her place the call to Uxbridge. Her nerves a little on edge as Wilfred smiled at her and took a seat behind his large English Oak desk to impatiently wait as if this endeavor was taking far too much time. She took a chair across from him hoping she was wrong. After a few moments, the phone rang and Member Eaton answered.

"Hello, Aubrey? This is Wilfred Eaton." He paused as he listened. "Fine, thank you. Aubrey, Livy Ashford is here asking about her friend, Jamie Wallace. Have you been able to find anything out?" He paused, nodded his head and said. "Hold on, I'll put you on the speaker." He fiddled with a switch on a box beside his hand.

"Aubrey, I have you on the speaker now. Tell Livy what you just told me."

"Livy, hello."

"Did you find anything about Jamie?" Tension made the words run out of her mouth.

"No, I haven't. I checked with Operations and they don't have any news. I'm sure he's all right—that's all I know right now. I wouldn't worry about it. The people at Ops would know if anything happened. If I hear something, I can call you later if you like."

She felt a wave of relief and said, "Thank you. Please ring me or even better—if you'd like to attend, we're having a crew party at Thirsty Bear tonight. It's right on Stamford Street a little north of Waterloo Road. Why not stop by? I owe you a pint for all the trouble I've caused."

"I know the place. What time?"

"Say, around eight or nine. Things should be well on their way by then."

"Thanks, I'll do that. I would like to see you."

"There, mystery resolved," Wilfred said and smiled at her. "Aubrey, thank you for your help. I know Livy appreciates it as well."

"Oh, you're welcome, sir. My pleasure." Aubrey's voice crackled through the box.

Wilfred rang off. "You see, Livy, it was only a feeling and nothing more. That should put you at ease, my dear." She stood as he walked around the desk and put his arm around her. "Please say hello to your father, will you? Tell him we'll get together for our breakfast soon."

Livy knew it was time for her to leave. "Thank you for your help. I'll be sure to pass your message on to him."

As she reached the outer office, she saw that 'I told you so' smile on Alana's face. One she'd seen many times growing up. "Okay, so I'm a fool."

"You got scared, that's all. Don't worry about it. I'm glad we could help."

"Why don't you come to the party tonight?"

"No thanks. Not interested." Alana got up from the desk.

"Come on, I'll be there; as will Aubrey. I would really like it if you came."

She cocked her head, "I don't think so. I'm not much for that sort of thing—how about I give you a maybe. Thirsty Bear between eight and nine, I believe you said."

Livy gave her friend a hug and said, "Please come. I think you'll have fun."

And after all of it, three steps into the hallway she knew Jamie was in trouble.

Chapter Fifteen

Aubrey Beck walked out of Uxbridge Headquarters as a squadron of Spitfires left the field and flew overhead with a deafening roar. Delighted that Jamie was dead, he opened the snaps on the tonneau cover over the baggage area of his new red Jaguar and threw in his leather satchel. It wasn't like the Aston Martin, but until he could get his hands on the ten thousand pounds, it would suffice. He needed to get to Livy and her money quicker. He thought of how he should approach her, with tragedy in his eyes and a soft regretful voice he would tell her Jamie was dead. He smiled as he slipped into the driver's seat and whispered to himself, "I'm coming for you, Miss Ashford."

A little over an hour later in the fading light, his journey concluded with a last turn onto Shoe Lane. A forgotten street wedged between others as if it were a map aberration. As the name suggested, many years ago the street had once been filled with cobblers, but now it contained boarded rows of dark run-down manufacturing sites that smelled of long-dead coal fires and the sweat of child labor.

Aubrey stopped the Jaguar across from number 46 pulling the car half off the cobblestones and onto the narrow sidewalk. Not a soul was in sight as he knocked twice on a door that almost caved in as if the slightest shove would push it off the hinges.

After a moment, it opened without a sound. Aubrey ventured down a single step into a black void. He heard shallow breathing over his shoulder as the Doctor's voice said, "Good evening, Mr. Beck, we've been waiting for you." The door silently closed sealing him in the emptiness.

Aubrey was startled when the Doctor ripped open the blackout curtain, the hanging rings screeched across the rod like fingernails on slate. A dim cavern appeared. Yellow light hung in the air from a kerosene lamp on a small round table in the center of a cracked concrete floor. The Irishman sat at the table surrounded by stacked wooden crates and several sixty-gallon black metal drums.

Aubrey felt the Doctor hovering behind him as the fat man said, "Mr. Beck, I've spent the last two days wondering what information you'd be bringing. You do have something for us, don't you?"

He looked over his shoulder at the Doctor a few feet away. "What I have will allow you to succeed where so far you've failed." Aubrey said as he walked toward a black drum, attempting to get as far as possible from the Doctor and present a confidence he really didn't feel.

"Is that so? Let me see it, Mr. Beck," the Irishman said.

Aubrey stood next to the drum and rested his hand on its metal top. "You asked for something that is not only impossible to retrieve but useless."

The fat man shifted in his seat and nodded at the Doctor who slithered in close to the black drum and Aubrey. "Why is that, Mr. Beck?"

Involuntary beads of sweat popped on Aubrey's upper lip. The Doctor now stood behind him, the translucent skin of his fingers tapping on the drum. Aubrey swallowed hard and said, "The order of battle isn't worth the paper it is written on. It changes almost every day. The RAF is constantly moving their forces to confuse you and from the looks of it they're doing quite a good job. Your Luftwaffe has utterly failed to destroy the RAF. You spend all your efforts attacking empty airfields. The RAF spot you as soon as you come across the Channel, they lay in wait and then devastate your clumsy attacks. If you continue as you have, you'll lose the war."

The Irishman looked past Aubrey, smiled and said, "And what is it you recommend, Mr. Beck? I assume you have an answer."

"I do. Radar is the key."

"Radar? I don't think that's crucial and Reichsmarschall Goring believes the same. He would certainly know if this radar was of any importance."

"Then Goring is a bloody fool." Aubrey said as emphatically as he dared.

"A fool, eh. Well, why not tell me this revelation you've come upon."

"I will, but first, I'll need a thousand pounds and some of my drug."

The Doctor leaned toward him, close enough for Aubrey to smell a faint odor of perfume.

After a moment while Aubrey sweat, the Irishman smiled. "I think your request for payment is acceptable." He said to the Doctor, "Give Squadron Commander Beck what he's asked for."

The horrible man slunk away and disappeared out of the weak light cast by the kerosene lamp. Aubrey walked toward the table. A few seconds later the Doctor returned carrying a small wooden box on top of two stacks of bills wrapped with yellow bands. He handed it to Aubrey and pulled out a stropped shaving razor, flipped it open, and slid his finger along the blade. The Doctor dropped his black eyes from Aubrey's and looked at his thumb on which now ran a small trickle of blood. The Doctor gazed up and smiled at him and Aubrey knew the next time he saw that razor; his own blood would be running from the soft underside of his throat.

The Doctor edged away as Aubrey opened the box and with a tasting spoon he pulled from his pocket, brought a scoop to his nose and inhaled the drug. He shivered as it rushed through his body. Feeling calmer, he began to tell them what he learned from Group 11 Headquarters. "The radar antennas you see along the coast are not individual, they're part of a system called Chain Home. They're all connected together, feeding information about your attacks in real time to a central point. From there, the information is delivered to group headquarters, down to sectors, and finally to the aircraft in flight assigned to intercept your incoming raid.

"That's why they've been so successful destroying your fighters and bombers, no matter what Herr Goring says. The weakness in the system is that all communications are connected by telephone routes that pass through centralized hubs, like spokes of a wheel. The locations of these hubs are a highly classified, but if they could be discovered and destroyed, you would blind the RAF for weeks, long enough to achieve air superiority."

Aubrey paused a moment, letting his words take hold.

"Somewhere there must be a master plan that includes the locations of the routing hubs." He continued, knowing he had their full attention. "If we can find that plan, or the one who created it, and pinpoint the hubs, they can be destroyed and the radar system will fail. At that point, your invasion can take place and most likely you'll win the war."

Aubrey paused, satisfied with their silence. "But first, there is something else I want. It's time I met with Electra, whoever's in charge of this little operation. I just gave you England, and that's worth a lot more than the ten thousand pounds you've promised me."

The Irishman got up from the table and came over to him. He smiled and said, "Your information sounds interesting, we'll review what you've offered us and be in touch. As regards to Electra or any others, you'll be meeting with them—I assure you of that. I'll let you know when we'll require you again. Good night, Mr. Beck." He extended his small thick hand and Aubrey shook it.

Following the Doctor's scuffling gait, Aubrey went through the dark room to the front door and gladly left the building, counting the thousand pounds. He took a deep breath, got into his Jaguar and opened the box. He sampled the contents, smiled and focused on Livy Ashford, thinking about her party at Thirsty Bear and how he would soften her grief and gently take her into his bed tonight.

Inside the warehouse, Electra watched as the Doctor returned to the table. Emerging into the lamplight from behind crates stacked in the darkest portions by a rear wall. She came to the table and said, "I'm surprised. The plan Mr. Beck put forward is a good one. We'll need to start action on it immediately."

The Doctor stared at her in disappointment. "How much longer must Beck remain alive? I'm getting anxious, I detest that man."

"Be patient until we have what we need," Electra said with a smile. "But I have one question for you—what did you do with Mary Bolton's body? She must not be found until after the invasion has begun."

"Oh." The Doctor grinned. "She's right here. In the barrel—cut in pieces and soaked in formaldehyde."

"My God, you fool! Get rid of her. I don't care where, get her out of here tonight. We can't have the slightest attachment to her death. Is that clear?"

"Of course," he said. "She'll be gone before midnight."

Electra gazed at the Doctor and thought, *you are a man with no soul, exactly what we need.* "Aubrey Beck doesn't appear to be as affected by your drug as you said he would. Have you attempted this concoction before?"

"Most certainly," the Doctor said. "I've experimented on SS prisoners many times before being assigned to this little venture. Believe me, it works." The Doctor's narrow face showed a wide grin.

Chapter Sixteen

Jamie lay on a bed in St. Thomas Hospital. Scrambled images returned in bits and pieces, out of order, not making sense. Sounds unattached to images swirled about his head, the confusion overpowering. It was as if he were without language attempting to describe an experience to others. All he could do was sort through the disarray, attach sound to image or image to sound and attempt to reconstruct a lost sequence in time.

He remembered falling, watching the ground and sky revolve around him, a dull roar of wind while he struggled against some unseen force as pain ripped through his body. And mud, sticky wet mud, with massive hands that attempted to drag him deeper into chilled water—but the rest was lost, out of sight like a destination over the crest of a hill.

The throbbing in his bandaged head lessened a bit, but the sting along the gash was rampant. He lay back against the pillows and stared at rumpled plaster on the ceiling and thought about what the flight surgeon said, about having a second chance for life. He kept thinking, a second chance for what? He felt as if he had barely lived and after twenty-three years he had nothing. He was still poor, at odds with his father, never really had a girl and as to his future—he didn't believe he had much of one. To get out of the war alive he would need several chances for life, not one.

He interlaced his fingers across his chest, breathing slow and deliberate breaths. Images fluttered in his mind, disconnected and foreign but with each pass, they became little clearer and more defined, until a commotion in the hall jarred him back to his hospital bed.

"I'm sorry, but you can't go in there." A woman's voice said loud and firm. "He is strictly on rest for the night and orders say no visitors."

"I'm his commanding officer, and I'll be only a minute or two." It was Eric Locke, his voice rang through the hall and barreled into Jamie's room.

"You heard me, I said no visitors and I mean it. Doctor's orders."

Jamie smiled, guessing what Locke was about to say.

"I don't really give a damn about your doctor's orders. That boy is my responsibility and I am bloody well going to speak to him. So, I suggest you carry on with your duties and close your flappin' mouth?"

"Excuse me?"

"You heard me. Now, where is he? Tell me, or I'll be checkin' every single room 'till I find him."

A few seconds later a dark face beneath a turban peeked around the door. "Lads, here he is." Raj Singh called out.

He popped into the room carrying a bundle wrapped in brown paper, followed by Billy Fiske and Harry Baum, and a few seconds later, Eric Locke. Immediately the joking started from Billy, who likened Jamie's bandaged head to Singh's turban. Harry kept shaking his head, reminding everyone, "Wow, we thought you were a goner, Jamie."

Locke stood a step back from the others, far more serious. After the teasing let up, he stepped over to the bed and said, "Jamie, I got the report from the flight surgeon—it's a damn miracle you're still with us. Can you tell me about what happened? Can you remember anything?"

Jamie looked down toward his chest and let out a breath. "It's all scrambled in my head. I can't make any sense out of it. I have glimpses of falling and being in river mud, but so far that's about it." He raised his head from the pillow. "By the way, where's Miles?"

Locke sat on the bed in silence for several seconds. "I know you and Miles were close and I'm sorry to tell you this, but Miles didn't make it. His Spit crashed into a field in Kent, no chute." Locke waited for the news to take hold as Jamie stared back in shock.

"I let him down, didn't I? My God, I got him killed."

"I doubt that, Jamie. Can you remember if you had any problems with your aircraft? Right before your plane exploded, I thought I saw the prop wind-milling. Did that happen? Think, Jamie. This is very important."

"I don't know. I sort of remember Miles climbing out of sight, but I'm not sure. It's all jumbled up. I only know I failed him."

Locke shook his head. "I'm not so sure about that Jamie. I don't think you failed him at all."

"I hope not." Jamie said looking at his hands.

"Stop thinking like that, Jamie." Locke stood up from the bed, he paused a second until Jamie looked up at him. "I spoke with the Flight Surgeon. He reported you have a concussion and told me to expect that you'd be confused and disoriented for a few hours more. What did they tell you here?"

"The same—a concussion and a ruptured eardrum. Also, that I wouldn't be flying for a while. I'm all right though, I can fly. I know it."

"Ok lad, that's fine. But you're grounded." Locke nodded. "After a few days, we'll talk again. But in the meantime, I'm also grounding each of the remaining new Spits. There's something wrong with them. Two pilots from other flights reported engine failure and I'll bet that's what happened to you. Now, let's get your tail out of here. We have a date to take you to a nice little place I know of. We're gonna celebrate."

"Celebrate? I can't go anywhere even if I wanted to. My clothes were ruined—all I have is this." Jamie indicated the green hospital garb.

"Not to worry," Raj said and he tossed the bundle in his arms to Jamie. "I brought a clean uniform for you, so I suggest you start dressing while Locke distracts the nurse. We're going to get you out of here." He beamed a smile.

Locke left the room as Jamie got into his uniform. When he was dressed, Raj peeked out the door and signaled for them to follow. They slipped into the hallway, hugging the far wall as Locke stood behind the nurse station on the phone. As they approached the station, Locke turned to the nurse while covering the mouth of the receiver. "I'm sorry I was so rude to you, it's inexcusable. But, the lad is part of my squadron and frankly, we all thought he'd been killed."

With her back now to the group slinking by, she said, "I understand. It's the war. We're all on edge and sometimes we forget we're in it together. I'm also sorry for speaking to you the way I did."

Locke kept her distracted, "Nothing to be sorry about and I promise we'll be gone in a minute. Thank you for understanding. The boy is my responsibility." He abruptly dropped his hand from the receiver, as the group slipped down the stairs Jamie heard him say, "It's what we thought. Something is wrong with the new Spits. I'm grounding 'em until we understand what's causing the failures."

Outside the hospital, Jamie stood with the group. A quick flash of light fell on them as Locke came through the blackout curtain and opened the door. Joining the pilots, Locke looked at the sky and said, "This could be a rough night, lads. The moon makes the Thames look like a silver ribbon wrapped around the heart of London. At altitude, they'll easily see it from fifty miles."

Billy Fiske looked at the sky to the southeast and said, "Locke, should we forget this? Go back to Hornchurch?"

"Not on your life," Locke said, "there's nothing of any importance around here. It's all civilian stuff. They wouldn't bother to bomb it. Come on, boys it's a short walk and we're gonna celebrate."

The dark streets of London were empty as Jamie and the group reached Waterloo Road. They turned right as a red Jaguar raced by on the left side of the street, its blackout lights barely showing. Harry Baum watched the sports car zip passed and said, "Wonder where the hell he's going so fast, he's gonna cock up that beautiful car."

Aubrey Beck reveled in the power of the wind in his hair as he sped along Waterloo Road toward Stamford Street and Thirsty Bear. He was elated, Jamie Wallace was dead. Aubrey's fantasy of passionately taking Livy was so close to becoming a reality, it stirred his blood.

The short drive from Shoe Lane gave him the opportunity to devise exactly how to tell her Jamie had been killed. He would wait until the alcohol had softened her and take her somewhere private. With a gentle hand on her shoulder, his eyes filled with compassion, his practiced words would come out. He smiled thinking of her with tears falling, needing warmth and solace. Tonight, he would lovingly seduce her, coax her into his bed. He wanted her willing but if she refused, he would simply drug her and take her. She would never know.

He slowed the Jaguar to a stop outside Thirsty Bear and took a quick look around. He reached below the passenger seat and retrieved the wooden box, smeared a nice quantity on his gums, slipped the box back into seclusion and switched off the engine. As he stood at Thirsty Bear's front door, Aubrey ran a hand through his hair and straightened his tie, preparing for his performance.

After he stepped into the pub, he moved off to one side and surveyed the crowd. He needed to locate Livy to properly plan his approach. Thirsty Bear wasn't all that crowded, but the hum of voices created a dissonance in his ears. To his right, some patrons stood at the polished oak bar, the pumps in action filling glasses with warm English beer. Small tables were placed orderly around the floor, mostly filled with working-class locals. Against the far wall, were the dartboards with several players testing both the beer and their skills at playing three in a bed. On his left, tucked into a private corner, he saw Livy with the film crew, the group laughing and toasting one another. Alana was seated next to her talking to the man with the white beard he remembered from the airfield. Livy sat as if she was alone, staring into her pint, almost oblivious to her surroundings.

Aubrey grinned and thought, couldn't be any better, my timing is perfect. She was into her cups and would be easy to console and manipulate. Stepping up to the bar, he had a full-figured girl pull him a pint. He watched her ample breasts bounce back and forth as she pumped and he smiled, took a deep breath and readied himself for conquest. Changing his demeanor, he made his way toward Livy's table as if the fate of the world was balanced on his shoulders. Halfway to his quarry, he froze as Peter Watt stood and raised his glass.

Watt held the glass in front of his face and tapped it with a butter knife, demanding attention. As the crew came to order, he said, "First, is everyone happy?" Applause and a few whistles from the crew gave him his answer. "I wanted to take a second to toast the finest motion picture crew I've ever worked with. To all of you, thank you for a fantastic job."

Some of the crew stood, laughing and toasting themselves. It was clear they had been sampling the pub's wares for quite a while. Watt laughed and continued, "I know I've asked a lot of you, and each and every time you came through. What we are doing here is not just making a film; our job is critical to the war effort. Every one of you should be proud of your contribution. You are making a difference. A hundred years from now people will be looking at our work and they'll know how we English responded to these Nazis. You've helped record that for our future generations, ones who hopefully will never have to experience what we are going through now and again I say, well done and thank you."

Aubrey let the applause die down and decided to wait a minute or two before he began to snare Livy. He sipped on his pint and watched the group settle into their conversations. Livy turned and said a few words to Alana and the white-bearded man. Another minute and the time would be right.

He watched until their conversation moved on and Livy once again settled. When she looked down at the table, he made his move.

Unfortunately, Alana looked up and saw him approach. Sarcastically the bitch said, "Aubrey Beck, I wondered if you were coming."

Livy's head snapped up and she stood from her chair. "Aubrey, have you found out anything?"

He had to be careful now. "Livy, let me speak with you alone."

"My God, Aubrey, what is it?" He could see fear in her eyes, exactly as he hoped. She was vulnerable now and he was ready.

"Come, let's go over here." He gently took her arm and walked her toward the bar. They stopped at the end with Livy's back against the wall. With no one near them, Aubrey laid his hand gently on her shoulder.

"Livy, I've got disturbing news. I'm so sorry, but Jamie is—"

Her anguished face lit up with surprise. "Thank God!" she exclaimed and pushed past him toward the door. He spun around, saw the open door and his jaw dropped. Jamie Wallace stood at the entrance with members of his squadron.

"Damn it." Aubrey slammed the beer down on the counter. That bastard has ruined everything.

It was time for him to do something drastic with this pest.

Chapter Seventeen

Relief flooded into Livy's heart. This was a man she wanted to know, to be with—she knew it as much as she knew anything in her life. She made a mistake pushing him away and now she would have a chance to rectify everything. They would start over and maybe create something very special.

He looked a little worse for wear. A stark-white bandage wrapped around his head and covered his left ear. It contrasted with a purplish color seeping down his face and neck. But his eyes were bright and somehow, she knew he was going to be fine.

She came to him, but he looked right through her with a blank expression.

She could feel her heart hammer this was not the way it was supposed to go, "Jamie, are you, all right?"

"And what would that be to you, Lady Ashford?" His words stung.

She opened her mouth to reply but the look on his face prevented her from saying anything.

"Someone of your class certainly wouldn't be seen with someone like me. Don't worry about it, you won't have to bother with me again." His words were emotionless, as if he was merely stating a fact.

Aubrey Beck came over, his hand extended. "My God, Livy and I thought you were lost. Ops told me you were shot down and killed. I almost told her that very thing right as you came in. I am so glad I didn't, is there anything I can do for you?"

"No thanks, I'm fine. Have a wonderful time with Lady Ashford." Jaime walked away to follow his friends. She stood next to Aubrey, stunned.

Aubrey put his arm around her shoulder, "That's all right, don't let it bother you. But he's right; he's not for someone like you."

She looked up at him and almost blurted out her thoughts but decided to hold her tongue. Livy wiggled out from beneath his arm and went to join the crew, she wanted to get as far away from Jamie Wallace as she could. She'd be damned before she'd let him see her cry.

Alana slipped into the booth as Livy took a chair across from Mickey McCarty who said, "That didn't go so well, did it?"

She picked up a red cloth napkin and daubed at her eyes. "That's an understatement. He doesn't want anything to do with me. He called me 'Lady Ashford,' almost as if my name was something repulsive."

"He's hurt lass and that's all. He's from a working-class family, isn't that right?"

"I think so, as if that mattered." A tear ran down her cheek and she wiped it away. "How can he think something like that?"

Alana looked at her from across the table. "If he's lower class let him go. It's for the best, believe me."

Livy stared at her feeling as if she'd been struck.

Mickey took a swig of his pint, looked at Alana and shook his head. He daubed at drips that settled on his beard and looked back at Livy. "He thinks you tossed him because of where he came from, not because of who he is."

"But that's not true. I was scared. All I could think was if he got killed, it would be horrid on me. Is that so selfish? I can't make sense of anything anymore."

Mickey smiled at her and it helped. "Well, when he comes over and I'm sure he will, you make sure you let him know about how you felt, how scared you were. He'll never show it, but I know he's scared too. I sure was."

"Come over? How do you know that? I don't think he wants anything to do with me. He made that very clear."

"If he's a gentleman and I'll bet he is, he'll be over to apologize and that'll be your chance."

She hoped he was right.

A chair scraped on the floor and Aubrey Beck sat down next to her, a pint in his hands. "Are you okay, Livy? I'm here to help if you'll let me. We can go somewhere and talk a bit if you want. We'll get this straightened out."

She stared at him, her mind went blank and then from over her shoulder she heard, "Miss Ashford, may I speak with you a moment?" It was his voice and her heart jumped.

She turned to look behind her and there he was, his light brown curls popping out from the top of the bandage. She couldn't help but smile.

"Let's go somewhere private." she said.

His face still wore a blank expression and there was a diffused sadness in his eyes as they walked out the side entrance of Thirsty Bear and stepped onto Broadwall Street. She stood in the moonlight as Jamie fiddled with the blackout curtain and attempted not to splatter light onto the sidewalk—another hated requirement of living during a war when the smallest slip could draw a bomb down on top of you.

Easing the door closed he turned to her and said, "I want to apologize to you for the way I spoke. Whatever decision you've come to doesn't excuse the way I behaved."

"Jamie, I understand. I don't blame you—really, I don't. But please hear me out before you say anything more, okay?" she pleaded.

She studied his eyes as he cautiously said, "All right."

"When I first met you at the airfield, in the middle of all that destruction and covered in mud"—that quirky grin crossed his face— "I felt there was something special there, something I couldn't put my finger on."

He started to say something but she gently put a finger to his lips. "You said you'd hear me out." He nodded and waited. "When I was young, my mother was killed in a horrible accident. I've never forgotten how much that hurt and every day that pain is in my heart. When you asked me to dinner at the party all I could think of was what would happen if I were to fall for you and lost you too. I was scared, very scared. I didn't want to get close to someone and lose them, feel that pain all over again. That's why I pushed you away."

"Livy—"

"Please let me finish," she took his hands in hers. "Somehow, today I knew you were in trouble. I felt it. I was scared that I'd lost you, that I might never have the chance to know you. It was an empty, terrible feeling. I made a mistake and I am the one that should say I'm sorry, not you. Please forgive me."

His face softened. After a few seconds, he said, "Livy, come walk with me. I think we have some discovering to do."

Chapter Eighteen

Hand in hand the two went north between century-old row houses toward the Thames River, a huge white moon glowing bright over the blacked-out city. Their footsteps echoed between the three-story homes like a slow heartbeat. It was as if they were the only two souls left above ground, a city of thousands hidden somewhere beneath.

"Eerie, isn't it?" Jamie said as they walked. "As if we're living in another world, the one we knew lost somewhere."

"It's this horrible war. When it first started, I was filled with patriotic fever, ready for anything, so eager to fight the Nazis and do my part. Now, all I wish is for it to be over, or for it to never have happened in the first place." Livy sighed, "It's as if it we're living in some nightmare we can't wake up from. But it isn't a nightmare, it's real and so very frightening."

He put his arm around her as they walked the empty street, the homes on either side looking tired, as if they too were contemplating the same bleak future. After a moment of silence, Jamie stopped and faced her.

"If it helps, I think we're winning. Just barely, but I think we're winning," he said. "They have the troops and the planes, but we have radar and that gives us the upper hand. I think we'll beat them. I really do." He smiled, but it didn't comfort her.

"Jamie, I saw pictures—maps on a table someplace we filmed. They're amassing an armada in France and the low countries, thousands of barges, hundreds of thousands of men all waiting for the order to come across the Channel. How can we stop that?"

"They'll have to knock us out first. As long as we're winning in the air, their invasion will never succeed. Unless they take out the radar, they'll never beat us and so far, they've ignored it. I guess they don't understand how important it is."

"If you think we'll win that's comforting, but what will be the cost?" In her mind, she saw the body of a seventeen-year-old airman.

"How many young men are going to die stopping them?" She cringed, "I don't want to think about it anymore; it makes me afraid."

As they started walking again toward the river, she slipped her arm around his.

"There's something I need to know. What happened to you today? Are you in pain? You're hurt, but you still look in one piece." She grasped his arm a little tighter.

Jamie smiled the same as in the trench and it soothed some of her worries. "I'm okay, got a bash on the head, several stitches and a ruptured eardrum. It hurts a bit, but not too bad. As to what happened, there isn't much to tell. I don't remember a lot of it. My friend Miles didn't make it, the Germans got him and it could be my fault."

"Your fault? No, you would have done everything possible to save him, I know that."

"I can't explain it. I need a little time. It's coming back, but slowly."

She put her head on his shoulder as they walked toward the Thames, the cool night air caressing them. "Of course, take whatever time you need. I'll be there to listen whenever you're ready."

They reached Blackfriars Bridge and she said, "Let's go out on the bridge. I want to look at the river. We'll be able to see Tobacco Docks from the center of the bridge. There was a massive attack there this morning; I could see the fires from the hospital roof."

"Hospital? What were you doing there? What hospital?"

She laughed at the shocked look on his face. "Oh, we were shooting a part of the film on the roof of St. Thomas. I wasn't in the hospital."

"Oh, you had me worried—that's where they sent me. I was stuck in there before the lads came to get me. There was this nurse that raised a ruckus with the squadron leader when he tried to get me out. I'll bet she threw a fit when she found I escaped," he laughed.

"You just left?" She shook her head. "Got up and walked out?"

He nodded, "The lads and I slipped out past her. She never even saw us, it was terrific."

"What if you have a concussion or something worse? We should go back." She stopped and gently pulled on his arm, coaxing him back toward the pub.

"I have one—at least that's what they tell me. But it's not bad and I don't want to go back. I wouldn't miss this chance to be with you." A warmth rose in her heart as he put his arm around her. "Let's see the river first."

They reached the center of the bridge and she pointed to the east. "There, look. You can still see the fires. Those poor people, that whole area around docks took a savage beating today."

They stood at the railing watching the orange glow flicker against the sky. "You know, on second thought, we should be careful," he almost whispered the words. "Maybe we should go back to the pub. On a night like this, the moon and the light from those fires is a beacon for the Germans. They'll see it from a long way off."

She moved closer and put her head on his shoulder. "Well, you should be in a hospital bed anyway." She looked up into his eyes, "Can we wait one more minute? There's something so peaceful about a river. It never stops, goes on and on forever. It makes me believe everything will be all right in the end."

"Of course," his arm tightened around her.

They stood for a minute silently staring into the river, watching silver ripples appear and disappear. Jamie took her shoulders and looking at her said, "I haven't had a chance to say this, but you look lovely tonight."

She looked up at him, feeling warm and at peace. She closed her eyes as he moved closer, awaiting his kiss, and the low sorrowful moan of an air raid siren began to wail. She flinched at the sound and opened her eyes. He was searching the sky to the south and east. She looked up and saw a bright glint of moonlight reflect off hundreds of dark-moving shapes headed directly toward them.

"We have to get off this bridge, quickly," he said, taking her arm.

They ran north as the screeching whistle of bombs falling grew louder and louder behind them. Explosions erupted on the south side of the river, hitting close to the same row houses they'd passed minutes before. Bombs fell into the streets, closing in on the bridge as they ran.

Livy struggled to keep up, her heart pounding from fear as he held on tight to her hand. A bomb exploded on the bridge behind them, sending chunks of concrete and steel into the air. A massive explosion landed in the river a few feet from the bridge, knocking her to the ground and sending her shoes clattering away. With some ten feet separating them, a plume of water fell from the sky and drenched her with cold, muddy water. As she started to crawl toward him, he scooped her up. In stockinged feet, she ran as fast as she could, her hand gripped his and she tasted the brown river.

The north bank passed under them as more bombs fell behind, coming closer and closer as they ran toward an Underground station, the sounds deafening and the concussions, a hot wind pushing against their backs. They bolted across the street as the top of a building buckled, raining down bricks and glass, the collapse detonating an angry orange fire. The next bomb fell in the center of the street not one hundred yards behind them and a third ripped open a storefront across the street, flames belched out, the heat scorching.

Jamie pulled her into the Underground entrance. They raced down the stairs as the bombs rained down, creating ear-shattering explosions. They scrambled down the first flight. Jamie turned a corner and pulled her into an alcove, wrapping his arms around her to protect her from the blast and flying debris.

She screamed into his chest as another bomb struck very close. The explosion roared down the tunnel stairs, carrying huge sections of concrete pillars and metal roofing. Yellow dust boiled like a sandstorm. The pressure wave slammed them against the blue and white wall tiles, hammered against their clothes, assaulting them. She screamed again and he held her tight as a single red brick bounced off the rubble. She watched it flip end over end down the stairs until it teetered on an edge as if holding onto life and ever so slowly fell with one final flop and at that moment, the world around them went silent.

They stood in each other's arms her back pressed against the cold tiles. He placed a finger under her chin and gently lifted her head. She gazed into his eyes, her breathing loud in the dust covered silence.

He whispered, "We're safe."

She could only nod as he came closer. She closed her eyes and he kissed her, his lips soft and reassuring.

Chapter Nineteen

Jamie opened his eyes and with his thumb rubbed some of the dirt from her cheek. She was drenched and her auburn hair hung dripping along the sides of her face. And yet, she had never been more beautiful. He couldn't detect any injuries, but her thin white blouse was smeared with grime and her right sleeve was torn below the shoulder. She trembled beneath his hands.

"You're soaked." He took off his heavy uniform jacket and wrapped it around her shoulders. "But it doesn't look like you're broken."

She put her hand on his cheek and turned his head to the side. "I'm fine, but you're bleeding, blood is seeping through the bandage."

"From the blast, I guess. It doesn't hurt though." He felt wonderful. "I'm sorry for putting you in danger. I was a damn fool for asking you to take that walk, but I'd do it all over again."

"So, would I." She smiled up at him, placed her other hand on his face, closed her eyes and kissed him.

A voice seemed to bounce around the shadowed tunnel. "Hey, you two! What do you think you're doin'? There's an air raid goin' on. Get in the Underground! You'll have time for all that later."

The voice of an East Ender, his words running together as if they spewed from a water hose. His torch swung back and forth between them. In the dusty gray light, the man appeared well into his fifties, wearing round black-rimmed glasses, a tattered military jumper and a dented Army helmet painted with a large faded white *W* on the front. An air raid warden. The man said, "Come on, we'll get you down below."

Livy giggled. She looked at him with a mischievous twinkle in her eyes and he started to laugh. Livy joined him and for precious seconds, the war, its destruction and horror dissolved away.

"Funny, is it?" the warden said, not amused.

He pointed his torch toward the bottom of the rubble-covered stairs, showing a path through the dim staircase. He turned and shone the light across the bloody bandage on Jaime's head and moved it onto Livy. He stared at the RAF wings sewn on Jamie's coat, and said, "You a pilot?"

"Yes, 41 Squadron."

"What do you fly?"

"Spits," Jamie said quietly.

The warden pushed his hat upward with his thumb and said, "Blimey, if that don't take it all. Come along, son. We've got a nurse down there. She'll fix you up and we'll take good care of your young lady too."

He helped Livy around some of the debris; the warden's light shining on the wreckage as Livy's bare feet stepped into the beam.

"Missy, where are your shoes? You can't be walking around in this mess dressed in your stocking feet," the warden said as if speaking to a child.

Livy shrugged. "I have no idea," and she started to laugh again.

Jamie smiled and quickly said, "Well, we'll take care of that, Mr. Warden." He scooped her up into his arms. "Ready when you are."

He carried her down the stairs, the warden in front, trailing the light so they could see. "On the looney side you are, both of you." Shaking his head and the warden began to chuckle.

Jamie stepped over jagged rubble as he carried Livy. With his arms supporting her legs and back, he felt the firm strength of her body, like the coiled power of an athlete. He was surprised. One of the first things any man would notice about a woman was the shape of her curves and this was the first time he'd thought about it. Even at the party he'd only noticed how the cream-colored dress perfectly set off her hair and eyes. "Are you a dancer?" he asked.

Livy smiled up at him, her arms around the back of his neck. "What a curious question. What made you ask that?"

"I can feel the strength in your legs."

She laughed. "One of the demands of my father, I was condemned to a ballet studio."

"Well, it did fine by you, that's for sure."

She smiled at him, her eyes soft and inviting and he was happier than at any time in his life.

The warden guided them through the last of the debris and turning a corner, they came into the yellow glow of electric lights strung along the blue and white tiles that lined the Underground Station.

Hundreds of people had fled the bombings to stake out tiny sections of the platform. Jamie looked at the people resting or sleeping on blankets stretched out on the concrete floor. He guessed that most had come to hide out of fear, but others because they had nowhere else to go—their homes destroyed by the bombs. Suitcases littered the platform, probably holding the sum total of their rescued belongings, including food rations and toys for the children—anything to keep the young ones occupied as thousand-pound bombs set fire to the abandoned streets above.

The warden gave a short burst on his whistle, commanding attention from those murmuring on the platform. "Ladies and gentlemen, we have a couple of visitors tonight," he said, "a wounded RAF pilot and his girl, so let's give 'em a welcome to Blackfriars Station."

He set Livy down on her bare feet to light applause that came from the crowd. Most of them, however, stared at the two newcomers with a blank look, rolled over and in the momentary calm of the night, sought sleep.

Tucked in near the entrance, a woman made room by scooting her two small children together. She said, "Sit down, we'll make room for you."

"Make yourself comfortable, son," the warden said as Jamie thanked the woman and accepted the space. "Miss, you come with me. We'll find you some dry clothes and get you some shoes." The warden looked at Jamie, patted his shoulder and said, "I'm also gonna fetch the nurse and have the canteen girl bring you a hot cup of tea."

Livy and the warden slipped away as he sat on the cold concrete floor. Somewhere off in the distance a fresh attack started. He heard the muffled sound of more explosions mixed with the sad bellow of a far-off air raid siren.

He looked up at the ceiling as if he could see through the earth above and said, "Must be the docks again." He lowered his head thinking of the people. "How long can they last through something like this?"

"As long as we have to—we ain't got a choice," the woman near him said with a tired, sallow face. "After they invade, it'll be much worse. Look at Warsaw—they destroyed that city. But they'll never get the chance to do that here. I know it—my Richard said so."

"Your husband?" Jamie asked.

The woman nodded, "He's a fireman in Silvertown. He's there now, at the docks."

"Then he's a very brave man," Jamie softly said.

"Aye, he is. And I pray every night that he'll come back to me and the children. We'd be lost without him, exactly like you'd be without your girl."

Jamie saw fear in her eyes and yet also an unwavering courage to see it through. "He's right—we're gonna win. They'll never invade, I'll promise you that."

A woman in her forties dressed in a volunteer's uniform came up to them. "Here, I brought you a cup of tea. Sorry, you'll have to share with your girl. I've clean run out of mugs. Would you like a scone?"

The woman beside Jamie whispered, "You don't want those—they're at least a week old and brittle. I've brought a little food I can give you, I still got a home and this morning I baked a few things for the night."

"Thank you," he said, her kindness touching him.

He wrapped his hands around the chipped mug and said to the canteen worker, "No thank you, the tea will be fine." He set it down next to his legs, saving it for Livy, leaned back against the wall and closed his eyes as images of Miles racing away from him tumbled about his mind.

He must have dozed for a second because the next thing he knew was the sound of his name. He opened his eyes and saw Livy in front of him, whispering "Jamie." Beneath his uniform jacket, she now wore a white blouse that was too small and Army pants that were too large, tied around her waist with a cord and rolled up at the bottoms, exposing black men's dress shoes.

Looking at her, he laughed and said, "My, that outfit will set off an entirely new fashion."

She laughed and sat next to him as he handed her the tea, still warm. She took a sip and wrinkled her nose as a tall, thin nurse came directly toward them, her medical bag in hand.

"That's awful stuff," Livy quipped as the nurse arrived.

"Evening," the nurse said, smiling at them. "My name is Lucy Wilkins. I'm the nurse on duty here. Let me take look at that bandage." She knelt in front of Jamie and started to remove the dirty gauze around his head.

"Lucy?" Livy said, looking up from the mug. "It's Livy, we met at the assignment office."

"My goodness, it is. I'm so tired—sometimes I doubt I could recognize my own mother. How are you? We all were wondering what happened to you after that man dragged you out of the office. We thought you might be in some trouble."

"Oh no, nothing like that, he's simply the man in charge of my assignment. What are you doing here? I thought you were working in a hospital."

"I am, I work in the emergency at St. Thomas. I come here after my shift to help out. If something were to happen, these folks wouldn't have any other care. So, I volunteered. I'm here three nights a week." She pulled the last few inches of bandage off Jamie's head and he flinched. She took a torch out of her pocket and shone it on the gash. "I'm sorry, I know that hurt. The blood stuck to the bandage. And what's your name?"

He turned his head as she gently pushed his chin to the side. "Jamie."

Livy leaned forward and winced at the gash on his head as air raid sirens started to wail, this time close by.

"Another raid on its way I guess. That's not the all clear." Lucy said, reaching into her bag. "They seem to come at least three times before the night is over." She looked at Jamie and asked, "Can you tell me what happened to you?"

This time, the images came back much clearer. His engine had quit. As Miles spun toward the ground; fireballs flew by and slammed into Jamie's plane. "This morning I was shot down." He said, forcing the images away. Like so many people in this war, his friend Miles was now dead. There wasn't anything he could do to change that. At least he knew it wasn't his fault, but it didn't make his death any easier.

Lucy blinked twice and paused, an iodine-soaked gauze in her hand. "Shot down! My God." She took a breath. "Sorry if this stings a bit." She daubed with the antiseptic. "You're bleeding a little, but that's normal for a gash that size. All your stitches are in place and I think you're okay. A little antiseptic, a new bandage and you'll be right as rain."

"Thanks, Lucy." He winced. The cold liquid burned like fire and he sucked in a breath. "So, you two know each other?"

Lucy smiled at him as she went into the kit and retrieved a new bandage. "We were at the assignment office at the same time. She was with another girl—Alana, I think. Isn't that right, Livy?"

"It is. By the way, how are your two friends?"

"They're fine. Rita, they put in lorry maintenance and Toddy—well, that's a different story. We don't know what she's doing. She won't say a word about it. See, she can speak German. We think she's with the intelligence service, but we don't really know."

Lucy finished wrapping the bandage and sat back on her heels. "There, that should hold you, but you really should be in hospital and not here. That's a nasty blow you got there—probably gave you a concussion."

From further down the platform, a voice called for Lucy's service. As she stood to take care of someone else, Livy said, "Good to see you again. Please take care and give Rita and Toddy a hello from me."

"I'll do that. Take care you two." Lucy smiled and winked.

Jamie stood, shook her hand and said his thanks. He sat down and turned to Livy, reached out and touched her arm. "It's all come back, or most of it anyway. I remember what happened."

"Go ahead, tell me."

"It wasn't my fault—I know that. My engine quit. There was nothing I could do. After that it's still a little foggy, but no matter what the reason, my job was to protect him and at that I failed. It cost Miles his life."

"I know you did everything you could to help him. I'm so sorry he was lost, it's terrible. But it's not your fault and I'm thankful you're here with me now."

After a pause, Jamie said, "I need to ask you something." Again, he paused and searched for the right words. "I need to go to home and pick up a car I bought. I want you to come with me, meet my family."

She turned to face him, surprised.

"Please don't get the wrong idea." He gulped and threw out the words. "We'll take the train there. It's a short ride and the next day we'll drive back. It's only for one night and you can stay with Julia. She's my brother's fiancée and I know she'd love to meet you. Would you come with me?"

She cocked her head and looked at him while apologetic thoughts raced around his mind. She smiled as he held his breath and said, "I'd love to. Where are we going?"

Jamie almost jumped. "Newent, the little town I'm from. It's close to Gloucester. You'll love it."

Her eyes twinkled and a smile came to her face. "I think that would be great. I'd be pleased to meet them."

"Wonderful," he said, thrilled she would be with him.

They leaned back against the tiled wall and sat silent for a few minutes. He put his arm around her and she nestled against his shoulder as the distant rumble of explosions filtered into the quiet safety of their shelter.

Chapter Twenty

A hand shook Jamie's shoulder; the jostle woke them both. The warden stood over them, a soot-covered fireman behind him. He gave them a second to orient themselves and said, "Son, we need your help. There's a family buried in some rubble a few blocks from here. We're trying to dig them out and we need more hands."

As he pushed off the floor to stand, Jamie looked at Livy and said, "I've got to go. Wait here—I'll be back."

"I'm going with you. I'm not staying here." she said, getting up.

"Livy, stay here. It's much safer."

In a voice not to be questioned, she said, "Oh no, I'm scared enough as it is. I'm going with you. I'm going to help and that's all there is to it."

He shook his head and turned his palms up. "Please be careful. I've gotten you into enough trouble already."

"Good. That's settled, come on you two," the warden said as they followed him out of the station's tubular cavern.

The cool night air smelled of cordite, scorched wood and concrete dust as they carefully stepped through the rubble and reached the top of the stairs. Smoke billowed into a sky glowing orange from the thousands of fires raging about the city. Outside the entrance, a bomb crater had exposed broken mains and water spewed high above the street to rain on torn electrical cables that snapped angry blue sparks across the muddy hole.

A few of the other men from the shelter joined in as they eased their way around the rim of the crater and up New Bridge Street toward St. Paul's Cathedral. Jamie kept his arm around Livy as they walked behind the group in the center of what was usually a busy street. Up ahead, the warden stopped as they reached Bridewell Place and waved for them to follow him around the corner.

They crossed over the street to the sidewalk and for a few moments white moonlight appeared through a gap in the roiling smoke. They could clearly see the destruction. Livy held onto him like he might vanish as they watched the hole in the sky collapse, swallowed by the strange orange clouds that tinted the mortar-and-stone buildings of Blackfriars a raw color unknown to him.

They turned the corner and seized at the sight. A half-block up, the street was covered with water and debris. Several of Bridewell's two-story row houses were demolished. Remnants of fire sputtered and died as an engine company shut down their hoses and prepared to move to another, more desperate location.

"This must be what hell is like." Livy said. "I never imagined I would live to see anything like this."

"I don't know how anyone could survive that. There's nothing left—just a mound of rubble." He said praying they wouldn't ask him to find someone buried by familiar walls that before tonight were their home.

A young woman caked in dust, a government blanket covering her torn nightdress, stood facing a fire captain. She screamed through blood-covered hands held up to her mouth. "Me Ella—it's me Ella that's in there! You've got to get her out. Please, you must get her out. She's me only child. She's only four—you've got to help me!"

She turned to run back to the rubble pile but was restrained by the fireman. "We'll find her, dearie. Don't you worry," the fire captain said as he held her and motioned for the warden to assist, care for her.

The warden nodded at Livy, who went to the bleeding woman and put her arm around her. "Come with me. I've got you." She helped the woman toward a waiting ambulance, where the medics were treating several of the other injured bodies of Bridewell Place. She looked back at Jamie with an expression of horror he would never forget.

A small group of men had formed up on the street. "You and you," the fire captain said as pointed at Jamie and a stocky man about his age in overalls. "Go in there, work your way back toward the right. That's where she reported the child."

The fire captain looked over at Livy and the young woman that was just pulled from the wreckage as they reached the ambulance. He leaned in close and in a low voice said, "There's not much chance the little one will be alive, so if you find the little girl's body bring her up, but by all means leave her in there. Don't bring her out. I don't want that woman to know that her child was killed—at least not right now. The gas mains have been shut off but there will be gas floating at the bottom of the rubble. Be careful, don't set off a spark or it'll blow. Okay, off you go. The rest of you, come with me."

As they walked away, Jamie and the other man began to climb the rubble pile. The man stuck out a thick, callused hand and said, "Billy's me name. What's yours?"

"Jamie."

"Well, Jamie, I got no idea what to do," he said. "Do you?"

"Why don't you take the center and I'll take the right. We'll dig till we reach the basement."

Billy shook his head. "That's a fool's errand. There's no way anyone survived in there. I'm not putting me self in danger for a kid that's already dead. There's gas in there, what if the Jerry comes back and it blows? We'll both be joining her on the casualty rolls." Fear bubbled in his voice.

Jamie stared at him. "What if she's still alive? She might not make it till morning. There's enough light to see inside and we've got to try, especially if there's gas in there. I can't leave a little girl in that kind of danger."

"She's already dead. Going in there is a ruddy mistake."

Jamie shook his head, wondering what the man could be thinking. How could he leave a child that might be alive in there to die? "No matter—you do what you must, I'm gonna give it try."

Jamie climbed the pile. He reached the top, knelt down and started digging into the twenty-foot-high mass of debris.

The woman was sobbing heavily as they reached the ambulance; blood flowed from her mouth and spilled onto her nightdress. Livy eased her down onto the flat rear bumper as a medic in a white coat with a red cross on his sleeve approached. He set a medical bag next to her and opened it.

"All right, my dear—let's have a look." He gently pulled her hands away from her mouth. As he shone a torch on her, she stared blankly at him and Livy recoiled, the young woman's face was torn apart. Her upper lip was split beyond her nose, blood dripped off her chin and her front teeth were missing. Tears had caused rivulets of black dust to dribble down her cheeks.

"You'll be fine," the medic said. "You got a nasty bash, but we'll get you fixed up right away."

He wrapped square gauze between her lip and the missing teeth and turned to Livy. "Use this to stem the blood. Gentle pressure, got it?" He whispered in her ear, "She's going into shock. Keep her warm and talk to her. She's gonna need more help that I can give her here. We'll get her to the hospital as soon as we can. There's others worse off I need to attend to."

Livy nodded and focused on holding the gauze in place, drops of blood falling off her fingers. The woman's bloody hands grabbed on to the rolled-up sleeves of Jamie's tunic, her eyes as big as saucers and she mumbled, "Me Ella they have to find her. Please, they have to save her." Tears continued to run down her face.

"They'll find her, I promise," Livy said and knew it could be a lie. She looked over toward the rubble pile and saw Jamie disappear inside.

"They have to. They have to find her she's all I have."

Her heart breaking, Livy searched for something to say. "What about your husband? Where is he? Can we get in touch with him?"

The woman stared up at her. Livy's hand shook but kept pressure on the gauze against the woman's mouth as she mumbled, "He's dead, killed at Dunkirk. He won't be coming home tonight."

Jamie eased his way down through the rubble, stepping on shattered walls, plaster and the remnants of bedroom furniture as he went deeper through the collapsed second story on his way to the basement. Broken timbers and exposed nails grabbed and tore at his shirt as he dropped lower and lower into the bowels of the wreckage. To his left, he could hear Billy scratching at the top of the pile as he tossed cracked lumber toward the street.

"Ella," Jamie called out. "Ella, can you hear me?"

He thought he heard a faint muffled cry that seemed to surround him, the sound coming from every direction. He paused, listened carefully to nothing but silence and the creaking of debris.

Jamie went head first through a large hole in what was the floor of the second story. He held onto a cracked beam, pulled his feet into the hole and dropped a few feet to a bunched carpet on a rubble-strewn lower floor. Unable to stand, he crawled deeper toward the basement. He called every few seconds and listened for the child's voice, but heard nothing. As he moved away from the opening, the orange tinge receded to leave only shades of gray and holes of black. Feeling his way, hand over hand, he inched across the rumpled carpet, the floor swaying and dipping beneath him. On his belly, he slipped below shattered beams as he moved lower when a loud crack of breaking wood filled the darkness and the floor abruptly sank below him. A large section of the ceiling above him fell and crashed into the basement. He froze, not daring to move and prayed the home wouldn't explode.

The waving floor slowed to a stop. Carefully, as if on brittle ice, he went on foot by foot, unwilling to give up on finding the child. With each move forward, the floor dipped and groaned, threatening to give way. Groping in the dim gray, dust and dirt choked his throat. His eyes burned and teared and he smelled gas trapped below in the rubble, ready to detonate. He pushed flat scraps of wood out of his way.

"Ella, can you hear me? Your mum sent me to find you."

Jamie froze in place listening, his breath short, coming in pants, it burned in his chest. Groans of the floor that rippled beneath him and timber cracking were the only sounds to touch his ears.

His hand reached out and found a hole in the floor where it separated from the wall. He reached into it and pulled himself across the floor deeper into the rubble.

Hand over hand he crawled lower into the wreckage until, his hand struck what felt like a small foot.

A tiny muted yelp erupted and Jamie's heart jumped. "I found her—she's alive!" he yelled, not knowing if anyone could hear him.

Lying on his stomach, he carefully removed the pieces of what had been her home from on top of her little body. He reached for an arm and pulled. In the silence, the child whimpered a painful cry as she slipped from beneath the rubble, out of the shadows and into Jamie's arms.

He cradled her as best he could and moved out of the hole to a higher, more stable part of the floor. Her foot was bent at an awkward angle, her leg broken above the ankle. Huge eyes stared blankly at him and yet, even in her pain, the little girl barely made a sound. He fumbled around for scraps of wood on the carpet and found two suitable pieces. He removed his shoelaces, tied a makeshift splint around her fractured leg, and pulled her close to his chest.

"It's all right, little Ella. You're safe now."

Gingerly he crawled with the child in his arms toward the opening above, ever so slowly crossing the floor as it moved in waves. It snapped and creaked at him in protest that he dared to take the child away from her death. When he reached the ceiling, he stood and pulled himself up onto the support. As he grasped a wood beam above him, most of the floor gave way and crashed into the black depth of the basement far below. He held her close as dust and gas billowed around them. It began to settle and he looked down into her face to check on her. Big dark eyes stared back at him and she started to cry. Silent tears ran down her face in streaks that cleaned away the dirt. Black droplets fell onto his arms.

"Mummy. I want my mummy?" Her little voice less than a whisper.

Jamie's chest tightened and a lump formed in his throat. He held the brave little girl close and said, "Mummy is right up there, waiting for you. I'm going to take you to her."

He struggled up to the opening in the rubble pile, stepping on the timbers and walls he'd used before. With his head below the hole in the rubble he called out. Billy's stunned face appeared over the hole above him. Jamie passed Ella to him and crawled a little higher, his head now peeked above the rubble. He watched Billy carry her down the pile amid cheering from the multitude of onlookers in the street.

Exhausted, Jamie hung on to the cracked home and watched as medics took Ella from Billy. He wiped his eyes with his sleeve. Ella's was one life the war wouldn't take, not tonight.

Livy kept pressing the gauze against the torn flesh of the woman's face. The bleeding had almost stopped when she heard an outburst of cheering. She turned around and saw a man clambering down the pile carrying the little girl. Livy's heart almost burst with pride. He found her.

As the man disappeared behind the crowd that gathered, Ella's mother pushed Livy's hand away and raced after her child. Livy ran behind her and slipped through the cheering people. She caught a glimpse of the mother sweeping little Ella into her arms.

Tears filled her eyes and rolled onto her cheeks as she looked over to the top of the rubble pile and saw Jamie's head sticking above it. For a few seconds, he didn't move. He wiped a sleeve across his face, climbed up and eased his way down the steep wreckage. She wiped blood from her hands on the Army pants and used the shoulder of Jamie's jacket to dry her eyes. Her heart filled as Jamie stepped onto the street. A few of the onlookers gathered around him, cheering him and patting him on the back. She ran as best she could in the heavy black shoes and threw her arms around him and held him tight.

They stood silent, arms wrapped around each other and in the orange light that hung above the tortured city, ash from a thousand fires began to fall like snow around them.

Chapter Twenty-One

The ambulance rumbled away with Ella and her mother inside. With the show over, the crowd moved on and in the silence of the street, the warden approached. He placed a hand on Jamie's shoulder. "Well done, lad."

"A second chance." Jamie said as he cradled Livy's head against his chest.

"What?" the warden said.

"She's got a second chance at life and I hope it's a good one."

The warden smiled. "Aye lad, that she does." He tilted his hat toward the smoke-filled sky. "And most of that is due to you, son."

"It was just luck, she was in a place where nothing heavy had fallen on top of her. That's what saved her."

"True, but you're the one that pulled her out. She had very little chance of surviving till dawn if you hadn't. The shock alone would have taken her."

Air raid sirens moaned, the volume warbling up and down, signaling the long-awaited all clear. The raid was over, at least for tonight.

The warden peered around the sky as if he could see through the orange smoke. "I'm off duty now. Can I take you somewhere? That's me real job—driving a hack."

He thought of Locke and the others and said to Livy. "We should go back to the pub. They don't know where we are, I'm sure they're worried about us."

She nodded. "We should go back as quickly as we can."

He looked at the warden. "Can you take us to Thirsty Bear? It's a pub on the corner of Stamford and Broadwall."

"You bet I can. I know the place well. We'll have to take a roundabout way though, they knocked out Blackfriars Bridge."

Chapter Twenty-Two

For the last two hours, Alana and the remaining patrons of Thirsty Bear had huddled together drinking spirits in the wine cellar. Most of the others in the pub and almost all of the film crew had gone their separate ways, leaving Locke and the pilots upstairs and a small group in the cellar. She sat on a wooden crate and watched Aubrey pace back and forth across the cellar as he scratched and twitched. After a sip of Burgundy from her glass, she said, "Aubrey, sit down. You're driving me mad."

"I hate being confined. I can barely breathe," he said as he started to pace once more.

"Then go upstairs!"

"I can't do that. There's a bloody air raid going on or didn't you notice?"

"We've all been going up and down the stairs for the last hour. So, either sit down or go upstairs. You're really getting on my nerves."

He glared at her but took a seat next to a bottle rack in the center of the room. She swilled the wine in her glass and recalled how he'd pined after Livy when she left Thirsty Bear with Jamie. She could see through Aubrey as if he were a pane of glass and what she saw was loathsome. Livy and Jamie hadn't been gone ten minutes when she had to leave the table. Aubrey kept interrupting her conversation with Mickey and the others. He feigned worry about them and their safety until she couldn't stand it anymore. She watched him fidget as he sat next to the wine rack.

Tired of his antics, Alana headed upstairs as far off in the distance she heard the low warble of an air raid siren, the all clear. She leaned against the polished oak of the bar, took a sip of her wine and noticed Locke and the pilots at a table near the entrance. As she approached them, one of the pilots stood and came over to her, "Hello there, miss. My name is Billy Fiske. What's yours?"

His accent was American and she laughed inwardly at the young man of about twenty. He had a look on his face that revealed he was more afraid of her than anything else. She forced away her irritation with Aubrey, softened and said, "Alana Eaton."

"It's a pleasure, Miss Eaton. Would you care to join us at our table?"

"Thank you, it would be a pleasure."

He pulled out her chair. She smiled at him and allowed her hand to brush against his as she sat. "Gentlemen," Billy said with a hint of triumph in his voice. "May I present Miss Alana Eaton. Alana, these are members of my squadron: Flight Sergeants Harry Baum and Raj Singh, and I know you've already spoken with our squadron commander Eric Locke in the wine cellar."

"Thank you for the invitation," Alana said. "I confess I was getting a little bored watching Aubrey pace back and forth. I should have come up with you a half-hour ago." She took a sip of her wine.

"Nice to see you again Miss Eaton, we met at that party," Raj said. "Are you a part of the film crew?"

"Oh no, I'm here with my friend. She's the one that works with the crew. I do remember seeing you at Mr. White's party though, you, Jamie, and another pilot."

Locke raised his glass and said, "Welcome, it's nice to have you join us. I didn't ask you when we had our chat in the cellar—what kind of assignment are you up to with the war on and all?"

She put on a smile and said, "I'm assigned as a slave to my father, he was also at the party. He's a Member of Parliament and unfortunately, I'm nothing more than his hireling."

"Somehow, I doubt that," Locke said. "I've got a feeling that you're the one that manages him."

She laughed and said, "Well, there's some truth to that." Seeing them start to relax, she knew the ice had been broken. "I noticed Jamie tonight. He's all bandaged. What happened?"

"He was shot down today and survived it." Locke said.

"Shot down?" She was genuinely surprised. Livy was right—he had been in trouble.

Harry Baum ran a hand through his dark hair. "He's the luckiest bloke in all of England. His Spitfire exploded, it's a miracle he's alive."

"Exploded!" She said, as if hit with an electric shock.

Billy nodded in amazement. "He was off to my right, there one second and boom, gone the next. I was sure he bought it. Poor Miles wasn't so lucky, they got him."

"Miles, wasn't he at the party?"

"Yes," Raj said, raising his glass with a somber expression. "To Miles—may he rest in peace."

They all lifted glasses and Alana said, "I'm so sorry, I'm sure he was a fine young man."

"They all are." Locke said as he drank his ale.

Alana took a sip of wine and said, "What about Jamie—is he all right? And for that matter, what about Livy, they're together somewhere."

"The mud girl!" Raj blurted out.

Locke gave him a surprised look. "That's her?" he said.

Raj nodded.

"Good. Maybe he'll stop talking about her now." Locke took another sip and shook his head, a smile breaking on his face. He looked at her and said, "Jamie won't be flying for a few days, but he came out of it okay. And if your friend is with him, she'll be all right too. He's quite a capable young man."

She shook her head. "It is a miracle he's alive." Alana looked in her wine glass and said, "And thank you for saying my friend will be safe— it takes some of the worry out."

Mickey walked over to the table, nodded at the others and said, "Alana, do you need a lift home?"

"I don't, I have a way, but thank you." She looked at the pilots and said, "Gentlemen, I need to take my leave. It was a pleasure to meet you all and Eric, thank you for the conversation in the cellar, very informative." They all stood as she got up from the table.

Eric looked over his group and said, "Boys, it's also time for us to get back to Hornchurch."

Alana left the pub, followed by the pilots along with Mickey and the last stragglers of the film crew. A cool night breeze filled with a scent of smoke swirled above her head, but all was quiet. The raid was over, however, pacing in the middle of the street was Aubrey, muttering to himself in the moonlight.

He snapped his head left and right, looking up and down the empty street as she and the others congregated along the sidewalk. Mickey came up and joined her observing Aubrey as he started to pace again.

He leaned over toward her ear and whispered, "What's up with him? He looks like he's about to tear a gusset."

"I don't know. He's been fidgeting like that since Livy and Jamie left. It's incredibly irritating," she said.

Mickey gave a small grunt. "Aye, it is." He paused a moment and continued, "I hope Livy is back soon though, I do need to get her home."

Behind her, Billy Fiske said, "Locke, are we gonna wait for Jamie or try to find him? I gotta get back to the airfield."

"We're gonna wait Billy," Locke said. "We don't know where they went, but they'll show up. Waterloo Station is not too far from here. We can catch the train back and be there before curfew—don't worry."

"Okay, if you say so." Billy said. "But I've been late twice already, once more and I'm in for it. I think we should try to find him."

Alana turned around and said, "Where would you begin? If you leave to find him and he comes back while you're gone, what good would that do?"

"The lady has a point. He'll turn up." Mickey said as Aubrey approached. "I'll bet they ducked in someplace and are on their way back right now."

"They're nowhere in sight. Why did she leave with him? In the middle of an air raid, no less!" Aubrey chattered above their whispers. "I am going put him on report. He should have never left the pub; he might have gotten her killed."

He was losing it, almost as if he was going mad. Alana stared at him feeling her stomach heave.

"You'll do nothing of the kind, Beck." Locke responded. "Are you really gonna spout off to the wing commander, tell him a pilot with nine kills, who's been put in for a DFC and is one of the best in all of 41 Squadron is on report for taking a girl out? Rather foolish of you, don't you think."

Aubrey's eyes widened. "Excuse me—a Distinguished Flying Cross for what!"

"Taking out four bombers and flying a wrecked Spitfire back to Uxbridge, a Spit that had no business being in the air at all. I'm the one that put him in for it and he deserves it."

By now Alana was fuming. "Oh, squash it, Aubrey. You're sure to look the fool doing anything remotely like putting him on report. Are you daft? It's not like he forced her to go with him—she wanted to. So, stop making idle threats."

"Hey, look at what's coming." Billy announced, pointing at an approaching black taxi, the blackout lamps looking like squinting eyes. "We could grab that and take it back to Waterloo, have 'em tell Jamie to join us there." Billy stepped out onto Stamford Street waving his arms at the approaching narrow beams of light.

The taxi slowed and stopped just past the corner. Billy Fiske reached the cab as the rear door opened and Jamie stepped out. Alana looked at him, her mouth open. He was a mess, covered from head to foot in dust and dirt. The bandage around his head was filthy and his shirt was torn across the shoulder. From the darkness of the backseat Livy appeared wearing heavy black shoes. She also was coated in filth, dressed in bloodstained Army pants and a tattered shirt that barely fit her. She was wearing Jamie's tunic, the rolled-up sleeves also stained with blood. Her auburn hair hung in long strands going haywire about her face, making her look as if she'd been salvaged from a flood.

"My God, Jamie," Fiske blurted out. "What the hell happened to you two?"

Alana was as shocked as the rest of them, "Livy, where have you been?" she said, looking at the blood covering her clothes.

Livy laughed at the shock on their faces, she wrinkled her nose and said, "It's a long story."

Chapter Twenty-Three

Irritation swelled in Aubrey's gut as Jamie put his arm around Livy's shoulder and she beamed with delight. The smile she gave him had an effect like needles jabbed into his skin. He was about to lose control. Jamie was now far more than a pest; he was an obstruction. And like all things that got in his way, he would do whatever necessary to get rid of him.

Mickey McCarty stepped through the group. "Well lass, you certainly look like you must have a story to tell but it'll have to wait for another time. I need to get you home." He looked at Jamie. "By the time I get her there, I'll know the whole story so I hope you've been good to my girl."

Jamie smiled. "It's been an experience." He looked at Livy tucked beneath his arm and kissed the top of her head. "But I think she's doing fine."

The way he said it sent a rage coursing through Aubrey.

Mickey smiled back at Jamie and shook his hand. "Lad, it's been a pleasure to meet you. Thanks for keeping her safe, she's quite special to me."

Jamie smiled, his eyes focused on Livy and he said, "Me too."

She looked at the cameraman, her eyes seemed to sparkle as she held onto Jamie. "Mickey, my father's in town. He has a flat near Westminster. It's the closest place with a bath." Livy laughed as she looked back to Jamie. "We might look a fright, but I wouldn't trade this moment for anything." She laughed again and Aubrey cringed. "I'll remember this night as long as I live."

"Ok, to your father's flat, it is." Mickey smiled at her and said. "But, we must get goin', for all we know the Germans might be back tonight and I don't want to get caught in it if they are."

Billy yelled getting into the taxi. "Locke, he can take us to Waterloo. We have fifteen minutes to get there. The last train out is at midnight."

"Okay, let's get going." Locke said. "Jamie, say good night to your girl—we have to go."

He leaned over and gave her a long kiss. "I'll meet you at Charing Cross Station. The train leaves at eleven, it's called The Welshman. I'll have the tickets and meet you on the platform."

Seeing him kiss her almost pushed Aubrey over the edge, he started to pace again, his anger boiled.

"I'll see you there. I hope your family accepts me." Livy said.

My God, she's going away with him?

"They'll love you." Jamie got into the waiting taxi and it started off on Stamford toward the station. Out the window as it pulled away he yelled, "Livy, I don't have your number."

"Stonebridge 2352." She yelled back.

Aubrey repeated the number several times, committing it to memory.

"Time to get you home." Mickey took her arm and escorted her to his Humber Super Snipe, a rather austere military livery on loan to the crew. "Come on, lads—we're off," he said to two tipsy crew members wobbling near the curb.

Aubrey watched the Humber pull off with Livy inside and the itch for relief became overwhelming. It had been almost three hours since he'd tasted the drug and now his body was demanding it.

He moved a little behind Alana, near enough to catch her scent. It was sensual and alluring, but there was something about the woman that unsettled him. Yes, she was attractive, but in a severe way that made him feel as if she were in disguise and behind her smile were the fangs of a viper. Inside she was calculating, cold like stone and his instincts told him to stay far away from her, to be wary.

It was time for him to quietly slink away and relieve the constant craving. He'd had enough of her at this point.

"Aubrey, where are you going?" Alana said as he slithered off toward his Jaguar.

"Home," was all he said.

"Well, I have something I want from you. I need a lift. Besides, we have some talking to do."

Talking? That was the last thing he wanted to do with her. He wanted his drug and if anything, he wanted to think about how to get rid of Jamie. "I've got things I need to attend to. You'll have to get someone else."

"Can't do that Aubrey," she said as she opened the door to the passenger side of the Jaguar.

He was trapped. There was nothing he could do but acquiesce. He slipped into the driver's seat and started the car. "Where to?" He snapped as he pulled away from the curb.

"Turn around, go the other way on Stamford and just drive. I'll give you instructions."

After a few minutes of silence, she said, "Go over Waterloo Bridge and take a right onto The Strand." About halfway over the bridge, Alana turned her head. "So, tell me—what do you want with Livy?"

"Me? Nothing, at least nothing that would concern you."

"You aren't telling me the truth, so I will ask you once more. What is it you want with her?"

"As I said, nothing that concerns you." He was angry, his nerves raw. He wanted to be rid of her.

Alana smiled at him. "All right, I'll tell you what it is. You want her in your bed and you'll do anything to get her there." He snapped his head toward her ready to deny it. "In fact, you'd take her forcibly if you weren't so afraid of her father. Hell, Aubrey, you've done that many times to other women, so why should she be different?"

He could only think about the drug box under her seat and how he wanted it. She continued, "You'd spend a very long time in the Tower for raping a Lord's daughter. Or would you murder her like you did that girl in Guernsey before the war? She never got the chance to go to the coppers, now, did she?"

Aubrey slammed on the brakes. The car screeched to a stop along the curb of the road. Shock struck him as if he'd been hit with a club. How could she know that? How could she possibly know about the girl in Guernsey?

"And another thing, Aubrey, go ahead and take your drug, you keep it here don't you?" She reached below her seat and pulled out his box. "You're getting far too fidgety for what you'll be doing next." She stared at him, a cold look in her eyes and held the box away from him as his hand went for it. "Take a left up there and the first left after that."

He slammed the car in gear, drove to the end of the block, took a left up a dismal street and then the first left onto a narrow run-down industrial street.

She tossed the box onto his lap and said, "You can stop now—we're here."

Livy waved good-bye to Mickey as he drove off with the drunken crew members. Not having her key, she used the spare stowed beneath a flowerpot on the porch and opened the claret-painted front door. As she entered, the midnight BBC news leaked into the foyer. She called out to her father.

"In here." His response trickled from open doors off to the right that led into his library. Livy stopped at the double door entry, surveyed the room and thought of the many times he'd called it his favorite place in the world. A half-filled glass of scotch rested on a small table between two over-stuffed wingbacks. From behind, she could see the top of his head poking above one of them. This room always had a rich feeling of peace, something Livy knew she would unavoidably shatter in the next few minutes.

"Well, don't just stand there—come in. I'm almost finished." He reached out from behind the chair and took a sip of the scotch. "Come sit down and tell me about the party. I hope you had fun."

Without saying a word, Livy walked around the chair so her father could see her.

"Good lord, what happened to you!" He sat up in the chair.

"I got caught out in the bombing."

"What! You could have been killed. What were you doing? Didn't you seek shelter when the air raid sirens began?" He looked at her as if she had lost any form of common sense.

"I was on Blackfriars Bridge with Jamie Wallace when it started."

"Who?"

"He's a pilot with 41 Squadron. You met him at Paul White's party. He was one of the boys that came with Aubrey Beck."

"I don't remember him, name sounds familiar, but I can't place him. Sit down and tell me how you ended the night looking like a vagrant." He laughed and then looked closer. "Is that blood on you?"

"It is." She said as she sat in the second wingback, amused by the shock on her father's face.

After speaking for fifteen minutes about her evening, she finished and leaned back into the chair. "There is one other thing I need to add. I'll be going with him to his home in Newent for a day or two."

"Who's going with you?" he asked, sounding a little suspicious.

"No one—just Jamie and I."

"A young, unmarried woman gallivanting about the country with a man, unchaperoned? That's something you shouldn't be doing. Think about what people will say. Women of your class don't behave like that." His hands gripped the arms of the chair, the knuckles turned pink but his voice remained calm.

"I don't care about what other people think. I might be in love with him." Livy said it from her heart. Her father's face turned red, his lips drew back thin and tight.

"What are you talking about! How long have you known him?"

"Not long, maybe three weeks or so." She knew this was going to be a problem.

"That makes it even worse. What are you thinking or are you? You can't do this. It goes against everything I've taught you." His hands gripped tighter.

"It's a short train ride from London and after that I'll be staying with his family so I really don't care about what people might say. It's none of their business anyway."

Her father closed his eyes briefly, took a breath and looked straight at her. "I want to meet this man. Who the hell is he to even ask you to do something like that?"

Resolute and firm she said, "He's a fine man. I told you about what he did tonight and what he's like. If he has the courage to climb into that destroyed home or a Spitfire and fight the Germans, he's far better than most."

"I'm not disputing that. But what kind of family does he come from? Who is he?"

"His father is a butcher. They own a little shop in Newent and he has a brother that was severely wounded at Dunkirk. Other than that, I don't know much more."

"What!" Her father shook his head, his ire rising. "You're not thinking straight. It's the war, the desperation, the intensity with which we're living that gives you young people the illusion you might be in love. Believe me, it won't last. Think about it Livy, where will this take you? Stuck in some little butcher shop passing out lamb shanks! How long will you do that? How long will it be until you run back to Kensington Manor, maybe with a small child in tow? Is that the world you'd choose? It's not the world you grew up in, not the one that's right for you. I refuse to let you do this."

"I expect you to trust me and believe in me." She paused, collecting herself. "I was brought up to believe in what's right and if this is the life I choose, so be it. But for now, I need to get cleaned up. I'm covered in filth." Hurt, as she knew she would be, Livy rose and started to walk out of the library.

"I have a breakfast meeting tomorrow with Wilfred Eaton. You will go with me, and we'll finish this conversation. All I can say right now is that I am very disappointed with you and what you're doing."

After ingesting a good measure of his drug, Aubrey felt better, but his heart pounded from the fear and shock. His mind raced as he attempted to make sense of this puzzle as Alana opened the passenger door and walked behind the Jaguar.

"Come along, Aubrey. You've had enough of that," she said, stepping down into the decrepit building. "I have a few tasks for you."

He followed her into the darkness and closed the door behind him. As Alana pulled the blackout curtain open from nowhere the Doctor appeared, dressed in his black suit and string tie with a sickening smile on his face.

Aubrey's chest clenched, choking off his air. He tried to swallow past the rock lodged in his throat as he gaped, horrified. The Doctor was smiling at her.

The terrible man took a step toward her and said, "Good evening, Electra. A spot of tea, perhaps?"

Chapter Twenty-Four

It was too much for Aubrey's drug-blunted mind to assimilate. He froze, motionless in the shadows.

"Well, don't stand there in a stupor Aubrey; we have work to do," she said, moving toward the table in the center of the factory.

He tried to make his feet cooperate, but the best he could do was to shuffle toward the yellow light coming from the table. As she moved away, unblocking his view, another shock penetrated his already shattered nervous system.

Seated at the table next to the Irishman was Wilfred Eaton, Member of Parliament.

"Beck, sit down." Wilfred said. He motioned to an empty wooden chair on the other side of the table. "There's much we need to discuss."

The Doctor pulled the chair back as Aubrey took a seat, his mind blank.

"I'm the one that brought you into our enterprise months ago, shortly before Alana went to Berlin. As you might surmise, she was quite against your being with us, but I assured her you'd be a fine addition. So far, I think I've been right, but"—he sighed— "I seem to be having a difficult time convincing her of your value." He lit a cigar, his eyes fixed on him. A chill ran up his spine.

He wiped the beads of sweat off his upper lip and attempted to form words, but none came. He stared into Wilfred Eaton's emotionless face and watched the tip of the cigar glow as he pulled on it.

"You see, Beck," Wilfred continued, "I think you did very well with the production figures. It sent me to Coventry to research the city before we act. I also thought you did a fine job mapping the locations of the radar installations on the coasts. On both of those tasks, you did quite well." He paused, took another long draw and exhaled slowly. "But you see, we've already paid you a handsome sum to bring us the distribution of RAF forces and you failed miserably. Don't you agree?"

Aubrey could picture the Doctor smiling as he stood behind him. "But what I've given you is a way to defeat the RAF and bring about your invasion. I did all I could to get the Order of Battle and it can't be done, it's impossible." Aubrey stammered.

"Now, now, that is so unlike the Beck I expected. Nothing is impossible—not if you apply yourself." The cigar between his fingers glowed cherry red as he puffed on it and then released a cloud of smoke toward the ceiling. "Several years ago, I realized that if the British Empire were to survive, it must align with the Third Reich. The Monarchy as well as the dilettante classes and the Jews need to be eliminated from our society and power seized so England can thrive." He casually picked a slice of tobacco from his tongue and flicked it on the floor, "I was told by friends of like mind, such as Lady Scott, Lord Rathermere, the Astors and of course, King Edward himself, that what I proposed could not be done, it was impossible."

He held his hand out, his fingers formed a basket as if he was holding a cricket ball. "At this very moment, I am one step away from accomplishing everything they said couldn't be done and I will allow nothing to obstruct my goal of a new and more prosperous England." Wilfred cocked his head, "Aubrey, nothing is impossible, especially if you've been paid to accomplish it." He looked over Aubrey's shoulder and nodded at the Doctor standing behind him.

A massive force smashed against his neck and a searing pain erupted. Aubrey went limp, his knees buckled. A garrote slipped around his neck and slowly tightened, removing any hope of breathing. Darkness seeped into the outer corners of his vision sealing him off from the world. A buzzing noise expanded in his head, growing louder and louder, washing out all other sound. This was his death he thought, unable to even struggle. The death he'd feared at the hands of the Doctor.

As his life force ebbed away toward a deep abyss, suddenly, it all stopped. He sucked in a choked breath and then another and forced back bile, his throat burning, his body limp like a cloth effigy dumped in the chair.

Wilfred's voice rang in his ears, "Aubrey, that is but a taste of what will happen if you ever disobey my orders or think of betraying us. The next time you fail, you'll will not survive. Do you understand me, Beck?"

Aubrey grasped at another painful, sour breath and feebly nodded, fear and horror gripped him. "I'll do whatever you ask," he croaked.

"Ah, that's much better. I'm glad we could come to an understanding. Get him some water." Wilfred said to the Doctor.

Aubrey closed his eyes, his body trembling.

Alana came close to his face and squeezed his chin. He opened his eyes as she said, "We are English, but we are also patriots of the Fatherland and we will not allow failure—not ever. Our mission is far too critical to have anyone destroy it. I will personally cut your throat if you give me the slightest trouble.

"If you decide to betray us, go to Scotland Yard, you'll be presented as a lunatic and a traitor." She gripped his collar with both hands and stared into his eyes. "A fool attempting to blackmail a Member of Parliament during wartime. Remember, we have the evidence we need to have you arrested for the murder of that fourteen-year-old in Guernsey, the one who was pregnant with your child. All of that evidence will surface and you'll be hung for her murder. A rather fitting end for the bastard you really are. Understand me Aubrey—this is your only warning."

"Oh, come now, enough of this," Wilfred said through swirling cigar smoke. "I believe Beck fully understands his responsibilities."

A glass of water appeared over Aubrey's shoulder and he snatched it, trying to quell the burning bile in his throat and calm his frayed nerves. There was no way out but to do their bidding, for now, he thought.

Wilfred's double chin folded as he nodded to the Irishman. With his heavy brogue he said, "The concept of breaking the RAF by bombing communication hubs is a good one, if we can discover the locations." The Irishman pulled his chair closer to the table and rested his thick hands on it, his fingers intertwined, his thumbs touching. "I have verified what Aubrey said. Their information about our raids begins with the radar stations which are impossible to destroy from the air. The observer corps is a secondary source. I went to one of the observation posts on the south coast and was able to see the phone lines they were using and tapped into them. I overheard their conversations on the phone and am sure there must be some sort of a central sorting location. It takes in the information and somehow distributes it to the fighter bases and ultimately to the aircraft. So far that's all we know."

"And it's a good start." Wilfred turned toward Alana. "What did you find out tonight?"

"I spoke with Eric Locke, 41 Squadron's Commander. Though he didn't say much, I gathered that there is an entire system that allows them to keep their fighters on the ground until the last moment. They send them directly to the location of our incoming aircraft. According to Locke, the system is fast and reliable. With it in operation, they believe they will defeat us."

"Well done. But let us not forget our enemy is a very clever one," Wilfred said. He sat forward in his chair, waving a finger. "They would have several places where the communication lines would converge. Therefore, we must discover the original plans used to construct the system and with that, destroy the locations. Without radar, we will destroy the RAF and achieve air superiority which is necessary for the invasion to commence.

"Our issue will be time. Berlin informed me the invasion is now scheduled to begin within the next two weeks—that is, if we can destroy this system. If not, it will be postponed. It's our responsibility to make sure that postponement doesn't happen.

"More than two hundred and fifty thousand officers and men of the Wehrmacht await the completion of our mission. With our success, we can end this war and dominate Europe. It all comes down to what we do in the next fortnight.

"This is how we'll proceed. Tomorrow morning, I have a breakfast meeting with Lord Ashford and will garner as much information as I can. He has known me for many years and believes me to be a loyal countryman. I have a suspicion he was involved with the creation of this radar. Alana, you will come with me."

Wilfred crushed out his cigar and directed more instructions to the Doctor and the Irishman. He pointed to two wooden crates stamped with the words Made in the USA— "Those crates contain radio beacon transmitters processed through His Majesty's Customs on the privilege of a Member of Parliament. You are to complete the construction of the beacons so we can position them at the communication hubs once the locations are known."

He looked at Aubrey with a calm that unnerved him. "Now for your assignment, Beck." Wilfred paused and scowled at him. "Tomorrow, you will receive orders to report to RAF Medmenham. That's the Photographic Intelligence Unit based in Danesfield House, a former resort in Buckinghamshire, some thirty miles west of London." He passed a tiny camera to Aubrey. "Use this to obtain copies of any relevant items you uncover. Steal or copy any photographs that will assist us to identify from the air the hubs we discover."

He pushed up and out of the chair. "Are there any questions?" After a moment of silence, he said, "Good. You have your assignments, and I expect them to be flawlessly executed. Alana, come, we have an early appointment."

"One moment," she said as she looked at the black drums by the crates. "There's one more item remaining, did you remove the drum with the Mary Bolton's body as I instructed?"

Aubrey glanced behind him wondering whose body they confined to one of the drums, positive he could end up in another.

The Irishman smiled. "We did. She's resting comfortably at the muddy bottom of the Thames."

Chapter Twenty-Five

Randall Ashford nodded toward a Footman as he held open the front door of the Mayfair Hotel on another beautiful late-summers morning. Livy fumed and thought about the silence they shared on the ride over. Even Harold, the family's butler, didn't speak during the ten-minute journey as he manipulated the black government sedan along the damaged London streets.

Harold held the car door and smiled a conspirator's smile at Livy as she got out of the rear seat, once more realizing how alike she and her father were—both headstrong and determined to prove to the other they were right. The only words spoken the entire morning were as she'd come down the flat's stairs. He looked up at her and said, "It's time to leave. Wilfred will be waiting." All it did was infuriate her.

Entering the hotel, they marched across the marble floor of the elegant lobby, passed the grand Victorian staircase and made their way through scattered settees of retired military officers still wearing uniforms from a past life and dowagers that took stations around the lobby and hoped to impress anyone who might spend the time to speak with them. They went through the open etched glass doors of the restaurant and her father was instantly greeted by the maître d', a tall thin man in formal dress who spoke with a discernible Polish accent, each "r" forcefully rounded.

"Welcome, Lord Ashford, how nice to see you again," he said. "And this must be Olivia. I've not seen you in years. My goodness, you're all grown. Good morning to you too, Miss Ashford and welcome."

"Thank you, Jacek," her father said. "Has Wilfred Eaton arrived?"

"No sir, not yet and I've been here all morning. May I seat you at the far window until he does? It is quite pleasant for a meeting, very quiet."

"That would be fine."

Jacek escorted them around a maze of linen-covered tables set with fine china and crystal to seat them on gold velvet chairs next to a large picture window that overlooked the oaks adorning Berkeley Square.

"Your waiter this morning will be Thomas and he'll promptly assist you." Jacek said as her father slipped him a one-pound note. "Thank you, Lord Ashford." As he turned, he snapped his fingers at a tall man approaching in a double-breasted white waiter's jacket. On a silver service he carried tea and freshly baked breads which he placed on the table.

"Oh my—butter," Livy said. "I haven't tasted real butter in weeks."

"It's quite good, I assure you," her father said.

She was shocked, those were the first words he'd spoken to her since they left the flat. "Livy, we will finish our conversation before Wilfred arrives."

She looked up from slathering butter on a hot piece of bread. "Certainly," she snapped the word out and bit into the bread.

He frowned at her as the waiter poured steaming tea into their cups. "I can't forbid you to go with this Jamie but I want you to think about the consequences to your reputation as well as that of your family. You're an unmarried woman and going across the country alone with this boy leaves you open to criticism. At least you understand that, I hope."

"It's a short train ride, that's all. After which I'll be with his family. If that is a problem regarding my reputation, I really don't care." She was still livid with him. "It's certainly not an issue to me."

"I didn't say it was. But, remember you're from a completely different world than that boy. A marriage to him would soon become a disaster. All I ask is that you think about that when you go off with him. He couldn't even relate to a world like ours. Look around this restaurant. I'd wager he's never seen a place like this—unless, of course, he was washing the dishes."

"Stop it!" She had to catch herself from shouting. "You know nothing about him. He's from a working-class family but he has finer qualities than all the dolts you've presented from Oxford or Cambridge. You might want to consider that when you speak about him. You're so very irritating right now."

"You might consider me irritating, but I'm attempting to save your future from a very reckless and foolhardy decision. You need to begin to think clearly about this boy and how he will affect your future, our family's future."

Before she could answer, Wilfred Eaton came to the table with Alana close behind.

"Randall, good morning." Wilfred smiled, shaking his hand. He sat across from him and next to her. "Hello, dear." He said, patting her wrist inches from the butter knife she held. "It's so good to see you in uniform. It suits both you and Alana very well. By the way, did everything work out with your pilot friend?"

"Yes sir, it did. Thank you. He was injured, but not too seriously."

Alana gave Livy a quick smile and sat down beside Randall who was still showing grumbling signs. Her father looked at Alana and said, "So nice to see you. I think the last time we saw each other was at Paul's party, before I had to so abruptly leave. I hope you're keeping track of my daughter and her travels with this film thing."

"Well sir, we haven't seen much of each other lately," Alana said.

"Let me ask you something." He tapped his mouth with a linen napkin. "Do you know this Jamie Wallace boy?"

Alana looked confused and glanced at Livy. "Yes sir, I've met him twice. He seems like a fine man young man and a very good pilot. He was almost killed yesterday when he was shot down, it's a miracle he survived."

Stunned, he looked at Livy. "Shot down? You didn't say anything about that. What happened?"

Careful to keep her irritation from showing she said, "He was flying in combat over the estuary and his engine quit. The Germans fired on him and his aircraft exploded."

"Exploded? Good lord, he is lucky to be alive. I wish you'd told me."

"Why, would it have made a difference?"

"Still, I wish you had told me," her father said in a tone that implied the conversation about Jamie was over. He shifted his eyes away from her and said, "Well, Wilfred, what's on your mind? Your phone call made this meeting sound somewhat urgent."

"You have no idea, Randall, just how urgent." Wilfred placed his heavy elbows on the table, it caused his coat sleeves to rise well above the white cuffs. "I'm of a mind where I believe our air defense system is of paramount importance to the war effort."

"I agree. Other than our pilots, it is possibly our most important contributor to stopping the Germans. That's not surprising nor that urgent. In fact, it's functioning quite well. I can't see what's caused your discomfort. The RAF is defeating the Luftwaffe and that's a very good thing. It might take a while, but we'll win this."

"Exactly my point! You're a naval officer, so please don't take this the wrong way. Some of the admirals, your naval colleagues, don't quite see it the same." Wilfred put his fingertips together and touched his lips as if in deep, troubled thought. "I'll be proposing dramatic increases to the budget for our air defense. I believe these increases are critical for the ultimate defeat of the Luftwaffe and the salvation of our nation. Hitler right now is preparing for an invasion—and that invasion is being stymied by the RAF. In some of my sub-rosa negotiations with several admirals, I have run into a thick wall of objection. The Navy believes building the ships necessary to invade the Continent three years from now is far more critical and therefore they oppose me. I need your help, in truth, I really don't know much about the system or how it operates, only that it's winning the war. I was hoping you would help educate me, so I may do a proper battle with the officers that oppose me. Randall, we've known each other a very long time, I didn't know where else to turn for assistance."

Randall Ashford smiled. "Of course, I'll help you. Without the defeat of the German Luftwaffe right now, we won't need any ships in 1943. We'll have lost the damn war. What do you need to know?"

Wilfred let out a long breath. "I feel as if I've been freed from the albatross, the cord cut from around my neck."

"Understand Wilfred, there are some areas I can't speak about, even to you, but I'll help where I can," her father smiled.

"More than I could ever ask, thank you. Let me start with a few questions."

"Certainly, go ahead."

Livy looked across the table at Alana and smiled. She rolled her eyes the way she did when they were children as if to say, "Here we go again!"

A waiter came up to the table and said, "I beg your pardon." He bowed slightly. It reminded Livy of the servants during a formal dinner at Kensington Manor. "My name is Thomas, I'll be serving you. As you know, restaurants no longer have the full menu due to our current situation. This morning we are offering fresh whipped eggs and bacon. Would that be suitable for all of you?"

"Does that suffice for everyone?" Randall said. They all nodded. "That would be excellent, thank you, Thomas."

Scribbling on a small strip of paper the waiter said, "Is there anything else I might bring you—tea or some more breads and butter perhaps?"

"For the present, I believe we are fine." Her father responded and Thomas sped off toward the kitchen. He turned back to Wilfred. "Now, for your questions, what is it you need to know?"

"Wonderful. First, how does this all work? A good start would be an overview, how it functions. I know some parts but I'll simply listen, quiet as a mouse."

Alana looked across the table at Livy and gave a quick motion of her head toward the loo, a signal Livy knew well.

"We're going to leave you two gentlemen to your conversation and freshen up a bit before our breakfast." Alana said as she got up from her gold velvet chair. Both men stood.

Leaving the table, Livy and Alana smiled at each other as they overheard Wilfred say, "Freshen up? They both just got here. I'll never understand why women must always freshen up."

Alana winked at her. Once out of hearing range she said, "Nice to know nonverbal communication still works. I didn't want to hear any more of that. You know, since the day I started my assignment, all I hear about is 'the damn war this' and 'the damn war that'—never anything else. I don't think I can put up with it much longer.

Alana took her arm and whispered, "So, now on to a completely different subject—what is going on with you and your father? Christ, the tension is so thick it hung over the table like a raincloud."

Livy sighed, "We've been doing battle since last night after I got back to the flat."

"That's another thing—you owe me the full story of what happened with Jamie. You weren't even in your clothes! God, you two looked wretched coming out of that taxi." She twisted her lips. "Everyone wants to know about it. Rumors abound." She said a little cheekily.

"That's for another time. I can't think about that. Right now, I'm still so infuriated with my father, I could throttle him."

They opened the door to the restroom and Alana held a finger in the air as if checking the direction of the wind. She took a quick glance under the stalls and seeing no one said, "Okay, it's clear. What's this all about?"

"Jamie invited me to his family's home in Newent."

"Newent?" Alana had a look of surprise on her face.

"It's the little town Jamie is from, somewhere near Gloucester. His father owns a butcher shop there and he wants me to come down with him, meet his family."

"I know it well. I've been there many times—it's only a few miles from Gloucester. Does sound kind of serious—meeting his family. You've taken to this boy, haven't you?"

Livy smiled and thought of his eyes. "I have."

"Why not have a quick tryst with him and be done with it?"

She sighed at Alana shaking her head, held a moment and said, "I think I'm in love with him and he might be the man to spend my life with."

Alana's eyes went wide. "Right Oh! Well, that's where we're different. The thought of marriage to one man and sharing a bed with only that man—that's something I can't fathom. It's not in my nature."

"It's in mine," Livy said. "It's what I want, what I've always wanted, to be in love like this."

"I can see it. But if you're in love with Jamie and vice versa, what's the issue with your father?" She held her hand up as if she said something absurd. "Oh, it's that he is from the working class, isn't it? Doesn't quite fit with your father's idea of the right man for you?"

"Precisely. He thinks I'll be unhappy and run home to Kensington Manor with a little one in tow after a year or two. He believes that I can't be happy with him, because he's of a lower status."

"Well, I certainly wouldn't give up Kensington Manor for a butcher shop but, to each their own. How long will you be away with him? Maybe that's another issue—being unmarried and all that rot."

"Not long. Two days maybe, that's all. However long it takes. He's going to retrieve a car he purchased."

"Livy, that should take about fifteen minutes, it's the rest of the time your father's worried about. He thinks you'll be in bed with him—that's his problem."

"Men are so mindless sometimes."

Alana laughed. "He's an Edwardian! He grew up carrying that. To the men of his generation, women are property—don't you understand that?"

"I've never been treated like property."

"Until now. You're a grown woman and you have a man that you might allow to sleep with you. That changes everything at least as far as your father is concerned. That's what all the fuss is, I mean at the bottom of it.

"A woman of his generation, from the upper class, would never consider going overnight anywhere with a man unless they were married. The ramifications to her reputation alone would have been devastating. If she actually got pregnant and wasn't married, that would be the end of it. I'll guarantee that's what he's roiled about. That and of course the fact he can't control his daughter anymore. He must be totally confounded about how to come to grips with that."

"Well, I'm going. I want to meet his family; I just hope they accept me." She said it firmly as if there was no other choice she would make.

"Oh, I'm sure they'll accept you. Your problem is, will your father accept Jamie and his family. That's going to be far harder, I suspect."

She sighed and said, "I think you're right. But he really won't have a choice, now will he? I've made my decision; he'll simply have to learn to live with it. Let's go back. The food has probably been served and I'm starving for fresh eggs and bacon. It feels like years since I had bacon. I can't pass that up."

Thomas had just placed the food on the table as they returned to their seats. "That smells wonderful," Livy said as she sat. "You never miss something as much until it's taken away."

Her father looked up from cutting into the eggs. "If the Nazis win this war, you'll miss our freedom too," he took a bite, "the freedom to go around this country wherever and with whomever you want."

He put the silver fork on his plate and turned to Wilfred. "I'll put you in touch with Sir Phillip Joubert. He's the one that designed the system and he'll be far better at answering your questions. As for the communication lines, I'm sorry but that's classified and I won't discuss it."

Chapter Twenty-Six

The clock on the platform showed eight minutes before eleven and Jamie was starting to get anxious. He felt he was in a dream, she said yes. The thought of this incredible woman being with him was something he didn't imagine possible. The way he felt when he saw her or touched her was something he never wanted to end.

What if she changed her mind? What would he do? Was he wrong to have asked her to go? What if she got the wrong idea?

From a distance, he thought he heard his name called, but the ringing in his left ear overpowered much of the sound around him. Once again, he scanned the platform. A second later he thought he heard his name again. He turned around and searched the crowd. Finally, two men in suits and bowlers parted from a queue boarding another train and, in the space, he saw her slip through, coming toward him. All his jitters vanished and the fear slid away.

"Jamie!" Her smile said everything as she ran into his arms. He kissed her and the tenderness he felt in his heart flooded through.

"Now that's a greeting." She said as she smiled up at him and Alana joined them. "I'm sorry we're a little late. Some of the roads were covered in rubble out and we had to scramble around a bit to find our way here."

"But you're here and that's all that matters. Let me have your bag, mine's already on board." He took it from her and smiled at Alana. "Thanks for getting her here."

"My pleasure," She nodded. "So, Livy said you're going to Newent," she said it to Jamie in a toneless upper-class voice.

It made him bristle. "Yes, it's my home."

"I know it well. I've been there many times. Our estate is outside of Gloucester."

"Oh, that's fairly close," he said. Livy slipped her arm around his back and it was wonderful.

Alana looked at him, a hint of a smile on her face. "I understand your family owns a butcher shop there?"

Again, there was something about the way she said it. "That's right. Wallace's Butcher Shop, right on Broad Street. You can't miss it."

"I know the place, across from a little pub. The Red Lion, I think."

Jamie was surprised she knew the place. "That's right—that's our shop." He could feel he was about to get short with her but when he looked at Livy, his irritation disappeared.

"Is that where you'll be staying?" Now she was prying, but he thought he should answer if for no other reason than to keep the rumors at bay. "Does your family live above the shop? So many of those little merchant places are like that."

"They do, and that's where I'll be staying. Livy will be with my brother's fiancée."

"How nice," Alana said with a flat smile on her face. She turned to give Livy a hug. "You two have a train to catch—don't let me hold you up. I'm sure you'll have a smashing time." Over Livy's shoulder, she looked at him in a way that made him defensive.

Livy pulled back from her and said, "Thanks for bringing me here. For the first time in weeks, I haven't a care in the world. I'll ring you in a few days after I'm back."

"Well, I hope things stay this way for you," Alana said. She took a step back and looked at him with a blank expression. "Don't let anything disagreeable happen to her." Alana smiled at Livy, turned and walked toward the exit. She quickly disappeared behind a queue on the station platform.

He paused a moment, shook his head and looked at Livy. "Well, that was interesting."

"She gets like that sometimes, don't pay her any mind." Calm settled over him once again. "I can't wait to meet your family. I'm so happy we're doing this."

He smiled, kissed her once more, and put his arm around her shoulder. He picked up her suitcase and they boarded *The Welshman*, bound for Newent.

Lord Randall Ashford checked his watch and noted it was two minutes past eleven. He gnashed his teeth as he stood with members of the War Cabinet and others at the foot of Sir Winston Churchill's bed. A late riser, the prime minister had a dour look on his face as he read from a unique sheet of paper, the type used for secure government communications.

Churchill looked up and gazed at them all over his spectacles. He picked up a snifter from his bedside table, swirled the contents and took a sip. After a moment of staring at those standing beside his bed he said, "I've brought you here to inform you it appears the little corporal has made his decision. Intelligence coming from France and the lowlands indicate the ships, barges, and matériel are in place and currently being loaded. From this point on, you may expect the invasion to commence sometime within in the next two weeks. Any further information as to the timetable Herr Hitler plans to follow will be made available to you as quickly as possible. This is most secret and for your ears only. As to the future actions of your respective departments, you are to execute plans under the defense classification *Invasion Imminent*."

Chapter Twenty-Seven

Cotton-ball clouds hung on hooks, motionless in a transparent blue sky. Livy rode in the carriage, looking out over green hills spotted with yellow daffodils where sheep and dairy cattle grazed oblivious to the war. Yet, even with all the charm and peace, she was far from settled.

Her mind drew pictures of a life with Jamie, images of where and how they would live. His integrity and honor would never allow her wealth to enter their marriage. That wasn't who or what he was. They would make a life based on what he could provide, but would that be enough? After a few years, a child or two, would she resent him? Suppose her father was right and what they were feeling was the intensity of war, making them believe they were in love. Doubts and confusion rose up in her heart, like water below the surface of a brook tumbling over stones.

He was seated across from her, his gaze fixed outside the window unconsciously rubbing his hand over the bandaged gash in his head. In spite of the bruises and the bandage, he was quite handsome. He had a slightly upturned nose, long lashes above his green eyes and lips that a woman could only call inviting. It was a wonderful combination. A gentle, confident man and much like her father—one of great courage. She could only imagine the horror and fear of being shot down and the pain his injury must have rendered and yet he never complained. She looked at the sadness currently on his face and wanted to reach out to him, comfort him. Warm thoughts filled her heart and made the doubts vanish like an ocean wave after it breaks on the shore. In her heart, she knew she loved him and no matter what happened, she always would.

"A penny for your thoughts," she said.

He turned from the window and looked at her as if he arrived from a faraway place. "I'm sorry. Did you say something?"

She smiled. "I did. A penny for your thoughts."

He looked at her with that quirky grin. "I was thinking of how happy I am and how wonderful it will be to spend the next two days with you."

She knew that was only partly true, but she looked into his eyes and couldn't resist. She slipped over next to him, gently took his face in her hands and kissed him. Her body reacted with a passion, warm and wonderful.

"I have a request to make, Mr. Wallace." She whispered, rolling a soft curl that wiggled out from behind the bandage around her finger.

"Anything at all." He smiled at her.

She ran her finger down the side of his face, tracing the bruise and the outline of his lips. "While we're here, no more talk of the war. I've had my fill of it. I want this time we have together to be about you and me and what we're sharing."

"I'd like nothing more." He took in a breath and smiled again. "If we were both out of uniform, might be easier to forget the war that way."

She tilted her head back and laughed. "And what is it you're asking for Mr. Wallace." He blushed and joined her laughter as she put her arms around him and whispered in his ear, "It's been so long since I've laughed like that." She leaned back and said, "No uniforms for the remainder of our stay."

She fixed on his eyes and as their lips met again, the door at the end of the carriage slammed, the sound made her jump. The next thing she heard was the conductor bellowing, "Newent, next stop Newent," as he made his way down the passageway outside their compartment.

The Welshman's wheels let off a high-pitched squeal and the engine exhaled a long breath of steam as it slowed to a stop. Jamie stepped off the train, set down their suitcases and helped her to the platform. He closed the carriage door behind them and said, "A little less than three months ago, I arrived here from a different place on a different train and it feels like that was a lifetime ago."

The station house on the wooden platform was small, rural and quaint, made of white clapboard with green trim around the windows and doors that glowed in the sun. The platform was empty except for a sole porter who stood beneath a white round clock above the ticket window, his arm comfortably resting on a hand trolley, a lazy cigarette hung from his lips.

The train let out a long hiss. It rocked forward and began to pull away toward another destination as two men in dark suits jumped from the last carriage. *Odd, they have no luggage,* she thought as she looked at Jamie who had seen them too. "Must be secret agents," she winked at him.

He started to laugh as he picked up the suitcases and grinned at her. "Welcome to Newent." She linked her arm with his and they started toward the double doors leading to the interior of the station.

As they reached the doors, a short, thin man popped through, dressed in of all things, a second-hand brown suit a size too large for his slender frame. Unruly curls sat on his narrow head that poked out of a collared shirt with a yellow and white striped necktie that lay around his neck in a knot as big as his Adam's apple.

"Squeaky," Jamie said, "good to see you, but a suit? I don't think I've seen you dressed like that in all the years I've known you."

"'Ello. Sorry I'm a little tardy. I've been behind all day. This suit"—he held his arms out, turning back and forth as if modeling the clothes— "well, it's because of my new position. Have to give the right impression. I'm no longer a part-time grease monkey, I'm a salesman." He announced it with pride. "You're looking at the salesman for the Newent Garage and Motor Car Sales Company." He laughed, his crooked teeth gleaming. "But, enough about me." He looked in her eyes and said, "You must be Livy. I'm Paul Jenkins, the folks around here call me Squeaky and I hope you will too."

He extended his hand, a tiny bit of leftover grease hiding under a fingernail. She smiled and took it, "Nice to meet you, I'm Livy Ashford."

"After Jamie told his mother you were coming you've been the buzz around here, Miss. She told me all about you. Actually, she told everyone, but don't let that worry you. Little towns have big mouths as they say, mostly because they have nothin' else to talk about, but anyway, welcome to Newent. It's nice to meet you."

He held her hand, pumping it up and down and as he let go, he stuck out his lower lip and nodded. "Ashford, eh. Been wondering what your surname was. No one seemed to know. Sounds royal, if you don't mind my saying so. I like it."

She laughed and said, "I do too."

Jamie chuckled. "What do you say we take a look at this car I'm about to buy? This'll be the first one I've ever owned."

Squeaky reached out toward one of the suitcases Jamie was carrying. "Here, let me grab one of those for you."

"Take this one," Jamie said, offering him his own. She knew it was much lighter.

After a few minutes of traveling through the beautiful village Livy felt like she belonged there. They reached the Newent Garage and Motor Car Sales Company located on the top of a hill at the end of Bridge Street. It was a tall single-story whitewashed construction with three faded red barn doors built to house the horse-drawn carriages of the last century. Inside the gaping spaces several cars sat on lifts or were scattered around in various states of repair, their bonnets raised. To the right, lined up against the side of the building, used motor cars were parked in the afternoon sun. Squeaky turned his green and white Vauxhall off the street and stopped it on the packed clay in front of the garage.

"Here we are. I've got one all picked out for you, Jamie. We'll see if you like it," he said.

"There must be ten or fifteen cars here, Squeaky. Are all these for sale?" she said, happy for his success.

"Well, not all of 'em. Some are waiting to be picked up or to go into the shop for repair. I got about seven for sale right now."

As they all got out, one caught her eye—a small dark-green MG Roadster that was almost hidden among the less-attractive sedans. Squeaky took them both to a Ford Anglia parked off to the right of the other cars, a few weed stalks scratching at the tires. It was maroon and slightly faded. Inside, it smelled of dust and the vinyl of the front seat was cracked and sagging in places that made her believe an over-sized person had done most of the driving.

"This is the one I picked for you. Not very fancy but her innards all work like new. I know—I replaced 'em," Squeaky smiled.

Jamie looked in her direction and she shook her head no and went straight for the roadster.

"I don't know," Jamie said. She turned and saw him looking at her. "I don't think Livy would be happy with this one."

"What about this one," she pointed to the green MG. "I think it's cute and fun. What about this one, Squeaky?"

"I don't think you're gonna want that one." He paused a second, running a hand through his curls. "It runs great, like new, but it's out of the price range we spoke about."

"Isn't that Tommy Lackman's car?" Jamie said.

"Yeah, it is. Or, I mean, was. Elisa wants it sold."

"His wife, how come? Doesn't Tommy want it? Or is she trying to get rid of it? I can see it's not very practical with the kids, only has two seats." Jamie reached the little green car and started inspecting it.

"It's not that. Tommy won't be using it anymore. Elisa and the kids need the money." Squeaky eyes looked toward the ground.

"What happened?" Livy said, waiting for the answer she already suspected.

Squeaky took a deep breath. "Tommy stepped on a land mine somewhere in Egypt. He's not coming back." He looked up and added, "The family needs the money bad. They're asking fifty pounds and I can't take anything less. A little more than it's worth, but that's the price she needs. It makes me feel awful when I think about Elisa and two little ones. What are they gonna do?"

The war was doing the same thing to countless thousands. She looked over at Jamie and knew he was feeling as terrible as she was.

"I'll take it." Jamie reached into his jacket pocket and pulled out a check register. "I've given you thirty already and I'll write you a check for the other twenty right now."

"Have you gone mad? You don't have to do that, I'll find someone that'll buy it."

"I'll take it, Squeaky. Write up the bill."

Chapter Twenty-Eight

Livy used a hand to gather wayward strands of hair as the MG scooted down the hill. She winced as Jamie gnashed the gears for a second time. When she looked at him from the passenger seat, that grin flashed back at her. "Don't worry I'll get the hang of it." He smiled as he said it.

She laughed and turned to look through the windscreen at the town below them, bathed in a color like honey from the dying sun. "When were we supposed to be at your home?"

"Oh, a little more than an hour ago. We'll be there in a few minutes." She turned toward him and his smile vanished. "What's the matter? Something's bothering you" he said as he took her hand.

She stared at their hands, his fingers intertwined with hers. "I can't get the Lackman family out of my mind. What's she going to do? How will they live? It's so sad, two little children, their father dead, their lives torn apart." He let her hand go to work the shift, smoothly sliding into to a lower gear. "It's horrible."

Jamie kept his eyes on the road, braking for a curve. "It is, and that kind of thing is happening all over the world right now."

She watched him inhale a long breath thinking of the toll on them both the war had begun to exact. "Is that a church?" she said, pointing toward a glistening spire rising above apple-green maples, shining in the sun as if were made of bronze. "It looks like a tower from the middle-ages."

"The spire of St. Mary's and it is from the middle ages. Legend has it the church was started in the eighth century with a Celtic cross in a field and that same cross is still there in the same place, the church was built around it. Growing up, my brother and I were altar boys there. How about I take the back way and we'll go right by it."

They reached the bottom of the hill and Jamie took a left onto a road that ran beside a long narrow lake about a quarter the size of the one behind Kensington Manor. It was rimmed with willows and reeds, dotted with purple and canary flowers that seemed to float in the air, waving in a breeze that rippled the golden glass-like water.

Jamie crossed a little bridge to the south side of the lake and turned onto a narrow, unpaved lane running parallel to the shore. Trees formed a canopy over the road as the little roadster bumped along the uneven rich-brown soil until a graveyard appeared on their left, the church tower soaring above it and he stopped the car.

The sun had dipped below the sugar maples, turning the spire a soft rose. "Doesn't it feel ancient?"

"It does. It's beautiful and sometime I'd like to see inside it. But, right now your mother is waiting for us and I think we shouldn't tarry anymore."

His quirky grim appeared. He put the car in gear and drove away from the graveyard, along the narrow lane now edged by a chest-high ivy-covered wall. After about fifty feet, Jamie followed a curve to the left and seconds later parked behind a three-story white building, the window trim painted black to match the thick thatched roof.

He laughed and said, "This is it. This is where I grew up."

She started to laugh. "I had no idea we were *that* close."

They entered through the back door, the warm aroma of baked bread filled the alcove. A single naked bulb glared at the end of a long electrical cord and forged deep shadows around a narrow wooden staircase that led up to the family's kitchen. Livy started up the stairs and stopped, turned around and looked into his eyes. "What did you tell your mother about me?"

"Nothing really, I told her how stunning you are. How we met and about the night we got caught in the bombing."

"That's all—nothing about my family?"

"No, nothing about your family. I don't know much about them. I've only met your father once, at the party. At the time, I didn't even know he was your father."

"Nothing else?"

"Only how I feel about you."

A melodic woman's voice came from the top of the stairs. "Ah, there you are!" A smile burst onto her face as she came out of the kitchen and stood on the landing above. "You must be Livy. Welcome to our home, my dear. I'm so excited to meet you." She appeared to be about fifty and was wiping her hands on a blue-and-white checkered apron. "Where have you two been?"

Jamie smiled. "That's my mum, Rachael." He looked up at her and said, "I bought a car from Squeaky."

His mother paused a moment and stared at him, a look of exasperation on her face. "Did you say you bought a car?"

"I did."

"Well, if that doesn't … and of all things, right before you bring Livy home. Jamie Wallace, sometimes I don't know what's to be done with you." She laughed and shook her head. Livy felt a special warmth radiate around her. It brought back an almost forgotten feeling, one she had bottled up since she was a little girl. "Come on up here, my dear. I could use a little help."

Rachael stood at the entry above them with her hands on her hips as they climbed the stairs. "Jamie, you told me you took a little thump to the noggin and here you are bandaged like a mummy!"

"I'm fine, mum. Looks much worse than it is."

"Well, you're here now and that's all that matters." She shook her head and entered the kitchen.

The two climbed the remaining stairs single file, Livy holding on to Jamie's hand behind her. As they rounded the landing's corner and came into the kitchen a beautiful olive-skinned woman with shiny ebony hair popped a piece of sausage into her mouth. Jamie laughed as she put both hands in front of her lips and said something that sounded like, "It's so good."

"Yeah, it is, mum makes the best sausages in the world," Jamie said as they came into the kitchen. "Livy this is Julia, my brother's fiancée." She nodded, still chewing and covering her mouth.

Livy smiled at her. "Julia, I've heard so much about you."

Julia swallowed and said, "Nice to meet you, Livy. You'll be staying with me tonight, we'll get to know each other." She had a slight accent, but her English was perfect.

Rachael came over to Livy and gave her a hug and a kiss on her cheek. Wonderful memories of her own mother flooded into her heart. "Here, my dear," Rachael said, slipping a piece of sausage into her mouth. "It's something I always did for my boys—a little taste for the appetite."

A world of flavor gushed into her mouth as she bit down. She closed her eyes in delight. "It's wonderful." She mumbled covering her mouth.

"I told you—there's none better," Jamie said as he scratched at the bandage around his head. "You'll never have another without thinking of this moment."

She nodded her head as she chewed and stifled a laugh.

The kitchen was a tenth the size of the one at Kensington Manor. A single window on the rear wall above a steel sink overlooked an alley, not acres and acres of grounds. Knife-scarred butcher-block counters lined the back and side walls set on top of too few white metal cupboards. In a corner, a small round wooden table with four chairs took up most of the space.

But in that small unadorned kitchen, Livy felt a warmth from so many meals cooked with so much love, very different than the cold formality of the manor. There was a comfort about it, with the old porcelain-covered stove chugging along, sending wonderful smells into the air. She smiled and to her surprise, felt right at home.

Standing by the little round table, Julia cocked her head and said, "Jamie, let me look at what's under that bandage. It looks like you're uncomfortable. I may be able to do something; after all, I am a nurse. How long has it been since you changed it?"

"I don't know—two days, I think."

"Come, let's have a look." Julia motioned for him to sit next to her.

Livy followed behind him as he took the chair next to Julia. She scooted her chair around to his side and started to remove the gauze bandage. Livy winced as the last of it peeled off remembering the night they were caught in the bombing and the blood that ran from the gash. This time, however, the bandage came away clean and the swelling was almost gone.

"That looks so much better," she said, "a long way from our night in the Underground."

"Jamie, she's right—this looks pretty good. For as bad as this must have been, it's well on the way to being healed. You're young and there's so much blood flow in your head a wound like this can mend quickly. Another few days and the stitches can come out," Julia said. "I can't do much for all the hair they cut off but I can dress this, make it feel a lot better."

Jamie nodded. "I'd like that. The itching is driving me mad."

Rachael stood next to the three of them and stared at the side of Jamie's head kneading her hands. "That's far worse than what you told me, Jamie."

"I didn't want to worry you, Mum," he said and showed her a bright smile.

"Not worry me? Now that's a thought. I've been worried about you since the afternoon you were born." She laughed and patted Julia's shoulder. "I'll go get the kit, it's got everything you'll need."

Jamie sat in silence as Julia leaned back in the chair watching him. His eyes were lowered, fixed somewhere else. Livy rested her hand on his back sure he was reliving the horrible images of a Spitfire exploding around him. Images she knew he would never forget.

Rachael came in and handed a medical kit to Julia. "This should do it. Here's a torch too. It'll give a little extra light."

"That's perfect. Livy, will you hold the light please." She handed it to her and said, "Okay, Jamie, you ready? I promise this won't hurt a bit."

He smiled at her. "I am—have at it."

Livy shone the light on the gash and watched as Julia gently cleaned the wound and applied a coating of antiseptic gel. In a few seconds, she had finished.

She wound a long strip of gauze around Jamie's head and said, "That's it—you're done."

"That's so much better, the itching has stopped." He leaned over and gave her a quick peck on the cheek. "Thank you."

"In a month or so you'll have all your hair back and be none the worse." Julia smiled at him. "But sometime, when you're ready, I would like to know all that happened. That's a rather nasty gash."

Livy recognized the look that flashed over Rachael's face as her eyes dampened. Rachael had almost lost one son to the war and she was very aware she could easily lose the other. She went to her and put her arms around her.

After a moment, she stepped back and Rachael gave her a smile. "Thank you, for that, luv." Rachael whispered. She dabbed at her eyes with the checkered apron and said, "Come, you three, it's time to eat. And bring a platter with you. Mind you, they're hot."

Livy followed Julia out of the kitchen, through a short pantry hall and into the dining room, using two hands to carry a steaming bowl of boiled potatoes. The room was a rectangle above the butcher shop in the front of the home taking up more than half the depth of the building. The walls were dotted with saffron-and-blue-flowered wallpaper and between two windows on the long side a varnished hutch occupied most of the space. A photograph in a pewter frame placed on a shelf showed the family years ago, when Jamie was about three. He held a teddy-bear in his arms, the top of his curls barely reaching his brother's waist. He was the kind of adorable little boy you wanted to pick up and squeeze. She smiled as she set the bowl on the table thinking how little that had changed.

Rachael came in from the kitchen carrying a basket of freshly baked breads that filled the room with that fresh-baked aroma. Rachael placed it on the table and pointed to the single window on the front wall. "Livy, be a dear and draw the blackout curtains."

Livy slipped behind a chair at the end of the table and took an edge of the thick black curtain in hand. As she slid it over the window, in the last of twilight, she saw a patron cross the street, climb a single stair and disappear into a pub called The Red Lion.

"You must be Livy." The voice was deep, strong and intimidating.

She turned around to find a tall, broad shouldered man. His eyes fixed on hers.

A smile came to his face. "I'm Jamie's father, Robert. Welcome to my home."

She extended her hand and he took it. "I'm Livy Ashford—a pleasure to meet you, Mr. Wallace." His hand was callused, thick and strong and yet there was a delicate precision in the way he held hers.

He gestured to the chair on his right and said, "Please sit. Well, Livy, looks like I finally get to meet the girl who has stolen my youngest son's heart."

As the remaining guests filed in from the parlor, Jamie smiled at her and pulled back her chair. His father gestured at the others entering and said, "Livy this is Michael, Jamie's older brother."

His father's voice continued about a medal for something he had done at Dunkirk and she did all she could to keep an expression of shock off her face. Michael looked like a ravaged copy of his father. They had the same beautiful sky-blue eyes, but Michael was much thinner. The gray suit he wore drooped at the shoulders and hung in the middle as if owned by a prior man, his skin tinted with a pallor. With his right hand he moved his cane, the left leg not cooperating. He was a shadow of the rugby player Jamie spoke about.

She forced her mind back into the dining room to follow Robert's introductions as he said, "You've met Julia and Rachael, my wife. And, these two are Simon and Rebecca Weiss, Julia's parents."

After they all settled and a blessing was said, steaming platters of sausage, potatoes and vegetables made their way around, passed from hand to hand, spoons and forks clanking. Jamie lifted a wine decanter from the center of the table and filled her glass. When everyone was settled, and had started to eat, Rachael rose from her chair and went into the kitchen. A moment later she returned carrying a small white platter she carefully placed on the table.

"Mein Gott, Eier kann ich es nicht glauben!" Rebecca, a heavy-set woman in her fifties with streaked gray hair almost came out of her seat next to Michael, her eyes fixed on a dish filled with a dozen deviled eggs.

"Speaking German at my table? We've got to teach you English, my dear." Robert laughed and said to Simon, "What did she say?"

Simon smiled. "'My God, eggs—I can't believe it.'" He looked across the table and said something in German to his wife as she shyly nodded.

"English, I try learn. It speak hard." Her Teutonic accent plowed heavily through the words.

Robert laughed and said, "You bet it does, Rebecca. Believe me, there's many an Englishman that can't speak a word of it. But I've made sure both my boys could speak the King's English as well as any toff."

Everyone laughed as Rachael picked up the dish and with a kind smile on her face offered it to Rebecca.

She took an egg and looked at her husband. "Was ist toff?"

Simon was a pear-shaped man, with dark inquisitive eyes set in a round face that expressed a silent burden beneath. His gray-tinged black hair wrapped around the sides of his head ignoring the crown. He was a little older than his wife and dressed in an immaculate, well-tailored dark navy suit. His hands came together to form a little temple and he said, "I'm sorry Robert, but we do not know your word toff. What does it mean?" His accent was Austrian and his English remarkably good.

Jamie's father gave a laugh as big as his frame. "Toff, well . . . it's a name we call the upper class." Livy swallowed a gulp of wine, a knot growing in her stomach. She glanced towards Jamie and noticed both of the brothers looking at each other, their mouths turned down at the corners. "The people that have ruled this country for centuries and run it to ground in order to line their own pockets. That's a toff."

"Oh, I see. Thank you." Simon nodded and in a hushed voice spoke to his wife in rapid German.

Jamie rubbed his forehead in almost the same way his mother did. He turned to her and said, "Mum, how do you do it?" He grinned, "I haven't seen this much food on one table in forever. And eggs—where did you find them? No one can get fresh eggs anymore."

"Well, let's just say I did and leave it at that. Don't want the bobbies sniffing around. That would be a fine thing—your mother arrested for hoarding."

Livy looked over the top of her glass at Jamie as he reached for a deviled egg. She thought back to breakfast two days ago, the last time she had eggs. They'd been placed on fine china, on linen with crystal and sterling-silver tableware. Her father's comment about Jamie washing dishes stung in her ears.

She looked at the table—the glasses that didn't match, serving platters with a chip or two, and a meal that was nothing like the meals served at Kensington Manor. But she also felt a family, something that was missing at the long formal table where she had often taken meals alone with her father during her visits home from boarding schools.

Thoughts about Jamie and the kind of life they would create churned in her head, until Robert Wallace posed a question to Simon. "Before the Nazis came, you were a professor back in Vienna."

Simon daubed a cloth napkin at his mouth. "I was Dean of the History Department at the university. That is, until we were forced to leave on a very cold Thursday, March 10, 1938. Two days before the Nazis came. We obtained some of the last tickets available to Bern."

At the mention of the Nazis, Rebecca glanced at her husband with dread on her face. Jamie looked at his dinner plate and said, "Thank God you got out."

"Yes, Jamie, we were very fortunate. I was warned about what the Nazis would do with the Jews of Austria, I had friends in the government. Our story is sad enough, but it will be nothing like the stories I fear will come later, the stories of those who stayed. Those stories will be far more frightening."

"Julia told me some of what you went through." Michael said. "It was terrible."

Robert's palm hit the table making the dishes clink. "None of this should have happened. The Nazis should have been taken out in 1935. It could have been done had we a leader with a backbone, instead of that toff-appeaser Chamberlain. And what do the toffs do now that the world has come apart? They go to the opposite end and appoint a warmonger like Churchill."

Michael snapped his head toward his father, "Rubbish! It doesn't make a difference! What we might have done or who might have done it doesn't mean a damn thing."

Livy saw a fury rise in him.

"The Nazis are a vile lot, something evil. I know them. I fought them." Michael said and took a long swig of his wine.

"You're finished with your part, Michael," Robert said in a quiet voice. "You stood up to the Jerrys at Dunkirk. The king even pinned a medal on you. You're a hero, son, and I'm proud you had the courage to stand up to 'em."

Rachael looked at her husband. "What about Jamie? He's fighting them too."

"He is." Robert said.

With his fork, Jamie pushed a potato around his plate. "I'm no hero."

"Of course, you are! You're standing up to them, giving the Jerrys hell. You're fighting them same as Michael did," his mother's voice a register higher.

Jamie looked at the plate in front of him and as if simply stating facts said, "I'm fighting them, but a hero, no I'm not. I'm petrified. I shake like a frightened rabbit every time I fly."

Michael looked across the table at his brother. "I know that shaking Jamie, I've done it a thousand times, that's after I'd wet myself."

"Enough! I'll not have that kind of talk at my table." Robert said in a way that told everyone the conversation was over.

Michael took another swig of the wine as a heavy stillness settled over the room.

Robert set his glass down, looked at Livy and broke the silence. "We haven't heard anything from you, Miss Ashford. Tell us a little about your family—where you're from."

She sipped from her glass, forcing the wine through her constricted throat and thought about what to say. It wasn't going to be received well. "My family lives in Kent, about twenty miles southeast of London."

"That's such pretty country. We went there once, remember, Robert? You liked it," Rachael said, her voice a little brighter.

"So, you volunteered as a WAAF. Where did they assign you—to Jamie's airfield?" Robert asked.

"No, I work with a motion picture crew, documenting the war— that sort of thing."

"Oh, I see. And what does your family do?"

She looked at Jamie. He smiled and winked at her.

This time the wine burned on its way down. "My father works for the government."

Robert's face went blank and he poured himself more wine from the decanter. He raised his glass, looking at her over the rim. "Really. What part of the government does he work for?"

She thought of her father and stared into Robert's eyes. Without a blink, she said, "He's a retired naval captain, a close aide to Churchill. His work is so secret, I'm really unsure what he does."

"Oh," Robert's chin tucked in and his eyes opened wide.

The room went silent again, leaving only the sound of a single fork and knife clanking on a plate and stunned looks on all the faces around the table except for Rebecca's. A smile was on her face as she carefully cut her deviled egg treasure into small bite sized pieces.

Chapter Twenty-Nine

With Livy in the passenger seat, they sped along George Hill Road on their way out of Newent. The sun above them and a beautiful day worked to somewhat settle his thoughts until he looked over at her. She was watching the countryside pass exquisitely dressed in a white collared shirt, open at the neck covered by a loose-fitting wool sweater, the sleeves pushed up above her elbows. Dark-brown riding pants that closely followed the sensual shape of her legs were tucked into brown boots an inch below her knees. She was stunning. A white scarf held most of her hair intact except for a few strands that managed to escape in the wind. He thought of how much he loved her, her strength and confidence, her beauty and grace and yet, he was in turmoil.

Echoes of their future together and how it would be scratched at the back of his mind. Was this a wartime romance destined to thrash their hearts? The thought stung and yet, he couldn't imagine being without her. But what would a girl like Livy want with him? He thought she loved him, at least for now and he knew he loved her, but what kind of life could he give her, would it be enough? Was it possible their love might lead to an unhappiness that would overtake them and drive them apart, leave a horrid bitterness in her heart? If he must, could he summon the courage to say good-bye and let her go out of his life no matter how painful?

Then in the next second, he would say to himself it didn't matter. They loved each other and always would and he should follow his heart. The confusion kept spinning around and around in his head until he looked at her, saw her smile and all of it would vanish. It was maddening.

"What are you thinking?" she said, probably noticing the wrinkle in his brow. "You look worried."

"I'm thinking about the road in front of us." He turned his head toward her. "I had a wonderful time. Thank you for coming to Newent and meeting my family."

She smiled, it was bright and filled with warmth. "Your mother is quite special to me, so caring. However, I'm not sure your father approved of me at all. He seemed to have rather strong opinions about my family."

"That's the Scot in him, hardheaded. I don't think he sees the changes going on around him. I don't think he wants to."

"I don't know if anything can be done to improve the way he thinks about those he referred to as toffs, but it was wonderful to meet Julia and Michael—all of them, especially your mother." He glanced at her, a playful look on her face. "She loves you very much. She made me promise to take good care of you and it was kind of her to give us all this food for our journey. Told me we should stop at some beautiful place, spread out a blanket and enjoy it." She laughed and it sounded wonderful.

"She's very special to me too, always has been."

Livy looked at him out of the corner of her eye and said, "Have you ever heard of Cliff's End?"

"Sure, my family would take summer vacation near there when I was a boy."

"Is it far from where we are now?"

"Not at all." He looked over at her, she was up to something and he was curious.

She curled her bottom lip under her front teeth, looked at him and said, "When do you have to be back?"

"I have to report on Tuesday morning. Go see the Quack and all that." There was look of mischief on her face that made him smile. "What's hopping around in that head of yours?"

"That gives us some time. I have a better idea than going back to London."

"What's that?"

"Near Cliff's End, we have a small cottage. It's on a bluff overlooking the Channel and I think it's my favorite place in the world. My most fond memories were created there during my childhood.

"There's a beautiful cove nearby called Winspit. It's a little carved-out section and if you're careful, you can follow a trail down the cliffs to the beach. Why don't we go there for a day or so? We'll be all alone, just the two of us. For the first time since we left we could really forget about the war. We can be back in London with plenty of time for your doctor appointment."

"With all the invasion preparations there won't be any road signs, but I think I know the way." He kissed her hand. "I don't want to go back yet. I'd much rather spend what few days I have with you."

Her face lit up. "It's a little south of Wareham."

He smiled hearing the excitement in her voice. "No problem, I can get us there and if we get lost, so what it'll be an adventure."

"We could always stop and ask someone for directions," she laughed.

"Have you ever asked an Englishman for directions? They can barely find their way to the loo. Just show me the way to the cottage after we get close."

A gold sun stretched toward the horizon as Jamie left the highway and pulled onto a crushed gravel road. They drove around a stand of European hornbeams and through rolling sea grass on a private drive that twisted toward Cliff's End. Off in the distance, perched on the landscape like a roosting white bird, a cottage with a high-peaked slate roof stood alone on the promontory, little windows overlooking limestone cliffs that fell vertically into the English Channel.

They drove closer and Jamie realized the cottage was larger than his first impression. The exterior was made of stone and whitewashed plaster, a technique used well over a century earlier. Windows with green shutters matching the front door were positioned to allow maximum light to enter. Two dormers jutted out from the slate roof and indicated the placement of bedrooms above the lower story. The cottage was tucked into the folds of the land so it looked as if it grew out of the soil. At the side of the home, unable to be seen from the curving drive until the last moment, was a carriage house with a square green door built for a horse-drawn coach.

The crunching of tires running over gravel stopped as Jamie eased the car to the front door and shut down the engine. As he gathered the food basket and suitcases from the tiny boot, Livy hopped out and went directly to a bed of little blue flowers that looked as if they had been pushed aside by the Channel winds. She retrieved a brass key from under a loose brick and set about opening the wooden door.

Jamie followed her in and halted a few steps into the entrance. He had entered a luxury world of comfort. The walls of the main room were plaster and perfectly corniced around each of the many windows. On a polished wooden floor covered with Persian rugs rested a long, overstuffed sofa with two matching chairs and end tables, each with its own electric lamp. There were places by the windows for reading or simply looking out at the Channel or grounds and best of all, a large hearth that beckoned for a roaring fire to warm body and soul. A short set of stairs led up to what Jamie guessed would be three or four bedrooms. The cottage was so different from his own home, the splendor of it made him feel as if he had just slipped his hand into a glove a size too large.

Livy lifted the basket from his arm and told him to follow her as she went to the right, through an open dining area where an ornately carved rectangular table and matching chairs were stationed with precision for dinner guests. Jamie left the two suitcases, went through the room and into the kitchen after her.

Livy stood facing a window above a large double sink, silhouetted by the late afternoon sun. She took the food from the basket, placed it on the counter, and pointed to a door that opened to fields behind the cottage. "If you'll go to the back of the garage you'll find the main water spigot and a power box," she said. "Please turn them both on and also gather some firewood from the bin."

He walked up behind her and slipped his arms around her waist. He placed a kiss on her neck and whispered into her ear, "Do you trust me to find them? I might get lost."

She tilted her head back and laughed. She kissed him and said, "I think you'll do fine. You can't possibly miss the spigot, the junction box or the wood. Now hurry along—we'll need the power and water on before the sun sets. Besides, it'll be much easier for a seasoned adventurer such as yourself to find them while it's light."

A few minutes later Jamie entered the kitchen carrying a load of firewood and headed toward the hearth. He set the firewood in a rack and seeing the suitcases missing, he called out. Livy answered from a room above and asked him to start a fire. He set about making it and watched with satisfaction as the kindling grew into flames.

In front of the fire, time seemed to vanish between them as they ate the dinner his mother packed and sampled the wine from the cottage's hidden cellar. They spoke of their childhoods and the magic of growing up, but not once did the war enter their conversation. Livy cleared the dishes as Jamie stood watching the fire crackle, awaiting her return.

She called out from the kitchen. "Please come here."

He entered as she finished the last dish, put it in a rack and wiped her hands on a towel. "Come take a walk with me. There's something I want to show you."

A yellow half-moon hung above the cliffs, a thousand stars brilliant in the heavens. They walked up a hill, hand in hand over the promontory, until they reached a point shielded by a jagged outcropping. Jamie walked around the jutting limestone and stopped. A gray-white Celtic cross shaped much like the one at St. Mary's stood near the edge on a stone platform.

"What's this?"

"Read it," Livy said. "You'll find it very special."

"Our Hearts Are Forever Woven." He read out loud the two lines etched into the stone. "That's beautiful—what is it?"

"My father placed that here one year to the day after my mother's death. This was her favorite place, their secret place. This is where he proposed to her."

"But it doesn't say her name."

"He said it was between the two of them and her name wasn't necessary, that she'd always know. It was his gift to her, his forever remembrance."

Jamie stood silently looking at the cross, thinking of the love they had for each other and feeling his own for Livy. "Your father's heart must have been torn apart when she died."

"It was. Both of ours were."

"I'm so sorry. That's something a child shouldn't have to go through. You were six years old. I can't imagine how painful that was."

"I wanted to show this to you because she lives in my heart. Sometimes I think I can feel her as if she's standing right next to me. I think she's here now and she's glad I've found you."

Jamie touched the cross, trying to understand why a child had to endure losing a mother she loved so dearly. It defied understanding. He turned back toward her and slipped a little on some lose rocks.

"Careful, it's over two hundred feet to the bottom. Below is Winspit and if you listen, you'll hear the waves crashing in the cove."

Jamie went to the edge, checked his footing in the moonlight and looked down. Far below he could see the whitecaps thrash against the rocks in a steady rhythm, the sounds rising above the cliff.

"If you want, we can come back tomorrow morning. There's a trail with some stairs we can take to the beach. The way down isn't too bad, but the way up is a chore." She laughed and the sound touched him.

"I'd like to try that. But for now, how about we go back and have a little wine by the fire?"

"That sounds wonderful." She placed her arm around his waist. He pulled her close and they headed back to the cottage, walking slowly in the moonlight.

The fire still crackled as Livy handed Jamie a half-filled wine glass and curled her legs underneath her on the sofa. He sat at the other end watching the fire.

She smiled and said, "What's in your thoughts."

He looked at her and thought of how much he loved her. "I was thinking about a little girl learning her mother would never return and not understanding why. How much that must have hurt you." He leaned back in the couch and gazed into the fire.

They sat in silence for a few moments and she said, "I have something I want to ask, something I need to understand." Her eyes gentle, curious.

Jon Duncan

"Go ahead."

"What's it like up there when you're flying?"

"Just flying?"

"Yes, what's it like to fly an airplane?"

He smiled. "It's wonderful. There's a sense of freedom that can't be duplicated. It's beautiful. After a while you aren't really flying the aircraft it becomes a part of you. Sort of like how driving a car becomes a part of you. You don't have to think about it, you just do it. I really can't describe it. It's one of those things you need to experience to understand."

"And fighting the Germans?"

"Oh, that's totally different. You're scared and simply trying to stay alive at that point. You hope you'll get back in one piece."

"When you were shot down, when your Spitfire exploded, somehow I knew you were in trouble."

He stared at his glass and swirled the red liquid remembering how she was in his thoughts the entire time.

Livy watched him for a few seconds, "Tell me about it. I really want to know what you went through. It's important to me."

He looked at her and said quietly, "I was chasing after Miles, screaming on the radio trying to tell him I couldn't keep up. The engine sputtered and quit. I was looking down in the cockpit trying to start the engine when I saw an orange ball whiz by. Another went by and the next thing I recall is being strapped to the seat, pieces of the cockpit still around me, spinning and falling. It was cold, very cold and I couldn't breathe. I thought of you and wondered why I was about to die."

She took in a deep breath.

"Somehow, I managed to unfasten the straps and was thrown out of the remains of the seat. The next thing I remember is how I struggled to pull the parachute cord and felt a huge jolt as it burst open. I saw the ground, little green squares that spun around below me and everything went black."

He looked into her eyes as she blinked a few times.

"I remember being in the mud, being dragged out into a river. I saw faces of people around me, pulling me back and that's about it. It's not words I remember. It's the images and those images come back in flashes. I never even saw the German who shot me."

Without saying anything, in her eyes he knew she understood how he felt each time he saw the images—the ones that haunted him, the ones that would never leave him.

She swallowed hard, "Will you go back? To flying in combat, I mean."

"I don't have a choice. I'm a fighter pilot. The lads in my squadron depend on me. It's my duty to fly. I can't let them down."

She placed her wine glass on the table in front of the sofa and moved in next to him, her head resting on his chest. "It frightens me, Jamie. I'm afraid that one day you might not come back to me."

He held her close, stroking her hair. "I know."

She moved her head closer to him, he could feel her breathing, soft and rhythmical. The desire he felt for her built, moment by moment. He tilted his head back attempting to quiet it. She moved, her legs straddled his as she took his face in her hands and kissed him, a long slow kiss.

She looked into his eyes and said, "In my heart, I know we will survive this war. But I can't wait a moment longer." She kissed him again and he could feel her passion, a passion that matched his own. "I want to know you, every part of you."

"Are you sure of this?"

"I've never been surer of anything in my life."

He held her face in his hands and kissed her, a soft gentle kiss.

She stood in front of him, her eyes never moving from his, her beauty taking his breath. A few seconds later, she took his hand, led him up the narrow stairs into a bedroom filled with moonlight, the sound of the sea below rising through the open windows. They held on to each other as the war receded to a distant memory and they shared joy of a man and a woman together, their lives and bodies intertwined in the peace and comfort known to lovers.

Chapter Thirty

In the sumptuous paneled library of Danesfield House, hunched over one of twelve identical drafting tables, Aubrey Beck peered through stereoscopic glasses set in a frame precisely four and one-quarter inches above the table's surface. At that distance, the aerial photograph, exposed by a twin lens camera, gave the illusion of being three-dimensional.

He pulled back from the glasses, his nerves twitching, and arched his back as he attempted to rub the kinks out of his spine. So far today, he'd studied hundreds of photographs and found nothing. Aubrey rubbed his eyes, reddened from strain. He tried to concentrate but couldn't. The time between relieving his anxiety had rapidly shrunk over the last several days and he needed comfort. With his hands shaking, he pushed back from the table to make his way to the loo and a quick indulgence when a woman's voice called him. "Aubrey, the Major sent me to find you. He wants to see you right now."

He looked at the young WAAF, a somewhat plain woman in her early-twenties, "What does he want?" he said, peeved he was being delayed from his comfort.

"God's truth, I don't know," she said backing away.

"All right." He snapped a little harsher than necessary, smiling at the impact it had on her. "I'm headed to the loo so if you want to join, that's fine by me. If not, I'll be there as soon as I can."

The girl almost trembled, the pitch of her voice higher, "Ok, but come right away, he's really insistent."

A few minutes later, feeling much better and certainly far more at ease, Aubrey approached the major's door. Placing his hand on the knob, he realized how much he despised the pompous fool. In their first meeting the man had been quick to tell him how important he was to the war effort and how he had been knighted for his work developing aerial photography during the Great War, as if Aubrey cared.

"Beck, there you are. I called for you at least ten minutes ago." Major Harvey Wald said, his gut almost bursting out of the belted officer's jacket. "Where the hell have you been? Dilly-dallying around somewhere?"

"No sir. I was involved in something that required finishing," he said, smiling to himself.

Major Wald shook his head, a frown on his face, "Well, so be it. I've been going over your file with Samson here." He pointed towards a thin man with graying hair and dark penetrating eyes leaning against a wall off to the side of his desk. His dark suit and tie looked somewhat rumpled and he had his hands shoved deeply into his pockets. He nodded at Aubrey but made no attempt to pull his hands out of the pockets. "I wonder how the hell you got assigned to me, Beck. You're completely useless as a photographic interpreter; you don't know a bloody thing about it." He rapidly clipped the words.

"In the short time I've been here, I believe I've picked it up quite quickly." Aubrey responded, irked by the arrogance of the man.

"You have?" The major lifted a thick arm off his belly and tossed an enlarged photo across his desk to land in front of Aubrey. "Then perhaps you can look at this and tell me what it is."

Aubrey felt uneasy as the thin man watched him closely. He chose to ignore him and with great care studied the photograph. It was obvious at first sight, but Aubrey waited a beat or two hoping to build tension in the other two men.

He waited a moment too long.

The major bellowed, "Bloody hell, Beck—what is it?"

"They're invasion barges."

"Good, good for you, Beck. That's correct; they are invasion barges—almost four hundred of them. And where are they, Beck?"

"I . . . I don't know, sir."

"See what I mean? You aren't very good. It's Boulogne, Beck. Boulogne, France. Now tell me how much draft each one takes, what's the clearance above of the water, both empty and fully loaded with troops?"

"I have no idea."

"That's our problem. The photographs are not good enough to tell us that, now are they?"

"I guess not, sir." Aubrey really hated him now as sweat began to squeeze out of the pores above his lip.

"Well, Beck, you're going to cure all that." The major said, as he rested intertwined fingers on his round gut.

"I'm going to cure it? I don't understand."

"Obviously you don't—we haven't told you yet. I picked you, because you have some experience with the squadrons and the pilots. Go ahead, Samson."

Aubrey looked at the thin man as he leaned against the wall, his hands still thrust deep into his pockets. "First off, my name's not Samson. But that's what you'll call me for the duration of this exercise. What you're about to hear is covered by the Official Secrets Act and subject to the most severe penalties for any breach. Do you understand, Squadron Commander?"

"I do. I've been through this procedure before."

"Good. You see, the reconnaissance photographs of German preparations are taken from high altitude. From the major's questions, it should be apparent that they don't quite give us enough information. For instance, if we knew the draft of their barges, both empty and full, we could determine invasion sites they would use. If we knew how high the gunnels were above the water, we could calculate the maximum wave height they could sustain and predict the weather required to land their troops." Sampson extracted his hands and folded his arms across his chest.

"These are just two examples of why we need photographs from much, much closer to the ground. We've attempted this twice. Both times our aircraft were shot down, the pilots killed and the film destroyed. The French Resistance can't get close enough to take pictures without being shot. We've also tried that and lost three agents.

"This information is critical to our being able to defend England from invasion and it looks like we don't have much time before that's going to happen. You with me so far?"

"Yes sir, I am. But I don't know how I fit into all this." Aubrey said.

Samson ignored him and continued. "A week ago, a young Luftwaffe pilot was flying a mail route from Cherbourg to Brussels in an old Gotha 145. That's a biplane trainer our Nazi friends use for mail delivery and they use their least trained pilots to fly it.

"On that night, there was a fairly brutal storm over the Channel. The pilot was young, inexperienced and flying in clouds and weather. Running low on petrol, disoriented and lost, he landed in a field, which, much to his surprise wasn't in France but Sussex. He was immediately captured and the Gotha went along with him. While the documents he carried didn't provide much in the way of intelligence, we did procure the aircraft and that's where you come in."

Aubrey twisted his mouth. "I don't understand how this could pertain to me."

Sampson stared at him for a moment, his head cocked to one side as if he was growing impatient.

"A few days ago, I approached the major with an idea of flying the Gotha low over the German debarkation areas as a way to obtain the photographs we desperately need. What we didn't have is someone like you, someone who has direct experience with the squadrons and can assemble the things we need to conduct this mission. We're interested in using you to set up the flight. It will require the utmost discretion and you will have complete authority to obtain anything you need to make it happen. That is, if you agree to take it on."

Immediately Aubrey thought of how much money and drugs he could demand for this intelligence. "Certainly, I'll assist the war effort any way I can," he said cheerfully.

"Good. First, you'll need to find a pilot. Find some way to get him safely from England to France and back again with the film. The Gotha still has the German markings, so I suggest the pilot and photographer be dressed in Luftwaffe uniforms.

"The flight will have to be cleared both ways across the Channel and I would suggest you have an escort ready for their return trip just in case the Nazis catch on and attempt to destroy the aircraft. We'll have a photographer assigned to the mission as soon as you have the flight scheduled. You have three days to accomplish all of it. The mission must take place within that time or it may be too late. Can you do this?"

He almost let his excitement escape but managed a calm, "I can."

The major leaned back in the wood rocker and said, "Good Beck, then you better get moving. You've no time to waste. Check in with me here when you have it all arranged. Samson will meet you at whatever airdrome you choose. After you finish this, Beck, I'm giving you back to that Parliament Member I got you from. Now, get going."

Aubrey was relieved to get away from the major and thought about how this could make him rich. As he spun on his heels, his eyes flashed by Samson. He'd returned his hands deep into his pockets, his expression as blank as the moment Aubrey first saw him.

He gathered his belongings, left the library and walked across the marble floor of what had been the resort's lobby. He smiled as he left the hotel feeling as always providence once again came to his aid.

He started the Jaguar's engine and raced down the road, leaving RAF Medmenham behind. He smiled, took a right onto the highway toward London and a great deal of money and drugs. Many miles later as he pondered how much Wilfred should give him for the secrets, his thoughts jumped to little Bethany. He felt a flash of regret knowing he could never see her again, never enjoy the young, subtle curves of her body.

The thought of Livy and Jamie alone together, her writhing against him, being pleased by a butcher's son, drove him mad. To relieve his anxiety, he'd gone to Bethany and in a drug-filled stupor imagined her as Livy. With his fists clinched, he pummeled her so many times he lost count, rendering her unconscious and bleeding profusely. He remembered howling with laughter as he roared away from the three bruisers chasing him—men who wanted revenge for little Bethany's blood spilled across the sheets of a dingy bedroom.

As the Jaguar barreled toward London, the warm sunshine and the wind rushing through his hair did nothing to stop his rage as it continued to build and seethe against Jamie. The bastard had stolen her away from him and he was not about to have some lower-class clod ruin all his plans.

His mind reeled in circles as he sped along until like a thunder clap, everything fell into place. He knew exactly what he would do. He wouldn't reveal the secret flight. He wouldn't reveal the information to anyone. He would order Jamie to fly the German plane and make sure the pest would never return. In a matter of days, Livy and her wealth would be his to take. He put his head back and laughed, shocked at how his voice cackled, how insane it sounded.

Chapter Thirty-One

Perfectly centered at the top of a gentle rolling hill, Livy's home looked out over manicured lawns and old growth forests that stretched across the countryside. It was his first sight of Kensington Manor and the view blanked out Jamie's thoughts.

"You look a little out of sorts." Livy said as if she could feel his comfort fading.

He realized he had slowed the car to a crawl. "It's, well, like something you see in a picture book." He pulled at the collar of his shirt and gave the MG a little petrol.

"This Manor has been in my family a long time. It was awarded by proclamation to one of my ancestors who helped capture and behead Charles I in 1649. What you see is the third home constructed on the property. The second one burned to the ground ten years before I was born and this is what replaced it."

The mansion was constructed from expensive Red Wales brick, with four sections of six towering French windows, black shutters on either side defining the white frames. In the center was a semi-circular marble entry porch, its carved Ionic columns supported an ornate polished brass balustrade surrounding a king's walk. Above the first story, on either side of the walk were two large oval windows, the frames surrounded by delicately carved stone that resembled soft draping from a Renoir painting. Dark-green ivy covered most of the first-story and on the curved lintels over each of the twenty-four windows, a white sculpted coat of arms complete with a gargoyle above that looked down at anyone daring to enter the home.

Jamie stopped the car and the tiny river stones of the drive ceased their whispers. "It's magnificent, stunning and at the same time more than intimidating." He rubbed his mouth. "And only you and your father live here? Doesn't that sometimes feel empty?"

"It's only the two of us that live here, plus Harold and Jackie, the butler and cook who have been with us since before my birth. Of course, there are domestic staff, as well as grounds keepers and maintenance workers, but they come and go, they don't live on the property.

"As to feeling empty, yes it can. There are many times it can feel very lonely, especially if I'm here by myself at night. But with all that said, I love it. It's my home. It's a part of me, a part of who I am." She smiled at him and said, "Come on, let me show it to you."

Jamie pulled her suitcase out of the boot and followed her up the stone stairs through the columns supporting the king's walk. He looked down, careful to step around the polished silver, black, and red family crest, three keys resting on a shield below a knight's helm. In shining bronze, Ashford was emblazoned on a scroll at the bottom of the shield, perfectly inlaid into the white marble.

As Livy reached out to open the door, it pulled away from her and standing in the foyer, his hand resting on the shining brass handle, stood the naval captain Jamie met at the party, her father.

He looked comfortable in dark-blue slacks, a formal white shirt with suspenders and an undone bowtie that ran under his open collar.

"Ah, there you are, Harold told me you were coming up the drive." He smiled at Livy as she entwined an arm around him.

"Father, this is Jamie Wallace. You met him at Paul White's party."

"I remember you."

Jamie stepped across the threshold. Her father closed the door and with his arm around Livy, he started across the white marble floor without shaking his hand or saying another word to him.

Soaring French windows lined the far wall. Through the glass, Jamie looked out on a stone porch lined with red geraniums and an expanse of lawn sloping gently into a lake that dwarfed the one at Newent. He felt small and completely out of place.

"So, how was the trip?" Lord Ashford said, his back receding as Jamie followed. He resented the way he said the word trip. It sounded to Jamie as if Ashford had directed the question to him, likening him to some sort of scoundrel.

"We had a wonderful time," Livy said. "I can't wait to tell you all about it." She stopped on the marble floor. "But more about that later—

you two go ahead. I'll catch up in a second. I need to freshen up a bit." She broadly smiled as she brushed by Jamie and ran up the stairs with a lightness in her step. Jamie felt quite alone as he stood in the huge room, awed by the surroundings and the man in front of him.

Lord Ashford's eyes narrowed and focused on him. "I'm still plying through papers Winston sent over this morning, come with me Mr. Wallace."

He turned his back on him, headed off to the right and opened a walnut door that led to his study.

As Jamie entered the room, Ashford went around his desk and looked directly at him. "Have a seat, young man." He said pointing to one of two leather armchairs.

"Thank you, sir."

Ashford sat, the back of his shirt bunched up around the suspenders. "Livy has mentioned you several times, looks like we're finally going to have a chat, get to know each other."

Jamie paused a moment, sensing something underneath the polite words that told him this chat was going to be difficult. "I'd like that. I remember meeting you at the party."

"You're from Newent, isn't that correct?"

"Yes sir."

"And your father has a little shop there—Wallace's Butcher Shop, I believe."

Taken aback, Jamie simply nodded, the direction of the conversation surprising him.

"Well first, let me congratulate you on your DFC."

"Distinguished Flying Cross? I don't understand."

"Oh, they must not have told you yet. Well, you've been awarded the decoration for getting your damaged Spitfire back, rather excellent flying Mr. Wallace. But I would ask that you at least feign some surprise when they do to tell you. It seems I've spoken out of turn."

"That's quite all right, sir. I am surprised, I knew nothing about it."

"Well, now you do. You have a fine record, Jamie—nine kills—and of course your extraordinary flying. I also understand you were shot down when your engine stalled."

This was far more information than the man should have known. Jamie was out of his league, wondering what else would be coming. "Yes sir. I lost a good friend because of it."

"Yes, Miles Stafford."

Jamie's eyes widened. "He was killed because I couldn't cover him, couldn't protect him."

"It wasn't your fault. An error was found in the manufacture of the fuel pumps. It appears there was a nick in a tiny rubber gasket that caused many of the newest Spits to fail, just as yours did. That error caused the deaths of three young men, your friend being one of them."

"I didn't know that."

Ashford paused for a long moment staring at him. "But that's not really what I want to speak about." He leaned forward, crossing his arms on the desktop. "I'm very glad your brother Michael made it home from Dunkirk. So many didn't, you know. I take it his recovery is going well?"

"Yes sir, it is." Jamie felt a spark of anger rise. "May I ask a question?"

"Of course." Ashford's eyes didn't move from his.

"You seem to have a wealth of information about myself and my family. How did you come by that, sir?"

"Well, a man in my position can't be too careful when his only daughter is involved. And, the cottage—did you enjoy that too?" Ashford stared into Jamie's now unwavering eyes.

He thought of the two man in suits without luggage and realized the man had them followed. "You know, Lord Ashford, we did. We had a wonderful time. I'll never forget it."

Ashford paused a moment, a red flush rising in his face. His voice became tense, each word carefully crafted. "As I said, Livy is my only daughter and someday, hopefully in the distant future, all this will be hers. The manor, the family estate, our holdings and over four hundred years of history will belong to her and be her responsibility. She'll need to do what is expected of an Ashford and that isn't always what she might want at the moment.

"While I'm not impugning your motives, a man of your somewhat modest means chasing after my only daughter will bring about suspicions. I'm sure you can understand that."

"You see Lord Ashford, I don't. Are you attempting to say that my interest in Livy is for some financial gain? Or that I even thought about it? If that's what you believe you're wrong, very wrong. I love your daughter and I don't give a damn about your money."

"Well, that's refreshing! You may not care about my money, but what happens in the future to my daughter is something I care a great deal about. What could you possibly give to her? I think this is a question you need to ask yourself because I will protect the sanctity of this family, our position and who we are. I assure you of that." He paused, continuing to stare at him. "I think it best that you not see her again, ever."

Jamie's fists clenched as he spat out the words. "I think that will be her choice and not yours."

"That's where you're wrong, Jamie Wallace. It is my decision. Yours is not one of love. Yours is some wartime romance built on passion and destined for failure. Livy doesn't have the vaguest idea of what a true love is."

He sat forward and gripped the arms of the chair. "You don't even know your own daughter. You have no idea of who she is or what she might want. To you, she's someone else, someone you've made up in your own mind. And whoever that is, it isn't Livy."

"How dare you speak to me like that?" He almost came out of the chair. "What could you possibly know? It's time you left my home and you are not to see her again—do you understand that?"

Jamie got up, knocking the chair backward. "I'll gladly go, but you'll not tell me I can't see her. That too will be her decision."

He stormed out of the study, followed by Ashford. When he arrived at the front door, he flung it open and strode to his car. As he slipped behind the wheel, Ashford shouted after him, "I promise you,

Jamie Wallace, if you see her again, I'll have you posted in the most godforsaken place I can find on this planet."

Jamie glared at him, knowing the threat was real. He started the MG and sped off down the drive, thinking of how this was going to break Livy's heart.

Ashford slammed the door as Livy reached the bottom of the stairs. "What was that?" Livy said, fearing the worst. "Why were you yelling and where is Jamie?"

"He's gone, permanently."

"Left without saying good-bye?" Livy opened the door and saw his little green car speeding down the drive.

"I don't want you seeing him anymore. In fact, I forbid it."

Livy stared at him a second, her mouth open, tears welling in her eyes. With fury in her voice she said, "What have you done? What the hell have you done?"

Chapter Thirty-Two

Armed guards stood in front of a black-and-white-striped gate barring all entry as Alana, dressed in the WAAF uniform Wilfred demanded she wear, sat motionless behind the wheel. In the mirror, she watched him make a show of disinterest from the rear seat while they awaited clearance to enter the clandestine facility. Northeast of London, far down a narrow honeysuckle-fringed lane, the campus looked more like an abandoned factory than a first-class electronic laboratory.

Alana scanned the several single-story flat-roofed buildings, gray government paint peeling away from the concrete blocks in many sections. All the windows had been blotted out with the sticky black sludge the government approved for blocking out light. Above the series of identical structures on long, thick wooden poles stretched camouflage netting specifically designed to make identification from the air almost impossible. It dappled the buildings and connecting pathways in shade.

Alana's eyes settled on a young and quite attractive sergeant who had now been on the phone for far too long. She drummed the fingers of her left hand on the steering wheel as her right closed around a .380 Beretta stowed in the map pouch attached to the door.

"Don't even think about it," Wilfred said, sensing where her hand had gone. "You're far too impetuous."

She didn't turn around or look at him in the rear seat. She shifted her eyes away from the sergeant toward the other guards by the gate, her hand never leaving the cold metal. "And what do you suggest if they try to arrest us?"

"We'll let them. Though, they'd be fools to do so. Arrest a Member of Parliament? And what would be the charge?" She watched her father in the rear-view mirror as he picked at a nonexistent fleck of dirt beneath a polished nail. "I don't think that would happen. There's no need for gunplay, I'll let you know if that becomes necessary. Now sit back and relax; smile at that fool of a sergeant. Use your guile—you certainly know how to do that." He laughed as if he had said something witty.

The sergeant finally placed the phone in its cradle and came out of the striped guardhouse toward Alana, holding their blue identity cards out, ready to give them over. She relaxed her hand as he approached and smiled flirtatiously.

"You're all cleared, Miss. Sorry for any inconvenience." The guard said smiling back at her.

Amused at his look of desire, Alana said, "No problem, Sergeant. You're just doing your job, I'm sure."

"It's the third building on the left—Room 104." The sergeant said as the gate pole lifted and the other armed guards moved aside. She put the sedan in gear and drove down the narrow sun dappled road to their meeting with Sir Phillip Joubert.

A short distance away, a middle-aged man in a white lab coat came out from the third building and held open the door. She stopped the car, got out and walked around to the left side to open the rear door for her father. As they walked toward the man in the lab coat, her father extended his hand, an effervescent smile on his face.

"Sir Phillip, a pleasure to meet you. I'm Member Wilfred Eaton."

"I'm sorry, sir." The man responded, replacing a ballpoint pen into a pocket that had several vertical blue lines above it from the many times he'd forgotten to retract the point. "I'm not Dr. Joubert; I'm one of his assistants. He sent me to collect you. My name is Stokes, Graeham Stokes."

Her father took the man's hand and shook it like a politician. "Not to worry, Graeham. Shall we get on with it?"

"Certainly, Member Eaton, please follow me."

He motioned them through the self-locking door, holding it open as they entered. Alana remained silent but politely smiled and nodded, making sure he felt the kinship—one struggling worker to another. She passed by him, thinking he'd be no problem and focused on a large, very fit, armed military policeman. He stiffly stood next to a table a few feet into the building, his eyes cold and staring back at her. On his side, a .38 service revolver rested in a holster specifically designed for a quick draw.

"Identity cards." The guard said in a monotone that meant business.

They held out their blue paper cards, both a little dog-eared at the edges. The guard checked them against his handwritten list.

He held on to the cards and said, "You have fifteen minutes. You are to return to me or I will come get you both and remove you. Do you understand?"

Alana stared at the powerfully built man, appreciating how dangerous he could be. Like a long-lost friend Wilfred said, "Most certainly, young man. We have no intention of causing trouble. We'll be back in plenty of time."

The man nodded and motioned for them to proceed into the building. He dropped their identity cards on his table. Alana reached out to pick up the blue cards but as she touched them, he pressed his hand down on top of hers.

"You'll have them back when you return. Now, you can move on or leave."

Seeing red but remaining calm, Alana smiled and removed her hand from beneath his. This man was someone she would keep at a distance if killing him became necessary.

She forced a smile and said, "I'm sorry, I didn't know."

"You have fifteen minutes." He said in the same monotone, his dark eyes staring without blinking.

She followed behind Wilfred and Graeham down the corridor toward the end of the building. With each step, she became more confident they were finally on the right track. The government wouldn't post such an experienced soldier to a desk checking identification cards unless the work going on was extremely vital. She was convinced that inside this laboratory they would find answers, answers that would launch the invasion and bring a new British Empire into the world—one that would rule under a new German paradigm. She smiled, thinking of herself as a liberator, someone worthy of serving the Führer and his new world order.

"Here we are, sir. If you'll follow me, please." Graeham said, opening a scratched wood-paneled door. He stepped aside, allowing them to enter and shut the door, closing off everything of the outside world behind them.

The lab was large and artificially lit, all the windows blacked out, the walls painted asparagus government green. There were several long tables covered with electronic equipment. Alana noted numerous oscilloscopes attached to thin wire-wrapped poles jutting up from the table that continued through the plaster ceiling.

Mathematical calculations were scribbled erratically on various chalkboards haphazardly strewn about, and none of it meant a thing to her. Swarms of silent men in white coats were busy at work, some staring at the flashing scopes, while others carted equipment or stood at the boards writing mathematic symbols in what looked like hieroglyphs. She felt as if she had escaped the real world and entered into a fantasy filled with mad, devious scientists invested in constructing some sort of death ray.

Graeham escorted them toward an area in a corner of the room with large frosted glass windows. As they entered, a distinguished-looking man with a full head of thick gray hair turned around and was introduced as Sir Phillip Joubert, the man responsible for creating the system currently foiling the Luftwaffe. He wore a well-fitting vested suit that had traces of chalk dust on it that surely also landed on his white shirt. His brown leather shoes made a slapping sound against the terrazzo floor as he came to greet them.

Joubert extended his hand to Wilfred and said with a smile, "Member Eaton, welcome to our dungeon."

"Thank you, Sir Philip. It's a pleasure to meet you and again, I thank you for offering your assistance." Her father gestured toward her, "May I introduce my daughter, Alana. Happily, I was able to requisition her as my driver from the WAAF Assignment Board."

She took a second to study Sir Philip. There was something about the man and his pale blue eyes sunken below unruly gray eyebrows that gave off the air of an immense intelligence, an intelligence that had been overworked and suffered from exhaustion. He shook Alana's hand with a firmness that surprised her.

"A pleasure to meet you, welcome." Sir Philip looked back at her father. "I don't mean to be rude, but our time is limited so I'll dispense with any small talk. Randall briefed me on your issue with the Navy and I am in complete agreement with your premise. If funding isn't delivered to this Department or is reduced, it may result in the Navy not needing any of the ships they're demanding. Quite simply, the German invasion will succeed and we'll have lost the war. So, how may I help you?"

"Is there another place where could speak in private?" her father asked.

"Private? There is no privacy here, Member Eaton. No one is ever allowed to be alone in here at any time. We always operate in at least pairs, if not more, the nature of our work demands it."

"Oh, I see." Wilfred said stroking his chin, which she knew would call for a quick rework of his plan for Sir Philip Joubert.

"However, I can assure you the gentlemen in this room are capable of the highest discretion and whatever we discuss will go no further."

"I understand, Sir Philip," Wilfred said nodding his head.

"Please go on—our time is very short."

"The work you're doing here is possibly the most important for our entire war effort." The flattery method, Alana reasoned as Sir Philip nodded and Wilfred continued. "To battle the arguments with the admirals that desire to decrease your funding, I need to have a better understanding of how the system you created works. I need more details to effectively combat their assault on your efforts."

Alana translated in her head, I am your friend, they are your enemy.

"What is it you want to know?"

"Mostly, how this radar system works. I want to be able to understand it and counter their arguments against its value."

"Well first, it's called RDF, Radio Direction Finding, not radar, only civilians call it radar. Powerful VHF—very high frequency—beams are sent out and bounced off incoming aircraft. We read the return signal and measure the time difference from sending and receiving. That is how we measure the distance to the aircraft. How we measure the altitude is an entirely different matter and that's classified."

"I see. You can actually know the distance and altitude from this RDF?"

"Most certainly."

"My goodness, very effective, I would assume. What happens from there?" Wilfred asked pretending astonishment. "How is all this information delivered to our aircraft?" His tone was almost reverent.

"You see, take an incoming raid and the information we gather about it. That information, numbers, altitude and direction of travel is sent to Bentley Priory, our central collection facility. From there it goes to each group's headquarters and sent down to sector commands and finally to the squadrons and the individual aircraft. The entire system is actually very simple and at the same time very complex, but most importantly it's fast, very fast. It takes mere seconds to update and distribute the information to our fighters intercepting the raid."

"How do you disseminate the information? That seems like quite a task. By radio, I assume?" her father said, knowing full well it wasn't.

"Oh, my goodness no. That wouldn't work at all. Far too much information to rely on radio and not fast enough. Except for the aircraft in flight, it's all done over phone lines which are far better and certainly more secure."

"Really! I'm surprised. I would have thought wires strung between telephone poles could be easily destroyed and shut your system down without much effort."

"Oh, it would if that was how it was done, but it's not. The phone lines are separate from the civilian ones and quite safe from attack." Sir Philip looked at his watch and frowned. "The pathway I assume goes through one or more hubs, distributed from there to Bentley Priory and back through those hubs to the groups and sectors. But, I really don't know how that's done."

"You don't? I thought you built it."

"I built the conceptual and technical aspects of the RDF, not the system. I'm surprised you're asking about this. Didn't you speak with Randall? He's the one that designed the system. He knows all of it, the rest of us only know pieces. He wanted it done that way for the obvious security it would provide. Outside of Randall and Churchill, there may not be another human in all of England that has seen or understands the entire network. You'll need to speak with him for information on the communications system. He may not choose to tell you but he knows all of it. He authored the actual plan."

"Wonderful, I'll ask him about it. As you know, he is very keen on helping me to acquire all the monies I can for you and your work here. One of the Navy's objections is paying for a large upgrade to all the communications, something I feel is necessary. No, let me say vital."

"Oh, I agree with you. The communications between my RDF and the aircraft is at the core of the entire thing. Without that, we have nothing. But as I said, you should ask Randall. He knows all the details."

"Thank you, I'll soon speak with him. I'm sure he'll be willing to help." Wilfred smiled at Sir Philip and extended his hand. "Thank you very much for all your assistance."

"Well if that's all, our time is almost up and I do need to get back to work. Graeham here will escort you out. I'm sorry I wasn't more help, but perhaps our meeting was of some value."

"Oh, Sir Philip, you've been quite helpful, more than you could possibly know." Wilfred said with a broad smile on his face.

Chapter Thirty-Three

Jamie left the flight surgeon at RAF Hornchurch, pleased the stitches were out and surprised to be back on flight status even if only for limited duty. He was restricted to low altitude and training aircraft for at least another week, for now a Spitfire would have to wait. He wouldn't see combat—for that he was thankful—but at least he would be flying and that helped to assuage the anger he felt toward Randall Ashford. It stuck in his gut and smoldered like a glowing coal. Overnight he had tossed and turned in his bunk, getting almost no sleep, hearing Ashford's voice utter those despicable words. He didn't give a damn about what Ashford thought of his character. He knew who he was and he was nothing like Ashford's assessment, especially where Livy was concerned.

What really stoked his rage was thinking how Ashford must be treating her, what he might be putting her through. The man obviously had no concept of the extraordinary woman his daughter was. As soon as he got away from meeting with Wing Commander Findley, he would call Livy and make sure all was well.

Outside the medical building, a light rain had begun to fall through a dark-gray overcast. He pulled the sheepskin collar of his flight jacket up around the back of his neck and set off in the direction of the flight line and Hangar 5. Walking against a stiffening breeze, he kept wondering about the meeting, why he had been ordered to attend and of all things why it was in a repair hangar and not Findley's office. Reporting to a wing commander, the highest-ranking officer on the base, in a dark hangar? That was definitely not standard procedure and if anything, the RAF was all about procedure. Something odd was afoot.

He tucked his chin down into his coat against the wet wind, counting his steps to keep his mind off Livy and her father. From the corner of his eye the long red snout of a Jaguar pulled up next to him and the horn beeped twice. From inside the car a hand waved, coaxing him over to the passenger window.

"Jamie, get in—we're late." It was a voice he knew well—Aubrey Beck's.

Jamie opened the door and leaned in, the rain coming down a little heavier now. "I've been trying to find you for the last ten minutes," Aubrey said.

"Find me? I don't understand."

"I'm the reason you're here," he said. "Get in."

Pelted with raindrops, Jamie slid into Jaguar's leather seat. "New car, Aubrey?"

"Yes. I couldn't find an Aston Martin to replace mine, so I picked this one up. She's great, isn't she? Twelve cylinders under the bonnet and fast—she'll do well over one hundred."

Jamie sat silently, looked at the car and wondered how Aubrey could afford it. After a moment he said, "How are you the reason I'm here? I was told a week ago to report to the Flight Surgeon when I returned."

"True. But you didn't know about reporting to Findley in Hangar 5, now did you?"

"Well, no, that is a bit of a surprise." Jamie said sensing something disagreeable was about to happen. "What do you have to do with that?"

"I picked you for a mission, Jamie. A very special mission, one only you can do. One that can change the way things are."

"What mission?" An uncomfortable feeling rose in him.

"I'll brief you in the hangar. Everyone else is there waiting on us. By the way, how was your trip? Did you and Livy enjoy it?"

"It was great. We had a smashing time." he said, wondering why he would ask.

"You went to see your family and caught a train back? Doesn't seem to me like that would be smashing."

"Well, it was and we took a little detour on the way back."

"Oh, where'd you go?"

"We stopped by her family's cottage near Cliff's End. Spent some time there, just the two of us." Jamie said, noticing Aubrey grip on the steering wheel.

"That sounds like a fine time. Did you stay there, overnight?"

"Aubrey, what are you asking about? It's none of your business what we did," Jamie said, annoyed with his questions. "Have you some kind of interest in Livy?"

"Oh no, nothing like that, consider me your friend, Jamie. I'm simply attempting conversation before you're told about the mission. I'm concerned for your safety, though I know this mission is nothing you can't resolve. I'm sure of that."

The red Jaguar sped down the slick tarmac faster than necessary, dodging tractors and people pulling aircraft in and out of the open hangars. On reaching the fifth of six cavernous white buildings, Aubrey parked the car along a corrugated steel side. As he got out, Jamie noticed that Hangar 5 was the only one closed, its massive doors buttoned up tight in the gray rain. Aubrey left the Jaguar without a further word and Jamie followed as Aubrey banged on the metal entry door.

It opened and they went in to an alcove filled with harsh artificial light. They were greeted by two armed guards, both no doubt happy to be in from the rain. The guards checked their identification, motioned for them to enter a briefing room and closed the alcove door.

The rectangular room had several long tables set in rows before a large map of southern England and the northern part of France and Belgium. Next to Wing Commander Findley, a thin man with his hands in his pockets and a tall civilian stood motionless in front of the map.

Jamie saluted the commander.

"Welcome back, Jamie," Findley said.

"Thank you, sir."

"I'm here for only a moment, to get you started and to give you something well deserved. I wish I could do this more appropriately—with a ceremony or something—but time won't allow it. Locke put you up for the DFC. I approved it and the Air Ministry agreed. Congratulations."

My God, he thought. Ashford knew all about this. He feigned surprise at Findley's words. "Thank you, sir. But, I'm not sure I deserve it."

"Well, I think you do, that's why I recommended you, one hell of a piece of flying getting that damaged Spit back. I've got the decoration in my office. Come see me when you're finished with whatever Aubrey wants and I'll try to do a better job of presenting it to you." He winked and shook his hand. "Okay, Beck, he's all yours. See you when you come back, lad."

Come back? From where?

Findley strode off, leaving only the four in the briefing room protected by the two guards outside in the alcove. The thin man pulled a pale hand from his pocket and motioned for Jamie to sit at the first of the long tables, a stack of maps and papers before him.

"My name is Samson—that's what you'll call me," he said in clipped speech. "Aubrey has selected you for this mission and I'm here to brief you. This mission is of critical importance to our entire war effort. I know this all is a bit of a shock but I must inform you by hearing this you'll be bound by the Official Secrets Act now and for the foreseeable future. Do you understand?"

Jamie nodded.

"I need an answer, not a nod, boy." Samson said, the man's dark brooding eyes staring at him.

"I understand."

"Good. This mission is code-named Glass Rim. Now, take a moment to look at the photographs in front of you."

Jamie leafed through several aerial images of what he thought was Boulogne, Calais and, of all places Dunkirk. They showed invasion barges stuffed into the canals by the hundreds, lined up against the quays and jamming the waterways. Full armies, thousands of men and matériel, all bivouacked in the nearby fields awaiting the order to invade England. The photos chilled his blood. He looked back at Samson.

"Where do you believe those photos were taken?"

"Northern France. Boulogne, Calais, and Dunkirk."

Samson smiled. "Excellent." he said. "To put it simply, son, we need better pictures—much better if we are going to stop the invasion." He pointed to the tall civilian. "Your job will be to get Harrison here over to France and back. It's that simple."

Jamie sat silent, he'd flown over France too many times.

"Harrison is our best reconnaissance photographer. He'll handle the camera and tell you where to go and all that. All you have to do is fly the airplane, low, very low. Just don't ask questions, clear?"

Jamie shrugged and nodded again.

"That'll do. Beck, tell him what you've planned."

"A few weeks ago," Aubrey said with a smile, "a Luftwaffe mail plane with all the proper Nazi markings was forced down and captured. Yesterday, the aircraft was dissembled and carted up here on lorries. Last night it was reassembled for this mission. It's a Gotha 145 biplane and you'll be flying that. That's why the hangar doors are closed—it's in there right now."

"A Gotha 145? I haven't the foggiest what that is." Jamie said. His irritation with Aubrey present in his tone.

"For a Spitfire pilot, flying a trainer, even one you haven't seen before shouldn't be a problem." Aubrey snapped back as if he were peeved about something.

Jamie leaned forward and almost said something to annoy him but decided against it.

Aubrey continued on. "We installed an offset camera into the front cockpit with a cutout in the belly for the lenses to look through. You'll fly from the rear cockpit and handle the radio. Once you're over there, Harrison will tell you where to fly. You'll need to be at two hundred and fifty feet, not more or less for the cameras to properly record what we need. That altitude is critical." Jamie looked at him with as blank an expression as he could form.

"That close to the ground, you'll be clearly seen by the Germans and that's why we'll have you dressed in Luftwaffe uniforms. If you weren't, they'd know something was wrong. The bad news is that if you are forced down or have a mechanical failure, you'll probably be shot on sight as spies."

"Well, that's comforting," Jamie quipped.

Aubrey picked up an instructor's pointer with a rubber tip and traced it over the map. "You'll leave tomorrow morning at 0500 and fly south until you pass Boulogne. You'll come inland from there. Harrison will direct you over the harbor and the areas we need photographed."

Again, the pointer traced the map.

"From there you will fly toward Calais, skirting the Luftwaffe base at Wissant. Be careful there—it's filled with ME 109s." He smiled as if he were giving him confidential information.

Jamie's irritation with him increased, Wissant was a place he knew all too well.

Aubrey waved his hand as if on parade. "If the Germans notice you or take an interest, make sure you wave."

Jamie gave him another blank stare. "The next area to photograph will be Calais. You will then proceed to Dunkirk and complete the photographic portion of the mission. From there, you'll head on into Belgium direct toward Antwerp, exactly the same course the real mail plane would fly. Clear so far?"

"That part I understand. What I don't is, how do I keep from being shot down by our own boys?" He rested his elbow on the table, his chin in his hand.

Aubrey smiled and said, "I've got that covered. I'll address your question in a minute. When you reach De Panne, just over the French border, you'll drop to wave height and make a beeline back to RAF Manston where we'll collect the film and you'll be done."

"This airplane is a sitting duck for a Spit." Jamie said in a tone as sharp as he could, "How do I survive this, Aubrey?"

As if he were placating a child, Aubrey said, "Like I said, I have you covered—here's how that will work. You're cleared through our airspace with Fighter Command in Group 11's Sectors C and D, which will cover your egress and ingress. They will be alerted and know you'll be flying through the sectors tomorrow morning. Nothing can go wrong if you fly it correctly."

Aubrey dropped his hands onto the front table, deep concern on his face. "Jamie, this part is very important for your safety. I've set up the following signals for you to transmit during the flight. When you are off the French shore transmit 623. No need for codes—the three numbers will be transmitted in the clear. Upon crossing the beach and over land as you make your run-on Boulogne, transmit 717 and when you leave Dunkirk use 884. When you are ready to cross the Channel at De Panne, transmit 175.

When we receive your code of 884, we'll have a flight of Spitfires nearby to meet you and fly cover. They'll take station to protect you after you transmit 175. That will insure your safety. Any questions?"

He shook his head. "Got it—623, 717, 884 and 175."

"Okay," Samson said taking his hands out of his pockets. "You and Harrison get acquainted. Beck, anything else?"

"No sir, I think that's about it."

Samson smiled at Jamie. "You better learn how to fly it while it's on the ground son, you won't get another chance. Your first and only flight will be tomorrow morning."

Jamie stood and Harrison joined him. Together they left the briefing room and entered the damp hangar. Alone, tucked into a corner like a criminal family member, a blue-gray biplane, complete with German crosses and a black swastika on its tail awaited its newest pilot.

After a few minutes exploring the aircraft, he felt comfortable with it and with Harrison—if that was really his name. The man had a sturdy competence about him. He explained about the cameras and why the altitude was critical to the imagery. In clear and concise detail, the man told him exactly what he needed to make the mission a success and never asked anything about Jamie or flying.

"I can fly this thing," Jamie said. "The instruments are in German and located in different places, but they're the same." He laughed, some of the tension relieved, "I even know enough German I can start the engine. I'll get you there and most importantly, get you back. No problem." He smiled at Harrison.

"You know what?"

"What?"

"I think you will." Harrison smiled for the first time and they shook hands.

A door slammed as if from a wayward wind and both of them flinched. Looking toward the source of the noise, Jamie saw Samson walking toward them along with an overweight pink-faced Army major who carried two light-brown flight suits, Aubrey followed behind.

As they approached Sampson said, "Gentlemen, there's a change in plans. This is Major Wald, commander of our photographic intelligence unit."

"This mission needs to go. Needs to go now, not tomorrow morning," the heavy-set major said, panting as if he'd run some distance. "We've received intelligence from the Resistance that the Nazis are moving their troops in droves toward the invasion barges. It looks like this is it, boys. We think the invasion is on and it will start in a matter of days, or hours." He tossed the flight suits, one to Jamie and the other to Harrison.

"Now? Right now?" Jamie said as Harrison stepped into his flight suit.

"It appears so," Samson said.

"I can't go now. I have a phone call I must make, a very important one," the frustration mounted in Jamie's heart. He must speak with her, make sure she was all right.

"I'm sorry, son. Your call will have to wait until your return," the major said. "It's only a few hours and you'll be back."

Aubrey came around from behind them and said, "I'll make the call for you, Jamie. What do you need? I'd be happy to help, if that's all right with you, Major."

"Not exactly protocol but I'll agree. Son, you tell him what you need, then get dressed and get going. You only have six hours or so of daylight left. You need to go and go now."

Jamie took Aubrey aside. "Call Livy—Stonebridge 2352—and tell her I love her and not to worry a thing about her father or anything else. Make sure you do it right away. Promise me."

"Of course, I'll do it as soon as you take off. I promise." Aubrey smiled at him.

Less than three minutes later, the cavernous hangar opened and the biplane taxied out. Standing by the open door, Sampson, the Major and Aubrey Beck watched the aircraft taxi across the wet field on its way toward France and the Germans.

"Beck, you'll need to make the calls to clear him right now." The major said.

Aubrey held his irritation with the Major in check. "Yes sir, first, I must get to a secure phone."

"Well, hop to it, man. Those boys' lives are in your hands."

"Yes sir."

Like an albatross, the Gotha gathered speed, left the ground and climbed away into a thick overcast sky much to the surprise of all those at RAF Hornchurch who stared at a German aircraft as it disappeared into a thick gray sky.

Chapter Thirty-Four

Aubrey gnashed his teeth as he ran from the hangar, hunched over against the rain. He slammed the door of his Jaguar and thought about how much he loathed the major and how much needed a quick moment with his drug.

A smile ran across his face as he started the engine. This wasn't quite the way he planned it, but, Jamie's demise would be a little sooner—that's all. No problem, in fact, almost perfect. He only had to make sure he made it to France and all would be well. Excited, he reached down beneath the passenger seat, pulled out his box. Seeing no one nearby, he inhaled a good portion of his drug and shivered.

Gray rain continued to fall as he parked the car outside headquarters and entered an office the young WAAF secretary directed him to. He snatched a black phone off the empty desk. With the receiver tucked tightly between his ear and shoulder, he blew on his hands to ward off the chill and waited.

A bright female voice came on the line. "Base Operator, how may I assist you."

"Uxbridge, Operations Section. Emergency priority. Secure line requested." Aubrey said, almost bursting with joy.

"One moment."

A slight pause followed by a crackle as the scrambler connected and then a bland male voice came on the phone. "Uxbridge Operations, secure line. Lieutenant Williams speaking."

"Lieutenant, Squadron Commander Beck here. Glass Rim has commenced. Clear airspace Sectors C and D." He said into the receiver.

"Operation Glass Rim underway. Departure time?"

"Less than five minutes ago, emergency priority."

"Roger that. Operation Glass Rim, clearance notifications out to Sectors C and D."

The line went dead and Aubrey knew the path to France would be clear. Uxbridge would inform the radar operators and observer corps they were underway and to expect Jamie's Gotha passing low overhead in the next few minutes. He thought about Livy and smiled. He had no intention of calling her. The second part of his plan was more important and it was not time to call her, not yet.

Half an hour later, about the time Jamie should be approaching the Channel, Aubrey brought the rumbling Jaguar to a stop and ran into the ready shack of 41 Squadron looking for Eric Locke.

"Where's Locke?" he demanded from a young airman sitting at the desk.

"Sir, uh . . . I believe he's in the base pub. I mean, with the weather and all, 41 is down for the day. May I call him for you?" The young boy said, nervously staring at Aubrey's uniform and rank.

"No, that's fine. Where's the pub? Direct me to it. Now!" Aubrey said the last word with emphasis to scare the boy.

"Five buildings down on the right, sir."

"As you were. I'll find him." He ran out.

Ten seconds later Aubrey popped back into the room and saw the young airman on the phone. He barked a sharp order, "Hang up that phone. If I wanted him warned I was here, I would have had you call him. Ring off and don't pick it up again."

He ran out of the shack in search of Eric Locke thinking it was too early for them to be drinking. That was all he needed to ruin everything. Aubrey jumped into the Jaguar fearful his entire plan would end in disaster. Less than minute behind the wheel, he arrived at the base pub and opened the door. He stood much like he had at Thirsty Bear, surveying the faces, searching for the one he wanted.

Long seconds later, he spotted him at a table in the far corner next to an old upright piano. As he moved closer, relief washed over him, they were drinking tea. Aubrey scooted through the crowd of flyers savoring their day away from combat and rushed over to Locke, who looked startled seeing him.

"Well, hello there, Squadron Commander. What brings you to our little piece of the world?" Locke said as he took a sip of hot tea, while the other members of Red Flight stared at Aubrey.

"Excuse me, gentlemen. Eric, I need to speak with you, right now. It's urgent."

Locke looked at him and furrowed his brow. "What could be so urgent on a day like this?"

"Come with me." Aubrey led him to a door next to the piano. He opened it and they entered a storeroom.

Locke stood in the room and said, "By the way, have you seen Jamie?"

"No," was all Aubrey said as he flicked on the bare lightbulb and closed the door. "I've got a critical mission and I need your flight to accomplish it, today."

"Today? We've been on duty for the last six days. We need a rest."

"You fly this mission and I'll promise you at least a full week from any duty."

"A full week, eh?" Locke paused a moment; his tongue ran over his teeth. "Well, okay. Let's hear it."

"We've received intelligence that a mail carrier, a Gotha 145 biplane is carrying documents obtained from the resistance. I can't speak about them, but if those documents are allowed to get to Berlin, it could be catastrophic. I need you to destroy that aircraft. I know exactly where it will be and when."

Locke scratched his head and skeptically looked back at Aubrey. "Have you cleared this with Finley?"

"No, this is a Most Secret mission. I have the authority to call for it and he knows that. He'll never hear about it and you and your flight will never speak of it again—to anyone. Official Secrets Act. Is that clear?"

"Are you ordering me to do this?"

"Not yet, but I will if I have to. I was hoping you would want to undertake this one. It's important Eric, very important. It could stop the Germans from invading—or cause the invasion, the mission is that critical."

Eric Locke looked at the floor and sighed. Aubrey knew he had him. "All right, we'll do it. Tell me about it."

Ten minutes later Aubrey and Locke walked out of the storeroom. As they approached the table where the members of Red Flight were passively sipping tea, Squadron Commander Eric Locke said, "Lads, we have a little job to do."

At Shoe Lane, a warm sun was beginning to peek through the gray overcast. Alana's father followed her down the single step into the abandoned factory and shut the door behind them. They came through the blackout curtain and Alana saw the Irishman at the table in the center of the factory soldering parts into one of the newly constructed radio beacons.

Hearing their footsteps, the Doctor, in a shadowed recess near the curtain, turned from a small electric heating plate and lifted a kettle. "Wilfred, Electra a spot of tea?"

"That would be splendid, thank you," Wilfred said, making his way to the table. "How many of these have you completed?"

"So far, four." The Irishman said, staring at the equipment strewn about the table.

"Four? That's all?" Alana said. "You've got three more to complete and almost no time to do it in."

"It's not as easy as you might think." The Irishman said, putting down the soldering iron. "It seems your friends didn't quite get the parts right. We had to reconstruct some of them and that put a damper on things. I'll need at least two more days to finish them."

Wilfred eyed the man and said, "I'm not sure we have the luxury of two more days. The last piece of the puzzle has come into place, I'm afraid you'll simply have to work faster."

The Doctor slinked over, his feet scraping the concrete floor. He handed a mug of tea to Wilfred and offered the second cup to Alana. She shook her head.

"I'll get some later. I've got a tin in my bag," she said, patting the gas mask bag slung over the shoulder of her uniform.

Wilfred took a sip from his mug and said, "We've got a little job for you tonight, but first let me tell you what we've discovered." The

Doctor nodded and took a seat at the table next to Wilfred, who sipped his tea.

"Our meeting with Sir Philip went extremely well." Wilfred said with a grin, placing the mug on the table. "Gentlemen, by this time tomorrow, we'll have the exact locations of the communications hubs and transmitted that information back to Berlin. Our invasion will commence soon after, primarily due to our efforts."

Alana could sense excitement mount in the Irishman and the Doctor as they looked at each other. She imagined they were thinking of how their lives would change under a German England. She smiled and went over to the recess near the curtain to prepare her tea, knowing what would be coming next.

"It appears, according to Sir Philip, my good friend Lord Randall Ashford was the principal architect of the entire system. Locked away in his office safe will be the complete plan for the radar defense of England and tonight gentlemen, you will obtain it. By the time, Ashford realizes the plan has been compromised, it will be too late."

Alana listened as she stuffed tea into a metal strainer. The blackout curtain screeched open and an older man carrying a clipboard marched in.

He pushed black-rimmed glasses up against the bridge of his nose, gray hair peeking out from beneath his tin hat. His olive-drab uniform was void of insignia except for a faded white armband stitched with a black W.

"Excuse me." The man said in an authoritative voice. His focus on the three men seated at the table. "What are you doing in here? This entire area is to remain abandoned. I don't mean to intrude, but the door was left ajar and that surprised me, so I came in. This factory and all the others around here are fire traps. No one is allowed to be here—Fire Marshal's orders."

"There must be some confusion." Wilfred pleaded as the older man approached him. "I purchased this building a few months ago."

"Purchased, you say? Impossible—these buildings aren't for sale. They're to be torn down—all these old factories are. With the dome of St. Paul's sticking up, this entire area is a prime target for Jerry. If those blighters drop bombs here, the whole thing will go up in flames. I must report this."

"There's no need for that." Wilfred said, standing up from the table and motioning for the Irishman and Doctor to remain seated. "I'm sure we can work something out."

Alana reached into the canvas bag next to the hot plate and grasped the weapon she constructed. She began creeping toward the man.

"Work something out? There's nothing to work out. You must leave and now." The man ordered. "It's far too dangerous." He looked past the table to the four radios lined up on a wooden crate. "What are those over there? What are you doing with those?"

She crept closer, her thumb resting on the safety.

Her father walked toward the man. "Everything's in order."

She was almost behind him, staring at the back of his tin helmet, finding the precise spot.

"I'll have to report all this and your presence in this factory as well."

"We're not leaving. I have rights, even in wartime."

She raised the weapon and unlocked the safety. Hearing the click, the old man started to turn toward the sound. "I'm sorry, you don't have a choice. You'll—"

Alana fired and a thick steel spike exploded from the barrel, smashing into the man's head just behind his ear. He was dead before he could blink. The spike had slammed upward through the cortex and jutted out his skull, pinning the tin hat to the top of his head as brain matter spewed into the air. He crashed to the floor, eyes open, his muscles twitched a few discordant spasms and went silent.

Wilfred stared at the blood-and-gray soup running onto the floor. "You designed that? What a horrible thing."

"Actually, it's rather humane. Death is almost instantaneous." She said matter-of-factly.

"Well, what do we do now?" Wilfred said, shaking his head.

She was fuming at his carelessness. "First, you close the door you left open."

The Irishman stood. "That door is a problem. It's rotted, and the latch won't close. In order to fix it we have to replace it with a new one and that would stand out like a sore thumb."

"Don't worry about it. Close it as best you can. We'll be permanently leaving this place in a few hours. You'll be going to the hunter's cabin. Get the completed radios packed and clean up this mess."

The Doctor stood over the body smiling and said, "Well, we do have another barrel. We can drop him into the Thames after we return. He should be comfortable sleeping next to your former secretary."

"A fine solution," Wilfred said, returning to the table. "So, gentlemen, it appears all we have left is to discuss a little theft."

Chapter Thirty-Five

Much to Jamie's discomfort, the overcast had lifted and left him flying low over white capped waves in a pellucid sky, the green coast of northern France three miles off to his left wrapped in a light haze. He was now perfect fodder for any marauding Spitfire that didn't get the message. He tapped out 623 on the transmit key and hoped Aubrey had done his job and cleared the Gotha with the RAF. If he hadn't, his would be a quick and violent death.

Jamie took a look around the sky, making sure it was empty and banked left, heading directly toward the coast a few miles south of Boulogne. He finished the turn and with his left hand tapped out 717 in Morse code.

They crossed over dry land and he banked north, lining up the aircraft with the tallest building—a grain elevator next to the docks slightly east of the town's center. He yelled above the engine noise, "Okay, we're here. Start your photo run, it's your aircraft."

Harrison turned around, waved acknowledgement and disappeared into the front cockpit. He imagined Harrison's eyes now looking through the camera and slowed the aircraft, side-slipping it to exactly two hundred and fifty feet as the canals and port of Boulogne—their first photographic assignment—filled his view through the spinning propeller.

After a few seconds, Harrison's hand popped up out of the front cockpit and waved for Jamie to turn a little right. His foot pushed on the rudder, coaxing the nose over until the hand motioned straight ahead, the aircraft's altimeter remaining as steady as a stone. Below, as the biplane flew up the canal, hordes of gray machines and uniformed troops made their way over the streets toward the quays, marching as if on their way toward some Teutonic festival with bottles of wine in their hands and a prancing in their step. Boats and barges floated in long lines on the still water, hundreds of them ready to carry the Nazis to England. A chill seeped through his Luftwaffe flight suit. Surely, within a week the invasion would begin and bring untold devastation and horror.

He scanned the German instruments and concentrated on keeping the aircraft steady and in position for the film to record all he was seeing. He followed the canal north to the open mouth of the port, where it spilled into choppy, deeper water. He thought of his homeland, all he knew of life and freedom only a few miles across the sea, where so many were about to die from the savagery of the Germans.

Harrison popped his head above the cockpit and gave a thumbs-up. Jamie veered the plane away from Boulogne and inland toward Calais. He looked back at the city drifting away behind them. It seemed so peaceful in an afternoon sun, not a brick out of place, as if completely untouched.

They crossed over miles of green fields dotted with vineyards and farms, places where the war seemed distant and remote. When they returned, and delivered the film, an attack on the villages and cities he was passing over would certainly follow.

In the distance, the Luftwaffe's primary fighter base of Wissant formed out of the haze, the narrow grass field partially obscured beneath a few scattered rainclouds. As an RAF fighter pilot, this was the last place he wanted to fly near. Far too many times he'd been in a life-and-death struggle with the flyers who called Wissant home.

He looked behind the biplane and a petrifying shock ran through him. Bright sunlight glinted off the saffron-yellow nose of a ME 109 bearing down on him, in perfect position for a kill. If he drifted off the mail plane's course, or accidentally flew too close to the field, flew somewhere he shouldn't, they would shoot him down. He may have already done that and had no way of knowing.

He fought every impulse to dive away, as he struggled with himself to keep the Gotha on course as if they belonged there, had a right to share the enemy's sky. Staring straight ahead, he closed his eyes, every nerve bristled as he waited for the stream of machine-gun lead that would end his life. He glanced back and saw the menacing yellow spinner closer now as the fighter sprinted toward him, the weapons extending like sharp pikes holding for a few seconds more, ready to strike.

With both hands on the stick, he summoned all the courage he could to hold the aircraft steady and concentrated on breathing a slow, deep rhythm to force calm into his stuttering hands as he waited for his life to end.

Jamie's thoughts drifted to Livy and how this would hurt her, the seconds passing like minutes as the sound of his engine receded and a calm surrounded him—the peace of accepting death. He opened his eyes and turned to face the incoming fighter, the black gaping hole of the 20mm cannon staring back, pointing directly at his head. Jamie braced himself for the inevitable when like a thunderclap, the fighter roared away overhead, its turbulent wake tore at the Gotha, tossing it like paper in a wind.

He wrestled to gain control over the flailing Gotha and as it settled down, Harrison peeked up above the rim of the front cockpit, his eyes huge and filled with fear as their tormentor streaked high in the sky above them bleeding off airspeed as the gear unfolded from the 109's belly. Perhaps it had been a joke, a combat veteran teaching a lesson to what he thought was a young novice, the difference between those that had faced death and a mail pilot that had never seen it. Jamie laughed out loud, relief filling him. Harrison looked at him, his mouth open, his eyes bulging and he sank back into cockpit to be with his camera.

Jamie brought the plane back on course, its blue-gray nose again pointing toward the horizon and the next part of their mission, Calais.

In a cramped concrete bunker, ninety-seven miles to the north of Harrison and Jamie, Aubrey Beck sat next to a WAAF radio operator, looking at his watch. It had been fifteen minutes since they received the 717-code. By now, Jamie was finished with Boulogne, they had to be well on their way to Calais.

The young woman removed her headset and switched the speakers on. "It should be another twenty minutes until the aircraft reaches Dunkirk." She said.

"Good," Aubrey's excitement showed as he anticipated the final stage of his plan. "Raise 41 Squadron and tell them to take station off the coast. Don't forget, you are under the Secrets Act. That little piece of paper you signed means I own you. A mention of this to anyone and you'll spend the rest of your life in prison. Do you understand that?"

"Yes sir, I do," the young woman said. "Since I'm bound by secrecy, can you tell me why a mail plane is so important? Why go through all this trouble for mail going back to Germany?"

"It's not the mail, there's more in that aircraft than you'll ever know, more than I can talk about and it must be destroyed."

"Okay, you're the boss," she said and shrugged as she put the headset back on. "Mitor, this is Redhawk, take position one."

The radio crackled over the speaker, static from weather disturbing the frequency. "Redhawk, Mitor here, wilco. Ten minutes out." Locke's voice came scratching through.

Aubrey was almost gleeful; the order told 41 Squadron to orbit a few miles off shore. His plan was going perfectly.

Calais had passed below the Gotha, the photographs complete. The huge port of Dunkirk, its ships and barges filled the protected waters beneath the plane. Jamie had given up in his attempt to estimate the number of barges and soldiers, there were far too many, more than a thousand barges, hundreds of ships and tens of thousands of men waiting for the order to load and sail across the Channel.

But unlike Boulogne or Calais, Dunkirk retained the scars of war. Entire sections, square miles of the city, had been reduced to rubble. Streets were littered with the debris of former homes, businesses and cafés that had been loved and cared for by the inhabitants before they fled and became those that clogged the roads with whatever possessions they could carry as German aircraft bombed and strafed them for sport.

Littered on beaches to his left, the wreckage of a defeated English Army lay strewn across wide white sand still pitted with craters from shells and bombs. The rusted hulks of guns, ships and tanks protruding from the dunes like morbid monuments to war.

Jamie flew the little plane east over the city. As it passed beneath them, Harrison popped up from the front cockpit and gave the signal his mission was complete. Jamie smiled and quickly transmitted 884 on the

Morse key. All that remained was a short hop into Belgium and then home, protected by Spitfires of the RAF.

"There's the code. The mail plane has left Dunkirk," the operator said.

Aubrey stared at her, thrilled. Everything was in place and soon the bastard would be dead. He smiled and conjured an image of Livy. "Tell 41 to intercept, now!"

She nodded and opened the microphone, "Mitor, Redhawk here. Cleared to intercept."

"Redhawk, cleared to intercept," came Locke's voice.

Seven miles off the coast, north of the shore, 41 Squadron turned to stalk its prey.

Locke brought the four Spitfires level, heading straight at the shoreline. He smiled thinking of a quick kill and a return to England, their mission complete and a week of leave awaiting them.

"All right lads, the time's here. Singh, you and Baum head east on the deck, hold position in front of the mail plane. Fiske, you're with me. We'll come in high and on his six. The biplane is maneuverable, so when he evades, we'll keep him looking back. Singh, that's when you and Baum will intercept, the last thing he'll expect is two Spits coming in low and head-on. Got it?" Locke said over the radio.

Singh opened his microphone. "Roger, flight leader." Singh's plane split off, followed by Baum heading east, getting into position for the kill.

A full minute passed with each of the flight crew searching for the Gotha, until Fiske came on the radio. "Got him, Flight Leader—one o'clock low, at about three hundred feet, running parallel to the beach."

"Got him," Locke replied. "Let's make this quick. I buy the first pint. Get ready for a week of leave, boys. Red Flight, tally ho!"

Locke eased the throttle forward and dove, rolling right and then left, getting behind and above the biplane. Screaming down, Fiske on his wing, Locke centered the biplane in his sight and pulled the nose slightly forward, where the plane would be when the bullets struck home.

Down they came as Locke eased off the throttle to slow their speed. He concentrated on the kill, while Fiske took the broader view, to scan and protect him.

"Bloody hell?" Fiske said over the radio. "The fool's waving at us."

Locke, looking through the sight, saw a single hand wave to his incoming death. "I see it. What an idiot! He thinks we're Germans." Locke squeezed the trigger and streams of glowing lead spit from his guns and slammed into the wings of the little plane.

The biplane jerked up onto its back, rolled once and slipped away, turning left and right, making it impossible for Locke to center the guns as his Spitfire roared by, the pilot glaring at him through his goggles.

"This one's good for a mail pilot, much better than I expected." Locke said as he pulled into a climb to set up for another pass.

"Singh, where are you? He's headed inland toward that long stand of trees. I hit him, but he's still flying." Locke yelled over the microphone.

"Twenty seconds out, Red Leader," Singh responded.

"Okay. On the next pass, I'll drive him toward you. Look for him to pop up above the trees." Locke kicked the rudder right, centering the stick as far back and right as he could pull it, G-forces shoving him deep into the seat.

Locke's Spitfire spun around on a wing and headed back down toward the Gotha now in front of him, fully showing its right side. The biplane was running south below the tree tops, parallel to a tall stand of trees along a hill. "Singh, he'll pop up over the trees right in front of you. Get ready."

The Spitfire shuddered as Locke pulled the trigger, tracer rounds walked from the right toward the slow-moving Gotha. As he expected, the pilot pulled up and banked hard left over the trees, straight into the trap. Locke saw flames leap from the guns of Singh's aircraft, tracers striking the engine and zipping back toward the pilot as fire erupted and curled around the sides of the Gotha. The target made it over the trees and went down into the valley on the other side as Locke banked left.

He came over the tree tops and saw the Gotha deep in the valley, headed down. It was burning as it bounced on the ground and back into the air. The bi-plane skidded and it plopped hard onto a road running toward a forest covered hill, the undercarriage smashed, the aircraft sliding on its belly. In a second the Gotha slipped up the hill, under the canopy of trees and disappeared, billowing smoke drifted above the green forest.

Locke pulled up and headed northwest. "I'll make another pass, after that, form up on me and we'll go home. Well done, lads." He switched the radio to the home frequency and calmly said, "Redhawk, the bird is down."

Aubrey Beck stood behind the young WAAF operator staring down her shirt, when he heard the words he wanted to hear, the Gotha was down. The plan to get rid of Jamie had worked perfectly, but he had to make sure.

"Ask if the pilot was killed." He ordered the operator.

"What?"

"Ask if the pilot was killed."

"How would he know?"

"Just do it. He'll know."

The woman turned away from Aubrey and opened the microphone. "Mitor, Redhawk, any knowledge of crew?"

A few seconds later, a much clearer voice, almost void of static, came on the speaker. "Redhawk, no survivors."

"Understood, Redhawk out." She turned and looked at Beck. "Well, there's your answer, Squadron Commander. The pilot was killed."

Aubrey did everything he could to conceal his delight. "Well done, Miss. Thank you, and don't forget—not a word of this to anyone." He pointed a finger at her, "You will be prosecuted if you say anything and I promise, you'll be a guest of the crown for a very long time if you do."

The young woman sighed, turned back to face the radio and said, "I understand, sir. Not a word of this to anyone. It never happened, as far as I know."

"Good girl."

Aubrey left the bunker and took the concrete stairs up toward daylight two at a time.

Chapter Thirty-Six

Livy climbed the eleven steps to the London flat, counting each one. It used to be a happy game, something she'd done many times as a little girl holding her father's hand as she learned to count. This time however, it was anything but happy. She was disappointed—not only with her father but also with herself. Once again, he had treated her like a child, and she allowed it.

Yesterday afternoon as she watched Jamie going down the drive at Kensington Manor she exploded with fury. The last thing she remembered as the front door slammed was Jamie's car passing by a black government sedan coming up the drive to collect her father and she knew she had lost. He would leave for London and some secret meeting without a word about what had transpired between the two. His meeting far too important to take time to explain to his daughter what he'd just done to the man she loved.

This afternoon she was calmer but still filled with anger. Her connection to Jamie wasn't tattered, it wasn't even bruised. Livy felt the bond in her heart as strong as ever. But she had to know why he left the way he did and what her father said to make him do it. He didn't even say a goodbye to her.

"Oh, there you are," her father said as he came down the stairs. "I thought you'd be here hours ago so we could have our little chat."

He was dressed in his Royal Navy uniform, the tailored coat closed, the double rows of brass buttons shining. One hand slid on the wrought-iron banister and the other carried a stack of red-edged manila folders. She knew he'd be leaving shortly.

"You're not to go anywhere until we speak."

"I beg your pardon? My driver will be here any moment."

"You owe me an explanation of what happened with Jamie. You're not leaving until you speak with me."

He cocked his head. "I have a meeting with the PM and the War Cabinet. That's a little more important than your Jamie Wallace."

"I don't care if your meeting is with Churchill and Hitler himself—you're going to explain your actions with Jamie yesterday!" She folded her arms across her chest, tapping one foot against the tile.

He crossed the landing without saying a word and came down the last five stairs to stop in front of her. To Livy, her shoe sounded like the banging of a hammer.

"You behave exactly like your mother did when she was peeved with me. I've heard that same voice and seen that same stance a thousand times." He shook his head smiling at her and held up a hand. "You win. Come into the library and we'll talk. But in all seriousness, I haven't got too much time. I can't keep the Prime Minister waiting. That is, if I want to continue in his good graces—and I do."

He walked around her and entered the library. Livy followed.

She rested an elbow on one of the two stuffed wingbacks as he dropped the folders into a leather briefcase. He faced her, nodding as if resigned to speaking about something he really didn't care to.

"I do owe you an explanation for the way I treated him. There were and are reasons for all of it," he said as he crossed over to her, his eyes on the briefcase.

"Reasons? What reason could you possibly have? I say rubbish!"

He looked up from the briefcase and searched her eyes. "I'm concerned. You say you love him. But, you don't really know him, now do you? You haven't had time to. There are so many of these quick wartime romances and in every one of them the couples truly believe they're in love and when they begin to know each other, it's too late. They find out they didn't love each other at all. It was just passion—not love. Worst of all, the children that come from these hasty commitments are the ones who really suffer; I refuse to have that for you."

"What you're saying doesn't apply to Jamie and I. We do love each other and this war has nothing to do with it."

His eyes narrowed. "If not for this war as you put it, you two would have never met. You'd be with a man of your class and Jamie would be selling sausage from behind a meat counter. You're from completely different worlds. I've told you that before. After your trip with Jamie and your night together in our cottage, I was furious ..."

"I can't believe this. How do you know we went to the cottage? Did you have us followed? How could you do such a thing?"

He grunted. "You've been followed for the last two months. All the senior staff families have. But it's not my doing. In fact, I made sure it stopped after you two came back."

"Not your doing?" She glared at him. "What do you mean? What gives anyone the right to do something as despicable as that?"

"I didn't have a choice. I couldn't take the chance of losing you, having you tortured or killed. I couldn't bear that, so I approved."

She stared at him, confusion and anger made her head swim.

"Livy, you're forcing my hand," he said. "Forcing me into a position I don't want to be in. Drop it."

"I'll not drop it. You owe me an explanation."

"There's much more to it. More than I should say." He rested the briefcase on the arm of the chair.

"I can't believe this! You've always hidden behind government secrets and I won't stand for it anymore."

He paused a moment. "All right," he said quietly. "However, you are not to repeat any of what I'm about to say. It's for your own good." He was giving her an order and it grated on her.

He took a deep breath and said, "Somewhere in our own government there's a traitor who's operating with access into very high places. Special Branch and MI6 have been investigating, working to uncover him. So far, all I know is that they've intercepted coded radio broadcasts, but they still don't have any idea who or where he is."

"In our own government? That's horrible, but what does it have to do with myself or Jamie?"

"I am in intelligence, that's what. They believed there would be an attempt to kidnap family members to extort information in exchange for their lives. They're the ones that didn't want you to have an assignment. They're the ones that put undercover men near you and had you followed, not me. It was done without my having any say in it. I was informed of it, and at the time, I approved."

Livy paused, trying to absorb all of it. "Why Jamie?"

"Anyone that came into your life was suspect, including your young pilot. When you came to me and told me you were going away with him, I knew they would have you both followed. It was to protect you. There's far too much at stake. I couldn't tell you. I didn't want to."

"But none of that explains what happened with him. Why did you do that?"

"When you came home, I had just rung off with Special Branch. They told me everything about your trip and when I asked, they also told me everything about Jamie and his family. To the inspector, it seemed like you were lovers and on hearing that, I wanted it stopped, for your own good.

"Our culture isn't something you learn. It's something you're born into and grow up with. No matter what happens, he'll never be a part of our society. He'll always be from the working-class. He'll never fit in."

He closed the briefcase with a loud snap.

"You are the last of my line, Livy, the final Ashford. I had to know if he was after the money and status that will come to you. I confronted him about it."

She defiantly glared at him, her arms folded across her chest. "You accused him of wanting my inheritance? My God, no wonder he left the way he did. That couldn't be further from the truth. We were in love with each other long before he knew I had anything at all. How could you accuse him of something like that?"

"I don't know him. I had to be careful."

"What happened?"

"He told me to go to the Devil and then the thought of him at my cottage alone with my little girl got to me. I still struggle to see you as a grown woman."

"Good lord, what did you do?"

"I forbid him to see you and that's when I ordered him to leave." He put both hands on the briefcase handle.

"All because I spent a night with him, alone? How can a man of your intelligence be so stupid?" She caught herself biting her lower lip, exactly like her mother did when she was angry.

He looked at her and his face softened. He took in a breath and said, "It all comes from a desire to protect those you love. That's a part of who I am, who any man is," he said defensively. "But there's still one more thing you should know. I threatened him."

"You what? I'll bet that went over well." She actually laughed.

"I told him if he ever saw you again, I would have him posted to the most godforsaken place I could find on the earth."

"Oh, no you won't! I love him, no matter what station in life he came from."

"You know what? I think you do." There was genuine regret in his voice as if he suddenly remembered memories he'd long forgotten.

"You'll call him and apologize." This time she was giving the order. She could feel her anger slipping away, her love for them both overpowering it.

"I will. But I want you to know that I did what I thought to be in your best interest. I still worry this might be wrong for you but even if it is, I understand it's your decision to follow that path."

She moved to his side and hugged him, kissed him on the cheek. "You've done nothing that can't be repaired but, I want you to stop interfering. I'll speak with Jamie this afternoon and I do intend to tell him about this. He needs to know all of it, even about being followed."

"I wish you wouldn't. But if you do, under no circumstances is he to say anything to anyone. It could hamper the investigation. We must find the traitor—make sure he understands that."

The door chimes rang. "That will be my driver."

"You have a meeting to go to." Livy took his arm as he picked up the briefcase and escorted him to the front door. "I'll see you later tonight and we'll finish this," she said as he started down the steps toward the waiting driver.

She stood at the door and watched the black sedan go around the corner toward Whitehall and went back inside. She locked the door and went upstairs to her bedroom and a welcome shower. Livy stood beneath the hot water, letting rivulets run over her hair, across her face and down her chest and back, remnants of her confusion and anger dissolving in the warm stream. While shampooing her hair, thoughts of Jamie and how he must be feeling came into her mind and she knew she had to speak with him.

He wouldn't be flying—he was to report to the flight surgeon and she knew he wasn't cleared for flight. Besides, over southern England the weather all day had been cold and stormy. Livy turned off the shower and decided to call RAF Hornchurch to find him and speak with him.

She quickly dried and threw on a robe, her hair dripping on her shoulders. After hurrying downstairs to the library, she dialed 41 Squadron's Operations. A second later a high-pitched male voice came on the line.

"41 Operations, Corporal Lester speaking."

"Corporal, this is Olivia Ashford. Can you please put Jamie Wallace on the phone for me? It's important."

"I'm sorry, Miss Ashford, I haven't seen him. He hasn't reported back from leave."

"Hasn't reported back?" That was odd she thought. "How about Eric Locke? Can you find him please? Tell him it's Livy."

"I'm sorry, ma'am. The squadron commander is currently flying."

"Flying on a day like this?"

"It's a special mission. I didn't even log it."

"Well, no matter. If you can reach either of them, please have them give me a call—Abbey 7719. Would you do that for me please?"

"Yes ma'am," the young man said. "As soon as I see either of them, I'll give 'em your message."

"Thank you," she said and rang off, certain something was amiss.

Aubrey Beck was thrilled as he entered 41's ready shack. He came up to a young Corporal who had finished writing on a tablet and said, "Have you heard from Locke? When do you expect Red Flight to return?"

"The last radar fix I know of was forty-five miles out, sir. That was a few minutes ago."

Aubrey looked at his watch and realized he needed to be back at Shoe Lane. He noticed Livy's name written on the note pad.

"What's that note?" He pointed at the pad.

"A woman just called for Jamie or Locke, an Olivia Ashford. I haven't seen Jamie, so I was going to give it to Locke when he reported in." The Corporal tore the top page from the tablet and placed it on the green blotter in front of him.

"I'll handle that. I know her. I know what she wants." Aubrey extended his hand to take the paper but the Corporal blocked him.

"Sir, she was clear it went to either Jamie or Locke," the young man said firmly.

"Give it to me, Corporal."

"I don't want to be in trouble with either of 'em when they find out I gave it to you." He held the note up for Aubrey.

"Don't fret, I'll speak to both of them." He snatched the note.

Ten minutes later, he was in an isolated office at headquarters. As he sat down at a scratched wooden desk, he noted the number Abbey 7719, a different one, he thought. She's not at Kensington Manor. Aubrey took a deep breath trying to settle himself, settle the excitement he was feeling about giving Livy the news. His hand shook a little as he picked up the receiver.

"Base Operator, number please," the woman's voice said over the line.

Aubrey swallowed and said, "Abbey 7719. Quickly, this is an emergency."

"Hold the line."

Aubrey could hear the connection being made and a moment later the staccato buzzing that meant her phone was ringing. As the buzzing reached seven he wondered if he missed her.

"Hello," Livy said, breathless, as if she'd had run to catch the phone. He inhaled sharply.

"Livy, this is Aubrey. Where are you?"

"What?" She was questioning him, he could hear tension in her voice. "I'm at our flat in London. What is it, Aubrey?"

"Livy, I've got horrible news. Brace yourself. Jamie has been killed."

There was silence on the phone and he waited, imagining she was in tears, needing comfort. He smiled.

A moment later she said, "Killed. How?"

"He was shot down over Belgium. His plane crashed." He said it far too quickly, he thought.

"He was flying? How is that possible? He was only to see the flight surgeon today. He wasn't even on flight duty."

"He volunteered for a special mission. It was dangerous and he knew the risks, but he was so courageous he flew it in spite of the danger. I'm very sorry to be the one to tell you, but I thought it would be for the best if you heard it from a friend, someone who cared about you and not from a stranger. I'm sorry, Livy—it's tragic. Is there anything I can do for you? If you tell me where your flat is I can come over there, make sure you're okay."

"I'm all right, thank you, Aubrey. Thank you for telling me." Her voice was flat, almost without emotion.

Shock, he thought as the phone went dead.

He looked at his watch, surprised she had refused him. Knowing he was already late to Shoe Lane, he forced himself to stop thinking about her. He had to leave. He was far more afraid of what the Doctor might do than anything else. *I'll call her afterward—go to her and comfort her*, he thought, very pleased with himself.

Chapter Thirty-Seven

The aircraft was on the side of a forested hill, the right wings had been sheared off. Aviation fuel leaked from a ruptured tank and spewed out onto the hot engine cowling. A massive conflagration erupted, the flames jumped over the front of the aircraft and onto the ground. Jamie freed the straps holding him to the seat and crawled out.

His first duty was to get Harrison out of the front cockpit before the fire reached him. Jamie found him slumped over, jammed against a shattered bulkhead that for the moment was holding off the inferno. He pulled the man's shoulders back and reached for the seat straps. He grimaced at the sight. Harrison's chest was gone. Nothing but a gaping cavity remained, his body torn to pieces by a torrent of lead spewing from the Spitfire. There was no time to pull his body out—in a few seconds the remains of the biplane would detonate.

Enraged that his own had shot them down and that Aubrey didn't do his job, Jamie grabbed the green canvas bag from the floor of the cockpit, hoping he'd salvaged the film. He ran, forced to leave Harrison's body to the pyre.

He got about thirty feet when the explosion knocked him down. It sent him sprawling onto the wet dirt and scattering the film canisters all over the ground. He rolled, heat from the fire searing. He crawled onto his knees and scrambled to pick up what remained of the film, snatched the gray metal cartridges off the earth and stuffed them into the bag.

There was nothing left to do but flee across the Belgian countryside, get as far away from the burning biplane as possible. He managed to get his feet beneath him and ran, staying under the trees and wending his way deeper through the stand. As he ran, slick mud and dread gripped him. From a distance, he heard the unmistakable howl of a Spitfire coming closer every second, searching for him. He dashed behind a wide oak near the edge of the forest as the Spitfire screamed by, tearing at the treetops, leaves scattered by the gale-force wind as the ground shook beneath him.

He crouched as low as possible and peered through the almost barren tree canopy as the Spitfire banked left and hurtled into the sky. He watched it until it disappeared behind scattered gray clouds. He searched back and forth across an empty sky and found his tormentors—four dark specks climbing higher, heading northwest toward England, their mission accomplished. They wouldn't be back.

Relieved, he took a deep breath and stood. He looked down and felt his wet knees, the tan Luftwaffe flight suit saturated with reddish-brown mud. He took a second breath, trying to gather himself knowing if he was captured in the German uniform, he would be shot. By now gray-clad troopers would be on their way to the crashed aircraft and he couldn't wait any longer. It was time to move.

He threw off the flight jacket and unzipped the tan flight suit He climbed out of it and stuffed the mud-soaked cloth beneath a broken limb, attempting to cover his deception with mounds of wet, decaying leaves.

Jamie scooped up the canvas bag and his jacket, noticing the lamb's wool collar singed and smeared with bits of Harrison's blood and flesh. After a quick glance at the Gotha's remains, he turned from the wreckage and set off toward the next hill, wanting to get as far away from the crash as possible before the Germans came and slaughtered him. He started running across fallow fields as fast as he could, having no idea where he was or where he was going.

Hours passed as he traveled from ditch to ditch or scrambled his way through thickets woven below clumps of dense trees. He was always hiding, intensely alert and hoping to live through the next minute. Twice he stumbled onto German Army patrols, forcing him to reverse his course or dive for cover until they passed, barely remaining concealed.

His mind blank, his next move unknown he pushed on, exhaustion his companion. He traveled step by step through sodden fields, each one more difficult than the last, heavy reddish-brown mud sucking at his boots. He reached a hedge-covered berm and crawled his way to the top, brambles and thorns tearing at his shirt, opening fissures in both cloth and skin.

At the summit, he lay on his belly in the twilight, his body failing, unable to go any further. Hidden in the thick foliage, he bunched the flight jacket under his head as his eyes closed and sleep overtook him.

Chapter Thirty-Eight

Jamie awoke with a start. Before he could utter a sound, he was yanked from beneath the brambles and pulled up, his hands swiftly bound. Confusion swarmed through his mind as a rag tasting of turpentine was crammed in his mouth and a gag applied to keep it in place. A short man dressed like a peasant motioned for him to be silent as he twisted a knife in front of his eyes. The man's face was thin and blackened with a woolen cap pulled down around his head. A second man reached down and picked up the canvas bag as a shove came from behind, throwing him down into the mud between the field and the berm. Their hands roughly grabbed his shirt, dragged him up and forced him to walk along the bottom of the hedgerow; the butt of a rifle continually prodding his back.

The little group moved in silence like a shade as the men forced him onward, the rifle butt reminding him they were right behind and would kill him for the smallest reason. Two or three times on the journey a full moon slid from behind high clouds, it provided enough light to find their way and show Jamie more armed people scattered like phantoms along the hedgerow.

They reached a corner of the field and an access opening to a gray road running along the other side of the berm. They stopped and he was thrown to his knees at the feet of a tall man staring down at him, his face blackened. He leveled a submachine gun between Jamie's eyes. The man leaned over as the short one whispered in his ear and showed him the bag with the film inside. He grunted and grabbed Jamie by the collar, pulled him within inches of his mouth, his breath thick. He reached for Jamie's face and tore back the gag.

"Qui es-tu?" The man hissed, his eyes threatening and Jamie knew he held the power of life or death, the decision to kill him or not.

The Resistance, Jamie guessed.

He took a chance and spoke in English, his French too poor to save his life. "My name is Jamie Wallace, I'm a RAF pilot. I was shot down earlier today." he whispered.

"Anglais?"

Jamie nodded. "Yes, RAF pilot."

"This we see." The man said with a heavy French accent. He shoved the gag back into Jamie's mouth and turned to mutter something in French to the short one that Jamie didn't understand. In a flash, he was jerked backward by the two and tied to a tree along the edge of the field, his arms and legs immobile. A hemp rope was wrapped around his neck, pinning him to the bark.

They threw the bag next to his feet and left him alone while the men scattered along the berm and took positions huddled next to the ground. Minutes ticked by and with each, the rag in his mouth gagged him. His legs felt heavy, the muscles burned as he stood rigid against the tree.

The men around him tensed. In the distance, carried by a light wind Jamie could hear the faint rumble of lorries. A woman came running into the field from the road access point and spoke to the tall man, out of breath, her voice a little too loud. The words ran together, spoken too fast. Jamie made out something about being ready as she pointed to the men. She stopped speaking and listened to the low voice of the tall man. She glanced at Jamie and continued speaking in a whisper far too quiet for him to hear.

Moonlight filtered out from a break in the clouds as the woman approached him. A thick ribbon pulled the dark strands of her hair back, exposing her face. As she came to him, he noticed her resemblance to the tall man—the same intense look in her eyes.

She placed her mouth close to his ear. "So, you're a pilot? An English pilot?" Her light French accent rounded the words into perfect English.

Jamie nodded.

"And you were shot down today?"

Jamie nodded again.

She pulled back.

"Liar!" she said and slapped him so hard it burned. She whipped a knife from behind her back and pressing it to his throat whispered, "I'll deal with you later, Nazi bastard."

Jamie shook his head; he was almost unable to breathe. The woman stared at him and smiled. As she walked away a quiet laugh came from her lips. She accepted a Bren gun offered by one of the men and slung it over her shoulder.

The black-faced phantoms began to move and took positions as if they had rehearsed them many times. His cheek still stinging, Jamie could now clearly hear the lorries as they approached, men singing, oblivious their lives were about to end. The moon once again crawled in behind a cloud bank, stealing light away and leaving Jamie to peer into the darkness. A square dark shape rumbled by the opening in the berm, the smell of exhaust rolled into the field. Jamie blinked, trying to focus his eyes, as a second shape passed along the road. He recognized it as a German troop carrier loaded with soldiers. Rising above the drone of the engine, he heard the sound of a Nazi marching song and he knew soon they all would be dead.

Another square shape followed behind the first two and after the fourth passed, the lorries slowed as if alerted to some danger. The singing ended abruptly as the troop carriers stopped on the gray crushed-shell road. Moments ticked by, the soldiers searching for an unseen enemy, bringing their weapons to bear on emptiness. As Jamie watched, knowing the next few moments could also be his last, a bead of sweat trickled down his neck.

The hands of a man some twenty feet from Jamie shoved down on a plunger, making generators whir and sending an electrical current into detonators wedged deep in plastique buried beneath the road.

A bright flash tossed away the night. The sound and concussion of the explosions tore into Jamie, his tattered shirt flapping in a hot wind. He watched as the entire rear cavity from one of the lorries filled with men flew high above the hedgerow. Burning bodies and pieces of bodies flew across the dark sky, turning over and over, a German boot attached to a shattered leg landed next to his feet.

He took in a sharp breath as the Resistance opened fire. Their submachine guns spewed, striking at any that survived the blast. Grenades sailed into the fury, exploded and sent shrapnel whistling in all directions, tearing through dead and living flesh. Men hiding behind the berm vaulted over the top and ran down onto the cratered road to finish the ambush, killing anyone that remained alive. In a matter of seconds, it was over and the world went silent, the German convoy annihilated.

Futilely struggling against the ropes that bound him, all Jamie could do was watch and wonder how many lives had just ended, certain his own would be next.

Through the dust and darkness, the woman came, followed by the short man and a young boy no more than fourteen. With quick hand signals, she directed them toward him. The short man pulled out his knife, the razor edge of his blade glistened white in the dim light. The young one reached down and picked up the canvas bag as the woman stood in front of him, smiling. The short man raised his knife to Jamie's throat. He closed his eyes, after all he had been through, his would be a horrible death.

Waiting for the strike that would end his life, he thought of Livy and what could have been as the cold steel rested on his skin, the blade digging in. He heard the woman laugh when he jumped as the blade slashed across his throat and sliced open the hemp rope.

Confused but alive, Jamie watched as the man cut his remaining bindings, freeing him from the tree. He pulled the turpentine rag from Jamie's mouth. The woman squeezed his chin in her hand and stared into his eyes.

"You make a little sound, one word and you'll be dead. You understand?" Her breath was sweet like licorice.

Jamie nodded. The short man took the cloth gag and wrapped it around his eyes, blinding him to the night. He was jerked away from the tree and they set off at a brisk pace, Jamie's hands still securely bound behind his back.

He could hear the fighters as they scattered, running in different directions to vanish before the Germans could arrive in force and retaliate. Shoved forward through the smell of burnt flesh and rubber, he felt the heat from the fires consuming the lorries. He stumbled several times, either on debris or pieces of bodies spread over the battlefield as the group hurried through the kill zone.

Urgent French voices whispered around him as his captors pulled him along. Several hundred yards passed beneath Jamie's uncertain feet. He blindly lurched over fields and ditches, trying in vain to keep from falling facedown onto the earth, his muscles failing, quivering with each new step. As he was about to collapse, they came to a stop.

Hands that gripped his biceps dropped away and he was left alone standing in the cool air listening to the sounds that surrounded him. Light footsteps on gravel, crickets, hushed voices and the gurgling of a stream found a way into his consciousness. He heard a door open, the thin sound of metal barking in protest. A few seconds later, a rough engine sputtered to life followed by the sound of someone slamming a tin door that didn't close properly and the acrid smell of over-rich exhaust.

The hands returned, tossed him into what he thought was the back of a lorry. He fell hard on his back and something gouged his hand. He heard his captors climb up and bang twice on the cab. A second door slammed, gears ground and with lurch, the vehicle started to move.

A foot pushed on his shoulder, rolling him over on the wood as the bindings wrapped tightly around his hands were checked. Facedown, his head struck the floor as they bounced along the road. Someone pulled his head up by his hair and stuffed a scratchy cloth beneath his cheek, one that smelled of potatoes and vegetables and musty earth.

After what seemed like an eternity of hitting every pothole and rut the driver could find, the lorry slowed to a stop and he was lifted out. Jamie heard the woman's voice giving orders in rapid French. The pungent odor of recently crushed grapes assaulted his nose. Someone grabbed the ropes binding his hands and used them to pull him along. He stepped over the uneven ground and behind him heard the squeak of rusting hinges on heavy doors.

Gravel crunched beneath his feet. His hands were shoved up his back, forcing him to hunch over. After a few moments, he heard the boy whisper, "Étape."

Jamie stopped and reached out with his toe, striking something hard. He raised his foot and placed it down on a step. He climbed another and his feet found a smooth floor. From the temperature change and the smell of food, he knew he had crossed a threshold and was inside a home.

A knife sliced through his bonds, freeing his hands. Abruptly, he was shoved down into a straight-backed chair and the blindfold was ripped away. He opened his eyes and blinked back amber light. He turned his head and squinted at the glare coming from an oil lantern.

"Rat," the woman said as she turned away into darkness, "regardez-le attentivement." Jamie guessed that meant watch him closely. The short man—Rat—pulled out a chair next to him and sat, his knife now spinning on its point next to the green canvas bag holding the film. Rat's eyes never left him as the knife spun in circle after circle.

With his eyesight adjusted and his hands free, Jamie went for the sliver of wood jammed into his flesh just below the thumb. His hands were covered in mud and dirt and his fingers felt thick with wet soil as he futilely picked at the exposed quarter-inch of stinging wood.

"I'll get that," the woman said as she set a bowl of stew in front of him. She grabbed his left hand and pulled it across his body, blocking him from the stew.

Jamie opened his mouth to protest, but upon seeing her clearly for the first time, he could only stare at her face, she was beautiful. The woman looked up from his hand, her eyes frigid, unforgiving. She paused as she saw him stare at her, as if she had seen the same look from men far too many times. She dropped his hand and without a word went to the sink to pump cold water into a shallow bowl.

He went for the spoon sticking up from the stew and attacked it. He shoveled the food into his mouth the taste thick and rich. The woman came back and sat next to him. She grabbed his left hand and thrust it into the cold water. A few seconds later she yanked it from the water and scraped off the grime with a rough cloth.

"So, you are a pilot," she said in English.

Her eyes were a soft brown but belonged to a woman that was closed to feeling. Full lips without color covered white teeth that couldn't stay hidden as she scrubbed at the dirt on his hand. Her charcoal-colored hair was tied with a black bow behind her head.

"Yes," he whispered through a mouthful of food.

"And, you say you were shot down today?"

Jamie nodded, swallowing.

"Where?"

He shook his head. "I don't know. Somewhere near De Panne, I think."

"Well, I think you might want to start over—if you want to live through what's left of the night. You see, right now we think you're a Nazi spy, one that's trying to infiltrate our little group. The only plane shot down near De Panne today was a German plane."

He finished chewing another bite. "I'm not a Nazi. I'm a Royal Air Force pilot. My name is Jamie Wallace and I was flying that German plane." The man she looked similar to watched quietly from the other side of the table.

Jamie jerked back as she finally got the splinter out. He looked down at his hand, a rivulet of blood flowed from the hole.

She smiled at him and pulled the stopper out of a bottle of iodine. "This will hurt more."

She put the reddish liquid on a cloth and daubed at the hole as Jamie winced.

She looked at him and daubed again. "Now as I said, can you explain why the English, your own people, shot down the airplane you were flying, a German airplane?"

He let out a grunt as she continued torturing him with the iodine. "No, I can't." Anger boiled in his heart as he thought of Aubrey, "I guess someone failed to tell them not to shoot my plane down. I don't know why."

She spoke in French to the others around the table who looked at him, none of them believed him, he could see that as Rat spun the knife around and around.

"I'm telling you the truth," Jamie said. "I was flying that German plane on a mission. We were photographing the invasion barges. The film is in the green sack right there." He pointed to it lying on the table.

She put her hand on Rat's wrist, bringing the knife back to the table and said, "So if I understand, you're a British pilot flying a Nazi airplane shot down by the RAF, who didn't get some message not to shoot you down while you were taking pictures of the Germans, is that right?"

He paused a moment thinking how absurd all that sounded. "It's the truth."

"A little hard to believe, don't you think? I think you need to do better than that." She pointed to the others. "The Nazis will do almost anything to gain our trust, infiltrate us and kill us. I'm not sure I believe your story, neither do they." She grabbed his collar, her face close to his. "It's much safer and easier for us to kill you."

Jamie pointed at the green bag. "In that bag is film we took of the German staging areas, the ones they'll use to invade England. My mission was to take the pictures and get them back so we can stop the invasion." He paused, wanting her to believe him. "Get in touch with London. You must have a radio. Ask them about a mission called Glass Rim. They'll confirm everything I've said."

"We might have a radio and we might not. We might be able to get in touch with London, but why should we."

"I'm telling you the truth. Those films must get back to England. It's critical. They could stop the Germans from invading my country and help yours to be free again—someday."

She looked at him as if she was deciding what to do.

"Please, what's your name? What do I call you?" he said softly.

"We don't go by names here. You have no need to know mine." She looked up at the others across the table and they argued excitedly for a minute in French.

She stood, turned her back to Jamie and said, "I've decided to give you a chance at least for tonight. We might get in touch with London and see if they know about this Glass Rim or Jamie Wallace"—she turned to face him— "and for your sake, you should pray they do."

Chapter Thirty-Nine

It was well after dark when Aubrey pulled the Jaguar onto the sidewalk outside 46 Shoe Lane. He took a quick lift from his drug and slipped the wooden box back under the passenger seat. Feeling light and thoroughly on his game after killing Jamie, he stepped down off the sidewalk and went to knock on the door. To his surprise, it readily opened.

He pushed through, struggled to close the door and walked into the alcove. The hangers screeched across the metal rod announcing his arrival as he yanked the blackout curtain open. Aubrey saw the Doctor standing off to one side by a metal drum carefully sealing the top with light strikes from a ball-peen hammer. At the table were the Irishman and Alana, both of them staring at him.

He started toward them when Wilfred Eaton's voice echoed over his shoulder out of the gloom.

"Aubrey, how nice of you to make it, we were expecting you much earlier."

"I was assigned to a special mission. I came as soon as I could." He said with an authority that pleased him.

A hammer strike crashed down on top of the drum making him jump. The Doctor spun the hammer in his hand and came over to the table, a thin smile on his face as he glared at him.

Wilfred motioned for him to sit with the others. "Aubrey, tonight you'll have the honor to serve the Reich in a manner few will ever have. What you're about to obtain will set the invasion in motion and secure the final and complete defeat of England."

Wilfred unrolled a crude drawing showing a floor plan Aubrey recognized as the Palace of Westminster. The Doctor placed weights at the corners to keep it flat.

"Aubrey, here is where you will take the Doctor and the Irishman." He pointed to a room almost at the end of a corridor.

"That's Randall Ashford's office, I know where it is," he said.

"I expect that you do. I'm pointing it out to the others." Wilfred said as if lecturing a boy. "Now, with Aubrey's permission, I'll continue.

"Use the St. Stephens entrance. The contractor passes I arranged for you and Aubrey's uniform will allow you to pass through the security station without any problems. I've informed them you'll be coming to evaluate some work I want done in my office. Aubrey, make sure you take them from the security station toward the Commons side before you go up to Ashford's office. Not until you reach the second floor should you start heading the opposite direction.

"Randall's office is on the third floor and you'll notice on this drawing there is a stairwell at the end of the corridor. That is the one you will take after you have the documents, it leads to a door through which you'll access the garden square by the clock tower and Westminster Bridge. You know which door I mean, Aubrey."

He nodded.

Wilfred pulled his finger off the drawing. "From there, you are to come back here, making sure you haven't been followed."

He paced around the circumference of the table, stopped behind the Irishman and placed his hands on the man's shoulders.

"My friend," he said. "Yours will be the job of opening the safe. It's located on a wall behind a painting of a schooner sailing on rough seas—rather appropriate, don't you think?"

Pleased with himself, Wilfred let out a chuckle and continued. "I've seen Lord Ashford put classified papers in there many times."

He looked across the table at Aubrey. "You will search the safe's contents. Find and retrieve only the defense plan without disturbing anything else. This point is critical. Do not disturb anything in the office— not the papers in the safe or on his desk, or anything else. I do not want Ashford suspecting something might be missing until it's too late."

He went behind the Doctor and patted his back. "You, my friend, will provide the security for this operation. If you're discovered, you must deal with it quickly and effectively. Leave nothing that could be discovered at least for a few days. After that, it won't matter."

Wilfred put his hands on his hips. "Right now, Ashford is at a War Cabinet meeting and should be there for at least another hour and a half. The timing couldn't be better."

He scowled at Aubrey. "After you have collected the papers and verified them to be the defense plan, return here and give them to Electra. I'll be leaving for Gloucester to coordinate the invasion from there. She will bring the plan to me and I'll get the information to Berlin. Do you have any questions?"

Alana looked at her father and said, "It seems I've been left out of the operation. What am I to do?"

"We have a few other items to discuss. I need you to remain here and assist me with the final preparations." He looked at the others. "Questions?" No one spoke.

"Good," Wilfred said. "I think it's time you began your journey. Just remember—leave no evidence you were there."

Aubrey rose from the table. "My car's right outside. It might be a little cramped, but I'll drive us there."

"No!" Wilfred said firmly. "You'll walk. If for some reason you're discovered and followed, you'll be able to spot it. It would be far too easy to track a car back here and that could be catastrophic for all of us, especially when we're this close to victory. Aubrey, you'll carry the document and you two will protect him. You shouldn't be in Ashford's office any longer than five minutes. It's a short walk and you have a little less than an hour to complete your mission, so I suggest you get started."

Chapter Forty

Livy finished pinning her hair under the WAAF service cap and stepped out of the flat. She needed to get to her father's office. The call from Aubrey didn't feel right. He wasn't telling her the truth and she knew something was wrong. A phone call to 41 Squadron from a Whitehall exchange would get an answer and quickly.

She pulled the collar of her coat up and set off in the direction of the office under a yellow moon and a clear sky. Though warning bells went off, she felt she could take the chance. Any attack would come much later and several miles away near the docks. Being caught in a bombing again wasn't something she wanted to entertain. She lengthened her strides to shorten the ten-minute walk.

As she came through the St. Stephens entrance at the Palace of Westminster, Livy crossed the familiar marble tiles to the security station, where armed military guards stood by the desk in battle dress and watched her with disinterest.

"Excuse me," she said, holding her blue identity card out to a gray-haired man writing on a lined sheet of paper. His hand reached out and she slipped the blue card into it. He took it without looking up, continuing to write notes on the ledger. When the blue card passed beneath his eyes, his head popped up.

"Miss Livy Ashford, I haven't seen you in years and look at you now, all grown up and so beautiful."

"Sam! It's good to see you. I thought you retired to a gentleman's life in Hastings."

"I had, Miss Livy. But it's the war, you know. They asked me back part-time as most of the men got called up." He gave her a broad smile. "I only occupy this desk a few nights a week, but it gives me a chance to do my part, however small. It's certainly good to see you. Your father isn't here though." He checked the ledger and said, "I have him at Downing Street for another hour or so."

"I hope it's not that long—I need to speak with him. I thought I'd go up to his office and wait for him there. I need to make some phone calls."

"That's fine, Miss Livy. Just sign in please."

He passed her the ledger and as she signed it, she noticed Aubrey's scribbled name four lines up.

"Thank you, Sam," she said. "Is Aubrey Beck here?"

"I'm sorry, who?"

"Aubrey Beck. She pointed at his signature, "His name's written a few lines above mine."

He took the ledger from her and studied the page.

"Oh, him. A squadron commander, I believe. He and two other gentlemen came in to look at some work needed for Member Eaton's office."

"Oh, I see. Well, please say hello to your lovely wife for me."

"I will, and you take care of yourself. It's good to see you again. I'll tell your father you're here when he comes in."

"Thank you, Sam."

She left the security station and went around the corner thinking of Aubrey Beck and his phone call. Nothing fit. What would Aubrey be doing here? He had lied to her and she knew it, but she didn't know why. Rather than go to Wilfred's office, find Aubrey and confront him, she decided to stick to her plan and make a few well-placed calls from her father's Whitehall phone. When he came from his meeting with the War Cabinet, she'd go over everything with him and see what he had to say.

Livy climbed to the third floor via the back stairs and went down a short, darkened hallway. When she turned the corner, she froze. Down the long corridor, coming out of her father's office, was Aubrey Beck and two other men—one short and heavy and the other tall and dressed in black with a birdlike face.

Livy jumped back around the corner. She took a breath and wondered why they broke into her father's office as she peeked around the corner still covered by the darkness of the hall. The three looked down the long corridor and Aubrey closed the office door. He led them across the hall to a stairwell that would lead out to the north side of the Parliament buildings.

Livy leaned back against the wall and wondered what to do. She thought about summoning security, calling them from the office but by the time they could get anyone there, Aubrey and the other two would be gone. With no other option, she decided to follow them and find out what they were doing and why they had broken into her father's locked office. When she knew, she would return and report it.

Livy went down the hallway passed the office and gently opened the door to the stairs. Below, she heard their footsteps going down and she followed, carefully moving, not making a sound. At the landing on the second floor, she chanced a peek over the banister and saw the three men as they reached the ground floor. The heavy door to the gardens opened and slammed closed. She picked up her pace and scrambled down the stairs. As she opened the street door, Big Ben began to chime. Scared and out of habit, she counted.

On the first strike, she was at the garden square searching the night, trying to find them. On the second, about two hundred feet away, she spotted them crossing City Center, toward Charing Cross Station. Staying on the fringes of sight, she heard the third ring as she hurried after them. She counted seven more from Big Ben's huge bell and silence hung over the blacked-out city.

They took back streets, always looking behind them as if they knew she was following. She carefully darted in and out of alleys or doorways, always keeping hidden. The three passed Charing Cross and headed north onto The Strand as two people walked by, their heads down, braving a fast walk home in the blackout. The three crossed the street, Livy shadowing them on the opposite side, relieved that in the darkness, her gray-blue uniform helped to blend her in with the gloom.

The Strand curved and dissolved into Fleet Street. The three turned and headed into a maze of narrow lanes, remnants from centuries past. As she ran from cover to cover, a sound returned like a nightmare, air raid warnings started to moan in the distance announcing an imminent attack.

Livy stopped at the corner where they turned and let one eye peek around the tattered bricks. They came to a stop on the sidewalk where the street bent to the right. After a few seconds, two of them—the shorter man and Aubrey—continued on, leaving the hawk-faced man somewhere deep in the shadows. All she could do was wait. Confident the man would emerge after a few moments and carry on.

The darkness seemed to press in on her as she looked up the street. The man was out there somewhere in the gloom waiting for her. He would kill her if she dared to make a move to follow them. She would chance a look and hide behind the safety of the corner, wait a few seconds and peek around again risking only the smallest exposure to eyes she knew were searching for her.

Muffled explosions from far away came slowly rumbling over the rooftops like thunder as she stood against the cold, dusty brick wall. She peeked one more time around the corner and saw the man step out of a shadowed shop entry and walk up the cobblestone street away from her. She backed up, took a deep breath, her heart pounding. After several seconds, she gathered her courage and slipped around the corner.

It was as if he had vanished. Not a soul was visible on the street. She started up St. Dunstan's Court, knowing that from any doorway or alley entrance the man could jump out, seize her and most likely take her life. Alone in the darkness, her fear tasting sour, she carefully continued until she came to a dingy run-down intersection that was deserted.

She'd lost them in the blackout.

Hidden deep in shadow, Livy looked up and down the street wondering what to do, her hands shaking. They could be anywhere. The only thing she could think of was to return to Westminster, see what damage they had done and why. She started off, creeping through the blackout, across Wine Office Court toward where she believed Fleet Street would be.

Many uncertain steps later, the sharp bells of a fire engine rang out behind her and a red pumper raced passed, its headlight blinders showing only a narrow slice of road in front of it. Livy watched from inside a doorway as it slowed where Wine Office dead-ended into another street and in the dim lights of the fire engine, she saw Aubrey look back.

She ran toward the intersection and stopped at the corner as the three men disappeared into a ramshackle factory a little way up a cobblestone road called Shoe Lane.

Livy crept past brick windowless façades with identical rows of rotting doors set one step down off the sidewalk until she came to the one they entered. She went down the single step and put her ear to the weathered door. It moved silently, a crack opening into a void darker than the night. Her heart racing, she eased the door open and entered to the sound of a raised voice she instantly recognized that came from behind a blackout curtain.

"I am telling you there was nothing there!" Aubrey Beck vehemently said.

She reached the curtain as air raid warning sirens began to blare close by.

"That's impossible! It must be there. You missed it." She heard Wilfred Eaton's voice say, the pitch high and agitated. She wondered what he was doing here.

"The Defense Plan is not in his safe," Aubrey said, a hint of fear in his voice. "It must be at Kensington Manor. He wouldn't hide it anywhere else."

Panic snapped Livy's throat like a vice. "Then, we'll have to go there. We must obtain the communication hub locations." Wilfred said.

Livy peeked through the crack at the side of the curtain, her shaking hands barely able to hold onto the cloth. Wooden crates and metal drums were stacked in the gloom against the walls. In the center of a concrete floor next to a round wooden table she saw Wilfred Eaton standing and staring at the ceiling.

He moved and she gulped a breath, trying to comprehend what she was seeing. Alana was there seated at the table, the bird-faced man and the short heavy one on either side of Aubrey

"Go on to Gloucester as scheduled," Alana said to her father. "I'll take care of getting the document from Ashford."

The contempt in Alana's voice brought a rage that began to burn in her heart. She couldn't believe her eyes. Alana had betrayed her—and what was more important, she and Wilfred had betrayed their country and all it stood for.

"And, my dear, what do you propose to do?" Wilfred said as he ran a hand through his thinning hair.

"I propose to go to Kensington Manor when he's there and get the document."

"Oh, and I suppose he'll simply give it to you because you ask?" Wilfred retorted.

"No, I plan to persuade him to give it to me and then, eliminate him—along with Livy if she's there." Alana said as if nothing could be easier.

Livy gasped and her hand snagged the curtain, making it screech as it slid a foot or two across the curtain bar. Wilfred and the others whipped their heads around at the sound, their faces frozen like statues.

"Get her!" Wilfred screamed. "She's Ashford's daughter!"

Livy ripped her hand away from the curtain and ran out the door and down the street. She could hear the sound of bombers coming, like the rumble of a thousand trains rolling through a station. As she ran, she dared a quick look behind and saw the bird man and the fat one racing after her. There was a flash and a bullet whizzed by, exploding into bricks inches above her head. She screamed and veered into an alley, her heart pounding against her ribs as she sucked in breath after breath through her choked throat. She had to get away, find some way to stop them.

As she ran over cobblestones, between the narrow alley walls she caught a glimpse of St. Paul's as a bomb exploded and splashed angry amber light into the dark sky.

St. Paul's, help would be there . . . if she could make it.

She reached the end of the alley as another bullet buzzed by. She sped around a corner and ran across Farringdon Street, the dome of St. Paul's a little larger. Another bomb exploded nearby, the blast shattering windows and stone, the deafening concussion bounced her against a wall. She turned into another narrow lane that seemed to close in on her. Sounds of explosions and the sharp wail of bombs dropping filled the night around her as she screamed and covered her ears, the terror making her feel as if she was running on sand.

Flames erupted in bursts around her, the concussion and heat flailing at her, almost knocking her to the ground as she ran down Bear Alley. She looked behind her and saw her pursuers gaining ground, getting much closer. She ran, calling on every last bit of strength, through the alley and onto a street when the world around her exploded. Heat seared her skin and her body was thrown against stone as a terrible weight cascaded down on her.

The Doctor stopped abruptly as the bomb exploded and a wall come crashing down on top of the girl they were chasing. Debris fell from the sky in huge slowly spinning pieces. Fires erupted in several places as he and the Irishman stood in the center of the alley.

"Did you see that? There's no way she could live through that," the Irishman shouted, his breath coming in spasms "The entire wall came down on her."

"Let's get out of here before we get killed," the Doctor hissed. "We'll go back and tell them she's dead."

They turned and ran away from the fires and the shrill screams of falling bombs.

Chapter Forty-One

A mortuary van pulled into the emergency drive of St Thomas Hospital as Lucy Wilkins was coming to work. She wondered why it was at a hospital. Here they dealt with the living, not the dead. The driver ran around the van and opened the passenger door for another man, who climbed out with a dust-covered body. If the woman wasn't dead, she was close to it. *Another one ready to buy it.* It was going to be a busy morning.

She opened a side door and entered into chaos.

Four and a half hours later, Lucy came out the same door and lit a cigarette, inhaling deeply as she thought about the morning's activity in the operating room. There were several patients with broken bones that needed to be pinned—painful injuries, but they would survive—many with burns and others that hadn't fared so well. They were the ones with massive internal damage from bomb concussions. The majority of those couldn't be saved. Eight out of ten never made it off the table.

Last night's raid scored a direct hit. Three floors of the nurses' home on the hospital's north side had collapsed, crushing several of the girls billeted there. Lucy was lucky. By chance, she had agreed to spell another girl and spent the night working in the underground shelter near Blackfriars Bridge. All she lost was everything she owned, except the clothes on her back and two sets of scrubs in her locker. Today, she had no home and would have to find a place to sleep but at least she was alive.

She took another drag on the cigarette, rested her head against the brick wall, and closed her eyes, the sun warming her. *In a few more days I'll be twenty-one and the only present I want is a full night's sleep.*

"Oh, here you are," a voice called from around the side of the building. It was Mary Hooson, the charge nurse. Lucy let out a long breath.

She had to be in her mid-forties or older. Her graying hair was pinned beneath the triangle cap and a white bib apron with a red cross stitched to it stuck out over her ample bosom. Her face formed an almost perfect circle with eyes set too close together, nearly touching a pointed nose. "What is it, ma'am?"

"Haven't you seen what's going on in there? I need you inside, not out here smoking."

"I was taking a break. I've been in the OR for the last four hours." Lucy said.

"And I've been here for six. I've got two with broken limbs, five with burns and one that doesn't know who she is. Look in on those and after, take your break."

"Yes ma'am."

Lucy sighed, trying to gather the energy to keep going and slowly followed her back into the turmoil. At the file-littered nurses' station, Mary handed her a clipboard with summary records attached. Lucy thumbed through the cases, stopping at the third in the stack, an unusual one. A woman had been brought in by one of the mortuary disposal units after being dug out alive from a rubble pile. That alone was unusual. It had to be the same woman she saw this morning, the one that was carried from the van.

Making her way down the crowded corridor, Lucy stepped around or over the injured waiting their turn. She stopped at the open door inside one of the wards lined with beds on either side of a long room. Turning her attention to the case, Lucy began to read.

The woman had arrived semiconscious with multiple contusions over her extremities and torso. No breaks were discovered with X-rays, but there was the possibility of unknown internal damage from bomb concussions. A little more than an hour ago she regained consciousness and had no idea who or where she was. The doctors call it concussive blast syndrome, a temporary condition where signals in the brain were jumbled from the patient being in the proximity of a bomb explosion. The Doctor recommended that she be held for observation over the next twenty-four hours and that attempts made to find her next of kin.

Fate, that's what it was. Lucy thought as she started toward bed twelve. She'd seen this same condition too many times—the blast should have got her, but it simply wasn't her time to die.

She was lying on her side facing away from her. "Excuse me, Miss. My name is Nurse Wilkins. I need to ask you a few questions." She looked down at the clipboard and her records.

As she looked up from the clipboard, the woman slowly turned to face her. Lucy gulped in a breath, the woman was Livy Ashford.

Chapter Forty-Two

Locked in a wretched root cellar, Jamie spent the remainder of the night and by his watch, many more hours alone in darkness. He lay on a straw-filled mattress with yesterday's events revolving through his mind. He thought of Livy and what she must be thinking, wondering if he was dead or alive? He had most likely been reported killed in action by Aubrey and that thought sent him into a rage. The next time he saw that bastard, he would throttle him.

He attempted to bring some coherence into his thinking as he listened to movement in the kitchen above, the floor creaking under footsteps. The muffled voices that filtered down into the darkness were of an argument between the woman and the man Jamie believed was her father. It came in rapid-fire bursts, the French spoken far too fast for him understand, but one phrase the man kept saying stood out: *L'exécuter.* That, he understood. They were planning to execute him.

The door to the cellar burst open, a painful light slashed onto the clay floor. The woman's father came down the wooden stairs, followed by Rat carrying a Bren gun. He aimed it at Jamie's heart and motioned for him to stand.

His mind now raced, trying to devise a plan, something to save his life, but he could come up with nothing. The men forced him up the stairs and shoved him forward, making him spill out of the cellar onto the kitchen floor. He rolled over, trying to get his feet underneath him and found himself looking up into the brown eyes of the woman.

"Get up," she said.

She motioned to Rat, who yanked him up and sat him in a chair at the table. The woman circled behind him, the muzzle of a pistol lightly rubbing across the back of his shoulders.

She sat on the edge of the table and stared at him, her face like granite.

Frustration mounted in him. "I told you the truth! Haven't you contacted London?"

"We have. In a few minutes, the BBC news will be on and we'll see if Jamie Wallace told us the truth." She rested one hand on the table, the other holding the pistol aimed between his eyes.

"It is the truth." He pointed toward the canvas bag still on the table. "The film in that bag must get to England. It may be only a few days before they invade and if they do, that will doom any chance France has to be liberated. You must believe me." He softened his voice, "Please tell me your name. I'd like to know; it's important to me."

"Why?" She laughed at him, cocked her head and paused. "But, you'll probably be dead in the next few minutes so if it makes a difference to you, my name is Amalie. And while we wait to see if Jamie Wallace is who he says he is, let me tell you a little story so you understand who I am." She folded her arms across her chest, the black Luger tapping her shoulder.

"I'm from a little village near the German border. I had a beautiful life, happy and peaceful with a wonderful family. Until the day the Germans came. I happened to be here, at this farm visiting my uncle and that's the only reason I'm alive."

He looked at the man he'd thought was her father.

She stared at him for a moment and continued. "The black shirts came late in the morning and took all of the men, every single one of them, to a field outside the village. In that field, they slaughtered them and left their bodies to rot in the sun. After that, they took the women and children. They marched them all to the church and locked them inside. Then, the bastards burned the church to the ground. If any tried to escape from the fire, they shot them and all the while they drank our wine and laughed as our women and children were burned alive.

"My entire village was destroyed. My mother, my father and my little brother all died that day. And because of that, I fight the Nazis. Nothing, except my own death, will stop me from slitting the throats of every German I can find, including you."

There was nothing to say. Jamie remained quiet, looking into her eyes, in the soft brown he saw only pain. He knew she could never restore her life, it was over. Even if she survived the war, she was already dead.

Amalie unfolded her arms and pointed the Luger at him. "So, if you're not who you say you are, this night will be the last night of your life."

She narrowed her eyes, studying him, the Luger now inches from his forehead. "The Germans will do anything to find us, go as far as plant evidence and make up stories as wild as yours. I almost believe you, Jamie Wallace, but we'll all know the truth very soon."

Amalie looked at a clock in the kitchen and motioned with her head towards Rat. He disappeared into the root cellar and a few long moments later, he returned with a forbidden item, a standard issue short wave radio. On his way to the table Rat connected the electrical cord and placed it in front of Amalie. She raised the antenna and switched it on. Inside the wooden box, he could see between the cooling slats the glow of tubes warming.

Amalie stared at him and said, "If in the next few minutes you hear, 'Le monde est á moi de tenir, in English, 'The world is mine to hold,' you are who you say you are you'll get back to England. If not . . ." She shrugged and lowered the gun.

Chapter Forty-Three

Randall Ashford stood by the windows of his office, his hands shoved into the pockets of his black suit. He looked out across the Thames where hundreds of thick plumes of smoke expanded over his city, graying out what should be a blue sky. The smell of charred wood and singed flesh hung in the air, scratched the throat of everyone still breathing. He focused on the devastation at St. Thomas Hospital across the river, the women's resident wing and all the young women killed there. It added to the anguish in his heart, Livy was missing.

This morning as he left the flat, he'd stuck his head into her room. She wasn't there and the bed hadn't been slept in. Thinking she must have gone back to Kensington Manor, he went into his library and gave her a ring. She hadn't gone home. His next attempt was to her friend Alana Eaton. She said she hadn't seen her in days. That's when the fear started.

He thought over his actions, wondering if there was anything he had missed, anything more he could do. The waiting was killing him. Hours ago, the intercom on his desk had come to life.

"Lord Ashford, Scotland Yard returning your call."

He grabbed the phone. "Gordon?" he blurted out.

Sir Gordon Howell—the Metropolitan Police Commissioner said, "Randall, what's wrong, I can hear it in your voice."

"Livy's missing. I need your help. I didn't know who else to turn to."

"Missing? Are you sure? How do you know that?"

He went over the morning in detail and received a promise that one of the Yard's best inspectors would be assigned to find her. Ten minutes later a detective, Chief Inspector Brooks phoned and Randall went over all of it again, since then nothing.

The hours had passed in turmoil. He turned away from the windows and sat at his desk, staring blankly at the silent black phone. Images of a rainy night in London, a drunken taxi driver and the lifeless body of his beloved cradled in his arms flooded back, the pain as real and intense as the moment it happened. He couldn't lose Livy. She was all he had left. She was everything in the world to him. There was nothing more he could do. The phone rang in the outer office and he jumped, snatching the receiver.

"Ashford here."

"Lord Ashford, this is DCI Brooks." Randall stiffened, awaiting the news. "Sir, we haven't found your daughter, but there's at least some good news. At this time, we don't believe she is among last night's casualty roles. Most have been identified and among the remaining, there are no young women. The mortuary people are on alert, but it's doubtful they'll see any more additions and your daughter isn't among the dead."

Randall closed his eyes, his worst fear abated.

"We spoke with Westminster Palace Security," the Detective said. "Last night she signed in, reportedly to use your telephone. We checked with the switchboard operators and no calls were made. Security reported that she didn't check out, so we're looking into that. We also spoke with all the hospitals in the area and none reported having an Olivia Ashford. So, at this time we don't believe she was injured.

"As we move forward, sir, we'll need your help. Is there anything else you can tell us? Such as whom she might be seeing—a friend or relative, a young man? Anything you can think of, something you might have forgotten?"

"I can't think of anyone except a young pilot she knows. But I doubt she saw him."

"Well, that's a start. What's his name?"

"Jamie Wallace. He's with 41 Squadron stationed at Hornchurch."

"Good. We'll check on that and get back to you. Don't give up hope, sir. We'll find her."

Brooks rang off, leaving Randall feeling slightly better. She was alive, or at least they thought so. He began to play back the entire morning, where could she have gone? And of all things, what was she doing at his office last night?

The squawk box erupted.

"Sir, while you were on the phone a hospital nurse phoned, a Lucy Wilkins. I have her on hold. Will you take the call?"

"Who?"

"Lucy Wilkins, sir. She wouldn't say anything to me. Said she will only speak to you."

He had no idea who she was or what she wanted, but since she was calling from a hospital maybe, "All right, go ahead and put her through."

He picked up the receiver and said, "Randall Ashford speaking."

"Good morning, sir," the voice said. "My name is Lucy Wilkins. I'm a nurse at St Thomas Hospital."

She had an obvious East End accent. "What can I do for you, Miss Wilkins?"

"I don't mean to be impudent, sir, but do you have a daughter?"

The blood drained from his face.

"I do. Olivia is her name."

There was a pause on the line. "I have her here."

He choked back tears. "She's in the hospital? Is she . . ."

"Livy is okay. They found her this morning buried in a rubble pile."

"My God!" The words stuck in his throat.

"She has quite a few bruises, but nothing's broken. Except she's quite confused and disoriented, sir. Right now, she doesn't know who she is or where she is. But in time, she'll be fine. The doctors say she'll get everything back in a few days or weeks. They think it's from a bomb concussion. We have her under observation right now to make sure she has no internal injuries."

He didn't say anything, trying to process what he heard. "If . . . if she doesn't know who she is, how do you know she's my daughter?"

"I met her twice before—once when we were getting our assignments and once when she was with her pilot friend in a shelter I volunteer at. As soon as I saw her, I recognized her. That's how I was able to find you. She told me her father was a Lord."

"God, bless you. Where can I find her?"

"If you come to Emergency, just ask for me, and I'll bring you to her."

"I'm on my way. I'll be there in a few minutes. And, Lucy thank you."

Aubrey Beck cleaned a few grains of white powder from beneath his nose and stepped away from the mirror in the loo. As he reached the door he held it open, allowed two men focused on each other to enter. *What impeccable timing,* he thought as they passed by. He smiled at their backs and started down the corridor toward Ashford's office.

The news from last night seriously disappointed him, it destroyed everything he wanted from Livy. When the Irishman and the Doctor reported back saying she was killed, Alana sat stone-faced as if nothing had happened and Wilfred was giddy. What distressed Aubrey most was that he'd never have her or her money. He was devastated, all his plans gone awry. There was nothing for him to do but move on to another girl, hopefully one as rich.

He knew he needed to be more careful. Alana had blamed him for Livy following them back to the factory. It wasn't his fault, but they blamed him for almost exposing their operation. He quivered, knowing that if anything else happened, she would turn him over to that psychopath Doctor. But, this job was simple—nothing could go wrong. All he had to do was find out when Ashford would be at Kensington Manor. They would invade the home and force him to give up the document and then eliminate him. Easy, but he had to be careful how he phrased it, Ashford might not know his daughter was dead.

As he approached the office door, rehearsing what he would say, Randall Ashford burst out. They almost ran into each other. "Lord Ashford," he said, surprised.

"I'm sorry, Aubrey, I haven't got time. Livy is in the hospital, injured."

He froze. Livy was alive? How could that be? Thoughts to do something and quick rushed in his head. If she spoke to her father, she would immediately inform him that he was a traitor. He'd be arrested and hung. "In the hospital?" he stammered.

"Yes, I can't explain it now. I'm on my way over there."

"Is she, injured?" He could hear the panic in his voice and hoped Ashford didn't.

"Yes, possibly seriously. She doesn't know who or where she is."

Fantastic, Aubrey thought, as relief settled over him. This might work out, he would still find a way to have her.

"I'll take you over there. I've got my car parked by the entrance. It'll be much faster than waiting for a government driver."

For a split-second Ashford paused. He grabbed Aubrey's arm and said, "Good idea. Come along."

On the way to the hospital, Aubrey kept thinking how providence always worked in his favor. Livy was alive and best of all, she had no memory of him being a traitor, or of her being in love with a dead Jamie Wallace. Things couldn't be better.

He knew the game he was playing could be dangerous, but that was what made it so exciting. How little Alana and the others understood him—the fools. He would betray them all when the time was right—once he got his due. Hell, he thought, they would probably give him the Victoria Cross.

He made the turn into the hospital's drive, swung the Jaguar around and stopped, leaving the car in front of the Emergency entrance. Ashford almost leapt out of the car and ran into the building leaving Aubrey at the curb. He shut off the engine and got out as a grumbling security guard approached.

"Excuse me!" he said. "You can't leave this here. You're blocking the ambulance entrance. Can't you read the signs?"

Aubrey scowled at him. "That was Lord Ashford," he said, pointing at the closing entry door. "His daughter's inside, severely injured. You want to tell him we can't park here for a few minutes?"

The guard's eyes widened while he paused a second. "A Lord, huh." Aubrey could see the wheels turning. "Well, I guess it'll be all right. Just leave me the keys so I can move it."

Aubrey smiled and pocketed the keys. He turned his back on the guard and followed Ashford into the hospital.

Halfway down the green-and-white painted hall, he saw him pacing at the charge desk. A young nurse held her finger up, holding him silent as she spoke into the phone. As he came up to Ashford, the girl managed to end the conversation and rang off.

She looked up and said, "I'm sorry for the delay, sir. How may I help you?"

"I need to see Lucy Wilkins," Ashford said.

"To tell you the truth, I have no idea where she is. We don't have a paging system—it was knocked out last night and with all the patients that were brought in this morning, I don't know where she is."

"That's fine. I'll find her." He started to leave and stopped in his tracks. "What does she look like?"

The girl was surprised at his question. "You don't know her, sir?"

"No, I've never seen her."

"Oh. Well, she's tall and thin, and she'll be dressed in . . ."

"What's going on here? What do you want with my people?" a round-face nurse with enough breast for three barked. "I'm Mary Hooson, the charge nurse and she works for me. I can't have strangers milling about wasting the time of my nurses. They have far more important things to do than chit-chat."

Ashford scowled. "I need to see Lucy Wilkins."

"What do you need to see her for? You just said you don't even know her."

"My daughter is in this hospital and I need to find her."

"And what is your daughter's name?"

"Olivia Ashford."

The woman gazed at a chart, her thick finger slowly sliding down a list of names as Ashford grew more and more agitated.

"There's no one here by that name, so I suggest you leave."

Aubrey watched as Ashford's eyes became slits.

"I'm going to ask you one more time—where is Lucy Wilkins?"

"And I'm going to call security and have you removed from this hospital." the nurse snapped back.

Ashford turned from her and in a loud voice yelled out, "Lucy Wilkins!"

"That's enough!" Hooson's voice boomed out.

Ashford yelled even louder. "Lucy Wilkins, where are you?"

The nurse started to come around the desk toward him and yelled, "I want you out of my hospital!"

From behind, a man's hand reached out and clasped Ashford's shoulder.

"Lord Ashford, I'm John Whitcomb the managing director of the hospital. Your secretary called and told me you would be here. How can I help you?"

Nurse Hooson blanched.

"My daughter is here. Lucy Wilkins called me and told me. I need to find her."

Whitcomb turned to Hooson's plump face. "Find Nurse Wilkins and do it now."

"There's no need for that. I'm right here." a voice said.

Aubrey turned around and saw a tall, thin woman dressed in blooded nurse garb. He watched as Ashford wrapped his arms around the nurse and kissed her cheek, "God bless you, Lucy. Please—take me to her."

"She'll be fine, sir. I promise. The doctor is with her now." Lucy winked and took his hand.

As they headed down the hall, Aubrey chuckled when he heard Whitcomb say to the head nurse, "You report to my office, immediately."

Lucy and Randall were met at the entry to one of the wards by a doctor with thick jet-black hair combed heavily across the crown in a fashion that made it seem as if the whole mess might slip off and run down the side of his head. He was slightly shorter than Ashford, dressed in a dark-blue rumpled suit and white shirt with a stethoscope hanging around his neck.

"You must be Lord Ashford. Lucy told me you were on the way. I'm Doctor Pritchard, the emergency surgeon. Well, for today at least."

The doctor had a way of describing each word with a delicate wave of his hand.

Aubrey followed them into the ward, his eyes searching for Livy.

"Thank you," Ashford said. "Where's my daughter and what are her injuries?"

"She's right over there." He pointed to the sixth bed along one side of the room.

Aubrey saw her in the bed, her hair rumpled, but as beautiful as ever.

"As to her injuries," the Doctor continued. "She's extremely lucky. Nothing's broken. We X-rayed her from head to foot. She has some contusions, all of which are mostly minor but she's quite confused. Lucy said she'd told you that."

"Confused? What does that mean? How did that happen?"

"We're not sure. We don't know enough about the human brain to understand the reasons. I've seen at least five patients with exactly the same condition. We've named it Concussive Blast Syndrome. We think the shock wave from a bomb can jar the brain and cause a sort of scrambling of the electrical signals. But we're not sure."

"Will she get it all back?"

"I believe so. All the others have."

"How long? How long will she be like this?"

"That I'm afraid I can't answer. There's no way to tell, we simply don't know. A few hours, days, a month or more, but I doubt that. As I said, all the others recovered, but none of the recuperation times have been consistent. Right now, her short-term memory appears to be fine, but she doesn't know anything about her past. She doesn't know who she is. We believe something will come along and trigger her mind to rebuild the proper connections. She'll begin to remember her life before the trauma but when, that I can't answer."

I have a little time. Aubrey thought. *I'll find a way to at least have my way with her before they kill her.*

Ashford closed his eyes, "Thank you for all you've done. It's time I took her home."

"That's not a good idea. I can't agree to that," Dr. Pritchard said firmly, his index finger rocking back and forth.

"Why? I can take better care of her there."

Dr. Prichard shook his head. "Lord Ashford, she needs to be here at least until tomorrow morning. The blast concussion may have caused unknown injuries and we need to observe her for that. I don't think you're prepared to recognize the symptoms of damage to her internal organs. I don't believe there is any, but we need to keep her here to be sure."

"Then, I'll stay with her." It was a command.

Whitcomb dashed into the room and went over to the doctor. "We will take her to a private room and I'll assign Lucy to care for her until the doctor feels she can be released, if that is all right with you, Lord Ashford. It's what's best for her, sir."

Ashford looked at the two and said, "Thank you, thank you both. May I see her now?"

"Certainly," Dr. Prichard said. "But don't be surprised if she seems very confused."

Whitcomb reached out and patted Lucy's shoulder. "Stay with Lord Ashford, I'll get the orderlies to move her to a private room."

"Certainly, I'm happy to help," she said.

The doctor and Whitcomb left as Ashford went over to Livy. When Ashford reached the bed, he sat and took her hand.

"My beautiful Livy, I'm here."

She looked at him with a blank expression on her face.

Chapter Forty-Four

Amalie slowly turned the dial on the face of the radio. A scratched whistle accompanied by static filtered in and out until words spoken in French floated out of the speaker. Jamie had no idea what they meant as it droned on and on until there was a pause and he heard the accented pronunciation of a word he understood, messages.

Jamie knew the intelligence services used the BBC to communicate with the resistance. Twice each day they would broadcast messages, some real, some meaningless, depending on the content and the person receiving it. It was quite effective unless whoever listened was discovered. If they were overheard, the Gestapo would immediately shoot them and confiscate the radio, a very dangerous business.

Amalie sat at the table and stared at Jamie, her hand resting on the Luger. Sentence after sentence came over the radio until the voice paused and said, "C'est tout pour aujourd'hui."

Rat and her uncle looked at each other and smiled. They rushed over and jerked Jamie onto his feet, Rat's knife pushed on the skin above his kidney.

"It seems that is all they have for today, Jamie Wallace. The message concerning you was not delivered," she said. Amalie stood and pointed the Luger at his chest.

Jamie could feel his blood drain away. "Wait! It can't be. Something is wrong. I told you the truth."

A cold stare came from her and for his benefit she said the words in English, "Take him outside and kill him. Bury him in a hole."

He struggled against the two men but it was hopeless. They started to drag him from the kitchen to an unmarked grave in the French soil.

"Don't do this Amalie, I told you the truth. You're making a mistake!"

She turned away from him and sat, her hand reached out toward the radio to silence it. Not looking up she said, "Goodbye Jamie Wallace."

As her hand reached toward the knob, in rapid French the radio voice decibels louder said, "Attendez un message vient d'être livre."

"Arrêtez." she said, her voice an order.

Rat and her Uncle stopped. They thrust Jamie's back against the kitchen wall and held him there, Rat's knife millimeters from his throat.

From the radio speaker, the voice came again, the words spoken slowly, clearly, "Le monde est á moi de tenir. Répéter! Le monde est á moi de tenir."

Amalie switched off the radio and stood. "Relâchez-le."

The two released their grip.

Jamie took in a deep breath. "I told you the truth."

"Now I believe you, Jamie Wallace. We have a long walk ahead of us. You leave tonight, but first, you'll need a bath and a change of clothes."

Chapter Forty-Five

Aubrey watched Lord Randall Ashford wipe his eyes—a man he thought incapable of emotion held Livy's hand as she stared at him, her expression completely blank. He swallowed hard, abruptly turned from the bed to hide his tears. He left the room saying he had to arrange for an ambulance to take her home tomorrow morning and that he'd be right back. Lucy also said she needed to check on the orderlies that would facilitate her move to a private room, leaving Aubrey alone with her for a few precious moments.

He approached her bed and sat almost exactly as her father did, gently taking her hand and stroking it. She was nude beneath the loose-fitting hospital gown, her breasts pushing up against the thin cotton. A purplish bruise rode on a shoulder that seemed to spill out of the untied collar. Her auburn hair was tussled, but her eyes were clear and beautiful. Jamie would never pose a problem again and he knew exactly what to do. This was his opportunity.

"Livy, do you remember me?" he said softly.

She stared, void of emotion. "No."

Aubrey feigned pain, as if his heart had been pierced with a sword. "You will, my love. I'll be here to take care of you. You'll soon remember me."

Her expression was empty as she looked at him. He reached out and caressed her shoulder, his fingers running lightly over the bruise and down her bare arm pulling at the gown. She reached up and pushed his hand away.

"Stop!" she said, her eyes narrowing.

He held her hand, frustrated as he heard Ashford approaching with the orderlies. "I am your lover."

Aubrey got up from the bed before Ashford entered the room.

As he came to her side, Aubrey said with the deepest compassion, "Lord Ashford, I need to return to Whitehall. May I give you a ride back to Westminster?" Knowing he wouldn't leave.

"No Aubrey, I'll stay here until the morning and take her home."

"If I may, sir, I'd like to check in on her tomorrow. Over the last few months we've become very close."

"Of course, Aubrey—anytime." Ashford looked at him, the rims of his eyes red. "You've been of great assistance. It might even help her, seeing people she knows."

"Thank you, sir. I'll return to Whitehall then and see you tomorrow. If you need anything, please let me know. I'm here to help."

Aubrey smiled at him and quietly left the room, elated. Everything would work out as he'd planned.

He drove over Westminster Bridge and back to the Houses of Parliament after a quick pause at Archbishop's Park for a measure of his drug. He climbed the stairs to Wilfred Eaton's office two at a time. He straightened his tie and came through the office door. Alana stood behind her desk, her back to him. She heard him come in and turned to face him, a scowl came over her face.

"Aubrey's here," she called out to her father in the inner office.

"Good. Both of you come in here and close the door."

They went in together.

"All right Aubrey, what did you find out?"

"Lord Ashford will be at Kensington Manor tomorrow and for the rest of the week." he said with a cheerful tone.

Wilfred stared at him and scratched his forehead. "Very well, we'll use today to plan our assault. Alana, tomorrow will be the day. How unfortunate for Ashford, that will be his last day on earth."

He slipped his thumbs under his suspenders as he got up from his desk, "The Irishman and the Doctor are at the hunter's cabin finishing the radio beacons. As soon as we have the locations for the communication hubs, we'll place the beacons and our bombers will destroy them. Right after, the invasion will begin." He continued as he moved toward the window, his back to Alana and Aubrey. "Our success can be measured in hours now.

"A rather exciting time, isn't it?" Eaton rested his fists like hammers on his hips. "You two go to the cabin and fetch the others. I'll leave for Gloucester and direct things from our estate. The four of you will retrieve the document from Kensington Manor. Alana, when you have the document, deliver it to me. After I've radioed the hub locations, you and I will take the full document to Berlin by U-boat."

A thin smile came to Aubrey's face. "One moment, I wouldn't be so hasty. There is something else Wilfred."

"And what's that, Aubrey?" He said it as if he were exasperated, his back still facing them.

"Livy Ashford isn't dead. She's actually quite alive."

Eaton whipped around, the color drained from his face. "My God, that could mean the end of everything. She must be disposed of immediately."

Aubrey glanced at Alana and almost laughed at her expression of horror.

He looked back to Eaton and with a finger rubbed his lower lip. "Hold on, Wilfred. There's more I need to tell you before you run off and do something rash." He said it as if he were the one in charge. "She's alive all right, but she's completely lost her faculties. I don't think you have to worry about her saying anything." He almost laughed as he said it.

"How do you know this?" Alana said, her voice skeptical.

"I've seen her. I was with her a few minutes ago." Aubrey beamed a smiled at her.

"Where?" she said, her dark eyes staring beneath lowered brows.

"I went to Ashford's office exactly as you wanted and ran into him as he was rushing out. He said she'd been injured. I took him to St. Thomas and saw her there. She's no danger to you. Her mind is as blank slate. She doesn't know a thing."

Alana picked up a glass globe from the desk and studied it. "I should go over there and see for myself. We need to know if she's a danger to our mission and if she is, eliminate her."

"Aubrey's right. Let's not be too hasty." Wilfred said, playing with the bowtie beneath his double chin. He smiled at Alana and said, "Her being alive might work out very well for us. Suppose you tell Ashford you want to see her when she arrives home. That is a perfect way to enter the

Manor. He won't expect a thing, so you bring her in front of him and threaten to kill her. I promise you, at that point he'll cooperate. It's perfect don't you see, because after you have the document, you eliminate them both. Quite tidy, don't you think?"

"And the servants, Harold and Jackie—dispose of them also?" she asked.

"I'm afraid so," Wilfred said, nodding. "A pity though, I rather liked them both."

He walked over to Aubrey and put a thick hand on his shoulder. "When do you expect Randall and Livy to be back at Kensington Manor—later today, was it?"

"No. He'll be staying with her at the hospital overnight. They'll return to the manor sometime tomorrow."

"Perfect—that works very well. Alana, gather the other two, you know what's needed. Find a way into Ashford's home tomorrow. Say you heard about her injury from Aubrey and want to see her."

"I don't think that's a good idea." Aubrey said, thinking of what they would do to Livy. He didn't want them near her. "There will be people at the Manor everywhere, specialists and doctors, all sorts of people coming and going. Tomorrow would not be a good time to do anything. But I have a plan."

"Really!" Alana said with a sarcasm that angered him.

"Hold on, let's hear him out." Wilfred said stopping her. "Go ahead, Aubrey—tell me."

Wilfred Eaton sat down at his desk. Aubrey's eyes were focused out the window watching streams of smoke rise, the fires still smoldering from last night's bombing. He took a deep breath, his mind raced as he tried to create something to convince them not to kill her—at least not yet.

"He's expecting me at the manor tomorrow." He paused a moment, gauging their reaction and continued. "I'll find the location of his safe and make sure the document is in there. It might be possible for you to obtain the document without Ashford knowing you have it. That's a much better solution than murder and a police investigation."

Wilfred squeezed his bottom lip with thick fingers as he thought about what Aubrey said. "A very good idea, I like it." His head bobbed up and down.

Chapter Forty-Six

Like most things he wanted, desire had turned into an obsession and his obsession with Livy Ashford was particularly intense. There wasn't much he could do to save her life or for that matter Lord Ashford's, but he would at least relieve his obsession before she died. The anticipation made the drive down from London painfully slow.

The late afternoon sunlight glimmered off the ancient oaks as he turned into the stone-and-iron gate of Kensington Manor. Aubrey slowed, shifted down two gears and swung the Jaguar onto the long river pebble drive. He stopped in front of the manor and took a sealed manila folder labeled with a bright red 'Most Secret' from the map pouch He tucked it under his arm and strode up to the black double doors, clasped the bronze knocker and struck it against the plate. A few seconds later, Harold Rider opened it.

"Squadron Commander Beck, good afternoon," he said.

"Hello, Harold. I'm here to see Lord Ashford."

"Is he expecting you, sir? He didn't mention it."

"With all that's happened, I'm sure he has far greater things on his mind but I believe he's expecting me," Aubrey said as he entered the manor's grand foyer.

"If you'll wait a moment, I'll tell him you're here." Harold spun around and headed toward the study, his heels clicking on the marble floor. As Aubrey stepped down into the living room, Randall Ashford came through a doorway that led from a butler's pantry, holding a plate of finger sandwiches, one stuffed into his mouth.

Harold heard his footsteps and turned around, "Sir." He motioned toward Aubrey. "Squadron Commander Beck has arrived."

Lord Ashford looked at ease wearing light-brown slacks and a white open-collared shirt, but his face told a story of distress. Chewing on the sandwich, he nodded and signaled for Aubrey to follow him into the study. Reaching his sanctum, he leaned an arm on one of the maroon chairs and turned to offer him a triangle-shaped sandwich. With a hand in front of his mouth, he mumbled, "You want one?"

"No thank you, sir," Aubrey said, stopping behind the other chair.

Ashford finished and swallowed. "Good of you to come, Aubrey. Livy needs some company. She's been alone, in bed most of the day."

Aubrey smiled to himself. "How is she doing, sir? As I said, over the last few months we've become close. I've been very worried."

"She's the same, Aubrey—nothing's different. She still doesn't know anyone or remember anything. The Doctors told me to keep her quiet and resting, have her look at photos of places and people from her past. So, with Jackie's help, that's what we've been doing. In a little while, Dr. Rosier is bringing out a neurologist to have a look at her. Maybe he can help." Ashford set the sandwich plate on his desk.

"Dr. Rosier? Isn't he the doctor at Buckingham Palace—the king's doctor?"

"Yes," he said with a smile. "Looks like good King George finally forgave me. We spoke for the first time in years this morning. He heard Livy was injured in the bombing and sent his doctor to help."

Aubrey was impressed, but curious. "Forgiven you, sir? I don't understand."

Ashford smiled and said, "Yes, forgiven me for stealing Mary Taylor away."

"Mary Taylor?"

"My late wife—Livy's mother. She and the King were quite an item back then—that is, until I stole her heart and took her from him. And to think, she would have been the queen. She gave up everything—position, prestige, title—to marry me."

Aubrey saw a wave of emotion ripple across his face—like an epiphany mixed with deep sorrow.

"You know, I have an idea." Randall paused a second and said, "Can you get in touch with Jamie Wallace? I think it would be good for her to see him. Might help her to remember things, start the whole process of her memory coming back. Aren't you in his chain of command. Can you let him know Livy's been injured, have him come to her?"

Aubrey remained quiet for a moment, relishing what he was about to say. He took in a slow deep breath. "Sir, I have some unhappy news." He looked down at the Persian carpet and with sadness said, "Jamie Wallace was killed two days ago over France."

Ashford exhaled softly. "Does Livy know?"

"I told her as soon as I found out, but that was before her injury."

"Tragic—I think she loved him," Ashford whispered. "I'll mention it to the doctor when he arrives." He placed his hand on Aubrey's forearm. "Go up and see her—third door on the left as you reach the top of the stairs. Jackie is with her now, it will do her good to see you."

"Thank you, sir" He pulled the red-lined folder from beneath his arm. "But I need to do something with this. Actually, I was on my way to RAF Biggin Hill and thought to stop here first. I've been ordered to deliver these documents to the base commander and I can't leave them unattended in my car. Would you mind putting them in your safe while I see Livy?"

Ashford nodded and said, "You bring back memories. I've been in the same position myself, delivering secret documents to one place or another. Come with me."

Aubrey followed Randall to one section of the wall length bookcase. Just left of center, he reached beneath a polished shelf. Aubrey heard the snap of a metal clasp disengage. Randall pulled on a shelf filled with books and swung it to the side, revealing a square combination door, which he quickly opened.

"Put the document in here Aubrey."

As he leaned in, at the bottom of ordered stacked papers, he saw a blue covered document about two inches thick, the defense plan. He gently placed his folder into the safe and backed away.

Randall closed the square door and spun the tumblers. As he slipped the bookshelf into place he said, "All right, Aubrey—it's secure, it'll be here when you want it back. Go see her, but don't say anything about Jamie. That might make things worse."

"Of course not, and thank you, sir." Aubrey left the study satisfied, he knew the location of his safe and the defense plan was in it. He controlled his excitement and climbed the stairs one at a time. At the third door on the left, he gave a light tap on it and entered her bedroom. He nodded to Jackie Rider, who was seated in a chair by the windows.

Warm sun flooded the room with a light that seemed to dance across Livy's body. She was sitting up on the bed nestled into stacked pillows, her auburn hair brushed and falling around her shoulders. She wore a lace nightdress and heavy robe, not at all revealing, but it still served to tickle his imagination. She looked up from a photo album and gazed at him, her eyes blank.

"Hello, Livy." He gave her his most endearing smile.

Her beautiful indigo eyes remained vacant, unmoved.

Aubrey crossed the room and sat on the side of the bed. He looked over his shoulder and said, "Jackie would you make us a spot of tea?"

He could see from Jackie's reaction she wasn't happy about the request, leaving Livy alone with him, but she stood.

Jackie looked at Livy and said, "My dear, would you like anything?"

"Some tea would be nice and some of those scones you made this morning would be lovely."

Aubrey smiled. He would be rid of Jackie and alone with his prize.

"I'll be right back," she said, leaving the door open.

He heard her start down the stairs. After a moment, he got up and closed the door. He returned to Livy's bed and took her hand. Aubrey smiled at her with all the tenderness he could muster.

"My darling," he said, softly rubbing her bare forearm, "you'll remember us. I know you will. We were to be married."

Her eyes widened, but she didn't speak.

After a few moments, Aubrey stroked the side of her head, her silky hair running through his fingers. He smiled and said, "Do you remember our time at the cottage by the Channel? We made love in front of the fire only a few days ago. We went there after visiting my family. Try to remember, I can't bear being away from you."

Livy's eyes narrowed as if she was attempting to recall a memory. "I . . . I don't know."

"My love, it's me—Aubrey." He knew his face was painted with a look of deep pain, "Please try to remember, me."

He bent toward her, caressing her shoulder. She didn't move, only stared up at him as his lips reached hers and he kissed her. Aubrey burned with desire as he felt her soft, warm flesh. He attempted to kiss her again with the passion of a lover, but she pushed him away.

"Don't," she said.

His nerves raged. "I don't understand." The words came between breaths as his hand brushed against her breast. He pressed on to kiss her again, but she turned her head to the side. When he pulled back, her eyes were wide and frightened.

The sounds of approaching footsteps made him quickly stand. Her bedroom door popped open. Randall Ashford came in with two men in dark suits behind him. One Aubrey recognized from newspaper photographs as Dr. Rosier and the other he didn't know. He was of average height and underweight. He had thick gray hair brushed back over the top of his head, exposing a rather bland and wrinkled, thin-lipped face.

Aubrey moved away from the bed and slipped into the shadows, as Randall came to her.

"Livy," he said, "these doctors have come to help you. They're going to talk with you for a few minutes."

She nodded and pushed up a little in the bed, her eyes fixed on Aubrey. The two men came to either side of her bed as Ashford stepped back and motioned for Aubrey to follow him out of the room.

"Hello, Livy, I'm Dr. Stein. I'm here to help you," the thin man said.

Downstairs in the study, Aubrey took one of the wingback chairs as Ashford sat behind the desk, his hands intertwined and motionless on the blotter. They chatted in circles for a few minutes about the weather and small things of no consequence before silence overtook them.

He noticed how Ashford continually checked his watch, his minutes passing slowly, his life caving in. Aubrey felt a flash of compassion for him as he thought about Wilfred and Alana and wondered how many hours Randall Ashford had left to live.

His thoughts returned to his plans for Livy and how the murder of a Lord would ruin everything. It was one of the few times he felt completely perplexed, had no idea what to do. He was absolutely sure they would get the documents and also sure Ashford would never give them up. His conundrum was broken by the clump of footsteps coming toward the study.

Randall Ashford almost jumped from the chair as the doctors entered, his face held a shadow of anxiety and fear.

They stopped a few feet from the desk and Dr. Rosier said, "I think she'll be fine, Lord Ashford. Physically, she's doing very well. A few bumps and bruises, but all in all she's fine."

Ashford's face lost some of the anxiety. "Thank God."

"Dr. Stein's examination will address her other issue."

The thin doctor slipped his thumbs into his vest pockets. "Lord Ashford," he began, "her confusion appears to be a manifestation of what we are seeing quite a bit of right now."

Ashford came around the desk toward them. "What is that?"

"It's when the pressure concussion from an explosion overwhelms the brain. The electrical signals appear to become scrambled which result in disorientation and confusion. We're seeing this a lot since the Germans began bombing civilians. But there appears to be something else also in play. Has she suffered a recent traumatic event, beside of course her injuries from the bombing?"

Ashford nodded, "A young pilot she was very close to was killed. She was in love with him. Aubrey informed her about his death before she was injured. Other than that, there's nothing I know of." He looked at Aubrey. "Can you think of anything else?"

Aubrey thought of his phone call, when he told her Jamie was dead and the Irishman and Doctor chasing her from Shoe Lane, set on ending her life, trauma indeed. He frowned and shook his head. "Nothing I can think of."

Dr. Stein looked at Aubrey as if he didn't believe him. "From what I've seen, a trauma, such as what she experienced in the bombing as well as the death of a loved one might be the cause. I believe she has experienced some sort of intense emotional and physical shock. It appears to be delaying the brain from reestablishing the pathways after the explosion."

Aubrey ran a thumb over the armrests and thought of Jamie, thrilled at how effective his disposal plan had been.

Dr. Stein took a gold pocket watch from his vest, glanced at it and fixed his eyes on Ashford. "Until the confusion dissipates, we won't know for sure. Whatever the cause, I don't think this will be anything long-term." He returned the watch to his vest.

"Lord Ashford, your daughter is a capable, strong young woman. I believe she'll have everything in order in the next twenty-four to forty-eight hours. Go ahead with what you're doing. Give her some time alone with photographs and things from her past. Keep her quiet and peaceful. Her mind will begin to clear very soon."

"Oh, that's wonderful!" Ashford said, exhaling a deep breath. "Thank you for coming to see her. I truly appreciate it."

They shook hands and he escorted the doctors to the front door. Alone in the study, Aubrey began to twitch. Twenty-four to forty-eight hours was all he had and he had no idea what to do. He heard the front door close and Ashford exclaim, "Thank God."

He came into the study and went directly to the bookcase, opened the safe and motioned for him to retrieve his folder. Aubrey reached into the safe, his eyes focused on the blue bound document as he picked up the red lined folder.

Randall quickly closed the safe and looked at him. "Thank you for stopping by, Aubrey."

Chapter Forty-Seven

Livy stared out her bedroom window as the sun dipped toward the horizon. The pain inside her head had vanished, but confusion swarmed in her mind like fireflies barely visible beyond the dark edges of a campfire. She'd catch a glimpse of a memory racing by and then it would vanish like a shadow bathed with light. A sound or smell might bring back something disjointed or jumbled. But the worst part was, none of it made any sense at all.

The doctor had been kind and cordial, said he had seen the same thing many times. He took pains to assure her everything would soon be right, but he had no idea what she was going through. She felt as if she were living a nightmare. But it wasn't a dream; it was her reality and she knew she was lost. Photographs given to her meant nothing, the people and places unknown and distant. The stories Jackie told of her life as a child only served to confuse and disorient her. Nothing seemed to be as it should.

She conjured an image of the man who called himself Aubrey Beck. He wasn't her lover—she instinctively knew that. All she felt around him was a fear—an unexplainable intense fear for her life—and she didn't know why. Smatterings of images and sounds fluttered in her mind—orange smoke rushing toward a coal-black sky, fires and noises loud and frightening, concussions that reverberated against her body. She could taste dust and rubble, dry and choking, and feel the weight of debris on her back as it pressed down and attempted to suffocate her.

She took a step back from the window and closed her eyes. She touched her lips and felt his kiss, soft and full of desire, his strong loving arms caressing her and protecting her, he was the man that loved her. She could almost see his face. She strained to bring it into focus and struggled to remember his name. But the image faded like mist in a wind.

Tears flowed down her cheeks. She sat on her bed and sobbed, terrified and so very alone.

Chapter Forty-Eight

The hot water felt luxurious. Jamie lay back in the metal tub until the water Amalie had heated for him cooled. He began scrubbing the grime off his body. After several minutes, he pulled on the little chain and popped out the rubber stopper. As he watched the water circle and the tub empty, he thought about this afternoon when Amalie had had a pistol pointed at his chest. How he was held against a wall, a knife at his throat, until the right words came over the radio. French words that told them London had confirmed everything and like the water in the tub, his fear drained away.

He stepped out of the archaic tub and crossed the bathroom to the wash basin, leaving wet footprints on the rough wooden floor. He grabbed a towel, turned his back to the mirror on the wall and inspected his body as he blotted at the water drops. Not too bad, he thought. Several scrapes and bruises, but he was still in one piece. He toweled his hair dry and wrapped the towel around him.

A knock came on the door and he opened it. Amalie stood in the doorway. He watched her eyes focus on his, saddened at the life she had lost. The love of a man holding her, filling her was dead to her heart. All her passions had transformed into a steeled hatred, one that drove her with revenge for the murder of her family. All she had left was loneliness and a pain that consumed her and always would. Even if she outlasted the war, she could never love again.

"Here," Amalie said and handed him a stack of clothes. He heard a slight crack in her voice. "Get dressed—we'll be leaving shortly. An airplane is coming to take you home. We've a long journey, so hurry." She went out of the bathroom and he closed the door behind her.

Several hours later, with the green canvas bag slung over his shoulder, Jamie trudged across another plowed-under field, its cornstalks broken, feeding the earth for next year's crop. He stepped over one empty furrow after another as he followed Rat and Amalie with the boy behind them. They marched single file, silent, alone in their thoughts, toward some distant field where an aircraft would land to retrieve him and the precious film. A location and time—somewhere between two and four in the morning—was the only information they had for the rendezvous and according to Rat, they were running behind.

A three-quarter moon rose above the hills to the east, the pale light made walking a little easier. Three times he had stumbled on something and dark patches of mud now clung to the baggy pants Amalie had given him. A dark shirt and a threadbare coat with a black beret finished the look—that of a French peasant. He felt absurd wearing it as if he were in costume, but she had burned his RAF uniform knowing if the Germans found it they all would be killed.

They moved southeast through the night, as quiet as possible and traversed a forest along the side of a hill. In the silence, he pressed the bag against his chest to keep the film canisters from rattling and his mind began to drift. He thought about Livy and if he was lucky enough to survive, the kind of future they might have together.

She was everything he dreamed of, but her father's words about their vastly different lives haunted him. He might not be the right man for her—he knew that—but the thought of losing her, of never seeing her again, sent a burning ache into his heart. His mind rambled on as he searched for some kind of solution, a way out of the chaos when like the crack of a rifle, he was torn away from his thoughts and returned to a dark field in France.

Rat snatched his arm and jerked him to the ground. He put a finger to his lips and whispered, "Allemands!" Germans!

Chapter Forty-Nine

She ran on a street surrounded by fire, her shoes sticking to the pavement. Each step harder, slower than the last. From the shadows, death reached for her and she couldn't get away.

Livy awoke with a start, terror closed her throat. The dream caused her heart to beat like thunder in her chest. She got up from the bed, went to the window.

A soft moon glow covered the vast lawn and the stars still held their place in the sky as they peeked out between scattered clouds. She knew it had been a dream and yet in the deepest recesses of her mind, it wasn't. Those things had happened; she was sure of it but she didn't know why. She closed her eyes to shake off the images and did her best to breathe.

Livy threw on a robe and went down stairs, through her father's study and onto the rear porch. She placed her hands on the cold stone railing and she looked out on the lake. It was calm, barely a ripple on its surface, a reflection of the moon danced on the water. A remembrance came to her, the same night, the same waning moon and her mother's soft voice as she held her in her arms.

Livy's chin slumped toward her chest, her hands shaking, when like a dam breach, the confusion began to fade. His name was Jamie. She could see him clearly and wondered where he was. She needed him now, his gentle touch, his loving eyes that gave her so much comfort. Thoughts of Aubrey Beck and his phone call ran through her mind. He had told her Jamie was dead and she knew that was a lie. She remembered being outside her father's office as she followed Aubrey and two other men to a rank abandoned factory. Another image struck her like a hammer, the image of Wilfred Eaton at a table with Alana sitting as cold as stone, a horrid, calculating expression on her face. Alana, her best friend since childhood, spoke of murdering her father. Livy gripped the stone railing, her anger boiled over. Alana would kill them both and hand England's defense plan to the Nazis, a betrayal by her childhood friend of everything they shared together.

She knew Aubrey had come to the house not to see her, but to make sure she was no danger to their plans. A cold breath came through her teeth knowing he would soon return with the others, and when they came, they would attempt to murder everyone at the manor, everyone she cared for.

Livy was the only one who knew about them. It would be her word against theirs and she had no proof. Wilfred and Alana would say she was a confused, injured woman, her memories scrambled. Accusing a powerful Parliament member of treason without a shred of evidence—how would that play out? Even if she told her father everything she knew and he believed her, what could he do? Her story would be dismissed out of hand by the authorities. They wouldn't be arrested; they wouldn't even be questioned and if suspicions arose, they would simply flee to Lisbon and take refuge in the German embassy there. They would never pay for their crimes and at that moment, Livy knew there was nothing she could do except remain as she was and pretend her confusion continued. As long as they believed that, she and her father would be safe and it would give her time, time to think of a way to stop them.

"Livy," Her father's voice came from inside his study. "I heard you get up and was worried."

She collected herself and turned to face him. "I'm fine, I wanted some air, that's all."

He placed his arm around her shoulder and said, "Don't worry, it will all come back and soon you'll be right as rain." He kissed the top of her head.

"I know I will." She said, slipping her arm around his waist.

"A few hours ago, Aubrey called to check on you. He'll be over to see you tomorrow, if that's all right."

As long as he believes I am no danger, that's what he'll tell Wilfred and Alana. We'll be safe, if only for a short time. "That will be fine." She knew she would have to act soon, but she needed more time, more time to think.

"Let's get you to bed. The doctor wanted you to have as much rest as possible." He put his arm around her.

As they crossed the threshold into the study she said, "I'm sorry to give you all this trouble."

He squeezed her and smiled. "Don't be, you mean everything in the world to me."

Chapter Fifty

Jamie nodded and looked where Rat was pointing. He crawled with him to the top of the hill and peeked out from behind a fallen tree trunk into a valley below. It was filled with German troops, their tents set in orderly rows, the men drinking and laughing. Campfires dotted the spaces between the tents, spreading light for miles into the night sky, the troops unconcerned, milling around the fires as if the war was long over.

Amalie huddled down beside him and unfolded a map. She handed him field glasses and put her finger on an empty area a few miles southwest of small village labeled Le Cartonnerie. Leaning close to his ear she whispered, "We're here." She moved her finger further down the map. "This is where we meet the airplane." It was at least ten kilometers away, a long and hazardous walk.

Jamie put the glasses to his eyes and focused on the Germans. Scanning down the long lines of men and tents, he recognized the insignia. These were front-line troops fresh from sacking France now held in reserve for the invasion. He made a quick calculation, counting tents and the number each held, some eight hundred men—an infantry battalion waiting in the wings for their turn at England.

Most of them appeared to be drunk, singing and swinging wine bottles back and forth arm in arm, oblivious to any danger. None of them had any weapons, their rifles and machine guns had been left in the tents or were standing by crates outside the canvas. Jamie scanned further down the line to the mess wagons, little columns of smoke blowing away in the light breeze, speaking of hot food and victory.

He studied the men by the food wagons waiting in the queue, when his vision filled with the chest of a soldier, an Iron Cross pinned to the uniform. Jamie dropped the glasses from his eyes and peered into the woods, barely making out two soldiers as they climbed the hill, heading straight for their group. He held two fingers up and pointed toward the valley. They had company coming.

Rat grabbed the field glasses, sighting where Jamie had pointed. "Bosh," Rat said. He gave the glasses to Amalie and slipped away into the woods. Jamie looked around for the boy to warn him, but he too had vanished among the trees.

Amalie dropped the glasses, pushed them under the fallen trunk and said, "Kiss me. Wrap your arms around me and kiss me."

Jamie hesitated, confused by her request. She reached up and pulled him down on top of her. She grabbed the hem of her skirt and pulled it up, uncovering the inside of her thigh. She kissed him, her kiss cold, void of emotion. She let out soft sounds of pleasure as she clung to him. Her throated moans continued for a few seconds, each a little louder, and then Jamie heard a sound he didn't want to hear.

"Direkthilfe?" What is this? He looked up into the barrel of a submachine gun. "Bruno, komm hier rüber." Bruno, get over here, the soldier said.

Amalie sat up, brushing pine needles off her blouse and straightening her skirt as if embarrassed. Jamie held up his hands, surrendering.

The other soldier laughed. "Sieht so aus, als er immer mehr als wir haben, Werner."

The one called Werner jerked at them with his gun, telling them to stand as they continued speaking in German. Jamie only understood some of it, but he got the meaning. They were going to kill him and take her. After they finished with her, they intended to sell her services to the other soldiers of the camp.

It left no other option. Jamie vaulted over the fallen tree and seized the barrel of the closest weapon. Werner's hand moved to the trigger as he tried to swing it toward Jamie's attack, but he wasn't fast enough. His fist landed squarely, the blow smashing into the corner of the Werner's mouth. It sent him in a sprawl to the ground, his blood and teeth scattered.

He spun toward Bruno as he cocked the Schmeisser and leveled it at Jamie's chest, a vicious snarl on his face. But before the German could fire, Rat's knife flashed across his throat. Blood gushed down over Bruno's chest and his head flopped to the side, almost severed from the neck.

Jamie turned toward Werner as the soldier scrambled for his gun a few feet away. The German got to his knees, the weapon quickly centered on Jamie. From behind trees a few feet away, the boy jumped and plunged a knife deep into the center of Werner's back. He dropped the machine gun, struggled in vain to reach the knife, glaring at Jamie, seething. He fell with a thud, face-first onto the ground as the boy calmly walked over and extracted his knife from the lifeless body. He cleaned it on the dead man's uniform and spit on the back of his head.

Amalie looked at Jamie, her eyes aflame, a narrow smile came on her face. She pointed toward Bruno. "Help me hide the body. We need to be far away from here when they're missed."

As the boy and Rat disposed of Werner, they took Bruno's body and threw it over the fallen tree trunk. His almost disconnected head lolled from side to side as the body rolled into the impression where Amalie had been just a few seconds ago. They covered his body with dead branches and leaves.

Jamie stepped back, shaken. This wasn't the impersonal war he knew from the cockpit of a Spitfire. This was blood and gore, personal, and filled with hatred. Amalie snatched up the field glasses as he watched Bruno's blood drip from his hands on to the mound of leaves. The boy came up to him and patted his shoulder. He said in broken English, "The first worst. After easy." He picked up a small pine branch and brushed the ground, removing all signs of the chaos from only a moment before.

They left the cover of the woods, moving as fast as they could, trying to put distance between themselves and the eventual discovery of the soldiers. Minute after minute, field after field, they trudged on, sticky blood covering Jamie's hands.

After about an hour they slowed their pace. Jamie checked his watch in the moonlight—ten minutes before two in the morning. They had to be close.

Out of the darkness, a steep embankment came in view. They climbed and eased down the other side and came upon a shallow irrigation canal. Jamie knelt next to Amalie as they both scrubbed blood from their hands. On the other side of the canal was a large smooth field surrounded by trees. They crossed the shallow water and nestled in by a thick growth of underbrush to wait.

Rat moved a debris-covered tarp lying over a hole in the ground and pulled out a radio and a hand-crank generator. He and the boy assembled it and the boy began to crank the handle as Amalie expertly tapped out Morse code. Jamie understood it. She sent the word bluebird three times. Amalie held the headphone close to one ear and waited. A few minutes passed without answer and again she tapped out bluebird and waited.

From the size of the transmitter, he knew it had a very limited range, possibly one or two miles. It was made to be portable and easy to use, designed to contact aircraft almost directly overhead.

Amalie nested in the underbrush, the headphones never far from her ears. Finally, the set came to life spelling out the word swordfish.

She tapped out FC NE06—Field C, wind northeast at six kilometers per hour. Jamie knew the pilot was near. There would be no sound. He would use the dead stick approach, one he'd practiced in training—a difficult night landing that required the pilot to cut the engine when the aircraft was within gliding distance and silently slip into a designated field. No one would hear the pickup until he gunned the engine for takeoff and by then, it would be too late. The plane would be on the ground for less than thirty seconds.

Rat and the boy ran out into the field. They carried two small round pots and set them at opposite ends. A moment later, a small bright flame burst from each. Seconds after they lit the pots, Jamie saw the outline of a Lysander turn for final approach. The pilot guided the plane directly over the boy and touched down, heading straight toward Rat.

As the aircraft slowed and spun around waiting for its passenger, Amalie smiled at him and said, "Time to go home, Jamie Wallace."

He looked into her eyes and knew that was something she could never do.

Chapter Fifty-One

"She's no threat to you," Aubrey almost shouted, as if his voice belonged to someone else. "Today's not the day to go to Kensington Manor. You don't know who will be there. You're taking a foolish risk." He wiped his hands across the back of his RAF tunic.

The single window on the front of the hunter's shack was open, letting a mild breeze flow through the room and relieving some of the dank smell. The Doctor was standing with his back to a wall watching the Irishman dress a rabbit in the sink while Aubrey faced Alana, agitated at the thought of losing Livy.

Alana leaned back in the tattered armchair, squinting. "Aubrey, sometimes in war you have to take risks. We'll go there later today and take the defense plan from his safe. By tonight, the information will be in Berlin.

"Today will be Ashford's last day on earth—and for that matter, Livy's also. And, if there are others at the Manor, they'll suffer the same fate. Wilfred will receive the defense plan in Gloucester tonight."

Aubrey was almost in a panic. They had made their decision to murder them both. Livy was far too dangerous to be left alive. He had to think of something he could do to save her, to have his way with her even if just for a few minutes. After that, he really didn't care. At least he wouldn't have to worry about Randall Ashford, the man would be dead.

Frightened, jumbled thoughts raced through his mind. He wrung his hands together as one surfaced above the others, "Yesterday, I spoke to Ashford and told him I'd call on Livy. He's expecting me and that can work in your favor. I'll know who's there and then we can plan our next move." He paused a second, his disjointed thoughts a little clearer. "After you get the documents and Ashford, I want Livy. You owe me that much for all I've done for you."

"I owe you nothing. You've already been paid more than you deserve," Alana said with such venom it scared him. "I know what you want with her and that's fine by me. You can have her, but she dies just like that girl in Guernsey as soon as you finish."

There was nothing left for Aubrey to say. He simply nodded.

Alana stared at him, her eyes narrowed, "There is a little pub outside Badger's Mount called Toby's Carvery, near Shorham Lane."

"I know the place," Aubrey said.

"Good. We'll meet you there at four this afternoon, sharp. That will give you enough time to go to Kensington Manor and find out who's there."

Aubrey nodded.

"Do whatever you want until four o'clock." He started toward the door. "And, Aubrey, if you don't do exactly as I say, you won't be alive long enough to do anything with her."

Aubrey turned on his heels, the door screeched, the sound seared his ears like a shriek of a bird.

The Doctor waited a moment until he heard the sound of Aubrey's Jaguar leaving. He stepped away from the bloodstained sink and faced her. "Why are you allowing him to go," he said, "the man can't be trusted."

The Irishman nodded in agreement as he wiped rabbit blood from his hands on a threadbare towel.

Alana looked at them both and smiled. "Oh, right now he can be trusted, there are only two things he cares about—Livy Ashford and his drugs, he knows getting them both depends on us," she said.

The heavyset man, still wiping the blood and entrails off his hands, sauntered over to her and said, "I concur with the Doctor. He should be eliminated. He's a threat."

She smiled at the two of them, looked at the Doctor and said, "After I have the documents and Aubrey has authenticated them, I want you to take Ashford's life. But, however you do it, I want him to die slowly. It must be a lesson to the English. Before he dies, kill his little girl in front of him, then eliminate Aubrey."

A smile crossed the Doctor's lips.

Chapter Fifty-Two

A cloudy sky had swallowed the sun when the Lysander touched down at RAF Hornchurch and rolled to a stop outside Hangar 5. A long interlude in the flight from France had kept a very tired Jamie Wallace at a felt-covered interrogation table in the center of a smoke-filled room at RAF Medmenham. He and four intelligence types, that refused to give their names, went over every detail of his flight in the Gotha—particularly those dealing with being shot down by Spitfires. He repeated the events of the last few days so many times, he'd relived the entire journey.

Toward the end of his interrogation, the pudgy-faced major he'd met before the flight came into the room and apologized profusely for the cock-up that had resulted in the death of Harrison and almost his own. They were told by Aubrey Beck he had run into a Messerschmitt and was killed, the mission failed. The major had a few choice words for Aubrey and also let him know the authorities were searching for him right now. He told Jamie they would find him and promised Aubrey would face justice. The Major thanked him for completing the mission and told him the film was exactly what they needed. He shook his hand and said they would fly him to Hornchurch, return him to 41 Squadron.

On the flight from Medmenham to Hornchurch, Jamie kept mulling over the attack. A mail plane wasn't the kind of target a Spitfire would go after—it wasn't worth the effort.

He climbed out of the Lysander in front of Hangar 5, still wearing the ragged, mud covered clothes Amalie gave him and thanked the young pilot for getting him home. As he walked across the ramp, he was surprised by Eric Locke coming out of the open hangar toward him.

"Glad you're back, lad," He said, shaking Jamie's hand. "Aubrey told us you were killed, shot down on some mission over France. We didn't know anything else until ten minutes ago. Findley rang me and said you were on your way here. Come on, lad—I think this calls for a bit of celebration. The squadron's off flight ops for a week, so let's have a few pints and welcome you back from the dead, a second time."

Jamie hesitated. "Aubrey was right—that's exactly what happened. I was shot down, but by a flight of Spits."

"What?"

"A flight of our own boys, they killed my passenger too—almost ruined the entire mission. And by the way, Aubrey lied, he told them all I was shot down by a Messerschmitt."

"I don't understand." Locke said.

"I was on photo mission in a captured Kraut mail plane—must have been a mistake, his mistake. He was gonna cover it up."

Locke's face paled. He swallowed. "A little blue-gray biplane?"

Jamie stiffened at the frightened look in Locke's eyes. "Yeah," Jamie said, wondering how he knew.

"That bastard." Locke's face went from pale to red in a flash. "We're the ones that attacked you. Aubrey ordered us to destroy that mail plane, he told us exactly where you'd be. It was no mistake."

Jamie sucked in a breath. "Why would he do that? I mean, Christ." He ran a hand through his hair and looked at Locke. "He wanted me killed!"

Locke stared back at him, his mouth open. "All I can tell you is, what we did wasn't an authorized mission. Wing Commander Findley didn't even know about it. We were told not to ever mention it—official secrets and all that rot. He set you up, Jamie, but why?"

Jamie shook his head, trying to make sense of it all. "I have no idea. Why go to so much trouble to kill me?" He thought of Aubrey watching him with Livy at the party. The times he wanted to "help" with her and it all came into focus. "It's about Livy."

"The girl at Thirsty Bear—the Ashford girl?"

"Right."

Locke scratched his chin, "Jamie, there's something I need to tell you, she's been injured. It was in the *Times* yesterday—a story about how even the upper classes get hit. She was caught out in a bombing and got banged up. That's all I know. The newspaper said she's recuperating at her home, she's probably there now."

Jamie felt as if he'd been struck. "Locke, I have to go to her. I'll deal with Beck later."

Locke cocked his head and said, "All right, you go to her, I'm gonna speak to Findley about all this. Beck has some explaining to do."

"I'm going to Kensington Manor now. I've got to find her." He started in the direction of the barracks and his car.

"Wait a minute Jamie," Locke shook his head. "Before you go anywhere, change those clothes. You look like a bloody vagabond, you'd scare the hell out of her."

Chapter Fifty-Three

Livy closed the last button on her blouse. As she looked out the window a red Jaguar popped out of the forest by the gate. She took a slow, deep breath. What she did in the next few minutes might keep both herself and her father alive. As long as she was impaired, they would be safe at least until she came up with a way to expose Aubrey, Wilfred and Alana, get the other two men and make it stick. For now, Aubrey was the key to their safety and she knew it. She also knew what he wanted from her. With a shaking hand, she undid the top three buttons of her blouse and slipped a knife she had taken from the kitchen into her riding boot.

As she reached the grand staircase, she heard Aubrey and her father talking below. She stopped for a moment, forced a blank expression onto her face and went down the stairs toward them.

"Hello, Aubrey," she said as calmly as she could manage as she reached the last stair.

His eyes dropped to her chest and slowly came back to her face. "Livy, it's wonderful to see you. You look terrific. How are you feeling?"

"Fine, I think." She slid her hand along the collar, making sure it was open just enough.

Aubrey's eyes widened a bit. "You do remember me from yesterday, don't you?" She detected tension in his voice.

"I do, Aubrey."

He nodded and looked toward Randall Ashford. "Sir, if I'm in the way, if you have doctors and such coming, I could come back later."

"No, that's all right, Aubrey," Ashford smiled at him. "No one's coming, this is a day for Livy to rest."

"Fine, sir," he said as he turned and smiled gently at her. "Would you like to get some air, a walk in the gardens, perhaps?"

Livy struggled to keep the panic from her voice, her mind working furiously. "I don't know," she said with a caution she could hear in her voice.

"Go ahead, my dear," her father said as he put his arm around her. "A walk might do you some good."

She curled her lower lip under, fear rising. She looked at Aubrey. "All right, but only for a moment or two, I'm still very weak."

She wanted him dead. Not only for the treachery to her family but also for something else, his treachery to England. As they stepped out of the French doors and onto the porch, her hands stopped shaking, thoughts formed and an action plan developed. She would manipulate him—find out their plans, when they were coming, all without giving herself away. Then she would tell her father everything.

Heavy, dark clouds hung on the western horizon as they stepped past geraniums that had lost their blossoms, the blood-red petals falling in the light wind onto the stone stairs as they stepped down into the acres of gardens. Livy placed her hand on his arm.

"I'm so happy to be with you," Aubrey said. His smile made her stomach turn.

He put his hand over hers as they walked across the lawn and stopped near a blossom filled magnolia out of sight from the manor. He turned and leaned in to kiss her. She closed her eyes and turned away, revolted.

She thought of Jamie, his touch so loving and full of desire. She thought of the way she felt when she was with him and then thought of the call from Aubrey telling her he was dead.

He wasn't dead, she could feel it in her heart. Taking a breath and gathering her wits, she said softly, "I'm sorry, I'm so confused. I went through photos today, so many people. People I can't remember. I saw a photo of someone that was supposed to be my best friend—Alana is her name. Do you know her? Can you get in touch with her?"

He was flush as he looked at her. "I know her well. In fact, I'll be seeing her this afternoon." She had run out of time! He would report back to them. "I'd be pleased to tell her you wish to see her, if that's what you want."

She rested her hands on his chest as she pleadingly looked into his eyes. "Please, Aubrey, it would mean so much to me. Seeing people I should know is the only way I'll straighten things out."

"Anything, anything you want."

Livy gasped as he roughly grabbed her and pulled her close to his body. She could feel his arousal and steeled herself. She eased her head back and gave him a soft and loving look. Her hands gently pushed against his chest. "Not this way. Please, a little more time and I'll give all of myself to you."

The seconds dragged on and she made ready to scream. His grip slacked and he relaxed, his eyes never moving from hers.

"I want you so very much," the words panted.

"Soon," she said, her hand caressed his face, hoping she kept the hatred out of her eyes. "I must have a little more time."

He stood rigid as she pulled away, wishing she had reached for the knife and killed him. Livy turned and started toward the manor. "Come," she said over her shoulder, "we should go back. I need to rest."

Aubrey caught up, his hand found hers and she allowed it, his damp sweat and desperation repulsive as they walked toward the porch stairs in silence.

Chapter Fifty-Four

The petrol station at Badger's Mound was five minutes from Kensington Manor, but Jamie had pushed the MG as far as he could without getting fuel. He slipped the nozzle into the filler pipe and stared the pump, his fingers drummed along the boot as the tank took a lifetime to fill.

Livy was hurt, that's all he knew. He had to get to her. The blowup with Lord Ashford surfaced in his mind and he promptly dismissed it. To hell with him, Livy was all that mattered.

He finished with the petrol pump and handed the attendant the correct number of ration stamps. He pulled the canvas top up and fastened it to the snaps to seal off the interior from a light rain that was starting to fall. Jamie slipped in and brought the engine to life, drove around the pumps and eased the nose past a lorry that was blocking his view of the highway.

As he started to pull out onto the road, a Jaguar flashed by, its brake lights came on as it slowed to turn into Toby's Carvery, one hundred yards behind him. Jamie looked down the road, eased past the lorry and shot off on the slick pavement toward Kensington Manor and Livy.

Aubrey eased the Jaguar to a stop and got out, the light rain another irritation after his frustrating encounter with Livy. He would have to wait. In a few short hours, he'd do whatever he wanted with her. Ashford would be dead and Livy would be his to play with, until they came to take her away—and murder her.

He went into Toby's Carvery and spotted Alana and the others seated at a booth in a corner where they could see every approach. Aubrey looked at his hands. With each heart beat they seemed to grow and shrink. He cringed as he slipped in next to the Doctor, as always dressed in black with the string tie dangled around his thin neck. The Irishman sat next to Alana and looked as if he were a country gentleman, with a tweed coat and vest covering an open white shirt. Across the table was Alana, her face pale above a black turtleneck sweater, her dark hair tied beneath a matching knitted cap, her brown eyes glared at his approach.

Aubrey swallowed the lump in his throat and brushed silver raindrops from the sleeve of his uniform. He reached for the teapot in the center of the table. Alana pushed his hand away and he blinked. "Just the two of them are there . . . for now," he said.

"And what does that mean—for now?" She looked at him, her voice demanding more.

"When I arrived, only Livy and her father were at the Manor." He said slightly above a whisper. "The butler and the cook were out, but they'll be there when we return to take the documents. So, it'll be the four of them. I'm sure of it."

"That's better." Alana paused and said, "And the document?"

"It's still in the safe as far as I know."

"Good." She looked to the others at the table. "This is how I want it done."

A wisp of a smile came to her face. She nodded at the Irishman and said, "You and the Doctor will go around the manor to the left. Toward the rear, you'll see a door that leads into the kitchen. That's where their two servants, Jackie and Harold, will be. Eliminate Harold first and do it quickly. He's a former soldier and will be armed—he always is. Take out the woman next. She won't be a problem, but do not leave either of them alive.

"When you've finished, go around the back of the home and onto the porch. At the far end, you'll come to doors that lead into Ashford's study. Aubrey and I will be in there with his daughter. He'll be seated at his desk, his back to you. Overpower him and Aubrey, you restrain Livy."

She looked at the Doctor. "After I have the documents, end Ashford's life. But, do it a way he dies slowly. You know what to do, we've discussed that."

The Irishman nodded and the Doctor smiled.

"Now," she said as her eyes bored into him, "a spot of tea, Aubrey?"

Chapter Fifty-Five

Jamie careened up the drive, his MG tossed river stones as he ground to a stop outside the manor. He ran up to the door and opened it. Randall Ashford stood in the foyer looking as if he'd seen a ghost.

"Where is she," he said, heading toward the stairs.

"I thought you were dead!" Ashford said as he grabbed his arm, the look on his face shocked, as if he had been struck with a hard blow. "Aubrey said you were killed."

He jerked his arm out of his grasp. "Where is she?"

"Upstairs, in her bedroom."

"Where is it?" The words jumped out of Jamie's mouth.

"At the top, third door."

He flew up the stairs two or three at a time and found the door. Livy turned toward him as it burst open. She was standing a few feet from the window dressed in riding pants, boots and a cream-colored blouse. Jamie's heart almost broke as she looked at him. Her hands covered her mouth, tears welled in her eyes. He ran to her and took her into his arms. He held her close as relief washed over him.

"Aubrey said you were killed, but I knew you weren't. I knew it." She gasped as he held her.

"I'm here now and that's all that matters." He said as he heard Ashford entering the room behind him.

"Jamie, they're going to kill us. She said it was rainy in Chicago, it wasn't. It was hot and muggy! She was in Berlin!"

"Who was in Berlin," he said.

"Alana! They're spies, German spies. They're going to kill all of us. They may be on their way here right now."

"What's this?" Ashford came next to them and looked at his daughter. "Alana a spy?"

"Alana, Wilfred and Aubrey they're all German spies! There are two others I don't know. They're the ones that attempted to kill me.

Everything came back last night, I was afraid to let you know. If you called the police and told them, they would think I was a ranting fool. But it's true, you have to believe me! They all are Nazis; they plan to kill you. They want a document you have in your safe, a defense plan, something about the radar system and communication hubs."

Holding her head close to his chest, Jamie said, "Aubrey working for the Germans, now it makes sense."

Ashford, clearly distraught, said, "Livy, get a coat—you'll need one. When you have it, come down to the study and tell me everything. Jamie, follow me." He started out of the room. "Aubrey was just here. They'll be back soon and we have no time to waste."

He ran down the grand stairs calling for Harold and into his study with Jamie following. He spun around, his heels digging into the Persian carpet.

"Jamie, I'm sorry. I was wrong, about so many things. You must protect her. They will try to kill her."

Jamie stood in the study, shocked and fearing for their safety. "Call the police, let them know. We all need to leave, quickly."

Livy entered the room carrying a down jacket and as she reached the desk, Harold rushed into the study. Ashford looked at Jamie and said, "Yes, you do. You'll be leaving in a minute." He glanced toward Harold standing near the door. "Do you still have your shotgun?"

"I do," he said, his face sensing danger. "What's happening, sir?"

"Get it and come back here. I believe we're going to have some unwanted and very dangerous guests in a few minutes. Warn Jackie," Randall added, his words hurried but his demeanor calm. Harold turned and left the room.

He looked at Livy and said, "Tell me what you know."

She sat in an armchair and explained about the call from Aubrey, how he told her Jamie had been killed, the break-in of his office and how she followed them back to a dingy condemned factory. Livy went through the conversation she overheard and what Wilfred and Alana had said. She told she was discovered in the dark alcove and how she ran from the factory, bombs falling all around her, the unknown two shooting at her, how the bullets struck the bricks near her head and the explosion that almost took her life.

She took a breath and said, "A few minutes ago by the lake, Aubrey told me he was seeing Alana today. I expect he's with her right now, planning their assault. They will have the other two with them, a tall frightening man and a shorter heavy one. They're the ones that chased and shot at me."

"What is it they want?" Jamie said to Ashford, his hand on Livy's shoulder.

"The master plan for the defense system of England. With that, they could easily defeat our radar system and the RAF. With it, their invasion will succeed and England will lose the war. My God Livy, why didn't you tell me right away?"

"And what could you possibly do?" She sat on the edge of the chair. "The police would have done nothing. Wilfred would have called me mad, I have no proof of anything. They all would have gotten away with it."

Ashford closed his eyes, "Still, I wish you would have told me, I could have done something."

"Right now, none of that matters," Jamie said as his mind focused. "You have the document here, in this room?"

"Of course, I'm responsible for it. It's in the safe."

Livy jumped up from the chair. "Destroy it."

Ashford looked at her, went to the bookcase and opened a shelf. He spun a combination on the safe hidden behind the books, reached in and pulled out a document about two inches thick covered in a simple blue binding.

He held it up. "Right now, this is the most important document in all of England."

"She's right—you must destroy it." Jamie said.

"Not possible," Ashford said flatly. "This plan is how Churchill directs the entire conduct of the war. He has a copy, but his is missing the critical elements of the system, the location of the communication hubs."

Jamie stared at him, astounded. "How is that possible? The most important document in the country and there's no other copies?"

"Besides Churchill, only a very few others know it even exists. That's why it's here and not in Whitehall. My home was the only place we felt it would be secure. This is the blueprint of how we built the entire system as well as keys to all the secrets of how we obtain our intelligence. If they discover the contents of this document, the Germans will win the war."

"And they know it's here?" Jamie said.

"From what Livy said, they do. I took a call from Philip Joubert the other day but I didn't think anything about it. He told me Wilfred asked about the radar communication system, how it was constructed. Joubert thought Wilfred had my approval so he told him I designed the entire system. That's why the break-in at my office, they thought it was there. The only other place I would keep it is here and they know that. I would expect them to make a try for it."

Livy looked at her father, "It can't stay here." Jamie heard the fear in her voice.

"Why not call the police or MI5—give it to them?" Jamie said.

"As long as we're at war, the risk would be too great." Ashford's eyes locked on Jamie's. "Trust no one is the first intelligence lesson you learn. Mere knowledge of its existence is a threat. The contents can't be revealed to anyone, not even the police. The secrets in it must be preserved, it must be kept safe. That's why you're going to take Livy and the document away from here. Right now, it's far too dangerous to do anything else."

"I say we get you and the document out of here. Go wherever you think we'll be safe." Jamie wanted a way out for all of them.

"We may not have the time to do that. You take it away from here. I want to protect the document, but also Livy. As soon as you're gone, I'll phone Gordon Howell, have him send Special Branch here and to where you'll be. Keep it with you at all times until they come for you. From there, follow their instructions, but do not show it to anyone." Ashford said without blinking.

"No," Livy protested, the pitch of her voice rose. "They'll be coming here; they'll kill you to get it. You can't stay here; I can't lose you too."

Ashford smiled at his daughter. "You won't lose me. Remember, they don't think I know about them."

He held the document out to her and looked back at Jamie. "Go to the cottage, it's the safest place I can think of right now and wait for Special Branch. Gordon Howell knows where it is, he's been there. The document will be safe and by morning, this will all be over."

Jamie could feel the man's courage. Ashford knew if they came before Scotland Yard arrived, he might die. "What about you? I can't leave you here to face them alone."

"I won't go, I'll stay with you." Livy's voice was cracking.

"No, your safety is too important to me." Ashford said.

Their eyes met and Jamie nodded, assuring Ashford he would do all he asked. He understood him and the unconditional love he had for his daughter.

Randall smiled at her. "I'll be fine, I've got Harold. Before you're out the drive, I'll be on the phone to Gordon Howell. Now go, quickly."

Livy wrapped her arm around her father as they went out of the study. He stood at the open front door as she and Jamie squeezed into the MG. "Keep her safe."

Jamie felt a sense of doom as he started the engine and sped down the long drive. In the seat next to him, Livy was silent, looking back with tears running down her face. He glanced in the mirror and saw her father, Lord Randall Ashford, standing alone in the doorway of their home.

Chapter Fifty-Six

Aubrey and Alana rode in the Jaguar through the light rain. Behind them, the Doctor and the Irishman followed in Wilfred's black government sedan. As they made the last turn onto a straight portion in the road, several hundred yards ahead Aubrey saw a green MG crest a hill and disappear out of sight. He started to turn into the stone and iron gate of Kensington Manor.

"No, not here, go further," Alana said.

"But this is the gate."

"Not the one we'll use. Go further."

Aubrey eased his foot off the accelerator and passed the gate, the government car tucked in close behind, too close for comfort. "Where are we going?" His entire body was tense, his nerves raw.

"Just a little further, we're almost there." She sat forward in the seat, her hands on the dash.

A few seconds later, Alana said, "Turn now, right here."

Aubrey spotted a small break in the canopy and underbrush, but no road. He followed her orders and the car bounced over twigs and broken limbs that scraped like fingernails against the sides of the polished red paint. Through the windscreen, he saw an overgrown track in front of him, one he could follow.

He glanced at Alana, who was still leaning forward, the wipers flopping back and forth. "If it starts raining harder, we'll be stuck back here," he said, the tires already spinning loosely in the wet soil.

"Focus on the mission. We'll be gone long before anything like that will happen."

He shook his head, wondering if he would survive the next few minutes as they bumped through the old oak forest, the black sedan right behind.

The forest thinned and opened into a rolling meadow. Alana told him to turn around and stop next to a line of trees on the right, heading them away from the manor. She jumped out and motioned the sedan to park next to the Jaguar as Aubrey shut down the engine and slid out of the seat.

They checked their weapons, Alana and the Irishman twisted silencers onto black steel muzzles. He stood by them, his fear of confronting Lord Ashford seized his chest and froze his feet to the ground.

Alana grabbed his arm and jerked. "Focus, Aubrey," she said, slinging a bag over her shoulder. "Focus on the mission."

She turned and motioned for them to follow as they silently set off through the forest toward Kensington Manor and Lord Randall Ashford.

Chapter Fifty-Seven

Alana and the three men made their way toward the front of the manor, keeping low to the ground. As soon as she had the documents and Aubrey verified they were the right ones, his life would end. She would never let him take Livy, she would kill her first, she owed her that much at least.

They reached the pebbled drive at the front of the home undetected. She sent the Doctor and the Irishman to the left, toward the kitchen to eliminate the threat from Harold and Jackie. Holding her position, she crouched undercover as she waited for them to clear the corner. Alana looked at her watch as they disappeared around the corner, the seconds ticking away.

She could hear Aubrey's breathing behind her as a gray rain began to fall from the overcast and she smiled knowing it would cover their tracks. Alana looked at the Manor, a place that held memories of her childhood and long talks with Livy about hopes for their lives. She laughed, thinking Harold and Jackie would be dead by now.

She jerked Aubrey's arm. "Now focus Aubrey," she said. They ran across the wide drive, up the stairs to the front door. Slowly Alana pushed the handle down and to her surprise, it silently opened. This would be easy. She drew out the Luger, its silencer snagged momentarily on the elastic band of her pants. With Aubrey behind her, she silently crossed the foyer, turned right and headed toward the study. The door was ajar and as they came closer, she could see Ashford seated at his desk, a phone to his ear. He was speaking, looking down at the blotter as she pushed the door open. He looked up to see her pointing the black pistol at his heart and curiously, he smiled.

"Ring off." she demanded, her voice soft, but well above a whisper. Aubrey came into the room and stood behind her.

Ashford paused and, looked straight at her. He eased the receiver toward the cradle. "Come in, I've been expecting you," he said.

The words expecting you whirled around her head, how could he know we were coming? "Expecting me?"

"I know all about you and your father. We've been looking for a traitor, though I must confess, I never dreamt it would be the both of you."

He looked at Aubrey, disgusted. "And you as well Aubrey, a traitor too. You set up Jamie Wallace and got him killed. You had him shot down by our own people, didn't you?"

Aubrey's mouth hung open. She could see fear grip him.

"I have a surprise for you, Aubrey. Special Branch is looking for you as we speak. As soon as they get their hands on you, they'll hang you. That is if they don't shoot you first." He turned his gaze toward her. "And you—working for the Germans. I can't believe it." There was revulsion in his voice as he dropped his hands below the desk where she couldn't see them. He was going for the pistol he kept in the second drawer on the right side, it had been in that same place since she was a child.

"Put your hands on the desk or I'll shoot you right now." He slowly complied, his hands empty. She laughed at him as she came around one of the wingback chairs and sat, the Luger still aimed at his heart.

"Working for the Germans? I am, but more importantly, I'm an English patriot—one who knows our only hope for the Empire's future lies with a National Socialist Germany."

He smiled at her, infuriating her. "That's where you're wrong, you are nothing but a traitor," he said, "and I will see you hang, right alongside your father. That was Scotland Yard on the phone, they're on their way here right now."

She looked beyond him and saw the Doctor and the Irishman appear on the porch. "I expected that."

She nodded and the two men burst through the French doors. The Doctor wrapped a rope around Ashford's throat and pulled. Ashford tried to get up, his eyes fierce, his hands fighting against the rope. The Irishman jumped to the side of his chair and slammed his fist into Ashford's face, almost knocking him unconscious. He threw Ashford's dazed body down into the chair and pinned his wrists to the arms.

The Doctor eased up on the rope that was choking him, sliding it down around his chest while the Irishman held him fast. Quickly the Doctor bound him, until Ashford was unable to move against the thick hemp. They tied his head back, securing a rope across the bridge of his nose and attached it behind the chair. The Doctor pulled it tight and grasped one of Ashford's wrists, while the Irishman continued to hold the other.

Alana moved to the desk, "Where's Livy?"

His eyes fluttered from beneath the rope. Ashford looked down and smiled. With blood dripping from the corner of his mouth, he said nothing.

Alana whipped the pistol across his head. It opened a gash above the hair line, the crack echoing in the room. "I'll ask you one more time. Where is Livy?"

He winced, but didn't make a sound.

"Aubrey, go find her," she said and he rushed out of the room. She lowered the Luger and placed it on the desk. Leaning forward, putting both hands on the blotter she whispered, "Now, Lord Randall Ashford, time to open the safe."

He looked at her and smiled again, blood dripped off his lip. She was wasting time and they had to move quickly, she was positive it was Scotland Yard on the phone.

She heard Aubrey's feet clomping through the home as the Doctor and the Irishman held Ashford fast to the chair. A moment later, Aubrey burst into the study panting. In a squeal he said, "She's not here. She's gone!"

Alana scowled at him, noting the shaken, terrified look on his face. She turned back to Ashford and ordered Aubrey to expose the safe. She would find and deal with Livy later. She glanced at Aubrey as he went across the room, opened the bookcase and revealed the safe.

Her head motioned to the Irishman who went over to the wall and pulled a stethoscope from a jacket pocket as the Doctor held Ashford to the chair. The Irishman placed the stethoscope to the safe door and listened as he swiftly moved the dial, working the tumblers. She turned her focus back to Ashford, his eyes wide watching the Irishman at the safe. Within a minute, she heard a click and the door to the safe swung open.

Alana pointed at the safe. "Aubrey, get the document." Her eyes stayed on Ashford, the Luger now pointed between his eyes as the Irishman came to Lord Ashford's side and pinned his wrist to the chair as the Doctor let go.

A few seconds passed then more and more. She glanced back at Aubrey and wondered what could take so long. He was pulling out papers, examining them, and throwing them on the floor. He reached back into the safe, bent over and stared inside it.

He turned and looked at her, his face pale. "It's not here—only personal papers, bank records and such."

Furious at his incompetence, she glared at him. "That's impossible—it must be there," she said. "Look again, you fool."

"I looked at each paper before I tossed it. It's not here."

She turned back to Ashford, anger boiling over at her failure.

"Where is the plan? You have ten seconds to tell me."

Ashford smiled, bloody teeth showing and said "It's never been here, Churchill has it."

"That's a lie! We know you have it! Aubrey saw it in the safe. Where is it!" she hissed.

Calm yourself, calm yourself, she thought, struggling to contain her emotions. She slipped the Luger back into her waistband and picked up her bag from the wingback chair. She reached inside and pulled out her weapon. Smiling, she inserted a long steel spike into the shaft of the weapon and began to ratchet it into the barrel. She thought of the night she'd killed Jack Reed and how Ashford's death would not be as quick or easy for him. She would drag it out.

Alana came over to the left side of his desk, nodding at the Irishman. Ashford fought with the man's strength as he started to lift his hand, but pain and fatigue won as the Irishman slammed his hand onto the desktop, the palm facing down. She went over to Ashford's ear and whispered, "I will ask you again—where is the plan. Did you give it to Livy?"

Before he turned his head away, she noticed his eyes widen. Livy had the plan. Alana grabbed his chin and forced his head around to face her.

"I'll give you one more chance. I know Livy has the plan. Where is she?"

He tried to pull away from her, the rope across his forehead cutting him as he jerked away from her grasp.

"Where is Livy?" she said softly.

He only smiled.

She held the weapon close to his ear and cocked it. Inflicting as much terror as she could. She moved it before his eyes and down his arm to his hand held fast to the blotter. The weapon hovered, she smiled at his terrified eyes and fired.

Ashford screamed as the spike crashed into bone and flesh, the steel burrowing deep into the hard-walnut desk, it pinned his hand like a skewered insect on display.

She walked behind his chair, allowed her fingers to brush against his shoulder and up his neck. She softly slid them across his hair, tussled it and ran down the other side of his head to his shoulder. Alana came around his right side and took out a second spike. Slowly, she inserted it into the black knurled handle. In front of his eyes, little by little she ratcheted the spike down into the weapon.

"This is your last chance." Her voice was almost cooing. "Where is Livy?"

He said nothing.

Alana positioned the weapon over his hand as the Doctor firmly held his wrist.

Ashford kept vacantly staring at the photos on the table. She fired and Ashford screamed as the spike tore into his flesh and pinned his other hand to the desk.

She came around the desk and slowly backed up toward the table closely watching his eyes, her hand held above the photographs, slowly moving. She watched and listened as she passed each item. When it happened, it wasn't much, just an intake of air, a quick reaction in his eyes.

She stopped her hand and studied him, his eyes wide and filled with fear. She had the right one.

Alana looked down at the table, her hand above a silver frame and reached for it. She barely heard it, but the sound was there, a soft whimper escaped from his mouth as she picked up the frame and studied the photograph. It was of his late wife and Livy, both happy and smiling, looking into the camera. At the end, he thinks of them.

Alana glanced at Ashford and back to the photograph. It was of his wife and daughter, a spring day long ago, sunny and bright, the English Channel behind them.

Their cottage—their place by the sea where she and Livy had played so many times. That's where he would send her, a place where she would feel safe.

Alana looked back at him as a tear rolled down his cheek, an admission of defeat. She headed to the desk as Aubrey came toward her, his face filled with terror.

"Tell her where she is." Aubrey almost screamed at Ashford.

Alana stared at him. "Come Aubrey, your job isn't finished."

She did everything she could not to kill him right there. "We're done here," she said as her eyes met the Doctor's.

A thin smile came on the Doctor's face as he reached into a pocket and removed a large bore hypodermic needle. He pulled off the cap, shoved Ashford's head to one side and jammed it into a blue-gray vein in his neck. Blood dripped from the open end. "He'll be conscious for maybe ten minutes. He'll be dead in about twenty."

Alana nodded. Exactly how she wanted it—slow and with as much psychological torture as possible. A warning to all those she knew were coming.

She picked up her shoulder bag and said, "Let's go." She looked in his eyes and with a smile said, "Goodbye, Lord Ashford."

Chapter Fifty-Eight

As they passed through the village of Paddock Wood, the gun-metal clouds opened up. Huge drops pelted the canvas top of the MG, sounding like hundreds of drums pounding out a spluttered rhythm, the clacking of the wipers timed the inconsistent beat. Somewhere overhead, in the dense overcast a lightning bolt flashed followed by a crash of thunder. The weather magnified the tumultuous thoughts that leapt through Jamie's mind.

In the seat next to him, Livy sat staring out the windscreen, her hands squeezed around the document as if it might take flight. In the last fifteen minutes, maybe ten words had crossed her lips. He held back and didn't speak, respected her silence, he knew what filled her heart. There was a good chance she would never again see her father alive.

Jamie glanced at her. "He'll be all right. He's strong and resourceful; I'll bet the police already have them in custody." He grimaced at how hollow the words sounded.

She turned to face him. "Maybe," she placed a hand on top of his. "I do know this—he'll do what he must. No matter what they do to him, he'll never tell them a thing. He'll give up his life to protect us."

"I know, but it won't come to that." Again, the words rang hollow.

A distant thunder rumbled through the twilight.

"It may not," she turned in the seat as Jamie took his hand and placed it on the steering wheel. "Now that I've had a chance to think, it's not our best course to go to the cottage, but it's too late for that now. We must go there—that's where Scotland Yard will expect us to be.

"When Alana gets to Kensington Manor, she'll bring Aubrey and the other thugs. If the police aren't there and they make it passed Harold and my father—they'll discover I'm gone and so is the document. My father won't tell her anything, but she'll figure it out. She's been to the cottage many times and she'll know that's where I would go, where I would feel safe. They might be on their way right now and if they are—I want to be there when she's arrested, or better yet, killed."

Jamie turned on the headlamps in the fading light, glanced at her and said, "I understand, but for your safety, the cottage is the last place we should go."

"No, we have to go there. But, we don't have to have the document. We should hide it, if something were to go wrong, Alana wouldn't get it."

So much courage exactly like her father's. "It's far too dangerous for you."

"I know you're trying to protect me, but hear me out," she said, her voice resolute above the beating rain. "We have no idea how many or what kinds of secrets they've already passed on to the Germans. If they are coming after us and Scotland Yard isn't there, it's up to us to stop them, there's far too much at stake if we don't." She turned in the seat to face him, the document still clutched in her hands. "Hiding it means someone else needs to know where it is if we don't survive. Michael is the perfect choice. We'll tell him where we hid it. Newent is only a few miles out of the way and if anything were to happen, he could retrieve it and get it back to Churchill. Alana can't win."

Chapter Fifty-Nine

Aubrey sat in the backseat with Alana and looked out the side window of the black government sedan, his chin resting on a clenched fist. He'd been grumbling since she demanded he leave his car behind. This very moment, the authorities were looking for him, Ashford made that very clear, and the last thing she wanted was for them to be discovered because of his car.

"Stop sulking, Aubrey," she said. "I've had enough—are you daft?"

She sat forward as the sedan seemed to crawl through the darkness, the rain coming down in sheets. She pushed Aubrey to the back of her mind, attempted to contain her frustration. "Can't you go any faster?" She spat the words into the front seat.

The Irishman never took his eyes off the road ahead. "Faster in this rain? I can barely see what's in front of me."

"Wilfred expects to have the document tonight and I'm not going to disappoint him." As she sat back against the rear seat, she glanced at Aubrey and thought of shooting him right then. The fool had jeopardized the entire mission, the drug they gave him had worked a little too fast, destroyed his mind. The second she had the document and the information in it, then she would kill him.

"When we arrive at the cottage, we'll stop short and go the rest of the way on foot. Aubrey, once we have the document, verify the hub locations. After you've done that, you can take Livy and do what you will. When you've finished, eliminate her. Throw her body off the cliffs, the storm will take it out to sea." She leaned forward toward the front seat and gave her orders, "From the cottage, we'll go to Gloucester and Wilfred will transmit the information to Berlin." She reached out and touched the Irishman's shoulder, "While we're waiting for the invasion, you two take this car and go back to the hunter's shack. Get the radio beacons and place them at the hub locations, then go to ground until England falls."

Chapter Sixty

Headlamps swept across several black police cars and slowed at the open rear doors of an ambulance. Sir Gordon Howell didn't wait for driver to stop. He leapt out of the rear seat and headed for the front door of Kensington Manor. He stepped aside as three medics hurried out carrying a litter bearing Randall Ashford, one holding a plasma bottle high above his head.

"Is he . . ."

"Barely alive," one of the medics responded.

A blood-soaked bandaged hand lifted as the litter slid by, beckoning him to come closer. Gordon leaned over Ashford's bloody chest and looked into eyes almost void of life. Ashford's words came out like a vapor, weak and labored.

Sir Gordon straightened and held on to the whispered secret. "Go! Do not let him die."

"We'll do our best, sir," the medic said as they hurried down the stairs. Gordon watched them place the litter into the ambulance and race off into the night, the heavy tires shredding the manicured lawn.

He thought of the phone call with Randall Ashford and the faint voice of a woman in the background as he said, 'I've been expecting you." It sent a frigid shot up his spine as the ambulance raced down the river-stone drive. He turned away from the sight and walked to a man of about fifty dressed in a well-tailored gray suit standing inside the doorway.

"DCI Willis, sir," the man said with a look of horror on his face.

"What have we got?" It was a command, not a question as Gordon entered the Manor, fearful of what he would find.

Willis followed him. "When we got your orders, we sent two armed uniforms out. They rang back and reported two casualties, and Lord Ashford. He was tied to his chair, his hands pinned to the desk, very close to death."

"Pinned, did you say?" He could feel bile rising.

"Yes sir. He had a large-bore needle inserted into a vein in his neck. The only reason he survived is that he jammed his shoulder into the needle, forcing it through the vein, deeper into his neck. It slowed the loss of blood—kept him alive."

A flashbulb went off in the study. Gordon's head swung around.

"Fingerprints, Willis?" he asked.

"Not yet, they're just starting," the Inspector said. "But before I take you into the study, come this way."

They went through the living and dining rooms. Lying face down, Harold Rider was wedged against a swinging door between the butler's pantry and the kitchen, a loaded shotgun lay open at the breach next to his body. Gordon noted three small holes in the center of his back.

Willis stepped over the body and said, "This way, sir."

Gordon followed him into the kitchen, the smell of blood surged into his nostrils. The rear entry door to the kitchen stood open. A pane had been shattered and glass shards littered the floor. Harold's wife, Jackie, lay sprawled over the table, her throat cut from ear to ear. Congealed black blood pooled in large puddles on the floor and around her head. He stood a moment taking in the gruesome scene, his mind thinking through every detail.

"This was an assassination." Gordon said.

"Yes sir, these two were murdered in seconds and quietly. The man was shot through the glass of the door as he was leaving the kitchen and the woman murdered as she got up from the table. If they used a silencer; it would have been very quick and very quiet. It was over in seconds. Lord Ashford was in his study; he would never have heard it."

He stood a moment thinking of the fear Jackie must have felt.

Willis said, "This way, sir. Mind the blood."

Gordon stepped around the blood pool. They left the kitchen and headed toward the study. A photographer was leaving the room as they approached, he licked and inserted another flashbulb into the reflector.

"Finished?" Willis said to him.

"Almost Inspector, one or two more."

"Give me copies of everything." Gordon said.

The photographer nodded. "They'll be on your desk in the morning."

"Thank you," Gordon said as he entered the study.

A man in a white shirt and tie, his sleeves rolled up, was standing by the bookcase on the far wall dusting for fingerprints. The bookcase was swung back from the wall, revealing an open safe. Gordon stepped toward the desk, noting a long table against the wall with one silver picture frame unlike all the others—lying on its back.

"Have you found anything?" Willis said.

The man in the white shirt said, "Nothing so far. Just a few smudged prints on the safe and they're unusable."

Gordon looked at the man, "Have you dusted this table?"

"No sir, that's my next stop."

Gordon took out a handkerchief and picked up the silver frame lying on its back. The photograph was of Randall's late wife and his little girl sitting on a stone fence, wind in their hair. In the background was their whitewashed cottage and off in the distance, the English Channel. He took the frame and twisted it in the light, carefully placed it back on the table. "There's a single thumbprint on this frame. Dust it and the backs and arms of the chairs. You should find more there."

Randall's desk was covered in blood and the outline of his hands showed where they had been pinned to the wood. Deep gouges in the desk marked the center of each outline. His eyes stopped on two steel spikes covered in dried blood that lay on scattered papers. Gordon imagined the horrific pain he must have felt as the spikes impaled his hands.

He looked at the papers spread around on the floor by the safe. "What did you find?"

"Nothing sir, it was empty," a young officer standing by the safe said. "There were only those papers you see on the floor."

"This is Officer Ramsey." DCI Willis said. "He and his partner were first on the scene."

"Ah, so you were the one who found him." Gordon said as he knelt, picked up and scanned a few of the documents.

"Yes sir. And as the DCI said, he was pinned to the desk by those steel spikes. It was horrible. They stuck a needle in his neck too, the blood was flowing out. I pulled it out as soon as I saw it."

Gordon glanced up at the young officer. "Son, you probably saved his life." He studied Officer Ramsey for a second. "You found only these personal papers and things. Nothing marked 'Secret' or anything like that?"

"No sir. There were a few government papers among the personal ones, but nothing like that."

Gordon nodded.

A gray-haired sergeant rushed into the room, out of breath. "Commissioner Howell, we located a car hidden in the trees beyond the lawn—a Jaguar. We've traced the ownership to an Aubrey Beck. We also believe there was another car there earlier, a larger one but it's hard to tell. Rain has washed away most of the tracks. I'm sorry, sir, but we won't be able to do much more till daylight."

"Find this Aubrey Beck, whoever he is—he was involved in all this. When you find him, arrest him and bring him to me, directly to me." Gordon went over to the desk, picked up a phone, and dialed a number. A few seconds later a voice came on the line.

"Good evening, sir," he said. "I'm at Kensington Manor. Lord Ashford is alive, barely, but alive. As the medics took him away, he whispered he'd sent his daughter with it to their cottage. Whoever did this may be following them. I'm sending Special Branch from Gloucester straight away."

There was a long pause, and the voice came back, guttural, with a hint of slurring. "You'll have anything you need. The entire resources of this government are at your disposal. Call me immediately with any news." With a click, the Prime Minister ended the call.

Chapter Sixty-One

By the time they reached Newent, the rain had slowed to a light, steady rhythm. Moonlight streaked through clouds that ran before a fierce wind, tearing hordes of dying leaves from the enormous sugar maple over the graveyard. Jamie jumped from the car with the document held tightly to his chest and ran toward the doors of St. Mary's and a refuge for the plan. Livy watched him until he disappeared from the leaf torrent that twisted and spun through the turbulence above the graves.

Minutes felt like eons, as alone in the darkness her eyes watched the bottom of the spire where Jamie vanished, a place that seemed so far away. A roar of wind surrounded her, fear her sole companion as Alana's face formed before her mind like an apparition. She was an imposter, a traitor—every word, every gesture a lie.

Livy knew she would murder her father; most likely already had and she was powerless to do anything. Alana's betrayal was now complete and Livy vowed she would see her die.

The door on Jamie's side burst open and she screamed, fear overwhelming her. He slipped into the seat and took her hand, his voice calm and reassuring. "I didn't mean to frighten you."

She inhaled and whispered, "Where did you put it?"

"It's in the altar. There's a hidden opening at the back used centuries ago to store valuables. I think everyone has long forgotten it exists. I showed it to Michael at the time I found it and he knows exactly where it is. All we need do is tell him." The car started and they headed toward the butcher shop one hundred yards away.

Jamie stopped the MG behind the butcher shop and opened the door. Livy slipped a hand on his arm and held on to him. "I need to call my home. I need to know if my father's alive."

He nodded. "Make the call while I speak to Michael. The phone is downstairs in the store, I'll show you."

Yellow light from the naked bulb in the stairwell cast swollen shadows as they came in the back door and went into the shop. Livy followed him through the butcher's cutting room, struck by the heavy musty odor of animal blood. He led her into the front room which was colored only by faint blue moonlight coming through the plate glass windows like a vapor.

He showed her a phone behind the porcelain counters. "Go ahead—make the call. I'll tell Michael what we've done." He held her face in his hands. "I'll be right back."

She watched him leave the shop to go upstairs. Alone again, her heart filled with dread, she lifted the receiver and tapped the cradle a few times to alert the operator. A moment or two later, a woman's voice came on the line. Livy's voice shook as she gave the private number for Kensington Manor.

"One moment," the voice said as if irritated she had to place a connection at such an inconvenient hour.

Livy counted the rings. When she got to five, a man answered. "Howell here."

"Howell? Who is this?" she queried.

"And you are?" the voice ordered.

"Livy Ashford. Who is this?"

There was a sharp intake of breath. "This is Gordon Howell, the Metropolitan Police Commissioner, I'm a friend of your father's. Livy, we're looking everywhere for you—where are you? Are you safe?"

"My father . . . is he . . .?" The horror of Alana's treachery caused Livy's voice to constrict.

"He's on his way to the hospital badly injured, but we got here in time. He's going to be all right. Now, where are you?" Howell's intensity flowed through the phone line.

She closed her eyes. He's alive. Another pang jumped into her heart. "What about Harold and Jackie?"

"Miss Ashford," he said gently, "they weren't as lucky." Her heart sank. "I'm very sorry. However, I must ask you again—where are you? Are you at your cottage?"

"We're in Newent," she heard herself say, the death of Harold and Jackie heavy as stone.

"We? Who's with you?"

"Jamie—we're at his home."

"The Wallace boy?"

She cocked her head, surprised he knew his name. "Yes. Tell me how bad . . ."

"Livy, they tried to murder him, but we got here in time. He'll be all right, I promise you. Did your father entrust you with anything?"

"Yes, and there's something you need to know. Wilfred Eaton and his daughter are German agents. Aubrey Beck is with them and so are two others. They'll be going to our cottage by Cliff's End." She was surprised at how composed the words sounded.

There was a pause and Gordon Howell said, "I'm sending men there and to your cott—"

"Sending help? Haven't you done that already?"

She stared at the handset for a second and slowly placed it into the cradle as Jamie and Michael came into the room. "The line went dead," she said.

Livy turned and faced the brothers. "My father is alive." Relief came to Jamie's face. "Though they tried to murder him."

The two brothers stared at each other as she continued. "Scotland Yard is on their way here and to the cottage, I think. Michael, when they come, tell them where the document is. Retrieve it, but hold onto it. Don't show it to anyone, not even the police. Give it only to Churchill." Her voice fearless.

Michael leaned on his cane, "I promise I'll do just that,"

"We should go," she said.

Jamie came to her and took her into his arms. "It's safer for you here. We should stay."

She looked into his eyes and said, "It's not about us, Jamie. We must stop them. All of England is at stake."

Chapter Sixty-Two

In the last few minutes the rain came to a stop, but the night sky was filled with electrical charges. Hidden arcs flashed in the core depths of low-roiling clouds as thunder pealed across the promontory of Cliff's End.

Jamie backed the MG into the carriage house as Livy held the door, a vicious wind threatening to tear it off the hinges. They forced the carriage house door closed and Livy used the key to unlock the cottage. Once inside, Jamie lit a candle and placed it on a corner of the dining table as Livy came beside him.

"I thought Scotland Yard would be here by now," she said. Jamie saw the fear etched in her face.

"So, did I."

She went to a coat closet by the front door and retrieved a shotgun and a handful of shells. "Here, take this. We may need it."

She dropped the gun into his hands along with the shells and picked up the candle. They climbed the stairs to the second floor and went into a bedroom that looked out over the long gravel drive.

She stood in front of the window and whispered, "Alana used to stay in here with me. Before we fell asleep, we'd spend hours talking about what we would be, how our lives would turn out, how we would be friends forever." She put a hand to her temples and rubbed. "What happened, Jamie? Where did all that go wrong?"

He leaned the shotgun against the wall and set a chair from a nearby table to face the window, a perfect vantage point to watch any approach to the cottage. Livy sat, blew out the candle and stared out into the moonlight seeping through holes in the clouds.

He stood next to her, his hand on her shoulder. She didn't take her eyes off the winding drive. "Alana was raised to be what she is," he said. "I'll wager from a small child she was indoctrinated by Wilfred to become what she is, a traitor." He picked up the shotgun and opened the breach. It squealed in protest. "How long has it been since this was fired?"

"I don't know—years maybe."

Jamie let out a short whistle as he loaded two shells into the side-by-side barrels and snapped the breach closed. "I hope this works, even the shells look like they're old."

"Jamie — someone's coming."

"Scotland Yard?"

In the distance, turning onto the drive, the lights of an automobile winked out.

"No, they wouldn't have turned out their lights. It's them." She looked at him, "If we are going to get out of this alive, listen to me. I've thought about this all the way here." She brought his hand to her mouth and kissed it.

"What are you thinking?"

She released his hand. "Take the gun and go up to my mother's place. I'll wait here and before they get too close, I'll lead them up the hill to you. They don't know you're alive, so don't hesitate. Shoot them or they'll kill us both."

"I can't leave you alone. There must to be a better way."

"They'll follow me right into your sights and we'll be done with them. Believe me, this will work and we don't have time to argue about it." She stood and kissed him, laying a hand on his cheek. "Now go," she said. "I'll be right behind you."

Jamie went out the kitchen door and raced up the hill, fighting the wind. Leaving her alone went against everything he was as a man. Even though he felt as if he abandoned her, he knew she was right, until Scotland Yard arrived, her plan was their only chance.

He ran around the tall rock outcropping that shielded her mother's cross and found a perfect refuge between waist-high boulders that offered a clear line of fire. He climbed to the top of the outcropping where he could look down on the cottage. A flash of lightning showed Alana and Aubrey at the front as Livy came out the kitchen door and ran away up the hill. Alana pointed and a heavyset man with a tall one behind, sprinted after her.

Thunder burst over the promontory, shaking the ground. He scrambled back down the rocks and slipped into his hiding place, a cold wind tearing at him. He rested the shotgun between boulders, pointed exactly at the spot where he knew they would appear.

Above the raging wind, he could barely hear Livy's screams. She was close, very close. He cocked the two hammers and sighted down the barrel as Livy raced by the boulders. The heavyset man rounded the outcropping and stopped in front of the loaded shotgun, his pistol trained on her.

Jamie held his breath and squeezed the trigger. The two hammers slammed down on the primer. A tremendous explosion came from both barrels, the smoke vaporized in the wind. He saw the man stagger back and drop to the wet ground, his chest torn away.

Lightning cracked above the cliffs. From the corner of his eye, he saw the other man standing slightly above him. Surprise and fear flashed across his hawk like face. He snarled and rushed down the rocks towards him, a knife extended.

Jamie had a split second to react. He flipped the empty shotgun around and swung it hard into the side of the man's head, breaking the stock. The man crumpled like a rag doll at his feet.

He turned to find Livy backing away, horror written on her face. Jamie jumped from the rocks, flew across the few feet of her mother's sanctuary and latched onto her arm, drawing her away from the cliff. "Run!" he shouted as the wind gobbled the words.

Livy slipped and fell, bringing him down with her onto the slick mud. He managed to stand and reached for her. As he pulled her up, her eyes went huge and she screamed. A violent shove from behind sent him cascading across the ground, sliding on his back, headfirst toward the edge.

His arms flailed and finally caught hold of a cone-shaped rock as his legs skidded over the cliff, toward the foaming sea far below.

The rock wiggled as he turned over, his chest against the wet mud, his hands wrapped around it. Near the cross, the hawk-faced man jerked Livy up by her hair, his enraged face covered with blood. He dragged her toward Jamie with a vicious smile on his face. Two feet from him, he stopped. Livy scrambled to stand, wildly swinging at him, catching only air as he held her fast at arm's length.

The hawk-face glared at him as he stepped forward and kicked the rock. His shoe smashed onto Jamie's hands and pain shot up his arms. The rock twitched and Jamie slipped a few more inches toward the edge. She had to get away. "Livy!" he screamed, the sound tore away in the wind.

Blood ran down the man's face and dripped into the mud. He smiled and kicked the rock again. It wobbled and Jamie inched further down the cliff. The man began to laugh as Livy slipped to the ground. He jerked her up on her knees, his hand clutching her hair. He twisted her head to face Jamie as he clawed to hang on. The hawk-face put his foot against the rock and shoved.

His eyes met hers as the rock tore away from the mud and he slid over the edge.

Chapter Sixty-Three

Livy screamed as Jamie vanished, her heart falling with him. The hawk-faced man snatched her to her feet as she screamed Jamie's name again and again.

"Shut up, you," the man demanded as he yanked a handful of her hair and jerked her down the hill.

When they reached the front door, he threw her into the cottage, her back and head smashed hard against the floor. Dazed, she looked up into a face filled with fury and Livy's heart went black.

Alana stared at her. "What the hell happened up there? Where's the Irishman?" Her voice thick with anger.

"He's dead, this bitch had a friend with her. He shot him." The man stumbled out the words as blood dripped from his chin.

"What!" Alana screamed.

"Don't worry," he said through his teeth, "he went over the cliff. I made sure of that."

"Was he a policeman?" Alana said in a chilled voice.

"I don't know—he wore a uniform."

Alana glared at Aubrey. "You bloody fool! It must be Jamie!" She yelled. "Pick her up." Alana hissed.

With one hand, he grabbed her and tossed her like a rag doll into a dining room chair. Alana quickly tied her arms to the chair and then snatched another chair and turned it around to face her. She straddled it, her arms folded across the back as she stared into Livy's eyes.

The spinning slowed inside her head and finally stopped. The cottage was in shambles, everything scattered and torn apart. Aubrey Beck stood behind Alana shaking, his mouth open and his eyes wide, staring at her.

Alana said with a sneer. "Where is the document?"

Livy heard herself laugh. "You're done for, I'm going to kill you," she said, her mind seeing Jamie as he went over the cliff and feeling a rage colder than anything she had ever known.

Alana smirked. "I doubt that. Too bad about Jamie and your father—you know he's dead too." Her eyes were empty, void of emotion. "I'll ask you one more time, where is the plan?"

Livy set a grin on her face. "That's something you'll never know."

"Oh, my dear, I doubt that too." She nodded to the hawk-faced man, who smiled and rested the blade of his knife on her arm. "You see, the Doctor here will remove small pieces of your skin until you tell me exactly where the document is. It's a horrible and very painful way to die." The Doctor drew the knife back, opening a gash in her forearm.

Livy threw her head back and winced, but made no sound.

Aubrey jumped forward. "Tell her! I promise you'll live." His voice was high and screeching. "I can't have you hurt. Livy, tell her!"

She stared at him, disgust coagulating.

Alana nodded to the Doctor and the knife slashed another gash perpendicular to the first. Livy let out a sharp breath. She knew he would cut another and another, remove the skin layer by layer. Staring into Alana's eyes, she laughed.

"I don't have time for this," Alana screeched. She slapped Livy's cheek so hard it drew blood. It felt as if her teeth cracked.

Pain seared across her face as blood gushed into her mouth. She spat it onto the floor. "You're right—you don't have time. Scotland Yard will be here any moment. They know who and what you are. They know about your father too." Vengeance filled her voice, "And you, Aubrey. You'll hang with them." She smiled again, blood bubbling from her mouth.

Alana screamed and hit her again.

For a second the world darkened and then slowly cleared. Livy dropped her head down and ran her tongue across her teeth tasting the blood, stalling for time. Her mind dashed, rolling over and evaluating every option until she arrived at one.

As if defeated, she slowly lifted her head as the blood pooled in her lap. She glared at Alana. By now, Scotland Yard would be at the church, waiting. "It's hidden at a church in Newent."

Alana rose from the chair, the smile on her face triumphant. "She's coming with us," her eyes never left Livy's. "She might be lying." She turned away and said to the one she called Doctor, "Untie her and then wrap her arm. I can't have her blood soiling Wilfred's car and clean up yourself too."

Chapter Sixty-Four

The terror on Livy's face burned in his eyes as Jamie slid over the cliff. His legs grated along the mud-slick wall, stone gouging at his flesh as he clawed the rock, reaching for anything to stop his plunge toward the white-capped sea.

Inches stretched to feet as his hands scratched and burrowed for a hold, until nothing remained. Lightning ripped apart the darkness and he screamed her name as his last handhold broke and he dropped into the abyss.

Jamie's body crashed against the cliff like a stone striking flint, the wind pushed against him, his chest scraping along the crag. Then as if seized by the maw of a gargantuan beast, his right leg was swallowed up to the knee and his fall stopped. He grabbed at holes in the weathered rock, the rough limestone carving at his fingers. He hung on the rock wall, his only thought the look of horror on Livy's face. He had to get to her. They would kill her.

Stable, at least for now, he searched above him for a path to her.

Mud, slick and impossible to traverse, was all he could see. He would have to climb to his left, along the side—there was no other way. In the gloom, Jamie freed his leg and started to move around the side of the sheer cliff. He knew one mistake would end in a swift plummet onto the rocks below.

Moment by moment he inched along, his feet slipping, his hands burning and aching to release. A bolt cracked the sky. The flash illuminated another handhold as he struggled across the face, searching the cliff with his fingers, his progress a sluggish grind. Thoughts of her, alone and captive forced him on, forced his burning legs to follow.

Another flash of light streaked across the clouds. From the corner of his eye he saw a pale space, a twisted ribbon that faintly glowed against the black rock—the beach trail cut into the cliff several feet below him.

He labored across the cliff face toward it and dropped the last five feet, sprawling onto the path that led to the sea. Drained, he managed to get to his feet and stumble toward the sanctuary where he last saw Livy as thunder rumbled in the distance.

The path emptied onto rain-soaked mud and grass at the summit, a narrow trail hacked between the rock walls. Jamie emerged from behind a line of boulders and lurched toward the monument Ashford erected to his wife. His arm slid across the stone cross and he knew how close he was to losing Livy—if he hadn't already.

Scant moonlight leaked through the black clouds and his breath came in burning gasps. On his second step toward the cottage, his foot slid to the side. Beneath it, poking out of the mud, the barrel of a pistol stared back at him. He wrapped his fingers around the muzzle and pulled it from the mud. Jamie ran the pistol across his thigh to clean it as best he could and set off toward the cottage and Livy.

He stumbled around the outcropping, at the top of the hill and slipped, sliding several feet down the wet grass. The pistol slithered away. On his hands and knees, he crawled after it as a sedan whipped into the driveway and skidded to a stop. He froze, prone on the ground. Aubrey popped out and stood by the driver's door as Alana and the tall, thin man came from the cottage. The man shoved Livy into the backseat and slid in after her. Alana jumped in the front as Aubrey got in and closed his door. Jamie scrambled for the gun as the sedan spun around and bolted down the drive toward the highway.

Fear for her filled him, but she was alive at least for now. He scrambled down the hill to go after them, to save her. Against a fierce wind, he managed to reach the carriage house and brace open the door. Exhausted, he stumbled to the side of his car, fell into the driver's seat and started the engine. It sputtered and came to life. He slammed the car into gear and shot out onto the drive.

The MG skidded around the first corner as he sped after them, the tires chewing up wet gravel. Far ahead of him red taillights abruptly glowed in the moonlight as the government car holding Livy turned onto the highway, heading north—toward Newent, toward St. Mary's and the defense plan. It was the only place left she could go.

Chapter Sixty-Five

With his lights off and hugging the white centerline, Jamie followed far enough behind for the MG to dissolve into the night. Dark thoughts about his chances to save her haunted his mind, always returning to the highway where the road would split. If Aubrey turned left and followed the highway, he had a chance. He would go straight ahead and take the narrow road, one at least seven miles shorter. That would bring him into Newent on the north side, closer to his home and well before they arrived. By now, Scotland Yard would be waiting. Together, they would go to St. Mary's and Livy's night of terror would end.

Mile after mile in the broken moonlight he shadowed them, barely able to keep the right tire on the center line. Ahead, slightly glowing in the sedan's headlamps, the gray ribbon of road arched toward the left. He gripped the wheel, sticky with his blood, as their car approached the decision point, praying Aubrey would go left. His eyes fixed on the sedan's faint tail lights.

His breath came in rapid spurts. The moments crawled on as the sedan closed on the split, the headlamps pointing directly ahead at the narrow road. Jamie held his breath. If they went straight, Livy would die tonight. He shouted at his futility as their lights shined like a beacon on the road straight ahead when abruptly, the lights swung away. Aubrey had taken the turn.

Jamie jammed the accelerator to the floorboard and the MG shot forward. A few seconds later, the sedan took the curve and disappeared. Jamie turned on his lights and hurtled by the split, onto the road straight ahead.

The miles raced away until he reached the bridge over Newent Lake. Slowing the car, he took the turn onto Broad Street and into the alley across from the Red Lion. He stashed the MG behind the butcher shop.

He ran through the darkness, up the back stairs and into the kitchen, calling for Michael. A single lantern illuminated the parlor as his brother's voice came from the surrounding gloom.

"In here, Jamie." His voice was clear, questioning.

"Turn on the lights," he yelled as he ran into the parlor and reached to flick the switch, but the darkness remained.

He moved into the yellow glow of the lantern, his uniform shredded in places, caked in mud and his own dried blood. Squeaky jumped up from a chair, knocking an end table next to it, his ale bottle wobbling. "My God, Jamie!"

He turned to Michael, who set down a half-filled glass of scotch and struggled to stand as his cane clattered onto the floor. "Where are the police, Michael? Christ, man! They've got her."

On the edge of the chair, Michael said, "They've got Livy?"

"Yes, where are the coppers?"

"They never came. We've been waiting for them since you left." Michael snatched up his cane.

"Ring them! Get them to St. Mary's."

"We got no power—the phone's dead," Squeaky said. "You can't call anyone."

Michael pushed up from the chair. "The storm knocked 'em out."

"They're coming here to get the document." He wiped a sleeve across his mouth, tasting his blood. "Squeaky, go to the police station, bring them to the church. Tell them to come at once, tell them to come armed. Do it now!"

Squeaky held his hands up, palms out. "There may not be anyone there." He looked confused and scared. "There's only five of 'em in the whole bloody town."

"Squeaky, go, hurry! Find them!" Squeaky nodded and bolted from the room. His footsteps echoed through the back stairwell.

Michael picked up what remained of his scotch from the end table and handed it to Jamie. He downed the liquid in one gulp as Michael said, "What are you gonna do?"

Jamie slammed the glass down. "Go to St. Mary's. I have a pistol in the car; I'll be there when the bastards arrive and I'll shoot every one of 'em. They'll kill her if I don't."

He turned and ran down the back stairs, grabbed the Luger from the passenger seat of the MG and ran by the ivy-covered wall toward the church.

Moonlight blinked in and out as he rounded the corner and sprinted through the graveyard. When he reached the alcove beneath the spire, a black sedan slowed to a stop by the street gate some fifty yards away. He eased open one of the doors and slipped into the church.

St. Mary's was cold and damp. The stone flickered eerily, basted by yellow light from several tall candles that circled behind the altar, one in each window alcove. His footsteps sounded hollow in the empty church as he ran, knowing he had seconds before they arrived. He climbed the two steps of the chancel and went around to the back of the altar as the door to St. Mary's opened.

Jamie ducked down and gripped the Luger as their footsteps came closer, the sound echoed around the stone walls. In his mind, he could place them in the church as they marched up the aisle toward the apse, the sound grew louder and louder and then they stopped before the altar.

"Now," Alana said with venom in her voice. The fury deepened inside him. "Get the document, Livy. You've got seconds to live if you don't—the Doctor will see to that."

"And seconds to live after I give it to you." She was stalling, alone and praying for the police to burst in.

That was enough. He opened the small door in the back of the altar and retrieved the document. He rose behind the altar, holding it behind him, the Luger pointed directly at Alana's heart. Aubrey Beck stood behind her, the color drained from his face. To her left, the man dressed in black pulled a pistol from behind his back and aimed it at Jamie but he dared not fire or Alana would die first.

Livy froze at the side of the altar, her eyes wide. "Jamie!"

He shot a quick glance at her and focused on Aubrey. "You too?" he said, glaring at him as he shook his head. "You're pathetic—a Nazi." He held the document up. "Is this what you came for, Alana?"

In a flash, Alana snatched Livy and blocked his shot. She shoved something like a black torch beneath her chin. It pushed Livy's head back.

"Put the document on the altar Jamie or she's dead." Her voice frigid, empty of emotion, "And put the gun beside it."

He slowly stepped around the altar holding the document away from his body, Alana's eyes never leaving it. The man she called Doctor stood in the center of the aisle, his pistol tracking Jamie's chest as he came around the side of the altar opposite Livy. The Doctor started moving to his right away from Alana, in an attempt to get behind him. He had seconds to make a decision.

Jamie looked at Livy. Her eyes narrowed and he nodded.

"If you want this . . . come get it." He tossed the document on the floor and watched Alana's eyes drop. Livy tore away from her as he went to one knee, turned and fired at the Doctor. His bullet missed, wood splintered as it slammed into the side of a pew.

The Doctor fired. The bullet zipped past him as he rolled away, the Doctor fired again. White marble from the alter vaporized inches from Jamie's face. He crouched and pulled the trigger again and again, but the Luger jammed from the mud inside. The Doctor smiled and closed on him, his revolver trained between Jamie's eyes.

He threw the useless weapon as he got to his feet. It careened past the Doctor and clattered into the stone aisle behind him as the Doctor slithered closer and aimed the muzzle of his gun at him, a rage burning on his face.

Livy screamed and Jamie turned toward her. Alana seized her and rammed the black torch against the side of her head. As he took a step toward her, a vise grip from behind threw him against the altar. His head bounced off the stone, his vision clouded.

"You shot him, you bastard!" The hate-filled words floated into Jamie's ears. Spittle flowed from the man's mouth as he said it and he centered the gun on Jamie's forehead.

From over the Doctor's shoulder, a cane crashed down onto his wrist and the pistol skittered away.

Michael.

The Doctor spun toward Jamie's brother and with one nimble movement, he retrieved a knife and plunged it deep into Michael's abdomen. His brother staggered backward and sank into the aisle.

Jamie jumped at the Doctor, his fist landing a blow on the side of his face. The man recoiled as if barely touched. A menacing smile showed blood seeping from the corner of his mouth as he grabbed him, his hands latching onto his neck. Jamie tried to elude him, but the Doctor's strength overpowered him. The Doctor picked him up and threw him against the altar, his powerful hands clutched his throat, bent him backwards over the altar as Livy's screams filled Jamie's ears.

He struggled against him, throwing punches that landed nowhere. From the corner of the chancel, Jamie heard Aubrey screech, "No! She's mine!" He turned his head toward the sound as Aubrey rushed Alana, pushing Livy away from her. He grabbed the black cylinder Alana held in her hands and fought against her, violently swinging her arms back and forth, screaming, "No! She's mine!"

Glittering spots invaded the edges of Jamie's vision. The Doctor's hands cutting off his life. He craned his head to the side, fought to break the Doctor's grip and heard Aubrey scream and crash to the floor in a heap.

Jamie yelled for Livy, but nothing came out as he watched Alana scoop up the document and race away as a shrill buzz swirled in his ears. A gleeful rage on the Doctor's face filled Jamie's eyes as darkness closed on him, his vision fading.

A loud bang reverberated off the stone walls.

Shock flashed across the Doctor's face. He stood upright, his hands eased their grip and Jamie gasped for air. He smiled at Jamie, red foam bubbled from his mouth. The Doctor turned his head and looked over his shoulder as another bang filled the church.

He jerked upright, his mouth open, bewildered as he looked down at his chest. Blood spread out across the center of his shirt. He glared back at Jamie as life fled from his eyes and he crumpled to the floor.

Livy rushed from behind the altar, wrapped her arms around him and helped him to stand. Gulps of sweet air filled him as the blackness began to fade and the buzzing ebbed. Jamie wobbled and fell back against the altar. He drew in a slow breath and spotted his brother wedged against a pew, his blood running into the aisle. Michael's hand slowly dropped and the Doctor's revolver clattered onto the stone floor.

Chapter Sixty-Six

"Michael!" Jamie shouted.

He jumped over the Doctor's body, careened into the aisle and crawled to his brother slumped against a pew. On Michael's left side below his ribs, a blood-smeared knife stuck out, buried almost to the hilt.

Livy turned around and snatched the white linen runner from the altar. The gold cross fell backward off the table. She reached Michael seconds after Jamie and together they moved his body away from the pew and placed him on his back in the aisle.

Blood bubbled from around the blade as Michael's eyes opened. "I got him, Jamie." His voice was strong between gasps. "I got the bastard."

"You did," Jamie said, the words thick with emotion. He looked at her; fear of losing his brother for a second time covered his face. Jamie turned back to Michael. "The knife needs to come out. It's going in deeper."

Michael gripped his sleeve with a bloodstained hand. "Do what you need to."

Jamie grasped the knife and eased the blade out of the wound as his brother winced in pain. Blood now flowed from the gape in Michael's flesh as Livy struggled to tear the linen into smaller pieces. She took the knife from Jamie's hand and sliced the fine weave into strips and handed them to him. He folded them into rolls, inserting them one by one into the wound to staunch the blood.

With the wound filled, the blood slowed to a trickle. She cut and folded a larger piece the size of a small towel and handed it to Jamie. He took the bandage and applied pressure to the wound.

A howl erupted from near the altar, rolling off the half-circle of the stained-glass apse. A second howl and Aubrey screamed, "Help me. I'm dying!"

She ignored him and looked at Jamie. "I thought I lost you."

He glanced at her. "And I you." He clenched his teeth as he looked at his blood-covered hands pressing against the wound. "Alana has the document."

"I know. I saw her take it and run away. She tried to kill me. That thing she had was some kind of horrible weapon. It went off and hit Aubrey." She put her hand on his arm as he pressed on Michael's wound. "Where is Scotland Yard? I thought they would be here."

"We're on our own. I don't think they got the call from London; the phones are dead." He heard Aubrey screech again, he called for Livy. "They almost killed you." Jamie closed his eyes. He took in a breath, still applying pressure. "I almost failed you Livy." He said staring at a purple bruise on her cheek.

"We're still alive, they haven't got us yet." she said. "But we need to find out where Alana went and Aubrey will know." She picked up the knife drenched in Michael's blood and stood. "I'm going after her." Aubrey let out another wail, moaning and calling for her.

Jamie looked at Michael lying on the stone floor and back to her. "Livy, you can't do that alone."

Michael's head raised slightly, the words whispered but clear. "Go with her, Jamie. Go." He grimaced from pain. "It'll all be for naught if the Germans if she succeeds."

A loud bang filled the church as the main door flew open and Squeaky rushed in with an ancient policeman on his heels.

Livy looked back at Jamie. "You stay with Michael. I'll go."

He shook his head. "They'll kill you. You won't have a chance."

Squeaky ran up to them. "My God!" He yelled the words from three feet away. "What happened!"

The policeman came up alongside Squeaky, his face bright red from exertion. Out of breath, he panted, "Scotland Yard is on the way!" He pointed to the Doctor's body, "Is he ... dead?"

"Yes," Jamie said. "He's a Nazi and so is the one over there." He motioned with his head toward Aubrey, who squealed so loud Jamie could hardly hear himself speak. "Squeaky, put pressure on this wound."

Squeaky knelt beside Michael. His hands shook as he pressed down on the bandage. Jamie stood and scooped up the remnants of the altar cloth. He wiped Michael's blood from his hands. His eyes narrowed as he looked at Aubrey and said, "Livy, come with me."

She followed as he closed the distance to Aubrey. He stopped at the corner of the steps leading to the altar and picked up Alana's weapon. He turned it in his hands, shaking his head. "What evil could think of such a thing?"

As Aubrey whined, with each step toward him, rage and disgust intensified in Livy's heart. Aubrey would tell him where Alana went or she would kill him. It was that simple.

Jamie stood over him as he whimpered, a red stain on his shoulder growing.

Aubrey stared up at Livy and begged. "Help me, please help me, I'm dying. Help me!"

The whining voice made her grip the bloody knife tighter.

Livy knelt and pressed her free hand hard against the steel spike sticking from his shoulder. He screamed and looked at her, shocked. He squealed as she pressed again and said, "Where is Alana?"

Aubrey's eyes popped wide open and his body shook. "Livy! You can't do this. You . . . you belong to me."

She gritted her teeth and pressed hard against the spike. Aubrey screamed again as he reached for her and she shoved his hand away, the knife now against Aubrey's throat.

"Where is Alana?"

Fear covered Aubrey's face. "She's going to her father's home. That's all I know." He whined, "Don't kill me, don't kill me!"

She stared at him. "You'll live . . . you'll live long enough to hang, you bastard."

Softly he pleaded, "Livy, please, help me." His voice made her sick.

She looked at Jamie. "I know where she's going. Her home is a few miles from Gloucester; I've been there before."

Jamie closed in on Aubrey and held Alana's weapon in front of him. Aubrey's huge eyes followed the black cylinder as Jamie went to a knee in front of him and slowly turned the knob at the bottom of Alana's weapon, it clicked with each twist.

Aubrey flinched at the sound and his eyes bulged, never leaving the weapon.

Jamie grabbed the collar of his shirt, yanked him forward. "Why did you have the Gotha shot down, why did you try to kill me?" He shoved the weapon under Aubrey's chin.

He glared at Jamie, the red stain on his uniform spreading and screamed. "You don't deserve her. She's mine, she always will be!"

Livy was sickened and at that moment, she knew Aubrey was insane, completely insane.

"What's Alana's plan?" Jamie demanded.

Aubrey's huge eyes moved from the weapon to Livy's. "Help me."

She knelt beside Jamie and took Aubrey's hand and this time she softly said, "Aubrey, tell me her plan."

He smiled at her his eyes open wide. "They want the location of the communication hubs." The words were mumbled without reason behind them. "They're going to bomb every one of them, every single one!" He burst into cackled laughter. "They know where they are and they'll win. You'll never stop them." He began to shriek with laughter again.

Jamie called out to the policeman standing by Michael. "Come cuff this one."

The policeman ran over and jerked Aubrey forward. He squealed as the officer cuffed his hands behind him. "There," the policeman said as he shoved Aubrey against the wall. He looked at Jamie and said, "The phones are working again. I rang Scotland Yard before I left the station with your friend, but it may take a while for them to get us."

Jamie went back toward Michael. He tossed Alana's weapon into a pew and picked up the Doctor's gun. She stood next to him as he knelt by his brother. Michael was pale and though his eyes were open, he looked as if he was fading fast.

"Go on," Michael whispered. "Get the document and come back. I'll be waiting for you." He forced a smile and his eyes slowly closed.

Jamie got up from his knees, the muscles in his jaw twitching.

The Policeman put a hand on his shoulder. "We'll take good care of him, son."

Squeaky looked up from the make-shift bandage. "I got him, Jamie. We'll get him to the hospital right away."

"When the police arrive, tell them to meet us at Wilfred Eaton's home. They should know where it is. We're going there," Jamie said.

She held out the Doctor's bloody knife and nodded. "Ready?" She said.

They ran from the church, across the graveyard and down the alley to the back of the butcher shop. As they got into the MG, in the distance, she thought she heard the sound of police cars, their bells ringing above the wind.

Chapter Sixty-Seven

Jamie slammed on the brakes. The MG slid on the wet pavement well past the opening, the Luger clattered to the floorboard. He shoved the gear-shift into reverse, the metal grinding.

"Sorry, it's been years since I've been here," Livy said as the MG shot backward. "The hedge is far taller than when I was a child."

He grabbed the pistol lying at his feet, put it back on his lap and turned off the headlamps, thrust the car into gear and released the clutch. They slipped through a gap in the thick laurel hedge and onto a packed clay drive.

Wilfred Eaton's two-story home was made of brick—square with windows on either side of a portal that gaped like an open mouth. Livy directed him to the right of the house, where a long thatched-roofed stable stood like an afterthought.

He slowed the car and shut off the ignition as she opened her door and said, "If Alana's here, she would put the car in the stables over there."

They ran toward the thatched-roofed building, staying low. She stopped at the first set of wooden doors and stood on tiptoes, peering through small glass windows set in a line.

"She's here. There's the car." Livy whispered as he wiped the dusty glass with his hand and peered in.

"That's it—you can still see raindrops on the boot," he said.

A gust fluttered the blackout curtains and light spilled on the ground by the end of the building.

"They'll be in there," she whispered, pointing toward the flash of light. "That was the one room we couldn't go in. Wilfred would never allow it."

As they approached the window, Jamie heard Alana's voice and the rhythm of a Morse code key. He turned the doorknob, eased it open and stepped into the room, Livy behind him.

Alana and Wilfred Eaton sat in front of a bank of radios, their backs to them. Alana typed on a machine with bulbs that lit up with every keystroke as Wilfred sat next to her and tapped out the Morse code.

Jamie pointed the pistol and fired three times. Sparks and flame exploded from the ruined radios, white smoke belched out and gathered at the ceiling.

Alana spun around and sprang at him like an enraged animal. He sighted the gun at her heart and pulled the trigger. The gun clicked, the magazine empty.

Before she could reach him, Livy flew at her. The blow knocked her sideways into a wall. As they grappled, Jamie pivoted toward Eaton as he snatched an Enfield revolver from a drawer.

Wilfred waved the gun back and forth, trying to get a shot off at Livy and yet keep Jamie at bay. His gun shifted to Livy, her back against the wall with Alana's hands wrapped around her throat, blocking his shot.

Jamie jumped to his right, forcing Wilfred to swivel the gun toward him, when a scream burst through the room.

Jamie turned, Alana's back was to him with Livy pinned against the wall. He hurtled toward them as Alana screamed again, cursing Livy. Alana took a step back, wobbled, and slumped backward onto the floor. Livy's eyes narrowed as she stared down at Alana, the Doctor's bloody knife in her hand.

Wilfred screamed, "You bitch!" He turned the gun on Livy. She ducked and the bullet missed, slammed into the wall inches away from her body.

In a fury, Jamie launched the Doctor's gun at him. It struck the side of Wilfred's head and opened a gash. The traitor stumbled back, the Enfield revolver crashed onto the floor in front of him. Wilfred scrambled for it as Jamie jumped to his left, placing himself between Livy and Wilfred. The bells of arriving police cars louder with each second.

Blocking his shot, Jamie glared at him. "You're finished, Wilfred. Even if you kill us, you'll never get the information out. Hear that? That's Scotland Yard coming for you. They know who and what you are."

Wilfred's mouth curled into a snarl. "We'll see about that." He raised the gun and pointed it at them. "You . . . killed her, you bitch," he screamed.

"She's a traitor like you and deserved to die." A fury in Livy's voice. She jumped out from behind Jamie and threw the bloody knife at Wilfred. It flew sideways, bounced off his chest and clattered onto the floor.

He glanced down at the knife and Jamie yelled, "Run, Livy."

She ran for the door and it was the opening he needed. Jamie rushed Wilfred to make sure she could escape. He aimed the gun and fired as Jamie closed in on him, the bullet smacked into the ceiling. Wilfred fired again as Jamie jumped to the side. The bullet whizzed by his head close enough to ring in his ear.

He smashed into Wilfred and the revolver flew from his hand, tumbling onto the table in front of the smoking radios.

"It's over. You're done for, Wilfred." Jamie yelled as they grappled.

Police burst into the room shouting orders for them to stop, their weapons drawn. Jamie shoved Wilfred into the corner hard enough to make him bounce off the brick wall. Jamie raised his hands and started backing away. Wilfred dove for the Enfield, jammed it against his temple and screamed, "Für Deutschland!"

He fired and gray matter splattered the wall.

Wilfred collapsed onto the radio table and fell to the floor. Jamie turned around with his hands raised and faced the police, their weapons pointed at his heart. Livy screamed and raced in, pushed her way past the officers. She threw herself at Jamie and wrapped her arms around him.

"I heard the gunshots. I thought Wilfred killed you." Her body trembled.

"It's over," he said, as he held her tight.

A baritone voice came from behind the policemen. "I'm afraid it's not over yet." They turned toward the voice as a man entered the room, holding a badge out in front of him.

"Inspector Roland Thomas, Special Branch," he said, taking in the carnage around him.

The inspector turned to his men and ordered, "Everyone, out!" He looked back at Livy and Jamie and pointed, his face completely blank. "You two stay where you are."

He was in his late forties, thick boned and dressed for his job. A rain speckled trench coat hung limply on his large shoulders and his tie and white shirt was a rumpled mess. His angular face needed a shave, but had a quality and air of authority. He moved passed them and walked around the room, observing everything, not touching anything. He used a pen to lift papers next to the coding machine Alana had used and made a clicking noise through his teeth.

He nodded and said, "Perhaps, you were lucky." The Inspector turned to look over his shoulder at Jamie, his eyes taking in the mud and blood covering his uniform. He looked at Livy and paused as his eyes surveyed the blood smeared on her hands. "Not often can amateurs disrupt a ring of traitors and yet you did. The odds were certainly against you."

Livy looked up at Jamie. Her shoulders were slumped with fatigue; a dark bruise had settled on her swollen cheek but the fear had left her eyes. "Hold me," she whispered.

Love and pride in her filled his heart. His arms enfolded her as her head rested on his chest.

The inspector pointed at the document stacked on the table. "Lady Ashford, is this it?"

She looked towards the Inspector and nodded.

He pointed to the machine. "Do you know what this is?"

Livy shook her head.

His eyes met Jamie's. "And you?"

"Some sort of coding machine, I presume."

The inspector scratched the stubble on his face and paused for a moment. He picked up a small green paper bound book and shoved it into his coat pocket. "Forget you ever saw it, both of you." He snatched the plug out of the wall socket and closed the machine in its wooden box. He lifted it off the table, looked at Livy and pointed to the papers, "Lady Ashford, gather those documents."

She left Jamie's arms and obliged. Carefully, she stepped over Wilfred's body and slipped several loose papers back into the blue binder. The inspector moved along the table, a thin smoke still rising from the radios. He picked up a phone and tapped the cradle a few times. A moment later he said, "One second."

He handed the handset to Livy. "I want you to ask for this number." He held a business card in front of her as she read the numbers into the mouthpiece.

She stood for a moment staring at Jamie. "Hello," she said and confusion came on her face. "Yes sir, I know who it is," she said tentatively. She listened intently, her mouth open.

"Yes sir." She placed the phone in its cradle and looked at Jamie, an expression of surprise on her face. "That was the Prime Minister."

"Churchill?" Jamie said, shocked.

Livy nodded and said to the inspector, "I'm to follow your orders, we both are."

The Inspector nodded and said, "Lady Ashford, within the hour you'll be on a plane to London. You are to carry this document with you at all times and surrender it only to the man you just spoke to. Do you understand?"

She nodded, "I do."

Jamie heard *Lady Ashford* was going back to London, and Churchill, the thought seized in his chest, the words burned in his mind.

"And you, Mr. Wallace—you are to report back to your duty station, to your squadron. We will take you there."

He looked at the Inspector, shook his head and said, "No. First, I'm returning to Newent."

The Inspector paused a few seconds, seemed surprised at his answer but said, "I understand and I'll not stop you, however, I will place a detective to guard you and you'll do exactly as he orders. Neither of you are to be left alone—at least for the time being. Your brother will be at the hospital. We had him on his way right after we arrived at the church."

Livy came to him, wrapped her arms around him and looked into his eyes. "I don't want to leave you. I'm scared for Michael."

Inspector Thomas shook his head. "I'm sorry Lady Ashford, the nation takes priority. You and I are leaving for London immediately." His voice eased a little. "The man I send with Jamie will report back to me as soon as anything more is known. I'll make sure to inform you."

"Go." Jamie said in a voice he felt wasn't his own. "There isn't a choice." The Inspector's *Lady Ashford* and the mention of Churchill had awoken his deepest and almost forgotten fears.

With the document in her hand, she stood on her toes and kissed him goodbye.

The inspector took Livy's arm and escorted her away. As they reached the door, he paused, turned back to face Jamie and said, "I sincerely hope the best for your brother, but go quickly son, he wasn't faring well when we left the church."

Chapter Sixty-Eight

The sun was barely above the horizon when Jamie eased to a stop in front of the only hospital in Newent. He slipped out of the car, the detective snoring in his seat. He pushed away doubts of what a future with Livy might hold and ran into the hospital to search for Michael.

Low murmurs filled the lobby. It had been taken over by the police, some armed and some not. Against the wall next to frosted glass double doors with No Admittance stenciled in black, his father and mother sat with Julia on a sagging blue sofa. Squeaky sat in a stuffed chair to the right, his hands still stained with Michael's blood. All four of them were staring at the floor. As Jamie approached, Julia looked up.

"Jamie!" She jumped up from the couch.

Her face revealed everything and he thought the worst.

"How is he," fear wrapped his voice.

"We don't know," Julia said shaking her head, her voice tottering as Squeaky and his family came towards him. "He's been in surgery for a very long time."

"He saved my life." Jamie held her close and knew she was petrified of losing Michael again, losing all their tomorrows.

"What the hell happened?" His father snapped out the words as he stepped in front of them.

Jamie turned around and saw the detective a few feet behind him, staring at him through sleep filled eyes. "I'm forbidden to speak about it."

The look on his mother's face broke his heart.

"Forbidden to speak about it? Rubbish!" His father raised his hand up and pointed behind him. "And who bloody hell is this following you?"

"He's my shadow—at least until I get back to Hornchurch and my squadron. Did they bring in anyone else?"

"That RAF Officer," Squeaky blurted out. "The Coppers took him away in a straight-jacket not long after we got here. He was squealing like a pig, cursing you and moaning for Livy. The coppers told me not to say anything." He looked defiantly at the detective standing behind Jamie. "But I will anyway."

One of the No Admittance doors opened. A woman of forty or so in blue hospital garb stepped out, her dark hair spilling from under a matching triangle scarf. She scanned the lobby and walked up to them.

"Are you here for Mr. Wallace—are you his family?"

Jamie's father faced her. "We are. Now, tell us what's going on." It was said as a command.

She looked over at the others and to Jamie. Her eyes moved to his uniform, a bewildered look on her face. She took in a breath, frowned and said, "He's still with the surgeon. I'm sorry, but I don't have any other information for you right now. Please be patient, it shouldn't be too much longer. The doctor will be out to speak with you soon."

The nurse took another look at him and disappeared back behind the doors. As they closed, Jamie felt as if they might be closing on Michael's life. He sat in one of the chairs next to the couch. Exhausted, pain settled in all over his body and he put his elbows on his knees and lowered his head thinking of Michael and the sound of the Inspector's "Lady Ashford" as it tore at his heart.

"Jamie. You don't look so good." His father tapped his shoulder. "In fact, you look terrible."

Jamie raised his head, "In the last twelve hours I've killed a man, saw two others die and watched Livy execute her childhood friend—I feel numb and alone." It was as if a bolt of electricity crossed their faces.

"That's enough. You're not to say another word," the detective barked.

Jamie ignored him and flopped back in the chair. "They took Livy to London, to Churchill."

His father blurted out. "What the hell is going on here? We come back from Cardiff to find all this! What have you done!"

A hand snatched Jamie's shoulder. He looked up and saw the detective's stern face, "Not another word son, don't test me."

A doctor burst out from behind the No Admittance doors, his light-blue scrubs splashed with blood, Michael's blood.

Jamie jumped to his feet and the family gathered, as if standing before a magistrate for an unwanted verdict. "I'm told you're here for Michael Wallace." His face void of expression, dark circles under his eyes.

His mother gasped as Julia's grip tightened on his arm.

"Go ahead, tell us," his father said, his arm tight around Jamie's mother.

The doctor took a breath. "He pulled through. He'll have a bit of a recovery and need some assistance, but he'll survive."

Julia's legs buckled. She toppled against him and gently, he held her up.

Chapter Sixty-Nine

Livy stood in the cemetery beside her father and his uniformed orderly as he folded a black umbrella. Huge raindrops would splash for a few minutes and then the clouds would scurry away to leave streams of sunlight that stippled the grounds. Wounded by the loss of Harold and Jackie, she found it hard to breathe and there was something else hidden low in her mind. It pecked at her like a voice from behind a wall, muffled and indistinct—she couldn't reach Jamie no matter how hard she tried. Five days had passed since she returned from Gloucester and it was as if Jamie had fallen off the earth. Call after call to Hornchurch went unanswered. Even the direct number Locke gave her to the squadron hut wasn't answered. The call wouldn't connect.

Yesterday, she decided to drive over to the airbase and find him, but she was stopped cold. For their protection, on the Prime Minister's orders, Kensington Manor was surrounded by armed guards. She wasn't going anywhere.

Frustrated and worried, Livy had gone into the kitchen. The crotchety nurse they had caring for her father sat at the table and horded the morning newspaper. She took a chair across from her and looked out the window, wondering what to do next. With the protection Churchill ordered, she was a prisoner in her own home.

A corner of the front page of *The Times* stuck out from beneath the nurse's discard pile. She stripped it from the stack and noticed a column off to one side. The headline read: MP KILLED IN TRAGIC CRASH.

Her mouth dropped open. The article read Member of Parliament, Wilfred Eaton and his daughter had been killed in an automobile accident outside Gloucester. The muscles in her jaw clinched when she saw, "MP Eaton was a man dedicated to the people of England, a hero." Livy slammed her hand down on the table. The crotchety nurse jumped and glared at her.

She almost tore the article to shreds. All of it was a lie. Anger burned in her when she realized no one would ever know what happened, that Wilfred and Alana were traitors and how close England had come to destruction. The Government would seal the truth away, keep all of it secret. The truth would never be known.

An ice-cold raindrop fell on her face, her eyes popped open and the memories from yesterday fled. She took in a deep breath and rested a shaking hand on her father's shoulder. The navy-blue wool of his uniform peppered with rain. He was pale, weak from loss of blood, far too weak to stand for the last part of the funeral for Harold and Jackie. His hands were wrapped in plaster and a blue-green bruise covered most of the right side of his neck and face, but his eyes were bright and that was all that mattered. He had survived.

A white-gloved military honor guard carried two coffins from the church doors toward side-by-side empty graves, their expressions solemn. Harold's coffin was covered by the Union Jack and on Jackie's, the polished mahogany had simple white roses resting on the lid—exactly what she would have wanted. The coffins were followed by a priest and his entourage that silently marched toward the waiting graves.

As the procession came closer, Livy glanced at her father, saw a tear roll down his cheek and her heart broke. The tear glistened in the sunlight as memories of these two, wonderful people flashed through her mind. The same emptiness she felt on the day she said good-bye to her mother returned to leave her numb.

Slowly the coffins were lowered together into the earth. The priest stepped back from the graves and three volleys of seven rifle shots split the silence, scattering birds from tree branches to circle around a hole in the sky. A lone soldier stood atop a small hill in the corner of the graveyard, the sound of his bagpipes filled the air over their graves in a final tribute.

She whispered a good-bye and followed the orderly as he pushed the wheelchair between the headstones. A deep sadness overtook her as she looked back at their graves being filled. Harold and Jackie were lost and for the time being, her home was inhabited with inconsequential people, ones she cared nothing for and the face she needed most, had vanished.

The trio moved up the hill away from the graves, toward the paved road and the armed men that waited to take them back to Kensington Manor. The wheelchair bobbled over thin roots as the orderly pushed the chair around low branches of an ancient oak toward the top of the hill. She plucked a faded leaf that told of the coming of fall as she came around the tree and there, standing alone on the crest, was Jamie.

Her heart leapt as she ran to him, her feet carrying her through the wet ground as if it wasn't there. That same grin she'd first seen in the air-raid ditch appeared on his face. He took her in his arms and held her.

"I'm so sorry for Harold and Jackie. I know how much you loved them." His voice touched her. "I wouldn't have simply shown up like this, not today, but it's the only time I have to speak with you. All pilots are restricted to base and I'm here without permission. I was going to leave the airfield anyway, but Locke insisted, he brought me here to protect me, they won't arrest both of us."

She held him close, "I've been so worried about you. I've been so scared." She looked up at him, "I've called you a thousand times."

He took in a breath and blinked as she said, "How's Michael?"

"A little worse for wear, but he'll be fine. He'll be in hospital for another week or so and after, he'll get great care from my mum. She'll either get him back to normal or drive him mad." She looked in his eyes and a sudden sadness appeared. Livy knew something was wrong. "What's happened?"

Memories seemed to flash behind his eyes. "The last five days I've flown twenty sorties. They came in force Livy, came with everything they had."

The hair on the nape of her neck stood.

"It was a struggle; it went on for days and many were killed, but we beat them. The battles won't end today or tomorrow, but I think we've won. They'll never mount an invasion and Hitler will lose this war."

She drew in a breath, her fear slinking toward shadow. "Is it true? Can the end have started?"

"I believe so," he whispered.

His hands, gentle and reassuring held hers. "Fighter Command closed off all contact with the outside world. That's why you couldn't reach me."

He pointed over his shoulder. Eric Locke stood leaning against a powder-blue staff car, smoking a cigarette. He stared at them both and pointed to his watch.

Jamie looked passed her. She followed his gaze and saw the orderly pushing her father's wheelchair towards them.

"Your father looks better than I would have thought. How is he?"

"He's doing well. Much better than expected." She turned back to him. "Somehow, he's different, his heart is . . . well open, as if he might be able to love again."

"Good, there was a loneliness about him I felt when I first met him. I didn't understand it until I saw your mother's sanctuary and knew how much he loved her."

"Yes, he did. Maybe the pain of losing her has eased, I know it's something he's carried with him a long time."

She tilted her head back and looked out of the corner of her eye at the pained expression on his face. "What's wrong?"

Locke's voice came from by the staff car. "Come on Jamie, we must go.'

He sighed. "I love you, you know that. But I'm not the right man for you." He swallowed, "I'm not a part of your world, I'm a butcher's son. You deserve more than someone who will be known as Livy's mistake. You deserve better."

Her heart pounded against her chest, a lump formed in her throat and she paused a moment to gather her voice. "You can't be saying goodbye."

He leaned over and gently kissed her. The softness and passion felt like their first kiss as she stood with her back against a wall in the Underground. She opened her eyes and saw the pain written on his face. He inhaled a deep breath and said, "I need time, time to believe a day won't come when we've become bitter, where our differences have destroyed each other and our love."

"Jamie, it's good to see you." Her father's voice came from behind them. There was a broad smile on his face.

"And to see you, sir." Jamie's voice spoke of the respect they shared. "I won't even attempt to shake your hand." He winced and she knew the detective told him how they found him, pinned to the desk.

Her father lifted his plaster covered hands as if each weighed several stone. "These are driving me mad. I have at least three weeks to go before I'm rid of them." He motioned to the orderly and said, "Take a break Thomas, I won't need you for a while."

The orderly's head nodded. "Certainly sir, call for me when you do, I'll be close by."

He thanked him and focused on Jamie. "When must you report back to your squadron?"

"Actually, right now. I'm absent without permission."

Her father looked at her and then back to Jamie, "As I came close, I heard you. I think I understand you Jamie, but you don't have to do this, in fact, I wish you wouldn't."

Locke's voice boomed from next to the car. "Jamie, we must go. Now!"

He looked at her, his shoulders slumped. "Goodbye Lord Ashford, take good care of yourself and of Livy."

Jamie held her hands for a moment his eyes searching hers. "I love you, I always will." He turned away, headed toward Locke and the staff car.

Livy stood silent as he opened the door and got in. He turned to face her as the staff car gathered speed, his eyes never moving from hers until the little blue car rounded a corner and Livy's heart came crashing down.

Chapter Seventy

The driver turned into the gates of Westminster Palace. In the rear seat, Livy noticed an old woman sitting outside the wrought iron fence, surrounded by buckets of wild yellow daffodils. Memories of Jamie and the fields around Newent flooded back and she quickly turned away, the sting still living in her heart.

The black Rolls Royce slowed to a stop in front of the St. Stephens entrance. A white gloved attendant opened the rear door and assisted her as she stepped out and waited for her father to join. They walked up the steps passed the two stone lions on either side of the arched cathedral doors and entered the palace. They were greeted by a guide dressed in formal morning attire. As they approached he bowed, came to attention and in a practiced formal voice said, "My Lord, My Lady, I humbly ask that at your pleasure, you accompany me."

He spun on his heels and with them following, the three traveled deeper into the rarely seen corridors of the realm. They went through pristine halls filled with the memories of lives that created the thousand-year history of England. The man stopped at a polished elm door tucked into and ornately paneled wall opposite a long bank of lead glass windows. He knocked three times and opened it, motioned with his hand for them to enter. They stepped through the portal and then from behind them, the door slowly closed.

The walls of the narrow room were filled with tapestries depicting St. George slaying the Dragon, mounted on his white horse heroically poised as the strike of his long lance ended the plague-bearing creature's reign of terror. A royal blue carpet woven with the hero's crest adorned the floor and matched the upholstered furniture. Artisan carved wooden sections covered in gold leaf patterned the walls between the tapestries. On a heavy oak table set before floor to ceiling windows that towered above the portly gentleman standing before them, a single piece of paper stood out.

Winston Churchill turned away from the windows and came to greet them, surprisingly agile and energetic for a man of his age and constitution. His dark blue suit and vest were dusted with tiny ash flecks from a cigar he held between thick fingers. On his cherub face, a smile of warmth and eagerness was overpowering. As he came to Livy, holding her right hand in his, he said, "Miss Ashford. I'm very pleased to see you again, our last meeting was under quite different circumstances." He looked toward her father. "And Lord Ashford, as always my friend, a pleasure."

He focused his attention back to Livy as she offered a clear good morning to him.

"Lady Ashford, on behalf of a grateful nation, I want to thank you for the extraordinary service you and your young man provided for all of us." The mention of Jamie echoed in the emptiness that filled her. "If that horrible man, Wilfred Eaton, had found a way to succeed, I dare say we could hear the sound of Jackboots in these very halls today. Catastrophe for our nation came too close, far too close."

He reached for the paper and slid it towards her.

"I wish there was more I could do for you and young Wallace, but unfortunately there isn't." He retrieved a silver pen from a pocket in his coat. "My Government has decided if word of a corrupted Member of Parliament became common knowledge, it would severely impact the faith and trust holding our nation together. It would damage that covenant at precisely a time we can afford it least, the result would be devastating to our war effort. Therefore, nothing of your exploits will ever be made public. The entire affair will remain a State secret under the Official Secrets Act." He lay the pen on the paper. "I ask that you sign this agreement, binding you to silence, just as young Wallace did a few minutes ago."

Her heart jumped, he may be near. Thinking of everything but the paper, she signed it. "Is Jamie here?" she said.

Churchill cocked his head and responded, "I don't know. I believe he has returned to his posting. Quite a young man you have there, he's been credited with five enemy aircraft destroyed during the German's last and most vicious attack. Quite Remarkable."

She allowed her eyes to close, her head down as she passed the paper back to Churchill. "I didn't know."

"I'm sorry Miss Ashford, you deserve much better but the needs of a nation at war take precedence." He extended his hand and she took it. "I personally ask that you be my guest in the next few minutes for my speech in the House chambers. I have arranged for a special place to be designated for you in the gallery." He put his arm around her shoulder, "The people of this nation are eternally in your debt."

Livy nodded as Churchill looked away and said, "And you Randall, how are you?"

"I'm fine Winston, a little worse for wear but healing nicely."

Churchill smiled as the door behind them opened and the same guide stepped in. "Lady Ashford, I have a few things to discuss with your father before my speech, but I look forward to your presence in the Chamber."

He gestured to the man in the spotless morning attire who said, "My Lady, if you would please follow me." He led her out of the room and walking a step ahead, escorted her through the halls of the palace and up narrow private stairs to the gallery. He removed a purple velvet rope strung across the end of one of the green benches directly above and facing the podium. He turned and gracefully offered her the seat.

Alone and in silence, Livy watched the House Members file into the chamber to await the arrival of the Prime Minister. In that personal silence, her mind began to drift from the disappointment she found so prevalent in her life. She remembered a day that felt like years ago, when she sat beside one she thought to be a friend. Vaguely, she could remember her heart filled with a fever for war and the quick and painless victory sure to come and how easy it was for people who knew nothing of war to praise it, as if it were some sort of glorious challenge.

There was no question Hitler must be stopped, the alternative was too bleak to comprehend. But until the day he was removed from this earth many more would die and the horror would continue, the road to the end paved with shattered lives and dreams. That was the truth about war and she knew it all too well.

A sound like thunder came to her as if from a distant world unlike her own. Her head slowly rose to see she was the only person in the Chamber not standing, applauding the sudden appearance of Churchill. Before she could stand, people took their places and the sounds of movement fell to a hush as Churchill stood behind the small boxwood podium.

Livy closed her eyes, working to quiet her heart when a familiar hand rested on her shoulder. She turned to look up into a face smiling at her.

Jamie slipped into the bench beside her. "My life is empty without you. I love you. Whatever might attempt to keep us apart will never succeed. Together, we can achieve anything. That is, if you'll have me."

She looked into his eyes, a gentle smile came to her face, "We belong to each other Jamie Wallace. We always have." He slipped his hand in hers and softly kissed her. She opened her eyes to that quirky grin she first saw in an air raid trench so long ago and then something unfamiliar and long forgotten began to fill the empty corners of her heart, hope.

She became aware of silence. They both looked toward the floor of the House and the portly man behind the podium. A corner of Churchill's mouth turned up. He paused a moment and then began to speak. "We are not at the end, nor the beginning of the end, but I dare say we are at the end of the beginning. On this day, it is more than fitting for me to acknowledge those brave souls prepared to sacrifice all for our freedom." He took a step back from the podium and his thumbs slipped under the edges of his vest and his graveled voice again rose to fill the House of Commons. "Those patriots of uncommon courage, those who remain unknown, unglorified, and yet are the core of our nation, the heart of the few." And this time, Livy knew he was looking directly at her.

About the Author

Jon Duncan is a Florida native who currently resides in Southern California. His background is in the motion picture/television industry as an editor and executive. He holds a BFA from Florida International University.

Heart of the Few is a fictional representation of life during the opening stages of World War II evolving from many conversations with individuals that lived during or participated in The Battle of Britain.

More information about Mr. Duncan may be found online at jonduncanbooks.com.